Central Park

DEBRA
WHITE SMITH

HARVEST HOUSE PUBLISHERS

EUGENE, OREGON

Cover by Koechel Peterson & Associates, Inc., Minneapolis, Minnesota

Published in association with the literary agency of *Alive Communications, Inc., 7680 Goddard Street, Suite 200, Colorado Springs, CO 80920.*

This is a work of fiction. Names, characters, places, and incidents are products of the author's imagination or are used fictitiously. Any resemblance to actual persons, living or dead, or to events or locales, is entirely coincidental.

CENTRAL PARK
Copyright © 2005 by Debra White Smith
Published by Harvest House Publishers
Eugene, Oregon 97402
ISBN 0-7394-5250-9

2004022091

Printed in the United States of America

To my all-time favorite boy,
my son, Brett Smith.

Special thanks to
LaRae Weikert and Nancy Toback
for all the NYC input.

Cast

Carrie Casper: Based on Mary Crawford in *Mansfield Park*. Ethan Summer's friend from Paris, the beautiful Carrie is rich, idle, and ready to fall in love.

Ethan Summers: Based on Edmund Bertram in *Mansfield Park*. He is the foster son of Tom and Mariette Barrimore. A serious-minded young man, Ethan declares an interest in being a pastor.

Florence Ponce: Based on Frances Price in *Mansfield Park*. Francine's mother, Florence is the mother of five. She struggles for economic survival in Rockaway, New York.

Francine Ponce: Based on Fanny Price in *Mansfield Park*. Francine, the daughter of a poor family, is invited to live with her wealthy relatives, Tom and Mariette Barrimore, when she is eleven.

Howie Ponce: Based on Lieutenant Price in *Mansfield Park*. Francine's father, Howie is more interested in how much beer he has left than whether or not his children are fed.

Hugh Casper: Based on Henry Crawford in *Mansfield Park*. Carrie Casper's brother, Hugh lacks good looks but makes up for it in charm and wealth.

Ike Gentry: The Barrimore family's trusted employee.

Julie Barrimore: Based on Julia Bertram in *Mansfield Park*. The youngest daughter of Tom and Mariette Barrimore, the flighty Julie embraces each moment.

Marie Barrimore: Based on Maria Bertram in *Mansfield Park*. The eldest daughter of Tom and Mariette Barrimore. Marie relishes being rich and craves even more wealth.

Mariette Barrimore: Based on Lady Marie Bertram in *Mansfield Park*. The Barrimore matriarch, Mariette's chief occupation involves listening to someone read to her and complaining about her health.

Nora Jamison: Based on Aunt Norris in *Mansfield Park*. Francine Ponce's aunt, Nora lives with the Barrimores on Central Park West Avenue in New York City.

Ricky Worthingham: Based on Mr. Rushworth in *Mansfield Park*. Ricky's family owns a chain of high-class hotels.

Sandra Ponce: Based on Susan Price in *Mansfield Park*. Francine's younger sister, Sandra is eager to see the world.

Tom Barrimore: Based on Sir Thomas Bertram in *Mansfield Park*. Francine's uncle, Tom Barrimore is the family patriarch.

Wade Ponce: Based on William Price in *Mansfield Park*. Wade is a hard-working, responsible brother who stays in contact with his sister Francine through the years.

Yancey Bates: Based on Mr. Yates in *Mansfield Park*. Yancey is Hugh Casper's actor friend.

One

❦ ❦

Francine Ponce hovered in front of the monstrous mansion's door. She tilted her head and examined the brown home lined with windows. The structure stretched toward the sky like a tower of doom. She clutched her Aunt Nora's hand and blinked against the June sunshine that baked the Manhattan concrete. Her watery eyes stung. During the whole two-hour trip, Aunt Nora had scolded Francine for her worried weeping. But Francine couldn't stop, no matter how many times her aunt referred to her as a thankless waif.

The girl couldn't imagine what a waif was. The way Aunt Nora's lined mouth turned down when she said it, Francine assumed the word must mean she was horrible. That would make sense because her father had told her she was horrible ever since she could remember.

A mockingbird swooped upon the edge of Francine's vision. She jumped and cringed away from the bird that targeted a yellow cat trotting from the city curb and up the wide concrete steps. Francine inched into the folds of Aunt Nora's broomstick skirt. The smell of the "bean stalk's" flowery perfume repulsed Francine nearly as much as the faint scent of vehicle exhaust shrouding the busy street. Francine had thought of Aunt Nora as a bean stalk ever since she overheard her parents' conversation a month ago.

"Okay!" her father had raged. "If you—you insist on sending Francine off with that bean stalk of a sister of yours, then make sure you understand I have no part in it! I *can't stand* your sisters! I've detested them since the day we got married. After the way they've treated us, I can't believe you—"

"Howie, listen to me!" Florence Ponce demanded. "She'll be living on *Central Park West!* This is an opportunity for at least one of our children to break out of this—this—"

"This what?" Francine's father raged. "This slum?" The crash of glass rattled Francine's bedroom wall. She assumed the missile was one of her father's ever-present beer bottles.

Now Francine covered her ears and tried to erase the noise from the corridors of her memory. The rush, honk, and whir of Manhattan's traffic merged with the remembrance of shattering glass. Francine wanted to disappear.

"What are you doing?" Aunt Nora complained. "Stop wrinkling my skirt like some thankless urchin! Stand beside me." Aunt Nora's skinny fingers dug into Francine's arm. She yanked her niece forward and released her with a jolt.

Francine's ponytail swayed from side to side. She whimpered, rubbed her arms, and stopped herself from wailing for her mother.

"Don't start that incessant crying again!" Aunt Nora snapped. "This whole thing was my idea, and all you've done is cry. Not one thanks have you given me. *Not one!* You need to remember your place and remember that you should be thankful for what's happened to you. You're moving into a brownstone mansion!" Aunt Nora pointed at the home. "Do you realize this place cost several million dollars? You don't deserve one scrap of this kindness, but it's being given to you nonetheless."

Aunt Nora's index finger targeted Francine's nose, and the child backed into the ragged suitcase near her feet. "Don't ever think you'll measure up to your cousins." Nora's stern lips pressed into a thin red line. "You'll do well to remember your place and be thankful for the good fortune that's befalling you."

Francine locked her knees and wondered how good fortune could feel so bad. She still didn't understand why *she* had been chosen to come live in New York City with an aunt and uncle she'd never even met. Or why Aunt Nora had been the one to take her from her home in Rockaway, New York. All Francine knew was that she'd far prefer being at the swimming pool, where her younger brother Wade was today.

"I can't imagine why they aren't answering!" Aunt Nora jabbed the doorbell and then pounded on the fancy brown door. "That sister of mine has several servants here every day. You would think one of them would have the decency to open the door." She wrenched the doorknob, but the thing didn't budge. "Well I'll be!" Aunt Nora huffed. "Some welcome this is!"

The fat cat now claimed the third step down from Francine. The squawking mockingbird dove toward the feline once more, and Francine jumped. This time she didn't make the mistake of turning to Aunt Nora for any kind of comfort. Francine knotted her T-shirt in her sweaty hands and prayed that maybe this had all been a huge mistake and she could go back home. She rubbed her palms across her red shirt's white letters that read *Children's Christian Association* and imagined jumping into the CCA pool with Wade.

"M–maybe we should just go—go back home," Francine suggested hopefully.

"Go back home indeed!" Aunt Nora stewed. "Just as I figured! There's not one thankful thought in that head of yours." The green-eyed bean stalk placed her hands on her hips and turned on Francine.

Francine's shoulders stiffened. Her eyes widened. She rubbed her feet against the soles of her flip-flips, and a fine layer of grit brushed the skin between her perspiring toes. Aunt Nora had griped about everything during the trip—including the fact that her sister, Florence, had allowed Francine to travel to the mansion in shorts and flip-flops.

The doorknob rattled. Francine's shoulders drooped. She stopped moving her toes.

"Well, it's about time!" Aunt Nora snarled.

Francine gazed into the face of the tallest man she had ever seen. Now eleven, she had long ago learned that giants belonged in fairy tales and not in the real world. But this man made her believe in giants all over again.

An annoyed grimace marred a face that was as shriveled as the tomato in the bottom of her mom's refrigerator. "We had an emergency in the library," the man explained in a voice that reminded Francine of a bass drum's boom. "Mr. and Mrs. Barrimore will be coming downstairs to meet you soon." The suit-clad giant opened the door wider and stepped aside.

Aunt Nora barged past him, stormed into the room, and left Francine to manage her beat-up luggage.

With a heave-ho, the child attempted to pick up the suitcase that held her meager wardrobe...along with her cherished rock collection. After Aunt Nora put the suitcase into her compact Ford, she asked Francine about the contents. Upon learning that Francine did indeed have rocks in the case, Aunt Nora refused to help her carry it another inch.

"Here, let me help you with that," the servant offered.

Francine gladly relinquished the case but shrank from his fingers brushing hers.

"My word, Francine," he gently teased. "What do you have in here, anyway, rocks?"

"Y—yes," Francine stammered. Wondering how he knew her name, she stiffened herself against more criticism.

The man chuckled, and his kind brown eyes assured Francine that a rock collection was acceptable for an eleven-year-old girl.

She ducked her head and stepped into the finest room she'd ever entered. It reminded her of the pictures of the White House in her fifth-grade history book. The day Francine's teacher made the White House reading assignment, the girl had stroked the photos and marveled that such luxury existed on earth. Now she drank in the chandeliered room. Tapestry curtains…polished wooden floors…thick rugs…paintings…a staircase against the left wall. Every rich element merged and struck Francine speechless.

The only thing that didn't fit her White House dreams was the smell of smoke. She wrinkled her nose as Aunt Nora plunged back into the entryway from a wide-open room to the right. Francine peered behind her aunt. A shiny black grand piano the size of her bedroom claimed the center of the room.

"Ike, do I smell smoke?" the bean stalk demanded. "I just checked out the music room because I thought it was coming from there."

"Yes, you smell smoke." Ike eased the door shut. He placed his lanky hands behind his back and faced Nora. "But it was in the library, not the piano room. That was our emergency." The giant gestured toward another room beside the piano room. Francine strained to peek past the doorway. She caught only a glimpse of books lining a shelf. "We had a small fire in the library—"

"A fire?" Nora shrieked and clutched her neck.

The giant nodded, and his eye twitched.

Francine imagined being trapped on the fifth floor of the blazing brownstone with no way to escape. She rubbed her toes against her flip-flops and couldn't calm her ragged breathing.

"Well, has it been put out, for pity's sake?" Nora stomped forward as if she owned the place.

"Of course," Ike stated, and a line formed between his brows.

"How did you manage to let a fire break out?" Nora asked.

The giant's mouth went hard like her father's often did, and Francine looked for a place to hide. "Mrs. Barrimore left an open book near a candle. She accidentally knocked it over. The flame got out of hand from there," Ike stiffly explained.

Nora gasped. "Did you call the fire department?"

"No. That wasn't necessary. We managed it with a fire extinguisher. I was just making sure the cleanup was sufficient when you knocked."

"And my sister…is she okay?"

"Yes, fine. Her sleeve caught on fire, but she isn't burned herself. She's gone back upstairs to change."

"That sister of mine is so absentminded." Shaking her head, Nora gazed toward the staircase. "I just hope she doesn't do anything so rash now that Francine is here." Nora's low-heeled pumps tapped against the polished wood as she stepped to the child's side. After laying her hand on Francine's shoulder, Nora continued, "I'm going to talk to Mariette about being extra careful while our niece is with us. This whole arrangement was my idea, you know. And I must be sure that Francine isn't in an unsafe environment."

"Yes, I understand," the giant agreed.

"And you servants need to remember to be extra careful, too." Nora pointed her finger at the giant's nose. "Florence would never forgive a single one of us if we don't cherish and protect her daughter."

The man's nostrils widened, and his mouth turned down like Aunt Nora's did when she called Francine a waif. "I understand," he said as he stalked toward the staircase. "I'm going to let Mr. Barrimore know you've arrived. Please make yourselves at home in the den."

"Well!" Nora huffed and glared at the giant's back. "Servants these days just aren't what they used to be. I at least expected to be *shown* to the den and offered a drink."

Even though the bean stalk's voice echoed off the vaulted ceiling, the giant never acknowledged her words. Instead, he paused in front of an elevator and pressed a button.

"The den is this way, Francine." Accompanied by the faint sigh of elevator doors, Nora grabbed her niece's arm and propelled her forward.

Two

Francine mutely obeyed her aunt and walked toward a huge open doorway that revealed a room full of antiques. Francine didn't need anyone to tell her she shouldn't even think about jumping on this furniture. Before stepping into the den, she cast a worried glance at the frayed suitcase that held her only possessions.

"Come *on!*" Aunt Nora nagged. "Nobody wants your old rocks. The servants will take care of the suitcase. That's what they're paid for.

"I can't imagine being so lucky to even have servants all the time," Nora continued. "Lord knows we can't afford such luxuries on a pastor's salary. But if I *did* have a servant or two, I'd make sure they were way nicer than that prune-faced Ike. I don't know *what* makes somebody's face want to be so wrinkled!"

Still walking, Francine gazed up at her aunt's face and considered the shriveled up tomato all over again. The edge of the thick rug rammed itself between her foot and her flip-flop. In an attempt to free herself, Francine lurched forward. A wing-backed chair stopped her fall. She toppled over the arm and into the cotton-covered seat head first. Her ponytail lashed sideways and smacked her in the eyes before her face smashed into a throw pillow the color of strawberries. A chorus of girlish giggles mingled with Aunt Nora's scandalized exclamation.

Her eyes stinging anew, Francine considered crawling under the chair and never coming out. But a startled canine growl from beneath the chair proclaimed that the space was already occupied. Francine scrambled away from the chair and stumbled into a camel-backed sofa. She collapsed onto red velvet stretched across a firm cushion, and a pointed-nosed terrier darted from beneath the chair and snapped at her ankles. Panting, Francine pulled her feet onto the sofa and shoved them beneath her, flip-flops and all.

"Get your grimy feet off the sofa!" Aunt Nora demanded at the same time a thin girl lifted the dog from the floor. The girl and dog so captured Francine's attention that she failed to obey her aunt's command.

"There now, Daisy," the girl crooned. "There's no need to get feisty. She wasn't trying to hurt you." The girl's gray eyes and dark shiny hair reminded Francine of one of the popular girls at school...so did her expensive-looking shorts set, her polished fingernails, and the frosty blush that tinged her cheeks. Francine decided the perfect-looking girl was a tad older than she.

Suddenly being eleven seemed inadequate. So did Francine's thin blonde ponytail and her faded clothes. She rubbed her toes against her flip-flops and now understood why Aunt Nora had been so upset over her clothing. But this was the best Francine had.

"I said, get your feet off the couch!" Aunt Nora tapped Francine's knee with her bony fingers, but the warning seemed to echo from a distant land.

Another girl with dark-brown hair every bit as full and pretty as the girl with the dog plopped beside Francine. "Hi! Are you Francine?" she asked.

Francine nodded and wondered how anyone could have blue eyes as bright as this new girl's. She looked older than the other one. She wore more makeup. And her light perfume smelled sweet—like the magazine perfume pullout that Francine had slipped in her drawer a few months ago. She had daily rubbed her wrists with the paper that featured a beautiful teenage girl with a cute guy until there was no scent left. Now all that remained was the pullout, tucked near her rock collection in her suitcase.

The dog's shrill bark sent a shock through Francine. She jumped and shrank into the couch when the yap merged into a snarl. Instead of moving the dog away from Francine, the younger girl leaned closer. Francine gripped her knees and stared into the canine's bulging, shiny eyes. The terrier bared its pointy teeth, and Francine imagined the razor-like enamel sinking into her neck.

The perfect brunette, ignoring the dog's tension, examined Francine's face as if she were a germ under a microscope. "Are your eyebrows and eyelashes always so white or did you bleach them?" she asked.

"Julie!" the older girl gasped.

Francine touched her eyebrow.

"Well," Julie explained, "I've just never seen anyone so—so blonde all over like this."

"I said get your feet down off that couch!" Aunt Nora smacked Francine's leg. A stinging burn blazed toward her knee with enough force to demand Francine's action.

She jerked her feet to the floor. The room blurred into a watery abyss. Francine wished she could erase her blonde hair, eyebrows, and lashes and then recolor herself to match the perfect girls.

"Hey, what's got Daisy in such an uproar?" a kind masculine voice asked from the doorway.

Aunt Nora and the girls glanced toward the voice. Francine scrubbed at her eyes and followed their gazes. A tall lad strode forward, his dark gaze sizing up the scene.

"She's here," the girl next to Francine said.

"And Daisy doesn't seem to like her," the younger girl explained.

Daisy barked and wagged her body at the newcomer, whom Francine decided was a little older than both girls.

"Hey, Daise." The teenage boy patted the dog on the head before focusing his brown eyes upon Francine. "You guys need to give her some space," he said and motioned for the girls to back away. "You've got her cornered here like a helpless mouse."

"Well, if the shoe fits," Aunt Nora's rigid voice floated from the wing-backed chair Francine had fallen into.

"Julie, why don't you take Daisy to Ike and get him to put her in the utility room for awhile. That will be a huge help for starters," the boy said.

"Okay," Julie agreed and ambled toward the doorway.

"I'm Marie, by the way," the other girl said.

"I—I'm Francine," she whispered.

"Yes, I know." Marie glanced at Francine's T-shirt and shorts.

Francine creased the hem of her faded denim shorts and felt like a droopy weed among a bouquet of fresh roses.

"And I'm Ethan." The lad extended his hand to Francine.

Her gaze trailed from Ethan's open hand to his relaxed face. Natural brown highlights streaked a head full of thick, dark hair brushed forward in a trendy style. She perceived no resemblance between Ethan and the perfect girls but assumed they must be brother and sisters. His low-riding jeans and buttoned-up shirt looked like the boy's on the perfumed magazine pullout.

"Well, are you going to shake his hand or not?" Aunt Nora prodded.

Francine's gaze faltered toward her aunt, who sat like the queen of the room in the wing-backed chair. The girl's face warmed while she placed her hand in Ethan's. During the brief firm shake, Francine felt safer than she had since she left her mother's arms.

Ethan's complexion was darker than the other girls. His eyes friendlier and softer. His smile ready and encouraging.

Francine clung to Ethan's hand until he released her fingers.

The doorbell's wheezing chime sent Marie to her feet. "Oh good! That's Patti!" she exclaimed. "We're going to Central Park for a play."

Ethan's frown reminded Francine of the giant's expression when he saw Aunt Nora. "Does Dad know?"

"Know what?" a masculine voice floated from the entryway.

Marie stopped and twisted her fingers together.

Soon an overweight man in a striped suit appeared in the room. Beside him stood a woman as thin as Aunt Nora. She was wearing a dark-blue house dress that sparkled like the first stars at sunset. While the lady was older than Florence, her wide-set eyes, thin nose, and broad mouth looked so much like Francine's mother that her heart wrenched. Except for their brown hair, Aunt Nora and Francine's mother didn't look a thing alike.

"What am I to know?" the man repeated and eyed his daughter.

"Patti and I are going to the park to see *Romeo and Juliet*." Marie shrugged as Julie stepped back into the den. "That's all," she added and meandered toward the doorway.

"I want to go to the park!" Julie squealed.

"Oh no!" Marie groaned and shoved her hair over her shoulder. "Why does she always want to go?" Marie stomped her foot, and her blue eyes sharpened as she glared at Julie.

The younger girl crossed her arms and protruded her bottom lip. "If I don't go, you don't go!" she said with a pout.

"Are we talking about Patti Towers?" Mr. Barrimore asked while his wife settled in the wing-backed chair beside Aunt Nora's.

"Yes," Marie mumbled.

"Isn't she seventeen?"

"I guess," Marie answered.

"You went out with her last week, didn't you?" The man's hard gaze suggested Marie shouldn't lie.

"Yes."

"Well, then, if you persist in going, you've got to take your sister with you," Mr. Barrimore insisted. When he nodded, his shiny, balding scalp looked like a crystal ball.

"But, Dad!" Marie placed both hands on her hips. "She'll ruin everything!"

"Exactly!" Mr. Barrimore said with a pointed smile and then gazed at his youngest daughter. "You have my permission to go only if you promise to tell me everything that happens."

"Okay," Julie agreed with a smug smirk that emphasized full lips covered in glossy glitter.

"Uuuuuhhhhh!" Marie erupted before she gasped at her father. "But Patti and I went out together last week and—"

"You were an hour late."

"But I called and told you—"

"This is the way it stands from now on with you and Patti," Mr. Barrimore explained. "Take it or leave it." He walked toward Francine who tensed her back.

The giant named Ike entered the room. For the first time, Francine noticed his hair was the color of the tired silver tinsel on last year's Christmas tree. "Patti is here for you, Miss Marie." The name "Patti" left Ike's lips with little enthusiasm. "She's waiting on the steps. She says you're going to Central Park to take in a Shakespeare play?" Ike turned the question toward Mr. Barrimore.

"Yes, Ike." Mr. Barrimore nodded and pointed a grateful smile toward his employee. "Marie and Julie are *both* going." He called toward Marie's retreating back, "Be home in three hours or this is the last time. Do you understand?"

"Yes," the girl responded in a tired yet respectful voice. "Ike," she continued, "tell Patti I'll be out in a few minutes. I've just got to go upstairs and get my purse."

"And don't forget your cell phone this time," Mr. Barrimore commanded.

Julie clapped her hands and squeaked, "I'll be sure to get mine!" She raced past her sister and the retreating Ike.

Mr. Barrimore swiveled his focus solely upon Francine. "Well, hello there!" he welcomed. "We've been expecting you, and now you're here!" His intense blue eyes shifted toward Ethan and then back to Francine. "I'm your Uncle Tom. What do you have to say for yourself?"

Francine's face heated. Her gaze fell to the red oriental rug she'd tripped over. She gulped and searched for something "to say for herself," but couldn't come up with a thing. The pronounced tick of the grandfather clock in the corner counted off the miserable seconds.

"Well, at least say hello," Aunt Nora suggested.

"Does she even speak?" Mrs. Barrimore questioned absently.

"Oh yes, she speaks when she wants to," Aunt Nora responded.

"I think she might like a soda." Ethan's kind voice floated across the cavern of Francine's shyness.

"Would you?" Mr. Barrimore questioned.

"Y–yes," she stuttered.

"Then I can get Ike to have the maid come—"

"Dad, why don't I take her to the kitchen and show her around the house on the way there and back."

"Of course! That's a great idea. Also, tell Katy that Mariette and I will have our usual Diet Cokes. Would you care for anything, Nora?" He lifted his brows and shifted his attention to his sister-in-law.

"Oh, I thought you'd *never* ask!" she whined and propped her head against the chair. "I'll take whatever you have. Just as long as it's cold."

"Okay," Mr. Barrimore agreed and looked back at Ethan. "Tell them to bring Nora a Diet Coke as well."

"Do you have Dr Pepper?" Nora questioned.

"Yes." The bald man nodded.

"Caffeine free?" Aunt Nora interjected.

"Yes." He raised one brow and observed Aunt Nora.

"With a twist of lemon," she finished.

"Anything else?" Mr. Barrimore asked.

"No. That's it." Aunt Nora lifted her head and leaned toward her sister. "How are you feeling these days?"

Mariette yawned. "Oh, I've had better days, I guess…"

As the ladies began a discussion about Mariette's health, Mr. Barrimore quirked his mouth at Aunt Nora and then looked at Ethan. "Did you get all that, Ethan?"

"Yes," Ethan said through a chuckle, "I think so."

Three

〜 〜

Ethan Summers ushered Francine from the den, beside the staircase, past the elevator, and through a doorway that led into a spacious kitchen. The smell of peanut-butter cookies obliterated all traces of smoke that lingered after the library fire. A plump woman dressed in black and white scrounged through an industrial-sized refrigerator. Ethan glanced down at Francine, whose lost expression and reddened eyes reminded him of the way he felt his first days at the home everyone referred to as Central Park.

The lad leaned toward Francine and whispered, "That's Katalina Gomez—the head maid. We call her Katy for short. If you get on her good side, she'll give you cookies." Ethan winked. Francine's faint smile and the glimmer of appreciation in her pale-blue eyes encouraged him to more kindness.

"Katy," he began as he stepped around the butcher-block island, "Dad and Mom and Aunt Nora are in the den, and they'd like some sodas." He repeated the order details, then turned toward Francine. "And what would you like?" he gently inquired.

Katy, wasting no time in her duties, marched to the other side of the kitchen and opened another refrigerator. This one held nothing but bottles and cans full of assorted beverages. Ethan smiled down at Francine, who stared at the sight.

The maid grabbed three cans from the shelves and plopped them atop a steel-gray counter. She turned to face Ethan, but her gaze slid to Francine. "Oh hi! I didn't notice you before. You must be our new guest!" she exclaimed with a Spanish accent tinged with New York flavor.

"Yes, this is Francine," Ethan explained and stepped to the maid's side. "And I have a hunch she's going to like your cookies as much as I do." He draped his arm across Katy's shoulders and said, "Hint, hint, hint."

"Get out of here, you!" Katy fondly pushed Ethan. "You're nothing but a no-good beggar."

"Yes, and you love it, don't you?" Ethan returned with a broad smile.

"You better watch this guy." Katy shook her finger at Francine. "He'll con you out of everything you own." The maid pinched Ethan's cheek.

"Ouch!" He covered his cheek and pretended injury. "Why do you always have to get so violent?"

"Come here, Francine," Katy urged and waved away Ethan as if he were of no consequence. "You need to pick out something to drink. I know what this beggar wants. These days he goes for Pepsi and nothing else. He used to drink milk, but he thinks he's gotten too old for it." Katy darted him a saucy glare.

Pressing herself against the ornate door facing, Francine lowered her gaze. Ethan's mind wandered back eight years to the day after his mother's funeral when his birth father brought him here. Pete Summers had handed Ethan over to Mariette Barrimore and her husband with no explanation of when he might return. Ethan had clung to the kitchen wall until Katy's fresh cookies and chocolate milk enticed him to sit in the breakfast nook.

"Would you like some milk and cookies?" Ethan offered.

Francine's doleful gaze rose to meet his and silently begged him to make the choice for her. "Come on." Ethan moved forward and gently took her hand. "I've got a good idea. Let's let Katy take the sodas to the den, and you and I will take the elevator up to the terrace for you to look around. When we come back, Katy should have the cookies ready. We'll get her to take them to the den with something for us to drink. Okay?"

"Wh–what's a terrace?" she asked.

"It's like a big patio on the top of the house. It's really cool. Dad has a set of binoculars up there. Since the house is five-stories tall you can see for miles. We might even be able to spot Julie and Marie and Patti in Central Park."

Francine nodded.

"Sounds like a plan," Katy agreed and busied herself with retrieving three crystal goblets from inside a glass-front cabinet. "Ike and I don't really care for that Patti person," she brooded. "I'd like to know what she's up to with our girls."

"Will you tell Dad and Mom we'll be back in about fifteen minutes?" Ethan requested.

"Yes, yes of course." Katy gestured toward the doorway. "You go and enjoy your new friend. One day she'll be twenty and beautiful, and you'll be as handsome as you are now. You'll be glad you were friendly today!" The maid knowingly smiled.

A veil of warmth crept up Ethan's cheeks, and he wished Katy wouldn't be so ready to insist he should be chasing girls. Ethan noticed pretty ladies just like every other guy his age, but he wasn't ready to think about a regular girlfriend now or in the future.

He'd known early in his teen years that the Lord's hand was on him. He was God's man now—a man who would one day be called "Pastor Ethan." With Tom Barrimore's support and encouragement, he had determined to keep himself sexually pure and as far removed from temptation as possible. Ethan stubbornly clung to the belief that he should allow the Lord to lead him to his mate when the time was right—despite the hints Marie dropped about her gorgeous friend Patti Towers.

Patti was two years older than Ethan, but that didn't seem to stop her or a few other older girls from flirting with him. Occasionally Aunt Nora had taken it upon herself to remind him that he was still just fifteen, even though he looked every bit of eighteen. Dad had even said he thought maybe Patti wanted Marie as a friend because it gave her access to Ethan. Apparently, these senior high girls didn't care how old Ethan was. All they were interested in was what Mom called his classic Latin looks—whatever *that* meant.

But right now, Ethan was more concerned about a *younger* girl—a new "little sister" who was in the same scary situation he'd been in before. "Come on, Francine," Ethan encouraged in a warm voice he hoped reassured her. "You'll love the terrace."

He extended his hand. After a brief hesitation, Francine raised her gaze and silently said, *I don't really know you, but I know I can trust you. You are a friend.* She placed her hand in his, and the two of them walked toward the elevator.

Francine's stomach lurched the second the elevator whined its way upward. She hung onto the rail and wondered if the White House had an elevator as well.

"This baby is *quick!*" Ethan explained. "Dad just had a whole new system installed a few months ago. The old one was slower than molasses."

"I didn't know houses even had elevators," Francine admitted.

"Oh, so you *can* talk!"

The elevator slowed and then hopped to a stop.

Not sure what to say now, Francine locked her knees and lowered her head.

"You're scared, aren't you?" Ethan asked. The elevator doors slid open.

"Not of *you*," Francine replied, her voice stronger than she'd expected.

"No, of course not," Ethan said, as if the whole world already knew she felt safe with him. He stepped onto the terrace and motioned for her to follow. "Come on," he urged. A cool summer breeze mussed his thick hair and enticed Francine to join her new friend.

Francine edged from the elevator onto the terrace. The north wind whipped at her ponytail as the smell of sun-kissed concrete tinged with exhaust testified to a busy city five stories below. When the elevator doors closed, Francine was overwhelmed by a bright blue sky the color of Marie's eyes. And in the distance stretched miles and miles of Manhattan and New York City. At once she realized she was standing only feet away from the terrace's edge. Even though the iron banister reached her chest, Francine felt as if she were being sucked off the top of the mansion. She turned to rush back into the elevator and bumped into the closed doors.

"Come on!" Ethan encouraged and patted her shoulder. "It's all as safe as can be." He walked to the railing. "See?"

Francine cautiously watched as he tugged on the rail with enough force to assure her that she really wouldn't fall through. After a reluctant grin, she stepped away from the elevator toward Ethan. For the first time she noticed the lawn furniture that looked nearly as fancy as the antiques in the den. Her flip-flops slapped against her heels as she slowly approached the edge, reached forward, and grabbed the rail before moving in close.

"Come over here." Ethan pointed to his left. "These are the binoculars I was telling you about."

Clutching the rail, Francine followed her new friend toward a large set of binoculars attached to a pole.

"See? They swivel." Ethan moved the binoculars in a circular path. "Look, I'll get a chair for you to stand on so you can look into them. We're lucky there's a north wind today. It's blown off all the smog, and we can see for miles."

Forgetting her fear, she peered at the binoculars and wondered how far she'd be able to see with them. Ethan dragged up a patio chair, and then he gazed into the binoculars. After a few mumbles and adjusting of lenses, he looked back at Francine. "There. It's all clear now." With his help, she climbed onto the chair.

"I've got them focused on Bow Bridge," he said as she placed her brow against the rest.

Her inhibitions easing, Francine strained to see the scene. A spectacular bridge overshadowed by majestic trees crested a lake that merrily sparkled in the liquid sunshine. "It's pretty," she said.

"Yes, very nice," Ethan replied.

She swung the binoculars to the left and spotted a large open space full of nothing but grass and a group of boys playing touch football. "My brother would like to play baseball over there," she continued.

"You have a brother?" Ethan asked.

"I have three. But I'm talking about Wade. He's just a year younger than I am." The wind toyed with her ponytail, and Francine pulled her face from the binoculars. "I also have a little sister named Sandra," she added with a lump in her throat. Her gaze never rose above the top button on Ethan's shirt.

"You're lucky," he said. "I didn't have any brothers or sisters."

Francine glanced into his kind, dark eyes. Confusion swirled upon her like the stream swirling beneath the bridge. "But—"

"The Barrimores are my second family," he explained. "My first mother was my second mom's personal secretary. Before Mother died—she had cancer—she asked Mom to take me. I've only lived here about eight years. I guess in some ways, I'm like you." Ethan's attention slid past Francine, and a dull ache marred his eyes. "I haven't seen my real dad in four years."

Francine didn't quite know what to say. While her father had never gone away for four years, sometimes he would go to work one morning and not come home for weeks. Often he showed up about the time she had stopped cringing every time the front door opened. She stepped off the chair.

"Oh well," Ethan continued with a forced smile, "Dad and Mom have really been good to me—especially Dad. And I guess I *do* have sisters if you count Julie and Marie."

He turned toward the binoculars. "I'm going to see if I can find them walking toward Shakespeare-in-the-park. Maybe we can spy on those three girls," he added with a sly tilt to his lips. "That oughtta really make them happy...Dad, too," Ethan asserted before placing his face against the binoculars. "We'll go over to Central Park in the next few days if you like," he offered. "There's all sorts of cool stuff over there...a carousel, a zoo, a puppet theater, and even a totally awesome castle."

Francine, already overwelmed, didn't answer. She lowered her gaze and examined the terrace floor. An annoying honk echoed from the streets below. Francine approached the terrace rail and grasped it before moving closer. She cautiously looked over the side and eyed the constant flow of traffic. Even though their home in Rockaway wasn't nearly this nice, at least they had a small yard and a beach nearby. A dull ache reminded her that she wouldn't be there to tuck Sandra into bed that night. Since her twin brothers were born a year ago, Mom was always busy with them at bedtime. Francine had taken over the tuck-in duties for her six-year-old sister.

Maybe Wade will do it, she worried and decided to write him today. Her mom had insisted upon packing a box of cheap stationary, and each envelope already bore its own stamp.

"No luck!" Ethan's claim, accompanied by a new gust of wind, cut in on Francine's fretting. "I didn't spot them anywhere."

She glanced over her shoulder. He shrugged.

"I guess you can't win them all," Ethan continued. He tilted his head toward the elevator. "Come on. Katy probably has the cookies ready by now, and Dad and Mom will be wondering if we're ever going to come back."

Silently Francine followed her new friend back into the elevator and braced herself for the ride. The trip down twisted her stomach more than the trip up. When the elevator hopped to a halt, she clutched the rail and swallowed hard.

"Don't worry," Ethan encouraged. "You'll get used to it. I did, and I promise this new elevator is way better than the old one." He rolled his eyes. "That thing jumped around so much it was like riding a mad bull." He mimicked the motions of a bull ride.

Francine giggled and lowered her head. Ethan's laughter mixed with hers as the two stepped from the elevator.

"I just took your cookies into the den." Katy's cheerful voice announced her presence.

The girl looked up to spot the beaming maid.

"Did you enjoy the terrace, Francine?" Katy asked.

"Y–yes," Francine stuttered and relived the sensation of being sucked over the edge of the building.

"It's high, isn't it?" Katy asked without breaking stride.

"Yes."

"She was a trooper," Ethan stated and placed a hand on Francine's shoulder.

Katy's grin broadened, and Francine wondered if the maid would make any more embarrassing statements about how pretty she'd be when she was twenty. But all Katy said was, "Duty calls!" With a cheerful wave she marched through the kitchen doorway.

A faint trace of smoke still lingered in the entryway, and Francine's curiosity trotted toward the library. She hoped no books were burned. And she hoped just as fervently that some of those books would appeal to girls her age. Francine had never claimed to do anything that well, but her teacher said she was the best reader in class.

Wade enjoyed reading, just not as much as Francine. Even so, after their swim in the pool, she and her brother would sit in her room and read awhile. She twisted her fingers until they ached and wondered if Wade was home from the pool yet.

A new wave of longing sent a sting to her eyes. *Stop all that sniffling!* Aunt Nora's retort crashed across her mind. Francine scrubbed her eyes.

The den doorway loomed ahead, and she dreaded having to face her relatives all over again. Something suggested Francine should latch onto Ethan's arm and lean on him, but she couldn't get her body to cooperate. When she and Ethan were within six feet of the doorway, Aunt Nora's shrill voice hit Francine.

"I really don't believe I've ever seen such a thankless child in my life," Aunt Nora fumed. "You would *think* she would be glad to move here and get away from that pit of a house where she's lived her whole life."

Francine stopped and went rigid. Ethan's hand rested on her upper arm.

"She's probably just scared," Uncle Tom claimed.

"What is there to be scared of, dear?" Aunt Mariette's languid voice was barely discernible. "From what I understand, *she* scared Daisy. Who ever heard of Daisy not liking anyone, anyway? She's a perfect angel of a dog. Yes, she is," Aunt Mariette's weak voice took on baby-talk tones. "And to think Ethan had you locked up in the utility room. Come here my pet," she crooned. "Do you want me to scratch your ears? Did that mean ol' girl scare you, huh?"

"That dog—" Francine choked out. Terrified, she turned to Ethan and silently pleaded for his help.

A veil of doubt wrinkled his brow. Instead of being the pillar of strength Francine so desperately needed, Ethan widened his eyes and shook his head.

"Well, Nora," Uncle Tom said, "I guess if Francine's staying here doesn't work out, she'll have to move in with you and Victor. After all, that was the original plan, as I recall."

"Oh no!" Aunt Nora squawked. "Whatever gave you *that* idea?"

"You did," Uncle Tom's blunt statement asked for no argument.

"W–w–well—" Aunt Nora stuttered, "I just assumed that since you'd taken in one extra child, you'd take Francine as well."

Francine winced and stared at the thick-piled rug, the color of raisins.

"Will you please not bring Ethan into this," Uncle Tom demanded. "He's an unusual exception, and you know it. We never had a son and—"

"We already knew Ethan so well," Aunt Mariette's cool voice cut through her husband's agitated words. "He'd been here with his mom ever since he was born. He already thought of Tom as a second father. You know that, Nora."

"Of course!" Nora injected. "But that doesn't mean I can take Francine now."

Francine imagined having to live with the mean bean stalk. She held her breath and rubbed the top of her knee where Aunt Nora whacked her.

"It would never work out," Nora continued. "You know about Victor's aversion to children. His nerves would never tolerate—"

"He picked the wrong profession to have the luxury of bad nerves and an aversion to children," Uncle Tom's sour drawl accompanied the rustling of paper.

Francine had no idea what "aversion" meant, but she sensed that it must be as bad as "waif." Feeling like an unwanted piece of garbage passed from one disgusted relative to another, Francine couldn't stop the fresh tide of tears. She covered her face and silently shook. The firm pressure of Ethan's hands on her shoulders proved the only strength that stopped her from collapsing.

"Of course, even if we *didn't* plan for Francine to live here, I'm sure she'll be of some use," Aunt Mariette conceded. "She can sit with me on the days I don't feel well. She'll be convenient."

Francine gulped, sniffed, and hiccoughed. Ethan mumbled something she didn't understand and patted her back.

"Don't forget that the child *will* go to school and *will* be expected to earn good grades," Uncle Tom asserted. "We can't have her growing up illiterate—not in this household."

A disgruntled bark erupted over Uncle Tom's remarks.

A shock stiffened Francine.

"Come here, Daisy!" Aunt Mariette's faint alarm preceded canine growls. "What is the matter with you?"

Francine lifted her damp face at the same time the pint-sized demon-dog dashed from the den and straight at her.

"Daisy, stop!" Ethan hollered. He released Francine and strategically placed his leg between the dog and his new friend.

Baring her teeth, the canine slipped around Ethan's leg and nipped at Francine's ankle. A terrified cry burst from the child. She scrambled backward with the angry dog bent upon new attack.

"Daisy!" Uncle Tom's voice bellowed across the entryway, but the dog ignored him.

Struggling to breathe, Francine turned and blindly raced forward. Only a few feet separated her from the staircase. She pounded up the steps as swiftly as her flip-flops allowed. Every other step Daisy's hot breath neared her legs and propelled Francine higher. The clashing of voices and surprised cries didn't rival her heart's pounding and the whirlpool of emotions that forced hot tears down her cheeks.

Never looking back, she topped the stairs and veered through the first open door she spotted. She rushed into a room that smelled of new fabric. With a frenzied cry, Francine slammed the door and locked it. She pressed her back against the door, slid to the wooden floor, and landed with a bump that rattled her teeth.

Shattered sunbeams flowing from a trio of narrow windows danced across her watery gaze. The mid-sized workroom, equipped with a headless mannequin beside a sewing machine, seemed an oasis of the familiar in a foreign country. She hugged her legs to her chest and buried her forehead against her knees.

Never had Francine felt so alone and unwanted. *Never*. Not even the time her father locked her and Wade in the closet for two hours. At least she'd had Wade with her. Now she had no one.

The doorknob rattled. Francine tightened her arms around her knees. A soft knock preceded Ethan's comforting voice. "Francine?"

Four

"Francine, are you in there? Hello…"

The masculine voice penetrated Francine's light nap. Her eyes slid open, and she tried to place the voice with a person. She drowsily peeked at the headless mannequin in the corner near the sewing machine, where it had remained since the first time Francine ran into this room nearly ten years ago.

Finally the sunshine piercing the trio of windows grew too annoying. She snapped shut her eyes and shifted amid the daybed's covers. A swish and thump announced her novel falling to the floor. A disgruntled woof from near her feet testified to Daisy's nap being disturbed.

A soft knock accompanied the man's voice this time. "Francine?"

Ethan! He's home from France! The realization broke through her slumber and left Francine gasping. Her eyes snapped open. She squinted against the sunshine. "He's here already!" she squeaked. Her attention riveted upon the brass alarm clock on her nightstand. She raised up on her elbow and grabbed the ticking timepiece. Closer examination proved that Francine had slept two hours.

"Oh no," she groaned.

"Francine?" Ethan's knock rang louder.

"Coming, Ethan!" she called and grimaced at the taste in her mouth. Francine swung her feet to the floor, stood, and scratched to the bottom of her linen shorts pocket for the peppermint left over from her lunch outing with Aunt Mariette.

Daisy's dainty paw stroked the back of her leg, and Francine offered a token pat to the dog's head. "Not now, Daise," she mumbled. "Ethan's home."

The dog hopped from the bed and raced toward the door as if she understood every word.

Fumbling with the mint wrapper, Francine scrounged her toes across the cottony rug until she encountered her leather thong sandals. She attempted to straighten her mussed ponytail and lambasted herself for falling asleep.

After lunch, Francine had gathered up Daisy and retired to her room to read until Ethan arrived. He'd been in Paris for six months on a special assignment missions trip. Francine had been so ecstatic about his return that the last thing she expected was to fall asleep.

Finally the mint was free of its wrapper. She popped it into her mouth and reveled in the explosion of cool refreshment before opening the door.

Ethan stood on the other side, his dark eyes alight with the brotherly affection that began the day he defended her from Daisy's jealous attack. The power of his Latin looks mesmerized Francine and brought back memories of the magical night he'd escorted her to her senior ball in high school. She'd been Cinderella. Ethan had been Prince Charming. And her feelings for him hadn't been the same since.

Now here he stood, dressed in a sports coat that smacked of Armani, smiling as if he'd been gone a mere week. Only his new, stylish goatee attested that his absence stretched much longer than a week. Added to that was the tinge of international mystery stirring his dark eyes that hinted that he was no longer "the same old Ethan." Even though Francine's heart rate increased at the sight of her best friend, she managed only a faint smile.

"Hello, Ethan," Francine said. "We've been waiting for you."

"Hello, yourself," he growled and swept her into his arms for a big hug.

Francine embraced the moment as tightly as she embraced the man. His warmth, his masculine scent, his strength stirred her quiet heart in a manner she could never—and would never—reveal.

Ethan and Francine had been nearly inseparable from the first of their acquaintance. After defending Francine from Daisy's aggressive welcome nearly a decade ago, Ethan had treated her like a cherished little sister.

"Listen, I've got someone I want you to meet," Ethan stated as he relaxed the hug.

"Oh really?" Francine questioned and detected an excitement in his voice she had never heard before. She scrutinized his dark eyes. This time the hint of international mystery left her uncomfortable…and made her wish more than ever that her Ethan had never gone to Paris.

Daisy's impatient yap interrupted the moment, and Ethan looked down. "I see you, too, Daisy," he crooned and scooped the rat terrier into his arms. "Hey there, little girlfriend, did you miss me?" The aging dog licked at his hand and panted her thrill.

"What's she doing up here with you?" Ethan asked. "When we got here, I expected her downstairs with Mom."

"She's acting like my shadow these days." Francine stroked the miniature dog's ears. "Julie and Marie are gone so much now—planning Marie's wedding—I guess I'm the only diversion Daisy has. Hard to believe I hated the sight of her the first year I lived here, isn't it?"

"I believe *she* was the one who started that little problem," Ethan said with an indulgent smile.

Francine swallowed hard, toyed with the waist tie on her sleeveless blouse, and focused on the dog. Confusion swirled across her soul as she relived the last few months without Ethan. His absence had revealed something she may have never realized in his presence.

Once, she would have spoken to Ethan with a freedom she bestowed upon no other. Francine would have told him of her success in last week's final exams during the summer semester...of the surety that she would graduate from Hunter College next May—one full year before schedule. But now, after his absence, after the realization that she was hopelessly in love with him, Francine could think of nothing to say. Nothing. Only desperate longing filled her mind...a longing that Ethan might one day return her love.

But haunting intuition suggested that the new mystery in his eyes might represent the presence of another woman possessing Ethan's mind and heart. The longer Francine stood with her Ethan, the more she sensed she no longer claimed his sole devotion. *Maybe I never did?* she despaired.

"There you two are!" Aunt Nora's sharp reprimand echoed from the stairwell. Francine never remembered a time when she had actually been *glad* to hear Aunt Nora's caustic voice.

When Nora's pastor-husband died a year ago and left her almost penniless, Tom and Mariette agreed to Nora moving into the second-floor room across from Francine's. During that year, Francine had silently endured more lectures from her aunt than she had from her professors. Aunt Nora's discourses usually involved lambasting her baby sister for having married Francine's father, that "no-good Howie Ponce." Before she was through, Nora was all but blaming Francine for the union while reminding her how lucky she was to have been rescued from "that wretched life in Rockaway."

Aunt Nora topped the final stair. "Mariette and the rest are waiting on you two," she huffed with the red-faced expression of an out-of-shape woman pushing sixty. Regardless of Nora's thin frame, Francine seldom saw her aunt do more than lift the foot of the recliner. "I'm heading to my room," Nora explained. "Forgot my blood-pressure medicine." She glared at Ethan and Francine. "It might do you both good to think of someone else for a change besides yourselves. There's a whole den full of people wondering where you are and what's taking you so long, Ethan!"

"Oh sure," Ethan said with a cheerful ease that suggested he hadn't been home long enough for Aunt Nora to start getting under his skin. He plopped Daisy down. Her toenails clicked against polished wood as she pranced near his side.

"Come on, Francine. There's somebody I want you to meet," he repeated with a light tap on her arm.

Silently Francine fell in beside Ethan and prayed this new acquaintance was masculine. "Is this someone you met on your trip?" she questioned.

"Yes, two someones, actually." His eyes bright, Ethan trotted down the stairs. "Carrie and Hugh Casper—they're brother and sister. They're actually Americans who had rental property next door to the church I was working with. We invited them to church one Saturday, and they wound up being faithful attendees. They have an uncle living an hour from here in Long Beach. When my term was up, they decided to come for a visit to New York. They flew in with me today and rented a car. They'll be heading to their uncle's in an hour or two."

Francine descended the stairs with less enthusiasm than did Ethan. By the time she took the last step, she was wondering why Ethan hadn't mentioned these new friends in any of his e-mails. However, his daily e-mails had eventually dwindled to one a week and then one every other week. Francine, intensely focused upon finishing her summer semester, hadn't worried about the lack of communication. She had simply assumed that Ethan was as busy as she. Now she suspected he may have been engaged in more pursuits than the mission trip.

She conjured willowy, glamorous, polished images of this Carrie Casper. By the time her imagination was through,

Francine had created a young woman fit for the cover of any fashion magazine. She touched her ponytail and wondered how much her nap had disheveled her appearance.

With Daisy on their heels, Ethan offered Francine an assuring smile that insisted nothing had changed between them…that the trip to Paris was just a missions trip and nothing more. Francine returned his smile and tried to control her suspicions.

Through the years she had watched more women than Marie's friend Patti Towers throw themselves at Ethan. But with the constant support of Uncle Tom, nothing had turned Ethan from his goal. He had always remained steady in the Lord and true to his calling. The trip to Paris had been part of a hands-on seminary assignment that earned him valuable credits toward completing his Master's degree. After finishing his last class this fall, Ethan would seek ordination as a pastor and begin looking for a church to fulfill his calling.

More than once during his absence, Francine caught herself daydreaming about what a wonderful pastor's wife she would be and how Ethan would see her with fresh eyes once he arrived back from Paris. Her fantasies had taken her through their simple wedding and into the first church they would take as husband and wife. Francine imagined how thrilled she would be to use her education degree in teaching Sunday school and helping Ethan increase attendance through children's church. Her dreams usually expanded to the day they brought home their first child—always a girl with Francine's white-blonde hair and Ethan's dark, merry eyes. Their life, as she envisioned it, would be a blessed extension of the friendship they'd shared…a friendship christened with love's sunshine and joy's gentle breeze.

But today the presence of this Carrie Casper blotted out the sunshine from Francine's dreams like a dark cloud promising wicked winds that would annihilate her and Ethan's special bond. Francine wasn't sure she could survive Ethan's rejection.

As an early adolescent, she had silently dealt with the gradual rejection of her birth family. First, her absentee father had never bothered to contact Francine once she moved to Central Park. Then her mother's initial correspondence had dwindled to eventual silence. Her brother Wade, now working as a restaurant assistant manager, remained faithful in writing and staying close to Francine. And her little sister, Sandra, now fifteen, did her best to keep up a sporadic correspondence.

Her mom, caught up in caring for four children while working, had encouraged Francine to make a life for herself with her new family. "You're the lucky one," she'd said in one of her few letters. Looking back, Francine realized that was her mother's way of saying she was too busy for her eldest daughter, who had it made with the rich relatives. Her mom's neglect intensified Francine's reticence and made her more desperate to please her aunt and uncle.

Francine rubbed her thumb against her forefinger and silently suppressed the tide of anxiety that swept across her soul. Through the years Ethan had become her family, her stability, the one she could count on to always be there. Together they had comforted each other when their birth families failed them. Ethan's father had only contacted him twice since Francine moved to Central Park. So Ethan had understood Francine's suffering as no other—and she, his.

Francine gazed toward the den. Alight with summer sunshine, the room emitted the faint scent of Aunt Mariette's signature raspberry tea. A chorus of laughter tottered into the entryway. Francine recognized Aunt Mariette's languid chuckle mixed with Uncle Tom's rich, masculine mirth. Among these familiar laughs frolicked musical giggles that testified to the presence of Ethan's new friends.

Knitting her brows, Francine eyed the den's entry. While attending Aunt Mariette, she had walked into this room hundreds of times. But now the familiar took on an ominous aura. The closer they grew to the den, the more Francine dreaded the meeting.

Ethan paused near the den's threshold and flashed her one of his traffic-stopping smiles. "Are you coming?" He extended his hand.

"Oh yes, of course," Francine offered and hurried forward to place her hand in Ethan's. The fit was familiar and snug and comforting.

He squeezed her hand and whispered, "Did I tell you I missed you?" The conviction in his voice sharpened the admiration in his eyes.

Francine's anxiety eased. Her trusting heart beat with new certainty. She offered Ethan a relaxed smile, flowing from years of faithful affection. *This Carrie Casper is nothing but a friend,* Francine firmly told herself before they stepped into the den. *My Ethan would never get involved with a woman now...not now. Not when he's supposed to be falling in love with me.*

Five

❧❧

Ethan Summers entered the den, and Carrie Casper casually smiled toward him. Nestled in the corner of the red velvet couch, she crossed her legs and strategically allowed her polished cotton skirt to inch above her knee, bare and tanned. Her feet, wrapped in strappy high-heels, felt as if someone were pounding nails into them. But Carrie refused to acknowledge that they were bothering her in the least. Every pain she endured was worth catching Ethan Summers.

The second she saw the good-looking, dark-haired guy working in the churchyard next to her parents' rental property, Carrie had been highly interested in him. So she agreed to attend church services. She got to know Ethan. The closer she grew to him, the more she liked. And once she learned that his foster father was a wealthy New York stockbroker and Ethan was an equal heir to a fortune, Carrie decided he was everything she wanted in a husband—an attractive, moneyed man she could fall madly in love with. While a few of her friends had married for money alone, Carrie had vowed to wait for money *and* love. Her father's vast fortune allowed her that luxury. Even though Carrie didn't want to marry a man of no financial status, she also didn't want to neglect love in the process.

When she met Ethan, she soon realized he was exactly what she had been waiting for. So she followed him to New York and planned to have his sizable engagement ring on her finger by Christmas. The rest was just details.

"There you two are!" Tom Barrimore exclaimed. As the balding gentleman stood to introduce the woman Ethan escorted into the room, his lethargic wife echoed his sentiment then lost interest in the newcomer. Mariette Barrimore, wearing a pretty housedress, nursed her cup of tea as her absent gaze wandered toward the terrier who hopped into her lap. Soon, Mariette set her tea mug on the lampstand and kneaded the dog's ears. Carrie assumed the woman's thoughts had left them once more. So far, she had only intermittently joined the conversation, regularly lapsing into meditative silence.

After a sip of her tart raspberry tea, Carrie placed the mug on the mahogany end table and carefully eyed the pale blonde. *So this is the famous Francine Ponce.* A few minutes ago, Ethan had asked where she was with too much interest for Carrie's comfort. Then again, Ethan always sounded a tad bit too warm when he spoke of Francine. From the first time Ethan referred to her and explained who she was, Carrie fully expected Francine to be a rival. Even though the young lady beside Ethan was far from a femme fatale, Carrie's abdomen tensed.

"This is my niece, Francine Ponce." The suit-clad Tom placed his hand on Francine's back and commanded the antique-laden room as if he were the sire of a luxurious castle. "Francine, these are our new friends, Carrie and Hugh Casper."

Hugh stood and readily greeted Francine with his typical warm handshake. "Nice to meet you," he offered with the faint French accent he exhibited if he chose. Today, he chose.

Francine, nearly as tall as Hugh, lowered her gaze. She returned his greeting and showed no signs of responding to

Hugh's carefree sandy hair, merry hazel eyes, or debonair appeal. Hugh, never accused of being classically handsome, made up for his lack of looks with bucketsful of charm and a wardrobe that testified to his impeccable taste and large budget. As a result, he usually made a conquest of most single women long before the drop-dead gorgeous guys had a chance. But Francine Ponce seemed oblivious to tall and masculine and captivating—even when he was dressed in 200-dollar low-riding jeans and a Ralph Lauren polo shirt that perfectly matched his hair.

Francine reminded Carrie of an albino mouse hovering in the corner of a den full of hungry cats. And Ethan lingered beside her like a protective brother. Carrie's tightened abdomen relaxed. She stood and casually smiled at Francine in an attempt to ease her bashfulness. The young blonde tilted down her head and sneaked an upward peak at Carrie, who received only a flash of pale-blue eyes before the two shook hands.

She assessed her own appearance in comparison to Francine's. Carrie's sandy-blonde curls were far more fashionable than Francine's straight, white-blonde ponytail. Her finely made-up, green eyes were more dazzling than Francine's wan eyes. Carrie examined Francine's simple, heart-shaped face bearing only a light brush of cosmetics. Then she candidly admitted that her own high cheekbones and full lips would snare more masculine attention any day.

Francine's athletic frame, crumpled linen shorts, and nondescript blouse sealed the friendship. Carrie smoothed her palms along the sides of her petite hips, adjusted her hot pink cropped jacket, and vowed to never waste another second worrying about Francine Ponce. A rival she was not.

"Here, why don't you sit by me?" Carrie was relieved her friendly offer could be genuine. She detested duplicity, and never more than when she was the one exhibiting it. Besides, Carrie deduced that Ethan would approve of anyone who showed an interest in his timid "little sister."

"We need to get better acquainted," Carrie added. "I'm going to be in New York awhile, and I need as many new friends as I can find right now."

"So do I," Hugh agreed. He reclaimed his seat on the couch's other end and patted the middle cushion.

Francine looked at Ethan.

With an encouraging nod, Ethan said, "Go ahead. I'll sit over there." He motioned toward the love seat near the row of gauze-swathed windows.

"No, son," Tom said, his deep voice demanding no objections. "Here, take my seat. I need to head to the office and take care of some business anyway." He politely nodded toward Carrie and Hugh. "If you don't mind my stepping out on you," he explained, "I've got a business trip to England scheduled in a few weeks, and I'm trying to square away some details before I leave."

"We'll miss your company," Carrie said with a warm smile. "But we'll be fine."

"Yes—don't worry about us," Hugh affirmed. "We understand. Our father has traveled all our lives. He owns a chain of restaurants," he explained with a nonchalance that understated the multicontinent food chain.

Carrie, tempted to mention the name of the highly advertised restaurants, decided to remain silent. *No sense appearing pompous,* she thought. *The truth will come out soon enough.*

"Glad you understand," Tom said. After a curt smile, he pressed his lips together, and his sharp blue eyes developed the keen gaze of a man already taking care of business. He stepped toward his wife and bestowed a respectful kiss upon her forehead. "I'll be back by seven. Tell Katy to have dinner waiting for me then."

"Of course," Mariette Barrimore acquiesced while he marched toward the door. Mariette crossed her legs and resumed her tea-sipping. After a swallow, she observed Francine and fondly smiled. "Franny, if you don't mind, be a dear and go tell Katy your Uncle Tom wants dinner at seven."

Debra White Smith

"Okay," Francine meekly agreed mere seconds after taking her seat.

Tom Barrimore stopped in the doorway and emitted a firm no. He turned toward his wife. "Francine is to stay where she is. She just sat down, for pity's sake."

"Well, who's to tell Katy then?" Mariette asked, her thin brows arched.

"I—I really don't mind," Francine insisted and scooted to the edge of the couch.

Carrie narrowed her eyes and started analyzing the undertones of this cozy little "family."

After a concerned glance toward Francine, Ethan began to stand. "I'll go," he offered.

"No," Tom repeated. "You just sat down, too."

Ethan didn't argue and settled back into the winged-back chair.

"I'll tell her," Mr. Barrimore groused. After shooting his wife a tart glance, he pivoted to leave the room again. "I don't know why I don't have an intercom installed," he mumbled under his breath.

"Well, I've taken my medication," Nora's voice preceded the scrawny woman's appearance near Tom, "now I can enjoy my tea."

"Nora," Tom stated without looking at her, "go tell Katy that I want dinner ready by seven."

"Isn't Francine able to do that?" Nora observed Francine with an accusatory glint in her green eyes.

Tom scowled at his sister-in-law while Daisy released a mild grunt before a yawn.

"Francine just sat down," Tom snapped and worked his jaw.

"I really don't mind." Francine stood. "I hate for everyone to be put out because—"

Mr. Barrimore's frown softened when he addressed Francine. "You're fine, Franny. Sit back down. Enjoy your new friends. Nora's taking care of it." He issued a silent challenge that suggested neither Francine nor Nora should argue.

Head lowered, Francine resumed her seat. A faint flush tinged her cheeks.

After a gape, Nora yanked on the front of her red smock and snapped shut her mouth. Her back stiff, she marched from the room.

Carrie watched Mr. Barrimore's swift exit before refocusing upon Francine. The woman she had assumed was a rival now evoked a flutter of empathy. Carrie was sure Ethan had told her that Francine was the Barrimore's niece and a blood relative. He, on the other hand, was a foster son. During the few seconds of awkward silence that settled upon the group, Carrie wondered if certain family members always treated Francine as if she were the family servant.

"Francine, how's college been this summer?" Ethan asked, leaning forward.

"Okay, I guess." She stole a glimpse of Ethan and stroked the hem of her linen shorts. Carrie detected the vague scent of a familiar fragrance—Ombre Rose. Carrie herself had worn that modest scent until a few years ago when she developed the taste for something more sophisticated. Now she admitted the simple fragrance fit Francine's quiet manner in a way it never fit hers.

"What college are you attending, Francine?" Hugh asked.

"Hunter College. It's here—on 68th and Lexington," she explained. "I'm majoring in elementary education." Francine lifted her chin with a speck of assurance.

"Wonderful!" Hugh responded and leaned closer to Francine. Carrie recognized the smile and the impish light dancing in his hazel eyes. Hugh was probably in the process of assessing how long it would take him to make the coy Francine Ponce come out of her shell and fall for him. Some men enjoyed hunting game. Hugh, on the other hand, specialized in hunting women. When he found one that posed a potential challenge, he began his game. The bigger the challenge, the more he enjoyed the sport. Hugh had relished this activity since he was an adolescent and realized the power of his personality upon the opposite sex.

For once, Carrie found no humor in Hugh's little pastime. A few times she had silently watched her brother break the hearts of some snobby Paris twits who deserved to be taken down a few notches. But already she recognized that Francine Ponce was different. Her guileless demeanor insisted she didn't deserve to have her heart broken.

"What grade do you plan to teach?" Carrie asked, and she hoped Hugh would find another diversion.

Francine's docile gaze took on the sharpness of a surgeon's scalpel. She looked Carrie in the eyes. Feeling as if her mind were being examined for any scrap of insincerity, Carrie tightened her fist and forced herself to hold the penetrating gaze. Once Francine glanced away and prepared to answer the question, Carrie relaxed her fist and realized her fingernails had bitten into her palm.

Ethan spoke before she uttered the first word. "She wants to teach first grade," he explained, his eyes aglow with pride. "We're all very proud of her—especially my dad."

Francine's eyes widened.

"Oh, don't look so surprised, Francine," Mariette drowsed. "You, of all people should know that Tom—"

"Oh no, I don't—or—or—I didn't!" Francine stuttered as a red flush crept from her neck toward her eyes. She shifted her gaze from Ethan to Mariette and back again. "I just assumed that—"

Mariette stroked her dog. "I believe Francine told us yesterday that it's all settled for an early graduation. Tom was nearly beside himself last night when we went to bed. He's all set to send her to graduate school as well, if she wants. She'll wrap up student teaching next spring and then be done with her degree a year early. Isn't that what you told me, Francine?"

"Well, yes." Francine's certain nod affirmed for Carrie that perhaps there was much more to her new acquaintance than met the eye. Maybe there was also much more to her position in the family than Carrie had first assumed.

For a few seconds, she was tempted to recant her decision that Francine Ponce could never be her rival. Then, she reminded herself that her size-four hips looked better in a pair of jeans than Francine's approximate size twelve would any day. The realization eased all worries.

Carrie rubbed her thumb along the base of her ring finger and cut a glance toward her brother. Hugh had asked Francine another question that Carrie missed, and he was in the process of appearing engrossed by her every word. Even though Carrie truly didn't want to see Francine hurt, she wondered if perhaps her brother's distraction might be a good thing. *At least when Hugh interacts with Francine, Ethan is more free to focus on me,* she thought.

She caught Ethan watching her and extended an inviting smile. "Didn't you mention showing me the terrace?" Carrie asked and hoped the top-of-the-house patio was as romantic as it sounded.

"Sure!" Ethan agreed and stood. "There are even binoculars up there." He stepped toward Carrie and extended his hand toward her. "You can see Central Park up close and personal."

"How neat!" Carrie exclaimed and placed her hand in his. She pulled on his slender fingers and allowed Ethan to assist her up.

"I just had Katy replenish the sodas up there." Mariette nudged a thick, graying lock of hair off her forehead and retrieved a pair of reading glasses from the lamp stand. "There's nothing better than sitting up there for a while, just sipping cola."

"That sounds great!" Ethan agreed and squeezed Carrie's hand just before releasing it. She stifled a sigh. So far, all Carrie could get the guy to do was hold hands for about thirty seconds.

"I wonder what happened to Nora?" Mariette mused and eyed the doorway. "Oh well," she finally said and dismissed the whole query with a yawn. After sliding the reading glasses up her nose, Mariette reached for a novel lying near her tea mug. The rustling of pages preceded her tuning out the room's occupants.

"I'd like to see the terrace." Hugh's admission both surprised and disappointed Carrie.

"Well, come on." Ethan motioned for him and Francine to join them and then offered Francine assistance in standing as well.

Instead of stirring any tinge of jealousy, Carrie was impressed by Ethan's old-fashioned, gentlemanly manners. None of the men she dated ever showed such consideration—unless they were simultaneously pressuring her for physical favors. Only a man of true character could exhibit honest respect with no ulterior motives. Carrie had never so desperately wanted to fall in love.

Six

Francine thought of four solid excuses for why she shouldn't accompany Ethan and his friends to the terrace. The problem was, the first one didn't pop into her head until after she'd stepped into the elevator and the door closed. By the time the elevator opened onto the roof, she had conjured the other three. After an intense mental battle, Francine decided not to voice any opposition. That would draw too much attention to her and require that she exert her will against pleas to stay. She chose to quietly endure.

Carrie stepped onto the terrace with the others close behind. "Wow!" she gasped and pivoted to take in the lavish outdoor patio, now replete with a glassed-in sunroom. "This is great!"

Francine sidestepped the chatty Carrie and moved toward the railing. She recalled the first day she'd come up here with Ethan. Even at fifteen, Ethan treated her with the same friendliness and concern he now bestowed upon Carrie.

Francine darted a glance toward Ethan as he bent toward Carrie and smiled into her eyes. Hugh was close behind them, and he chuckled at something Ethan said. It didn't take a genius to see that Ethan was on the verge of falling hard for Carrie. Francine had never seen him so animated in the presence of a woman. And Carrie had the same look on her face that dozens of other young ladies displayed through the years: *Wow! This guy's a jewel! Not only is he good-looking and charming, he's also a gentleman and, oh gasp, honorable! On top of all that he's going to inherit a lot of money. I have died and gone to heaven!*

But Francine knew so much more about Ethan than Carrie Casper or any other woman who had imagined herself in love with him. Francine had the advantage of nearly a decade of emotional intimacy with Ethan. Not only did she understand his strengths, she also recognized his imperfections…the occasional temper flair-ups, the constant nag of athlete's foot, his untamable stubborn streak, his scrawny legs. Francine smiled. These flaws only made her love him all the more. She wondered if Carrie's love might wane in the face of Ethan's shortcomings.

Francine rested her forearms on the rail and focused on the treetops that graced Central Park. At this point, she figured she had only two options. She could dissolve into a desperate heap of despair or deny her feelings and pretend everything was normal. The latter option proved itself the least messy. Francine had functioned in denial mode most of her life. She would continue to do so.

She examined the typical Manhattan haze blotting out any chance of a peek at the blue sky. Francine identified with the overcast sky. In her mind she opened her soul to the haze and allowed the haze to blanket her heart. No one would suspect that beneath her cool exterior beat the heart of a woman passionately in love. Soon maybe even she would grow numb to her own feelings and be able to function without the pain.

She closed her eyes and slowly inhaled the warm air. Midst the city smells of hot concrete and vehicle exhaust, Francine thought she detected the faint scent of one of Central Park's hot dog carts. She would have given her right arm for a chance to roll back time to the days when Ethan was all hers…to the times they'd enjoyed Central Park's horse-drawn carriages…to the hours they strolled the park together while munching their favorite treat—hot dogs with extra mustard. Her eyes stung. Francine swallowed hard and told herself to concentrate on something less heart-wrenching, like her fall class lineup.

"A penny for your thoughts?" Hugh Casper's voice penetrated her reverie.

Francine gripped the rail and opened her eyes. She lowered her head and shot Hugh a brief, upward glance. Earlier she had been surprised by Carrie's authentic offer of friendship. Hugh's eyes weren't as earnest as his sisters. Francine suspected that at best he was a flirt. She didn't know him well enough to consider the worst case scenario. What surprised Francine was that Hugh had taken the time to strike up a conversation with her. Most flirtatious men didn't waste a minute on her.

"I was just thinking about my fall class lineup," Francine explained and gazed back at the park. Not even the haze could detract from the park's beauty…or the beauty of the memories.

"That's a boring topic for a beautiful woman." The glib remark fell off his tongue far too smoothly.

Francine averted her face. *I'm not a beauty,* she thought. *Not like your sister, anyway.*

Despite her better judgment, she cast a glance toward Ethan and Carrie. She was standing on a stool looking through the binoculars. With his low, assuring voice, Ethan guided her sightseeing, just as he had once done with Francine.

Francine looked down and reminded herself that she had chosen not to react. She didn't. Not outwardly or inwardly.

The elevator's ding accompanied a burst of muffled laughter that Francine recognized well. She and Hugh simultaneously turned toward the elevator as the doors slid open. Julie, Marie, and her fiancé, Ricky Worthingham, invaded the terrace.

"Oh my word!" Julie gasped, "I've never laughed so hard in my life. Ricky, your jokes are all too funny!"

Marie, hanging onto Ricky's hand, was agreeing with her sister when she spotted Hugh. Her hilarity faded so swiftly Francine wondered if Ricky's corny jokes would only be half as funny if he were half as rich.

"Oh hi, you guys!" Ethan waved toward the group, then spoke to Carrie.

"Mom said you were up here and had some new friends we should meet," Marie explained.

"Yes, of course," Ethan agreed. "I was hoping you'd get to meet them before they left."

The group of six met near the doorway to the sunroom, which held a suite full of wicker furniture. Aunt Mariette had ordered the air-conditioned room's construction over five years ago. The structure guaranteed that Francine's aunts spent ample time on the terrace. Francine, who had long ago-claimed the terrace as her special quiet spot, had to endure the invasion of her territory. Since then she discovered a tiny, unused room on the fifth floor. The austere furnishings fit Francine's needs. The room's window overlooked Central Park. So far no one in the family had decided the room was perfect for one of their endeavors.

Francine examined the group of new friends, and then turned toward the elevator. She would rather be in her special room than here on the terrace watching Ethan fall in love. The man occupying her thoughts placed his hand on Carrie's back and leaned closer to hear what she was saying. Faltering wind tossed Carrie's curls like an invisible hand styling her hair. Francine flexed her fingers against the rail and forced herself not to feel. She concentrated on her cousins, who both centered upon Hugh. The heightened color flattering Julie's flawless face insisted that Hugh was already throwing around compliments like Ricky threw around money. But this time, when he said that his new acquaintances were beautiful, it would be true.

While neither of her cousins was as attractive as Carrie, they each knew how to get the well-bred look that turned heads. Marie's features were more classically proportioned, and Julie was often dubbed cute. The two, with their straight dark hair and top-dollar clothing had outshone Francine since the moment she moved to Central Park. Only the morning served as equalizer. Neither Marie nor Julie would attract much attention when they first crawled out of bed.

But Francine had never been so thrilled to look and dress exactly as she did—sleepy eyes, rumpled hair, simple wardrobe and all. She'd far rather Hugh focus on her polished cousins than her. Thankfully, Marie possessed the decency to act engaged and guard her expression, but Francine knew her well enough to recognize the interest in her blue eyes.

While Hugh Casper wasn't half as attractive as Ethan, he looked like a model compared to Marie's bony fiancé. Ricky, with his droopy nose, slanted shoulders, and unkempt dark hair, seemed unaware of his fiancée's discriminating appraisal of Hugh. Ricky was often oblivious of much—including where he'd placed his keys, whether or not he shaved, and what day of the month it was.

His shirttail, untucked in the back, sashayed in the mild breeze. Ricky had a knack for wearing designer clothing in a way that made it look like garage sale rejects. Francine frequently marveled that the guy actually graduated from high school, let alone college. Despite all his shortcomings, Francine also saw a man with a good heart. She hoped Marie would eventually see the same.

"No way!" Julie's exclamation erupted upon Francine's thoughts. "Your dad owns Addy's?" She looked from Carrie to Hugh. "All of them?"

"Yes," Hugh said, "all of them. He started with one small restaurant in Long Beach before we were born. One led to another."

"And now the chain is all over the world," Carrie added with a knock-'em-dead smile.

Ethan revealed no hint of surprise.

"Hey, I think one of my dad's hotels has an Addy's in it," Ricky mumbled and looked to Marie for confirmation. "Doesn't it? Or is that an Arby's?" he questioned and squinted into the distance.

"Both," Marie supplied without hesitation. "Remember, Addy's is in the Worthingham Renaissance and Arby's is in the Worthingham on the Harbor."

"Oh yeah." Ricky placed his fist in the center of his forehead as if trying to fuse the facts into his brain. "There are so many, I lose track."

"Your dad owns hotels?" Carrie questioned.

"Yes," Marie purred and stroked Ricky's arm. "Their family *is* Worthingham Hotels."

Francine slipped her hands into her shorts pockets and moved toward the elevator. The peaceful ambiance of her fifth-floor room beckoned.

"Worthingham Hotels," Hugh mused. "How interesting… and one of *our* restaurants is in one of *your* hotels!"

"We should go see that one!" Carrie suggested. "Ricky could give us a tour of the hotel, and we could eat at Addy's! I've never been inside the Renaissance." She looked at Hugh. "Have you?"

"No," Hugh said.

"That's a brilliant idea!" Ethan exclaimed. "I think we've all seen it at one time or another, but it's worth another visit any day."

Despite the sporadic wind, warm moisture dotted Francine's upper lip. She pressed the elevator button and anticipated the home's cooler air. She tensed her knees and glanced over her shoulder. So far the group seemed ignorant of her presence. Her escape was almost complete. The elevator's subtle ring proved her nemesis. Before she could scurry through the opening doors, Ethan called her name.

"Francine? Where are you going?" His nearing footsteps prohibited her from slipping into the elevator.

She turned toward Ethan and smiled weakly. "I was just getting a little warm," Francine explained, "and thought I'd head back into the house." A keen glance over Ethan's shoulder revealed the other five were focused upon her.

"Francine!" Julie exclaimed. "I didn't even see you when we came up. Did you, Marie?" She looked at her sister, whose negative nod insisted that Francine's presence, or lack of it, mattered little in the scheme of her world. Besides, Hugh mumbled something to Marie and snared her attention. She released Ricky's hand as this new volley of private conversation engrossed her.

"She was hiding over there by the rail, right beside Hugh," Ethan explained. With a sly smile he pointed toward the highly visible section of terrace straight across from the elevator's opening.

"Hiding?" Ricky questioned and looked where Ethan pointed.

"It was a joke," Julie explained. "Francine was right out in the open. We should have seen her. I guess we were just distracted."

"Oh...okay," Ricky said and absently listened in on Marie and Hugh's conversation.

Francine determined that that little exchange was turning into a quick-witted battery of banter—if the swift words and Marie's delighted smile was anything to go by.

Ethan took Francine's hand. "You can't run away, Franny," he admonished and tugged her toward the group. "I won't let you."

When he smiled into her eyes, Francine reminded herself she was no longer allowed to feel. But she was quickly learning that true love was as stubborn as Ethan on a bad day. It refused control.

"We're talking about a trip to one of Ricky's hotels," Ethan continued.

"Yes, I heard," Francine admitted.

"So you also heard about Carrie's father owning Addy's?"
She nodded.

"Good. We want you to go with us. We only have to decide on a day and time," Ethan concluded and urged Francine to step into the circle of friends between him and Carrie.

"Of course we want you to come with us," Carrie agreed and patted Francine's back. "Have you ever eaten at Addy's?"

"Yes, that's one of Aunt Mariette's favorite restaurants."

"Oh, mine, too," Hugh commented with a laugh.

Marie and Julie's hearty laughter lacked even a trace of the forced shrill some of Ricky's jokes incited.

"Very funny," Ethan drawled.

While Ricky draped his arm along Marie's shoulders, Francine couldn't resist another eye-to-eye scrutiny of Carrie's motives. Once again she saw nothing in her exotic, green eyes but the offer of guileless friendship. The reality was at once relieving and disconcerting. Francine hated the thought of her Ethan falling for a schemer, but she also realized that the more pure Carrie's motives, the more likely Ethan would genuinely love her. Furthermore, while Francine's goal was to always exhibit a Christlike spirit, she would have far preferred not to like Carrie. So far, the only thing Francine could find not to like in Carrie was the fact that she was enamored with Ethan—and that seemed an unfair and shallow basis for despising a kind woman.

What single woman isn't enamored with Ethan? Francine reasoned. *How can I hold something against Carrie that I have fallen victim to myself?*

"So, when do we take this little trip?" Hugh asked. "Tomorrow?"

"No, Hugh, that won't work at all," Carrie scolded and shook her head. "Uncle Al will want us to himself for a few days. Remember, he said he was going to take us to New York Harbor tomorrow."

"Oh goody!" Hugh rubbed his hands together as if he were five. "I'd way rather do that than hit the town with four hot babes!"

"Oh Hugh!" Carrie grabbed his arm and kissed him hard on the cheek. "You're such a tease!"

When Carrie pulled away, she left a lip print in glossy pink, the exact shade of her jacket.

"Did you just put lipstick on me?" Hugh touched his cheek and examined the end of his index finger, now shiny pink. "Uuhh," he huffed. "Now, I've got to get someone to match up the other side or I'll be lopsided." His gaze rested upon Marie.

Francine assumed Ricky missed the tantalizing lift of Marie's brow just as Julie exclaimed, "I'll match it up!" She lurched across the circle to plant her lips against Hugh's other cheek. Before she pulled away, he grabbed her and went into a dance dip. Julie clung to him and squealed her delight while the rest of the group laughed—everyone except Francine.

When Hugh lifted Julie, his arm lingered along her waist for several seconds. Her tight T-shirt stopped about two inches above her snug hip-huggers and revealed a glimpse of tanned abdomen. Francine didn't have to wonder if Hugh noticed. Julie didn't seem the least bit offended that someone she'd just met was taking such liberties.

"Why don't we set our little trip for three days from now?" Ethan asked.

"That would be Friday," Carrie observed. "Friday's good, I think. If I remember right, Uncle Al is taking a weekend trip anyway. He works for Dad, by the way." She waved her hand in explanation of the connection and shifted her weight from one foot to the other.

Francine eyed Carrie's feet and winced. Those three-inch heels on her sandals looked like killers.

"Maybe we could leave around three," Ethan continued. "That would give us time for Ricky to give us the hotel tour. Then we could have dinner at Addy's and maybe even take in a movie."

"Okay," Ricky said with an eager nod that flopped a clump of dark bangs onto his forehead. "I'll call Dad's secretary and get him to make us some reservations." He fumbled along his belt loop, retrieved his Palm Pilot, and turned it on. "I'm making myself a note in case I forget," Ricky explained.

"There's a theater across the street," Marie mentioned.

"Across the street from where?" Ricky blankly stared at his fiancée.

"From the hotel," Marie enunciated. She lifted her straight hair and fanned the back of her neck.

"Oh!" Ricky nodded. "Yeah, right, I knew that," he said with a chuckle that no one shared.

Marie glanced at Julie's rosy lip print on Hugh's cheek, dropped her hair, and gazed into the distance.

Francine shared in Marie's growing discomfort. While summer in New York wasn't desert-hot, the terrace could heat up nicely in early August. She touched her cheeks and wondered if they had flushed yet—they certainly felt it. Given her fair skin, Francine seldom went out—even on a hazy day—without sunscreen. While her face was protected by makeup, her bare arms weren't as fortunate. She touched the edge of her shoulder, right where her sleeveless shirt stopped. Even though her skin was warm, there was no tenderness…yet. But she figured she wouldn't have to stand on the terrace much longer before she sported a mild burn.

"You're overheating," Ethan observed and examined her shoulders like an over-protective dermatologist. "I shouldn't have kept you out here so long," he worried.

"I'm okay," Francine said.

"Don't give me that," Ethan argued and delicately lifted the edge of her shirt off her shoulder. "I've seen you burn to a crisp while denying it the whole time. See there!" He dropped the shirt's edge. "You're already getting pink. I've got to get her in, guys," he said and took Francine's arm.

"Really, I'm fine right now," she protested, but saw this opportunity as the perfect chance to make her getaway. "I'll just go on inside, and you guys can—"

"Nice try," Ethan growled and tugged her toward the glassed-in room. "We'll just all move into the sunroom."

"Works for me," Marie said. "Mom even has a stash of drinks and snacks up here."

"She mentioned that earlier. Sounds great!" Carrie agreed and followed Julie and Marie toward the door.

Francine stepped forward, but Ethan constrained her progress while Hugh and Ricky awaited the ladies entering the room.

When Carrie reached the entrance, she looked over her shoulder. "What do you want, Francine?" she inquired. "I'll get yours when I get mine."

"Thanks, but you don't have to—"

"She usually goes for the bottled water," Ethan offered.

"And you?" Carrie asked.

"Don't worry about—"

"He'll take a Pepsi," Francine said with a trace of humor in her soft voice.

Carrie smiled. "I like the way you two look out for each other."

Shaking his head, Ethan chuckled.

As soon as Carrie slipped inside, he whispered into Francine's ear, "I haven't seen you in months, and I'm not going to let you hole up in your little room and leave me alone."

"You wouldn't be alone," Francine reasoned and managed to hide the thrill in her spirit.

"But I wouldn't be with you, either." Ethan raised his brows and challenged her to contradict him.

Francine smiled and dared to stroke his black goatee, as thick as his cropped hair. "What possessed you to grow a goatee, Ethan Summers?"

"Don't you like it?" he countered, and the two moved toward the sunroom.

"Of course," she said and didn't add how distinguished she thought it made him. "I just never imagined you'd—"

"What? Do something so fashionable?"

"Oh brother," she complained, "now you're putting words in my mouth."

The minute Ethan showed concern for Francine's welfare, her tension began to ease. Now that he was looking at her with all the old respect and love, she could almost hope that Carrie really meant nothing to him. But the love in Ethan's eyes wasn't the ardor a man held for a woman; it was the admiration of a brother for his sister. Her neck tensed anew.

He held open the door, and Francine walked inside where the rest had clustered around the miniature snack bar, replete with a refrigerator, a basket of fruit, and a shelf lined with chips and crackers. The air smelled of wicker furniture and cooled the perspiration along Francine's hairline and upper lip. A delightful shiver followed.

"It feels so good in here," she said.

"Better than outside, that's for sure," Ethan said. He pulled out one of the wicker chairs near a round, glass-topped table and motioned for Francine to take the seat.

She gladly accepted the kindness. When Ethan sat down, he leaned forward on his elbow, looked her squarely in the eyes, and said, "Tell me more about this early graduation. Sounds like you've got Dad swollen up with pride, here."

Francine averted her gaze and toyed with the silk ivy in the table's center. "I had no idea he even cared," she admitted.

"Cared? Are you kidding?" Ethan questioned. "Every time he e-mailed me while I was in France, he mentioned you. Dad thinks you have grown into a very wise young woman—and he thinks you're pretty on top of that."

She widened her eyes and held Ethan's candid gaze. While Marie and Julie, Hugh and Ricky exploded into a round of laughter on the other side of the room, Francine remained silent. She was so stunned, she didn't even blush.

Ethan shook his head. "Why do you always have to be so infernally modest?"

Carrie arrived carrying a petite tray laden with a trio of short bottles. "Don't criticize her, Ethan," she admonished and set the tray near the silk ivy. "A lot of people think infernal modesty is a wonderful trait. I know that's what I like the best about myself," she teased. Carrie settled into the seat between Ethan and Francine, gracefully laid her hand on her chest, and fluttered her eyelashes. "That—and my humility."

Francine didn't want to enjoy Carrie's humor. The very act seemed a betrayal of her own heart. She tried to stop the smile, but it wouldn't be denied.

Ethan laughed out loud, then grinned straight into Carrie's face with a fervency Francine dreamed he might one day bestow upon her. "I must be the luckiest guy in the world," he said. "I've got two modest women at one table—and one of them even admits she's humble." He picked up his Pepsi bottle and toasted both of them.

"Now you're starting to sound like Hugh," Carrie countered.

Leaning within inches of his new friend, Ethan whispered, "But I don't think Hugh means it half as much." This time his words and attention were all for Carrie.

Seven

Carrie Casper flexed her bare foot against the brake pedal and slowed the flashy sports coupe she and Hugh had rented. "This is the last light before we hit the Atlantic Beach Bridge," she said and tried to catch a glimpse of the Manhattan skyline in her rearview mirror. *No luck. Maybe when we hit the bridge, I'll get a view.* Carrie couldn't look at Manhattan enough and couldn't wait until Friday.

"Good," Hugh drawled, "I don't think I could take any more of your wild driving."

"Oh puuulllleeeezze." Carrie rolled her eyes and glanced at her heavy-eyed brother, who was reclining his seat. "At least we're still alive," she said.

"Yeah, that's a shock. I thought for sure eighty-five cars were going to run us over considering how slow you were driving," he said, his vague French accent now discarded. Hugh rested his head against the seat, closed his eyes, and yawned.

"And if you'd been driving, we would already have three tickets. My goal is to get us there alive—okay?" She fondly patted her brother's flat tummy.

He opened one eye, feigned a glare, then checked out the intersection. "The light's green," Hugh proclaimed. "Are we going to sit here all day or what?"

An angry horn from behind punctuated his question.

Carrie huffed and decided to put the new-smelling vehicle to the test. She pressed the accelerator with more gusto than normal. The Honda leaped forward. The tires squealed.

"Whoa!" Hugh sat straight up. "What are you doing, woman?"

"I'm driving like you!" she shot back and wove beside a Toyota before cutting in front of it.

His eyes bugging, Hugh slammed against the passenger door. The rental car revved and shifted with grace and gusto.

"Stop it!" Hugh cried.

Carrie laughed and slowed the car. One of her discarded shoes flopped beside her foot. She kicked it aside with her free foot and flexed her sore toes. There were times when fashion was nearly too costly.

"That's what you get!" she taunted.

"I've never driven that wild in my life!" Hugh defended.

"Could have fooled me," Carrie quipped and examined her brother.

"Keep your eyes on the road!" He groped beside his seat for the adjustment lever, and the seat's back clicked straight up.

"Of course," Carrie agreed and concentrated on the road, which was lined with businesses and restaurants. "At least you're awake now."

Hugh grunted.

"You know I can't stand it when you sleep while I'm driving." She tapped her bright pink fingernail against the steering wheel.

"Excuse me, but I can't sleep on the plane as well as you do. I'm zonked here! These international flights wear me out. The time change is a killer, and—"

"Too bad. We've only got ten minutes until we get to Uncle Al's. I don't want to have to listen to your snoring for even *that* long."

"I don't snore."

"How do you know, you're asleep?"

Hugh chuckled. "Okay, okay, you win!"

"And *you* were winning on the terrace, I'd say."

"Excuse me?" Hugh said over a yawn.

"The terrace," Carrie repeated.

"Oh yeah, the terrace. Hmmm…" he said, savoring the memories. "Ethan has some nice sisters."

"And you've still got lip prints on your cheeks." Carrie shivered and adjusted the air conditioner to low cool.

Hugh touched his face, rubbed his thumb across his fingers, and grinned like a grand-prize winner. "So I do," he admitted.

"If you don't take it off, Uncle Al's going to be asking questions. There's a tissue or two in the top of my purse." She retrieved her petite handbag from the console and tossed it into her brother's lap. "There."

"Like Uncle Al has room to talk," Hugh mumbled and unzipped her purse. "What mistress number is he on now, anyway?" He pulled a tissue from her purse and lowered the vanity mirror.

"I've lost count," Carrie admitted.

"Maybe I have, too," Hugh mused and rubbed at the lipstick.

"Like uncle, like nephew. Is that it?"

"You said it, not me." He flopped the soiled tissue onto the dashboard, flipped up the vanity mirror, crossed his arms, and looked out the window on his side of the car.

"So, which one did you like best?" Carrie asked. "Marie or Julie?"

"Marie's engaged…"

"Since when did that stop you?"

"…to a fool," Hugh finished and cast her a tart glance.

"He may be, but he seems to love her."

"Yeah, and she's wild about him…or is it his bank account?" Hugh drawled. "I would hazard to guess that Worthingham Hotels nets more than her father's stock brokerage."

"Ah, so you liked Marie the best?" Carrie calculated and clicked on the left blinker. She checked her rearview mirror and steered into the empty left lane. "That's what I figured. You're always after the one you can't have. Makes for a better game, doesn't it?"

"Of course not. I'm all about Julie," Hugh countered. "That *was* her lipstick."

"So? It was mine, too," Carrie reasoned. "And I don't think either shade was the one you really wanted. Besides, Julie was too quick to jump. That's no fun, is it? There's no challenge."

Hugh grunted. "What does it matter anyway? Easy come, easy go."

"Yes, but the harder they are to get, the better the sport."

"Are you talking about me now…or you?" Hugh's sarcastic smile heightened the devilry in his eyes. "Ethan doesn't strike me as the kind who jumps at every opportunity. I figure he hasn't even kissed you yet," he taunted. "Usually by this point, you're in the—"

"When he kisses me, it'll mean something," Carrie interrupted, not caring to hear her brother's testimony of her physical encounters.

"Hey, all my kisses mean something." Hugh raised his brows to a suggestive angle.

Carrie shoved at his arm. "The difference between me and you, brother dear, is this time I'm playing for keeps. And you're just playing."

"There you are, Franny." Ethan's soft voice penetrated the library's solitude.

Francine looked up from the Charles Dickens novel she had been reading aloud to Aunt Mariette. Her gaze first encountered her snoozing aunt, stretched out in her recliner. As usual, Francine had become so engrossed in the classic she tuned out Aunt Mariette's mild snores. Francine sighed and stroked the musty-smelling book's textured cover. She had read the same novels to her aunt dozens of times, and the dear lady never remembered them.

Daisy, on her mistress' lap, woofed a complaint, yawned, then jumped from the recliner and trotted toward Ethan. She dutifully sniffed his sneakers before whining to be picked up.

Francine shifted in the corner chair, and her attention drifted from Ethan's running shoes to his slender legs. She noticed his shorts and T-shirt before encountering his benevolent appraisal. Francine didn't have to guess what he was going to say next.

"Want to go for a walk in the park?" he whispered. Ethan's mussed hair and sleepy eyes testified that when he'd claimed he needed a nap to shake the jet lag he had meant it.

She checked her David Yurmon wristwatch. Uncle Tom had surprised her with the luxury last Christmas when he gave both his daughters David Yurmon's as well. While Julie and Marie had gloated over their diamond-studded trophies, Francine insisted Uncle Tom return her less ornate watch for something more practically priced. In the face of receiving only Wade's present from her family of origin, Francine had been touched by her uncle's generosity. She had also been overwhelmed to the point that she simply could not accept such an indulgence. With a rare dash of assertiveness, Francine actually voiced her concern to her uncle. He gruffly told her if she didn't wear the watch he would never speak to her again. Francine complied.

The fine timepiece insisted that dinner wasn't for another hour. Julie and Marie had gone to the country club with Ricky and his sister shortly after Hugh and Carrie left. Aunt Nora was taking her daily nap in her room. That left only Francine as a companion to Aunt Mariette.

"I better not go," Francine mumbled, despite the fact that she would have loved nothing more than spending time in the park with Ethan. She hadn't had him to herself since he arrived. Francine had entertained dozens of questions she would like to pose about Ethan's trip and the successes of his ministry efforts. "If Aunt Mariette wakes up, she might need me," she whispered.

Ethan wrinkled his brow and looked at his sleeping foster mother who was draped in a cotton coverlet. "She'll be fine," he softly pronounced. "You spoil her far too much as it is."

"But what if she wakes up and can't find me?"

"She's a grown-up," Ethan reasoned. Then his gaze rested on the library's corner. Ethan strode toward the oak roll-top desk near a towering bookshelf. He retrieved a notepad and pen from a drawer and scribbled a message. With a mischievous grin, he tore off the note, dropped the pad back into the drawer, and marched to Mariette's side. Ethan propped the small note between his mom's clasped fingers. The piece of paper stood at attention, waiting to be read the second she awoke.

"There!" Ethan hissed. "Problem solved."

Francine couldn't stop herself from returning his grin. Her desire to be with Ethan outweighed her sense of duty to her aunt. She laid the novel on the table next to her chair and stood.

"Go upstairs and change into your walking shoes," he insisted. "I'll be waiting outside on the steps."

After she nodded, Francine whispered, "Hold Daisy so she won't follow me upstairs. Aunt Nora's asleep in her room. If Daisy goes up with me and decides to bark, she'll wake her up."

"Heaven forbid!" Ethan responded and scooped the dog into his arms. "Let's get out of here before anything wakes Mom up."

Francine nodded. She trotted up the steps and silently stopped at her door. With a wary glance toward Aunt Nora's closed bedroom door, Francine cautiously opened the door to her room. Aunt Nora was a notoriously light sleeper—when she wanted to be. Amazingly, when Marie was an adolescent she could arrive two hours past her curfew and traipse down the hallway with a team of ostriches and Aunt Nora would never hear her. But if Francine's doorknob rattled too loudly at the wrong time of the day, Aunt Nora became the hall sentry, ready to stop her niece from wasting a moment of time on personal trifles.

When Francine reached the front door, she pronounced her sneak-and-change operation a success. She had not only donned her walking shoes, but she'd also switched into a floppy T-shirt and a more comfortable pair of shorts and slicked her hair into a tighter ponytail. The ponytail swayed as she slipped through the front door and into the six o'clock heat. She discovered Ethan on the front steps landing—right where he said he'd be, as always.

He straightened from a round of leg stretches and smiled as if Francine were the only woman in the world. "There you are!" he said. "Want to take some time to stretch?"

"Sure," Francine said and wondered if her lax muscles could take this challenge. "I just hope I can keep up with you. I've been nothing but a couch potato since you left. I think I've gained ten pounds."

"You? A couch potato? I doubt that." Ethan shook his head and placed his hands on his hips. "I'd be more likely to believe your aunts have kept you busy every second you aren't doing schoolwork—and I haven't been here to pry you away."

Francine touched her toes. Her muscles complained so much she didn't bother to answer Ethan. Besides, he sounded like he knew he was right anyway. He was, of course. She went through a round of token stretches and jogged in place a few beats. Even though Francine had never been a runner, she'd probably be trotting to keep up with Ethan's swift walking.

"Ready?" he questioned and patted her back.

"As ready as I'll ever be," Francine responded and eyed the hazy sky. A bright spot toward the west attested that the sun was still at its job. A rash of moisture was already dotting Francine's upper lip. "I'm looking forward to cooler weather," she complained.

"Did you remember your sunscreen this time?" Ethan asked.

"Believe it or not, I did! Oh gasp!" Francine covered her lips with her fingertips and smelled residual sun lotion. "It's a wonder I survived at all without you here!" she taunted and thrilled in the ability to wholly relax with Ethan for the first time since he arrived home.

Ethan smiled and trotted down the steps that stopped on the curb of Central Park West. Francine followed closely and halted behind him. Ethan shot a jaunty glance over his shoulder. "The rest of the world just doesn't know the torment you put me through," he complained. "Why is it everybody else gets the quiet Franny-mouse and I get the Francine-tease?"

Francine's throat tightened. If any other man looked at her with the same indulgence and flung such words her way, Francine would suspect he was flirting. Her heart ached for Ethan to do exactly that. Then she remembered all the years she and Ethan had enjoyed such banter—years when they were nothing but buddies. She gazed at the road. A trio of vehicles whisked by, leaving behind the smells of warm rubber and exhaust.

"Francine?" Ethan queried. "Is everything okay?"

"W–what?" Francine stuttered and peered past Ethan at a man walking a German shepherd through the historic neighborhood lined with brownstone homes. "I was just thinking, I guess."

He stroked his goatee. "Well, okay." Ethan shrugged and caught her eye for a searching stare that spoke his confusion.

She glanced up the road and back. No cars in sight. Only the scattering of sugar maples, ash, and hickories. "Beat you to the park," she challenged and darted to the corner of Central Park West, then across the street.

By the time Francine trotted to the park's entry, her legs burned in protest and Ethan was several yards ahead of her. She huffed to a halt beside him, only to endure his cheerful mockery.

"You're not as quick as you thought you were, are you?"

"Oh, go away," she groaned and clutched her abdomen while a trickle of sweat oozed down her lower back. "I thought we were supposed to be going for a walk anyway. What's with all this running?"

"You're the one who started the race, not me."

"I hate it when you're right." Francine placed her hands on her hips, tilted her head back, and gulped for all the air she could hold.

"Come on." Ethan tugged her arm. "I'll go slowly just for you."

Francine nodded and struck out beside him. Central Park was everything it had always been for her—a place where she and Ethan could close out the rest of the world and enjoy nature's haven in the center of Manhattan's confusion. The red and black oaks, sugar maples, and ash formed a canopy over the paved walkway that blotted out the hazy sun and eased the threat of more perspiration. They walked in silence for several minutes, and Francine grappled with what to say. After their brief banter, she was feeling like "quiet Franny-mouse" again. Before she challenged him to the sprint, Ethan had looked at her as if he suspected something had changed but he didn't know what.

What if he figures it out? she thought and retreated further into herself. *Or worse. What if I somehow reveal how I really feel?* A layer of fear settled across the haze covering her soul. If she inadvertently told Ethan she loved him by some nonverbal expression, he might reject her. The thought of no Ethan in her life made Francine's knees nearly buckle. After several joggers passed them, she was ready to feign exhaustion and retreat to her room until dinner. Francine was simultaneously elated and terrified. Elated to simply be with the man she loved; terrified that he might suspect the reason for her elation.

By the time they were near the Shakespeare Garden, Francine sensed Ethan's pensiveness. Usually when he grew thoughtful, Francine and he wound up enjoying a stimulating conversation about spiritual issues or the Bible. She was always fascinated with the results of his recent research or the historical context of scriptural passages. As Ethan learned all this and more, he shared it with Francine. Now he had returned from his first missions trip abroad. Francine had so looked forward to this moment…to the day they would talk about the new depths of spirituality to which this venture had probably led Ethan.

"So, what did you think of Carrie?" Ethan asked.

"Carrie?" Francine averted her face and hid the frown. *So much for spirituality!* She commanded her features to be still and looked straight ahead. Ten yards in front of them, a biker pumped her pedals as if she were losing a race. The poor woman looked as spent as Francine was beginning to feel. "Well, I—"

"She's very pretty, don't you think?"

"Yes, she is very pretty," Francine agreed and tried to cover her panting. "And nice." *But I wonder if she's very spiritual.* She noticed a hot-dog vendor, and then eyed Ethan. Francine studied his expression and wondered if he'd been able to get past Carrie's great figure and wonderful smile long enough to consider her spiritual depth. Had he pondered other important elements—like whether or not she'd make a good pastor's wife? Francine gulped. The smells of wieners and mustard made her wish for the less complicated days.

"I like her *a lot*, Francine," Ethan admitted. "I can't wait until Friday!"

Francine stole a glance at his animated expression. "I wouldn't have ever guessed," she wryly said and then concentrated on the biker, lest Ethan notice the longing in her eyes.

"Am I *that* obvious?" he queried.

Francine feigned a chuckle that came out more like a huff and puff. "Well, not as obvious as Julie, I'll say that much."

"Oh, Julie." Ethan sighed and never slowed in his forward trudge. "Now *she* was obvious."

"Yes, and Marie *almost* was."

"Huh?" Ethan's question was nonplused. "Really? I didn't notice."

"I think the only thing that stopped her from kissing Hugh before Julie did was Ricky. If he hadn't been there—"

"Poor Ricky," Ethan mused. "So, what are you saying—do you think Marie doesn't love him?"

"Who knows?" Francine said and jogged a couple of steps to remain abreast of Ethan. "Even if she is in love with Ricky, I think she was still attracted to Hugh."

"Dad wasn't that happy about the engagement at first. Did you know?"

Francine blotted at a trickle of sweat along her temple. "I gathered," she admitted. "I overheard a conversation between him and Aunt Nora right after you left for Paris." Francine panted awhile before continuing. "Since Aunt Nora was the one who introduced them while Uncle Tom was out of town, she was, like, bragging about it. Uncle Tom didn't sound as enthused as Aunt Nora."

"You got it," Ethan said. "He told me in an e-mail he thinks Ricky's an idiot. I think if Ricky wasn't worth billions, Dad would probably tell Marie to fish a little longer."

"But you know what Marie always said about marrying money," Francine replied and stopped before saying anything negative. She hated to make critical statements about people, even when they were true. Nevertheless, her cousin always said she was going to marry someone so rich he could use hundred dollar bills for wallpaper and that love could wait until after the marriage.

"I really feel a little sorry for Ricky," Francine said in an attempt to change the conversational direction.

"If anybody would, it would be you, Franny." Ethan looked her full in the face with a confidence and respect that made Francine love him even more.

Her pulse still thumping from exertion, she peered at the paved pathway. "I think he's got a good heart and means well. He just can't…"

"Seem to get it together."

"Yes. How much do you think Hugh is worth, Ethan?"

"I have no idea, but I would guess he could probably hold his own with Worthingham Hotels."

That's what I was afraid of, Francine thought.

The whisk of their sneakers against the concrete filled the thoughtful pause. "Money or not, I think Hugh and Carrie both have such dynamic personalities. They just draw people to them."

"Hmmm," Francine said and wondered when Ethan started labeling womanizing as "personality." Head bent, he seemed lost in his own thoughts. Francine scrutinized his profile. *Are you completely blind to what Hugh is?* she thought.

"They come from a good family," he said as if answering Francine. "They give heavily to a lot of worthy causes. They even donated to our missions project. I met Carrie's parents before we came home. I really like them."

"And they like you, I'm sure," Francine wheezed.

"Yep." Ethan focused on Francine and slowed his gait. She gladly followed suit. He neared a park bench and paused.

Francine decided now was not the time to be tough. She flopped onto the bench, propped her elbows on her knees, and hung her head. A cricket hopped into her line of vision and crawled along the concrete. "I've got to get back into a regular walking routine," she admitted. "I feel like a rag doll." She leaned back against the bench, hung one arm along the top, and pulled her T-shirt away from her sweaty torso. Thankfully the bird-infested oaks provided ample shade.

"We'll get you back into shape." Ethan laid his hand on her shoulder. "I guess this is what happens when I leave town. You just fall apart." He doubled his fist and touched her chin.

That's truer than you'll ever know. Francine gazed across the lush park bridge that spanned the creek. In the distance Bow Bridge spanned the lake and seemed to whisper memories of carefree days full of Ethan's friendship…days that might be gone forever.

Eight

By the time Friday arrived, Ethan felt as if the three-day waiting period had multiplied to a dozen or more. He was burning with anticipation. Ethan had never pursued a woman before. Oh he'd survived a few mild flirtations and even enjoyed a sprinkling of group and double dating in college. But there had never been a woman who lured him like Carrie Casper. Friday afternoon, when the group of seven entered the high-rise hotel on Park Avenue, Ethan decided he had known Carrie long enough to move a tad closer.

While Uncle Tom left his daughters' and Francine's etiquette training to his wife and Nora, he had exerted an abundance of effort in teaching his foster son the ways of a gentleman. Ethan, forever sensible, needed little encouragement to exert his considerate spirit. Therefore, he had purposed not to ever coldly break a woman's heart—never to imply by coziness or words that he was more interested in a deeper relationship than he was ready to commit to. That resolution had kept Ethan out of some of the messes he'd watched his friends suffer through. But, by the same token, now that he was ready to deepen his relationship with Carrie, Ethan's nerves reminded him he had never been here before.

With the imperial hotel's revolving door behind them, Ethan reached down and purposefully wrapped his fingers around Carrie's hand. This time he had no intention of ending the contact within seconds. He even stroked her supple palm with his thumb as if to say, "We're here to stay." As suspected, Carrie didn't reject his overture.

She smells good—really good, Ethan thought. The perfume she wore was every bit as sophisticated and pleasing as the lady. *She looks as great as she smells!* Ethan mused and didn't attempt to hide the appreciation from his expression. Today she wore a green silk pantsuit that made her eyes look like a mystical ocean, ready to ensnare, full of surprises.

Carrie's smile preceded her wink, and Ethan felt more like a man than he ever had. Given Carrie's blatant femininity, Ethan didn't even question why he should experience such strong feelings. Looking ahead, he imagined the increase of adrenaline when he kissed Carrie. Ethan barely noticed his grandiose surroundings or the flurries of a busy hotel. No exquisite hotel could ever compare to the vision of this woman beside him.

For several seconds Ethan was sucked into a hurricane of excitement and expectation. The force of his feelings left him holding his breath. While he longed to surrender to the swirl of emotion, common sense urged him not to move too swiftly.

One step at a time, he told his eager heart. *One step at a time.*

His foster father's repeated warning underscored his own logic: *Remember, there's never a need to rush. You'll have less to regret if you don't rush in.*

Ethan broke Carrie's lengthening gaze and swiveled to face the rest of the group, now stepping through the revolving door. Julie and Hugh had paired off early and wound up riding to the hotel in his and Carrie's rental vehicle. After a sibling haggle over who drove "this time," Hugh won. Carrie and Ethan rode in the back. While Hugh's spunky driving kept Ethan alert and Carrie on edge, he didn't think Julie would have noticed if they hit an eighteen-wheeler head on. She focused on nothing but Hugh.

Julie was as oblivious to the fancy hotel as was Ethan. She smiled up at Hugh, who whipped off his designer sunglasses and hung them on the neck of his T-shirt. He gazed around the fine hotel and whistled. Ethan could understand Julie's fascination with Hugh. He'd felt much the same soon after meeting Carrie.

Ricky Worthingham, who had somehow matched his pants and shirt that day, responded to Hugh's blatant appreciation with a broad grin and a glow of pleasure. "This is one of our nicest hotels," Ricky explained. "It was built in the 1930s. I can't remember the exact year." He squinted but soon continued, "We cater to people all over the world. The Prince of…" Ricky touched his temple and stared across the room. "Oh, what prince was that?" He worked his fingers, then pressed his fingertips against his temple. "I can't remember. Anyway," Ricky shook his head, "this prince guy says it's his favorite hotel in all the world."

"I can imagine why," Hugh responded and observed Ricky with new respect.

Marie encountered the luxury with a bored stare, glanced at Ricky, and then turned her full attention to Hugh, where it stayed through the next conversational volley. Ethan couldn't deny that Ricky looked like an advertisement for "skinny has-beens" beside Hugh, who could pass for a pop star in his trendy low-slung jeans and cutting-edge hairstyle. Ethan recalled Francine's comments in the park and began to debate whether Marie was committed to Ricky or just to his money. Ethan had never been that close to Marie. He'd spent more time urked over her superior attitude, which was enforced by Nora's doting. He wasn't as adept at reading her as he was Julie, who had been his playmate and pal even before his mother's death. Ethan never bonded with either of his foster sisters as he bonded with Francine.

Suddenly he realized Francine had yet to join their circle. He tuned out the group's light chatting and even Carrie's presence to search for his friend. Sure enough, she had done exactly what Ethan expected—purposefully kept her distance. Francine, her arms folded, stood thirty feet away near the marble waterfall, whose splashing mingled with the classical music drifting from an inky grand piano.

Silently she observed the plethora of hotel clients and uniformed staff taking care of business. Her serene stance suggested she had never known a problem in her whole life. Ethan knew differently. He understood her heartache over her birth family's neglect as much as his own.

Ethan leaned toward Carrie, whispered, "Excuse me a minute," and pointed out Francine.

Carrie's understanding nod, along with her general kindness to Francine, only heightened his respect for her. But then Ethan appreciated anyone who befriended Francine. He had plenty of friends in every area of life, from seminary to the golf course. But Francine had proven herself his steadfast confidante. No one could take her place.

As Ethan neared her, he admitted what had nibbled at his mind since he arrived home. Francine had somehow changed since he left for Paris. In the first place, he didn't remember her being quite as pretty as she was when she opened her bedroom door and bestowed her sleepy welcome three days ago. He understood why his dad had commented in a recent e-mail how Francine seemed to have blossomed.

Even today, with her white-blonde hair cascading down the back of her peach sundress, she looked like an attractive woman any number of men might notice in a crowded restaurant. Maybe the effect could be attributed to a new trick with cosmetics—that enigmatic art that went beyond Ethan's masculine mind. Or maybe Francine was simply embracing her womanhood.

Ethan scanned the crowd of patrons, and a protective urge he didn't bother to understand suggested that a few men in this room might have noticed Francine. Sure enough, a male sitting on one of the plush sofas near the waterfall casually glanced away from his newspaper. His gaze trailed across Francine and snapped back. Dressed in fine business gear, the guy looked like he could easily afford the hotel's 500-dollar-a-night executive suite. The man shifted, laid his newspaper down, and never took his attention from Francine, who remained innocently unaware of the distraction she was causing.

When the man stood, Ethan hurried forward. The last thing Francine needed was a smooth-talking, gold-watched, forty-year-old Don Juan hitting on her. Ethan could only imagine the lines the guy would use while Francine, naive and shy, might never realize he was up to no good. By the time the jerk was strolling toward Francine, Ethan stopped at her side.

He leaned close enough to smell her soft fragrance—as innocent in smell as Francine was in disposition. "Franny, what are you over here by yourself for?" He shoved a hot glare at the intruder and laid an arm across Francine's shoulder.

Francine jumped and turned toward Ethan. Their noses were only centimeters apart, but Ethan didn't back away. Even though there was nothing romantic between them, that gold-watched heathen didn't know that.

"You sc–scared me to death, Ethan," Francine stuttered and lowered her head. She darted an upward glance out of the corner of her eye. Her cheeks flushed. She inched away.

His arm still around her, Ethan glowered at the businessman again. But the guy didn't stop his approach. Ethan doubled his fist and hardened his scowl. He sensed Francine's appraisal and glanced at her. An odd awkwardness cloaking them, Ethan whispered, "Sorry, Franny. I didn't mean to crowd you. But I think that guy was about to hit on you. I was trying to—to—"

Ethan observed the businessman as he neared Francine and then passed her. The man's focus remained targeted just past Francine. Ethan concentrated on him until he encountered a smiling woman near his age. The two enjoyed a discreet hug, and the man bestowed a light kiss upon the woman's forehead. She lifted her left hand to lightly touch his cheek. A diamond ring on her third finger big enough to choke a guerrilla sparkled in the crystal chandelier's blazing light. And for the first time Ethan noticed a wide gold band on the man's left hand that complemented his golden watch.

When Ethan shifted his gaze back to Francine, she was still watching the married couple. Ethan jerked his arm away from her shoulders and couldn't recall a time he'd ever felt so foolish.

"I can take care of myself," Francine softly asserted and returned her attention to Ethan. A hint of humor stirring her smile heightened his embarrassment.

"But some of these guys really know how to snow a woman," he growled, "especially someone as…as…" He started to say "as unsophisticated as you" but stopped himself for fear of insulting her.

"You haven't been here for months, Ethan Summers," she fondly mocked.

"I know," Ethan mumbled. He awkwardly slipped his hands into his slacks pockets and examined the tips of his loafers. After a few seconds, Ethan pinched the middle of his goatee and shook his head.

"I'm acting like you're twelve, aren't I?" he admitted and laughed. "And on top of that, I'm imagining things." He motioned to the couch where the businessman had been sitting.

Francine remained silent. Ethan possessed no idea what *that* meant. When he tried to interpret her expression, there was no clue to her thoughts. Even the humor had vanished. *And now I can't even read her anymore,* Ethan thought and marveled that the one woman he believed would never change was going weird on him. Life was so much simpler before Paris.

"Here comes everyone else," Francine commented.

Ethan turned to encounter the noisy cluster just as Julie wedged herself between Hugh and Marie. Julie's hips, wrapped in tight bell bottoms, swayed in victory. Marie frowned at her sister, but the challenge went unnoticed because Hugh was asking Julie a question.

Ethan had been so engrossed in the conversation—or whatever it was called—with Francine he hadn't even noticed this talkative bunch approaching. Nevertheless, when Carrie arrived at his side, all traces of confusion over Francine dissolved into nothingness. He reclaimed Carrie's hand and smiled into those bewitching eyes that promised her lips tasted every bit as sweet as her smile. While life before Paris may have been simpler, it wasn't nearly this promising.

"Okay, everyone," Ricky said over their voices. "I thought we'd start here first since," he shrugged, "that's where we are, right?"

Ethan's chortle blended with the rest. Only Marie didn't join the mirth. Instead, she took in the grandiose lobby and stifled a yawn.

"This is the lobby, in case you haven't figured it out."

"Well, I was wondering." Hugh injected and feigned a dumbfounded gaze across the room.

Marie and Julie exploded into a round of giggles. Carrie pretended to punch her brother's arm. "Oh you," she said.

Ricky ignored them. "If you'll look up, you'll notice all the painted panels in the ceiling."

The whole group obeyed. Ethan encountered a multitude of scenes from around New York City.

He leaned toward Francine. "Look, it's Central Park," he said.

Francine barely acknowledged his claim, but Carrie tightened her grip on his hand and said, "That's *so cool!*"

"I think so, too," Ricky added with an eager nod.

"That brownstone looks just like ours," Francine mused.

"It might be," Ricky replied. "My dad hired this famous painter…" He pressed his fingertips to his temple, and his droopy eyes took on a pathetic strain.

As he turned to Marie, she blurted, "Julio Artemis."

"Yes, yes, that's the guy's name. Julio Ar-Ar—"

"Artemis." This time Marie's voice held the edge she occasionally used on Francine. Her lips turning down, she picked a piece of lint off her linen pantsuit and flicked it aside.

Ethan narrowed his eyes but admonished himself to keep his nose out of Marie's business. If Ricky could put up with her high-handedness, then more power to him.

"Anyway, this painter painted scenes from New York on the panels, and then they inserted them into the ceiling. Fortunately for Dad, Julio what's-his-face overdosed on cocaine and died like two weeks after he finished the project. So the ceiling alone is worth over a million bucks now."

"Very fortunate," Hugh mumbled.

Ricky continued his monologue, and Ethan assumed Hugh's sarcastic remark went unnoticed by everyone except him...until a choked cough escaped Marie. Ethan observed her as she swallowed a laugh and exchanged a wickedly humorous glance with Hugh.

"Now, let's move this way!" Ricky's voice echoed with importance.

As the small group trailed Ricky, Ethan didn't know whether to be annoyed or to pity him.

"We'll tour the chapel next," Ricky continued. "It's really something. It's my mom's favorite."

Focusing on Hugh, Ethan strained to hear if he made any more remarks. His suspicions were confirmed.

"Mommy dearest," Hugh breathed and grimaced.

Ethan decided Ricky was more annoying than piteous. The last thing he wanted or needed was someone irritating his new friends. Ethan studied Carrie's expression to see if it mirrored Hugh's opinion. She caught Ethan watching her and grinned.

"This is a *great* hotel," she oozed, her high-heeled sandals clicking along the marble floor. "And I've seen some of the best. It looks more like a palace than a hotel. I can't believe I haven't been here before. This is the kind of place a woman dreams of having her wedding at, then just staying for the honeymoon."

Relieved that Carrie didn't join in Hugh's scorn, Ethan barely registered the hint. "I can believe that," he replied. "I think Marie said they even have a small pool in three of their honeymoon suites—along with jacuzzis."

"I could live with that." Carrie puckered her lips, nodded, and shot Ethan a sassy smile. "Couldn't you?"

Nine

The full meaning of Carrie's innuendo socked Ethan between the eyes. He groped for a response. Even though he knew Carrie really liked him—and he certainly liked her—he had constrained his thoughts against pondering a honeymoon. Her comment, coupled with the invitation in those enchanting green eyes, prompted Ethan to tighten his fingers against hers. His heart began to thud at a disconcerting rate, and a startling, primeval force demanded he grab this beautiful creature and kiss her until the room spun.

"Let's keep the noise down as we go in," Ricky called over his shoulder, "in case someone's in here praying or something."

Ethan tore his gaze from Carrie and stared straight ahead at Ricky. He stood in front of a door that bore a brass plate with the words, "Chapel. Quiet Please," etched in black. Without realizing the path they were taking, Ethan had blindly followed the group through the hotel lobby and down a hallway leading to this sacred room. His hand trembled against Carrie's. Somehow this didn't seem the appropriate moment to enter a chamber dedicated to the holy.

Ricky opened the door, peered into the room, then flipped a light switch on the inside wall. "Coast is clear."

Ethan couldn't remember being less comfortable stepping into a chapel. Usually, any time he entered any church-related structure or chamber, he sensed he was embracing his divine destiny. Right now he was more interested in the feminine destiny standing beside him.

Carrie and Ethan, who had dropped to the back of the group, moved through the doorway behind everyone else. Ethan didn't notice a thing about the chapel. He was too busy admiring Carrie's profile and wondering how soft her casual curls would feel against his ready fingers.

"This is perfect!" Francine's voice cut through Ethan's ardent daydreams. "Don't you think, Ethan?" She looked over her shoulder toward Ethan, who encountered her guileless appraisal before he comprehended one element of the special room.

Guiltily, Ethan scanned the chapel and gathered the swift impression of one of the historic churches he'd toured while in Europe—only on a smaller scale. The Sistine Chapel came to mind, and Ethan stood speechless in the sacred splendor. The numerous pews lining the room appeared to seat a couple hundred people.

"We host a bunch of weddings here," Ricky's voice, floating from behind a panel near the front, accompanied the igniting of half a dozen spotlights that illuminated hallowed artwork along the walls and ceiling.

"I guess you do," Carrie's faint voice barely drifted across Ethan's awe. Even though he'd attended some business meetings with his foster father at the Worthingham Renaissance, he never realized there was such a chapel in the place.

A final light illuminated a life-sized brass cross behind the pulpit. Candles in brass floor holders awaited someone to employ the butane lighter resting on an oak stand. A spotlight behind the cross shone upon a stained glass depiction of the image of Christ. Jesus' nail-pierced hands reached toward a lost world. Christ's eyes, brimming with love, invited Ethan to remember his special call. The smell of warm wax suggested a recent occupant. Dots of glistening moisture on the altar's oak rail spoke of a heart blessed beyond words or broken in grief.

Ethan released Carrie's hand and strolled toward Francine, who was close to the ethereal image of Christ. "I love it," he said and meant it. Ethan inhaled the essence of the room in a cleansing rush. He relived the first glory he'd known when embracing his call to ministry and relished the awareness of being exactly where he belonged...in the house of the Lord, surrounded by the things of God.

"I could stay here for hours," Francine's whisper echoed the cry of Ethan's soul.

Carrie's sarcastic laugh invaded the reverent moment. Hugh, Marie, Francine, and Ethan all looked at her in silent question. "I just had a thought," she explained. "This is a wonderful idea." Her wave encompassed the impressive room. "A chapel at an upscale hotel." She laughed again, and tilted her head. Her face ignited with an impish light. "I guess all the overpaid clergymen who have affairs on the tenth floor come here to repent before going back home to their wives, huh?"

Hugh's abandoned laughter bounced off the vaulted ceiling. Marie joined him. Ethan tried to chuckle, but couldn't quite appreciate the jaded humor. Francine ducked her head and drew even nearer the image of Christ. Julie, still at the back of the room examining a mural, didn't acknowledge the remark.

"What's so funny?" Ricky stepped from behind the panel and lumbered toward Marie.

"Never mind," Marie waved him off while he joined her at the altar.

"Carrie was just expressing her...appreciation...for the cloth," Hugh said with a derisive snort.

"Well, I've seen enough to lose all respect. That's all," Carrie added.

Ricky, not the least interested in anything Hugh said, asked Marie a question, and she turned to answer him.

Carrie moved to Ethan's side and looped her arm through his. Her sophisticated fragrance that earlier lured him now seemed to mock Ethan's honor. "Aside from the adultery factor," she continued, "I think pastors are about the most boring bunch of people I've ever met. Who would think any woman in her right mind would agree to an affair with one—forget marriage! Somebody deliver us all!" She pretended a delicate yawn.

Hugh chuckled again.

Ethan stiffened against the verbal punch. He looked straight at the carved pulpit and didn't blink. Sensing Francine's scrutiny, Ethan glanced toward her. Her anxious expression testified her understanding of every emotion now rolling over him. Ethan searched his memory of the last two months. He possessed no recollection of telling Carrie about his call to ministry.

I guess I just assumed she knew, he thought and wrinkled his brow. *I told her I was on a missions trip. She should have known!*

"Well, well, well…isn't this a snug setup?" Julie's voice echoed from the back of the room.

Ethan welcomed the diversion.

Striding down the aisle with a mischievous twist of her lips, Julie didn't stop until she reached Ricky and Marie in front of the altar. Before Marie could stop her, Julie took her sister's hand and placed it on Ricky's. She clasped them with her own hands and turned toward Ethan. "Too bad you aren't ordained yet, Ethan. They could plight their fate today."

Carrie gasped and released her hold on his arm. Ethan's neck warmed.

With no clue that she'd just dropped a verbal grenade, Julie shoved a silent challenge toward Marie: *Don't forget you're engaged!* Then she brazenly winked at Hugh. "You could be the *best* man." Julie wiggled her index finger at him. Her straight, dark hair fell across her shoulder, and she looked like a cutesy chick on a sitcom.

"Of course, I'll be the maid of honor." Laying her hand across her chest, Julie fluttered her eyelashes.

Even though everyone was observing Hugh and Julie, Ethan still swirled in a sea of dismay. The woman he thought might be "the one" despised the clergy! Francine stepped to Ethan's side and gripped his arm. As always, she was the one who supported him, who understood him when life got tense.

Meanwhile, Hugh raced toward Julie and grabbed her around the waist. She squealed her approval. "So when Ricky kisses the bride," he stroked her back, left bare from her short T-shirt, "do I get to kiss the bridesmaid?"

"Absolutely!" Julie agreed.

And Ethan expected her to lay one on Hugh he wouldn't forget, regardless of the audience.

After a discreet glance toward Marie, Hugh backed away.

"Thank goodness," Francine murmured.

Ricky turned his head, but not before Ethan noticed a sneer. "I think it's time we move along. I wanted to show you guys the executive suites next." He worked his fingers like a nervous five-year-old. "Oh, and the ballrooms. They're the finest in New York. And then there's the twin towers and starlight roof on the top. After that, we can eat, if you like. Arby's is off the lobby."

"*Addy's!*" Marie snapped and gazed after Hugh and Julie, who were heading toward the door. Sighing, she stroked her forehead and shook her head. "Arby's is a fast-food chain in the cheaper hotel on Long Beach, remember?"

"Of course I do," Ricky grumbled and pushed at a section of dark bangs that flopped forward. "I just slipped, that's all."

"Well," Carrie chirped, "I say let's move along then." She directed a brittle smile toward Ethan. He tried to grin, but in the wake of Carrie's clergy comment, the gesture felt as stiff as hardened clay.

"Okay," Ricky said. "Come on, dear." He grabbed Marie's hand and hurried up the aisle. "We need to stay in the lead so no one will get lost." He peered over his shoulder at Francine. "Are you coming?"

Ethan gripped Francine's hand and silently urged her not to leave him. "Don't worry. We'll keep up with you," he said. Ethan dreaded the thought of being alone with Carrie. What could he say? What was there to say? She had publicly detested everything he ever planned to be.

As soon as Ricky turned his back, Carrie touched Ethan's arm. "I guess I put my foot in my mouth, didn't I?" she whispered.

Francine's fingers tightened around Ethan's. For the first time since Carrie made her remarks, Ethan dared look her full in the eyes. He encountered a sea of remorse and a soul that begged forgiveness.

"I don't know what made me say all that," Carrie rushed. "If I'd known, I would never—I'd never do a thing in the world to embarrass you or hurt you. It's just that I—"

Ethan's disappointment slid away. Her comment was just a terrible misunderstanding! His Carrie, capricious and charming, spoke without thinking. Everything was going to be fine. No one with her angelic face could really disrespect clergymen. Like her brother, Carrie was simply going for laughs.

Ethan released Francine's hand.

He studied the pulpit and imagined speaking behind it, with a rapt, receptive audience drinking in his every word. Many in seminary told him he was a gifted communicator...that the Lord's anointing was evident in a powerful way when he spoke. And Ethan felt that anointing, that fire in his soul, that propelled heaven-sent words from his mouth and quickened the hearts of listeners.

An annoying inner voice told Ethan that he should seriously seek God before moving forward in a relationship with Carrie. Ethan acknowledged the idea. But for now, he determined to enjoy this group date.

"Ethan?" Carrie cooed. "Are you never going to speak to me again or what?" She nestled one hand into his and stroked the side of his face. A well of delicious longing sprang from his gut and threatened to take him under. Breaking his focus upon the pulpit, Ethan received the vague impression of Francine's departing. But he couldn't gather his wits enough to ask her to stay.

"It's okay," he said and peered at Carrie.

She moved directly in front of him and placed both hands on his face. "I really like you a lot, Ethan," she whispered, her eyelids heavy.

Ethan's mind roared with the effect of her closeness. Never had he been so enchanted…so ensnared. He examined the chapel. They were alone, now. All alone. And Carrie Casper—his dream woman—was begging to be kissed. A primal fervor insisted he fulfill her wishes, that he meld her honeyed lips to his.

Tom Barrimore's voice sliced through Ethan's mind. *Remember, there's never a need to rush. You'll have less to regret if you don't rush in.*

As much as Carrie's soft mouth beckoned, Ethan somehow found the willpower to bestow only a light kiss upon her forehead. "Everything's fine," he whispered. "I know you didn't mean it." Ethan backed away, and the disappointment in Carrie's face nearly weakened him to the point of reversing his decision. "I thought I'd told you about my call."

"No, you didn't. I had no idea." She shrugged. "I mean, I knew you were in Paris on a missions trip, but my dad has gone on those, and he's not a pastor by any means."

"Well, I'm scheduled to be ordained next spring—as soon as I wrap up my last class this fall. I'm working through a distance education program with a seminary out of Indiana. I'm actually on staff at our church as an assistant pastor right now. I'm even scheduled to preach the week after next. As soon as I'm ordained, I'll be ready to take my first church."

"That's very special." Carrie once again slipped her arm through his, and the two of them began a slow trek toward the doorway. "I imagine you're a powerful speaker," she continued.

"Well…" Ethan shrugged. "I have been told that a time or two, I guess. But I know it's a gift from God."

During her pensive silence, Ethan tried to imagine Carrie at his side during his first church assignment. In the middle of this effort, he recalled the short skirt she wore all the way from Paris. *She'll need a few pointers on dressing the part. But other than that, she'd probably charm the whole congregation until they purred.*

"You know," she said, her words tempered and assuring, "there are other professions that require your special gifts."

"Oh?" Ethan asked. They paused in front of the doorway, and he placed his hand on the elongated knob.

"Well, yes." Carrie's firm nod swished her hair around her face.

Even the way she looked up at him made Ethan feel as if he was, and would always be, her hero.

"As a matter of fact, you have to be a good speaker for politics…to be a lawyer…or even a professor. There are all sorts of things you could do with that gift."

Ethan protruded his bottom lip and nodded his affirmation. He twisted the knob, tugged on the door, then held it open for Carrie. Stepping into the hallway behind her, Ethan said, "I guess there is, but I really feel that being a pastor is what God wants me to do. It's just one of those things, ya know?"

"Of course." Carrie stroked his arm. "And you've got to do what you believe is important."

"Well, matters of the soul are the most important thing in the world, aren't they?"

"Yes, of course." Carrie beamed up at him, and Ethan wasn't sure he remembered the last thing he'd said. Discreetly, she examined the hallway. "Oops! I don't see everyone else."

"I guess they just ran off and left us." Ethan hadn't expected Francine to disappear as well.

"Is that so bad?" Carrie arched her brows.

"Maybe not," Ethan agreed and respectfully draped his arm around her waist. "Want to go check out the gift shop?" he prompted.

"Sounds like a great idea!"

"Good. I thought you might like a souvenir or something."

"Why not?" Carrie said. "I'll let you do the choosing, okay?"

The way she tilted up her face and squeezed his arm, Ethan was ready to buy her anything she wanted—short of an engagement ring. He considered the excessive cash in his checking account and decided this was the time to make good use of some of the money he'd saved.

Tom Barrimore had long ago set up a hefty trust fund for Ethan equaling that of his daughters'. The money became available four years ago when Ethan turned twenty-one. Ethan's early childhood, far from wealthy left its mark on his psyche. He despised wasting a penny of his fortune. With the help of his foster father, he had chosen a strategy of wise investing that ensured a solid portfolio. According to Tom, Ethan wouldn't ever have to worry about his future.

In contrast, when Julie and Marie each turned twenty-one, they had invested only what their father insisted. From there, they each paid cash for a new sports coupe they parked in a 500-dollar-a-month private garage. And seldom a week went by that one of them didn't come home with a bag full of high-priced clothing.

Occasionally, Ethan wondered about Francine…whether or not her uncle would bestow a trust fund upon her at her twenty-first birthday party in November, mere weeks after Marie's wedding. He hadn't mentioned the subject with either of them because he didn't want to impose upon Tom Barrimore or embarrass Francine. However, Ethan long ago decided that if his foster father had overlooked Francine, he would share his fortune with her. A 50/50 split seemed the only fair amount. This decision reinforced his frugal habits.

Ethan's conservative spending pattern also meant he could splurge on Carrie if he so chose. He chose. The specialty gift shop that catered to the wealthy just might feature a pair of emerald earrings that would perfectly match Carrie's pantsuit...and her eyes.

Nothing too big, Ethan thought as they struck out across the crowded reception area. He didn't want to give Carrie the impression he was ready to propose. But at least she would understand that even though he had pulled away from the kiss, he was still interested. *Very interested,* he added to himself.

Ten

Francine followed Ricky, Marie, Hugh, and Julie as they wound around the balcony of the mezzanine floor. Below, guests dressed in fine attire scurried off to theaters or upscale restaurants. Business professionals carrying leather briefcases strolled across the polished marble floor to their next appointment.

Francine glimpsed a familiar couple entering the exclusive gift shop adjacent to the hotel's entrance. She slowed to a stop, gripped the nickel-and-brass handrail, and wrinkled her brow.

Carrie had wasted no time retracting her heartfelt statement about the clergy. As soon as she gurgled out her apology, Francine hadn't possessed the stomach to hang around and watch Ethan succumb to Carrie's wiles. For the first time, Francine had been presented with a legitimate reason to dislike Carrie. She was more like her brother, Hugh, than Francine had originally assumed. Even though Carrie appeared to genuinely want to befriend Francine, even though her eyes lacked the tainted essence Hugh's revealed, she wasn't the quality of woman Ethan required or deserved. Ethan needed someone spiritual...a woman committed to the Lord.

You need me, *Ethan,* Francine whimpered to herself as she strained to catch the last glimpse of the couple. *He's probably going to buy her something,* Francine deduced and braced herself for the expensive trifle she imagined Carrie displaying. *I just hope it's not a ring,* she inwardly groaned.

Earlier, when Ethan put his arm around her, Francine momentarily believed he might one day buy a ring for *her.* She had spontaneously hoped her prayers had been answered—that Ethan was awakening to her love...and his. But the hope died in its infancy. Ethan was just acting like his usual polite self and trying to protect her from that man. Although Francine couldn't remember a time when he had been so ensensed or worried about someone hitting on her.

She squinted and observed the busy patrons. There was only one word for the way Ethan acted by the waterfall: weird. But then, that word best characterized most of his behavior since arriving from Paris. The man she thought she knew better than anyone was proving to be unpredictable at best. Francine cringed with the prospect of what the future might hold.

Ricky's distant monologue alerted Francine that she'd been standing by the rail too long. She gazed after the group, now twenty-five feet away. Still following the balcony, they turned right and rounded the corner. Francine pursued them.

"This passage will take us to the private elevator that leads to the executive suites," Ricky said. "From there, we'll see the ballrooms." His commentary interested no one.

Julie watched Hugh, who divided his attention between her and Marie. Ricky appeared so engrossed in trying to prove that Worthingham Enterprises could out-money the Casper restaurants that he was missing Hugh's sly comments to Marie.

Despite Ricky's demonstration, Francine wasn't so certain which family might be the richest. According to the few barbs Hugh had strategically unleashed, Addy's had grown into a celebrated, worldwide chain offering an upscale feel at affordable prices. As Ethan had already established, each family had to be worth billions. A materialistic woman would label either man a good catch. Francine eyed her cousins. She could not deny that both Marie and Julie were materialistic and that both would be willing to ignore womanizing or simple-mindedness for the money behind the man.

Whatever faults Ricky might have, Francine knew he would be far more trustworthy, dependable, and honorable than Hugh. Of course, this elevated him as the better catch in Francine's estimation. *Too bad he is so pitiful*, Francine thought and shook her head.

Aunt Nora had been so proud of herself for introducing Marie and Ricky. Somehow, Nora acquainted herself with Ricky's mother at the huge church she joined after her husband's death. While Aunt Mariette never went to church, the rest of the family worshiped with the smaller congregation where Ethan was on staff. After Aunt Nora moved into the Barrimore's brownstone, she proclaimed that she was going to join a church that offered some connections, even if the rest of the family was blind to the need.

The devices she used to develop the friendship with Mrs. Worthingham remained a mystery to Francine. Aunt Nora's ability to worm her way into the lives of the prominent defied explanation. But she had done it, and done it so thoroughly that Mrs. Worthingham was thrilled to host a small dinner party for the sole purpose of introducing Ricky and Marie. With Nora's gentle encouragement and regular comments regarding Ricky's net worth, Marie had succumbed to "common sense" and agreed to marry him after they'd known each other a whole month. Once Ricky slipped the enormous diamond on Marie's ring finger, the society pages buzzed with nothing but their engagement. And Marie was in the limelight—exactly where she wanted to be, exactly where Nora wanted her to be.

Francine slowed and stopped just behind the foursome, who had halted in front of an elevator that read "Management—Key-Holders Only."

"I know I've got the key here somewhere." Ricky searched his bony body for some sign of the plastic key that fit into the slender slot above the elevator's button.

"Let's try the button anyway!" Julie pressed her coral-tipped finger against the button. The thing emitted an offended squawk. Julie squealed, jumped back, and bumped into Hugh.

He took advantage of the situation and gripped her bare waist. The two fell into a round of hilarity that made Francine wonder if they'd visited the hotel bar. But both of them had been with the group the whole time.

"Hurry with the key, Ricky," Marie exhorted and huffed toward her sister and Hugh, still snug and giggly. She didn't see the snug exchange between her sister and Hugh.

Francine, shifting from foot to foot, wondered why she had allowed Aunt Nora to talk her into the peach-colored sandals with two-inch heels. The simple flats she'd originally donned seemed so much more appropriate. But as usual Francine had taken the path of least resistance and acquiesced to her aunt's pressures.

Ricky plunged his scrawny hand into his left trouser pocket. He stirred his fingers around without results. "Guess I forgot it," he fretted with a sheepish smile.

Her back stiff, her head high, Marie crossed her arms and turned her back to Ricky. Francine could only imagine what might be on her cousin's tongue. To date she hadn't witnessed Marie verbally attacking Ricky, but that didn't mean there wouldn't be a first. She had certainly exhibited her share of fits at home, usually when her father was conveniently away and Aunt Nora was present to take her side.

Francine's shoulders slanted. The dynamics of this day were weighing heavier all the time. Last Tuesday, Ethan had insisted that she go with the group on this outing. Now he'd meandered off with Carrie. When she left Ethan and Carrie in the chapel, she at least expected them to attempt to catch up. Francine was stuck with four people who probably would have preferred she hadn't come. She crossed her arms and drummed her unpolished fingernails against her elbow. As much as she hated to admit Ethan's shortcomings, his behavior had been less than hospitable, to say the least. She looked over the balcony railing again. No sign of him or Carrie.

The vague scent of sweet, creamy coffee wafted from the ground floor and attested that Addy's wasn't far. *They're probably already at Addy's ordering Carrie's favorite latte or something*, Francine griped and felt anything but spiritual. Her fifth-floor hideaway back home beckoned, and she pondered the benefits of quietly hiring a taxi and heading to Central Park West. Her attention trailed back to the group.

His pant's pockets hanging out, Ricky said, "I'm sorry, darling. I'll go down to the manager's office and get the key."

Hugh's satisfied smirk made Francine think of a prized stud left with the mares. Marie, her back still to Ricky, cast a demure glance toward Hugh. Now free of Julie's clutches, he leaned against the wall near the elevator, mere feet from Marie. Only a dimwit would miss the meaningful tilt to Marie's brows or the craving in Hugh's eyes.

Francine, shocked that Julie didn't throw her body between the two, noticed the younger sister scouting out the different doors back in the direction they'd come.

Marie turned toward Ricky. "Well, hurry along, dear," she encouraged, her expression as indulgent as her voice. "We'll be waiting."

Ricky's tense face relaxed. "Okay, sure," he said. "I won't be gone but a few minutes."

"Don't rush," Marie encouraged. "We've got all afternoon, you know."

"Okay, okay." Ricky nervously wiggled his fingers and stuffed the pocket linings back into the sides of his trousers.

With Ricky shuffling off, Francine decided her feet couldn't take another minute's torture. How Carrie and Julie and Marie wore those three-inch spikes all day was anybody's guess. *I guess for some people, fashion rules,* she thought and sat down on an ornate bench facing the elevator. Francine, making sure her modest sundress remained below her knees, gazed at the gray and green terrazzo floor.

She laid her billfold on the bench and wondered if Carrie's latte was now getting cold because she was so busy talking with Ethan and basking in his admiration she forgot to drink it. Francine resisted the temptation to indulge in a catty grimace. Forever committed to taking the high road, she'd never worn the baser emotions with much grace. The fresh jealousy inflicted self-disgust as much as it did irritation with Ethan.

Why is he so blind? Francine fumed. *She's totally wrong for him!*

Julie's spike heels and wide-legged jeans appeared in Francine's line of vision. "I need to visit the little girl's room," she said. "Is there one around here somewhere, Marie?"

Her sister appeared to be earnestly contemplating Julie's need. "I think the closest one is downstairs, just as you get off the elevator."

The younger Barrimore narrowed her eyes. "Are you *sure* there's not one up here?"

"Absolutely." Marie nodded with a sincerity that nearly convinced even Francine. "This is the staff's wing. There's no amenities for patrons." While Marie's candid blue eyes thwarted argument, Francine barely shook her head. She could spot one of Marie's lies ten miles away. Marie even started fidgeting with the her linen suit's collar. She always fidgeted when she lied.

"Okay, then," Julie agreed, "I'll be back soon." With a confident swag of her hips, she blew Hugh a kiss.

He pretended to catch and hold the invisible missile until Julie turned away. When he snagged Marie's gaze, he made a monumental task of dropping the make-believe offering. His inviting eyes said, *Step into my parlor,* and reminded Francine of a blood-thirsty vampire ready to attack his next victim. Francine denied a shiver and suspected Marie was out of her league.

"There must be some stairs around here somewhere," Hugh said in a seductive tone. "Anywhere there's an elevator, there are usually stairs."

"Of course," Marie agreed with a calculating lilt. "The stairs are this way." She crooked her index finger at him and backed into a hallway that Francine hadn't noticed. "They're right beside the restrooms, actually."

"Ah, the restrooms." Hugh chuckled and followed Marie like a dog on a leash.

With Hugh at her side, Marie turned and walked up the hallway. Her long hair sashayed across her back and shone like polished satin in the receded lights. Keeping her gaze trained upon them, Francine leaned sideways and followed their progress until she nearly fell off the bench. Propriety and her commitment to her uncle's good name insisted she could not sit by as a silent observer. Before she could question her actions, Francine rushed behind the two escapees.

"Hugh! Marie!" she called just as Hugh was opening a swinging door with "stairs" posted above it.

The pair turned toward her.

Francine boldly hurried forward. "You mustn't go," she insisted and was surprised at her own bravery.

Marie looked at her cousin. "And why not?" she challenged.

"You…you could get lost," Francine sputtered.

"Lost?" Hugh scoffed. "In a hotel?"

"Don't be ridiculous, Francine," Marie added with a how-dare-you-interfere expression.

"Then I'll come with you," Francine asserted and placed herself next to them.

Marie sighed. "And who will tell Julie where we are?" she reasoned.

"You can call her on your cell and let her know," Francine countered.

Frowning, Marie looked to Hugh for another road block. "What about Ricky, then?" he hurried.

"He never remembers his cell," Marie alleged and crossed her arms with a satisfied swagger that said, *There! I won!*

Francine worried the clasp on her billfold and wished Aunt Nora hadn't insisted she cut costs and decline Uncle Tom's offer of a cell phone for herself. She could at least call Ethan and ask for his help. Her mind raced for a new mode of attack. "But why not just wait for Ricky? He'll be back before you know it. He'll be so hurt if you run off like this."

A tiny doubt nagged Marie's arresting blue eyes.

"It's not fair to him," Francine insisted.

"You and Julie do the waiting," Hugh persisted.

His voice annihilated all doubt from Marie's eyes. "Yes," she agreed, "*you* do the waiting."

Hugh grabbed Marie's hand and pulled her into the shadowed passage.

"But…" Francine began. The door closed in her face.

She slumped and rubbed her brow. "Boy, this group really likes to stay together, don't they?" she mumbled. Francine trudged back to the bench. She plopped down, crossed her legs, placed her elbow on her knee, and rested her chin in her hand. Francine didn't even bother to tug her skirt below her knee this time. She wanted more than anything to please Uncle Tom. He wouldn't be happy with what Marie just did…or with Julie's throwing herself at Hugh.

The sound of Julie's high-heels tapping the floor announced her approach. "So why so gloomy?" she asked.

Francine raised her head and observed her cousin, wondering how the latest news would affect her.

"And where are Hugh and Marie?" Julie continued. She slowed to a gradual stop, placed her hands on her hips, and pivoted while searching for her sister and Hugh.

"They took the stairs," Francine said without expression.

"Stairs? What stairs?" Julie whipped around to face her cousin.

"Down the hall by the bathrooms," Francine explained and pointed toward the passage.

Julie set her jaw. "By the bathrooms!" she shrieked. "I should have known! Well, if she thinks she's going to shake me so easily, she's got another think coming." She wagged her head and then started for the hallway.

"No!" Francine stood and trotted after her cousin. Her complaining feet insisted she stop before reaching her. "Please, don't go," Francine called down the hall. "I'll be alone when Ricky comes back."

"Meet us later at Addy's!" Julie called over her shoulder. She stepped through the stairway door, and it clicked shut.

Shaking her head, Francine hobbled back to the bench. *Maybe Hugh's the one out of his league.*

Francine plopped onto the bench and decided she and the shoes were officially parting company *now*. She unfastened the tormentors and slipped out her feet. Francine flattened them against the cool floor and groaned.

Ricky's rushed breathing preceded his appearance around the balcony's corner.

Francine stiffened and searched for the right thing to say. This wasn't fair—not fair at all. Not only had Marie slighted Ricky, she had left Francine to mop up the mess. She brushed her baby-fine hair away from her face and stressed over the appropriate thing to say.

Ricky, plastic key in hand, stopped short and eyed Francine. "Where did they all go?" he asked, searching for the others.

Francine nodded toward the hallway. "Through there…looking for another way to go up. They found the stairs." She attempted a wan smile.

"Well, I knew about those stairs," he fretted and hurried toward the hallway. Ricky stopped and faced Francine again. "I just figured nobody wanted to take them—especially not all you women in high heels." He looked down at Francine's feet.

She turned under her toes and nearly groaned again as her bones and tendons continued to ease. "How considerate," she commented, shaking her head at her cousin's cold-heartedness.

"Why didn't they wait for me?" he begged.

"Look, I—I'm sure everything's all right…I'm sure," Francine repeated. She lifted her hand, placed it back in her lap, and rubbed her palms together.

Ricky lowered his arms to his sides and hung his head. The key dangled from his index finger and thumb. "How could everything be all right?" He helplessly looked at Francine. A lost puppy had more spirit. Ricky approached the baroque bench and collapsed beside her.

"I don't know what everyone sees in this Hugh Casper." He turned down the corners of his mouth. "Do you?"

"Actually, no," Francine agreed. Her definite nod underscored her conviction.

"I don't have the eyes of a woman," Ricky continued, "but I don't think he's good-looking at all. Do you?"

"No—not at all," Francine affirmed.

"Well, what then?" He raised his hand and smacked his knee. "I'd bet this hotel my family's got more money than his," he declared.

"I don't look for him to stay long," Francine encouraged and swiveled to face him. She adopted as positive an air as she could rouse. "He'll probably go back to Paris within a few weeks. He doesn't strike me as the sort who stays in one place very long. And then," Francine rested her hand on Ricky's arm, "out of sight, out of mind. Right?"

Ricky lifted his head. His pensive gray eyes took on a ray of hope. "You're a good friend…" He trailed off and stared across the hallway.

"Now look," Francine urged, "you need to go after them. Don't let this guy win. She's your woman, and you should fight for what is yours." Francine blinked at the strength in her words. But she believed every syllable. Marie had promised Ricky she would marry him; she should stand by that promise!

"You're right." Ricky stood and crammed both hands into his mop of hair. He scooped it away from his angular face in a gesture that momentarily lifted his eyebrows. Francine didn't know whether he was pulling out his hair or trying to get control of it. Finally he removed his hands from his scalp and began working his fingers. Francine decided the guy was just worried about exactly how he should "go after his woman." He looked at her and silently begged for a means to evict Hugh out of Marie's space.

Francine could offer no specifics since she'd never attempted such herself.

"Okay, okay," Ricky panted. "I'm going—I'm going up there, and I'll stick to Marie like glue until he leaves town." With a decisive nod, he whipped around and approached the elevator.

"Oh!" Facing Francine again, he began fumbling through his pockets anew. "The key! I've lost the key."

She perused the floor where he'd stood, then examined the bench. A white plastic card lay where Ricky had been sitting. "Here it is!" She picked up the key, stood, and extended it to him.

"Such a good friend," he mumbled. "You're an angel." Ricky's eyes glowed with appreciation, and Francine wanted to shake Marie for being so blind to the good qualities Ricky did have.

He inserted his key into the slot and pressed the elevator's button. This time it didn't squawk. It dinged. And the door hissed open.

Francine reclaimed her place on the bench.

"Aren't you coming?" he asked.

"No—oh no." Francine shook her head. "My feet are *killing* me, and I need to just sit awhile. I'll meet up with everyone at Addy's, okay?"

"Well…okay," Ricky dubiously agreed.

Eleven

༄༅

Francine prepared to sit on the bench about an hour—long enough to give her feet a reprieve. By then she hoped Ethan and Carrie would have cleared out of the gift shop as well. Then she planned to peruse the store and hopefully find a decent novel to read. From there, Francine would go to Addy's and wait in the foyer while reading her book.

But soon boredom set in. After only thirty minutes lapsed, she decided to take her chances in the hotel store. The gamble paid off. There was no sign of Carrie and Ethan. She was even delighted and surprised to find a section of Christian fiction. She chose a Christian novel and dreamed that one day Ethan would love her. With novel in hand, she settled onto a padded bench in Addy's foyer, slipped off her sandals, and lost herself in the book's pages. Minutes blurred into nearly two hours.

"There you are! We've been looking all over for you!" Ethan's fond scold cut through the engrossing plot.

"Oh!" Francine looked up and discovered she was surrounded by the whole group. Marie and Ricky, Julie and Hugh, Ethan and Carrie. They stood in a cluster, each gaze focused upon her. While

Marie didn't try to hide her impatience, Ricky's warm smile was all for Francine.

Hugh, on the other hand, looked anything *but* worried or interested, for that matter. His attention was diverted by the attractive Asian hostess who was asking Julie how many were in their party.

The smells of a smoky grill covered with chicken breasts and steaks and shish kebabs sent a lazy growl through Francine's stomach. She checked her watch and widened her eyes. Five hours had lapsed since lunch.

"We were afraid we'd lost you," Carrie said, laying her free hand across her chest. "Ethan was getting really worried."

Francine noted the two were still connected at the hands. Her appetite waned, and she was tempted to delve back into the book and tell them she was skipping dinner.

Ethan indulgently shook his finger at Francine's nose and scowled. "You should tell someone when you strike out on your own like that." he admonished.

"Yes, I agree," Marie snapped.

I did, Francine thought. She observed Ricky and started to say, *Remember when you left me at the elevator, I told you I'd meet you at Addy's?* But the guy's nonplused demeanor insisted he didn't recall Francine's statement. She could only imagine Marie's exasperation with Ricky when she learned he'd known Francine was waiting for them at Addy's. So Francine chose to say nothing. She'd rather take the fall than make Ricky look more inadequate.

Then she had another thought. She wasn't the only one who had gone off on her own. And at least she was thoughtful enough to tell someone where she'd be—even if he did forget it. She barely flexed her brows and examined Ethan, and then Marie. *Maybe you should tell people where you're going, too,* Francine thought. Even though she didn't utter a word, both her accusers looked away.

"I guess several of us meandered off, didn't we?" Ethan finally admitted, and his scolding attitude was replaced with a shroud of shame. "Sorry," he added.

"It's okay," Francine's soft voice smoothed the moment.

She eyed Julie and wondered if her cousin even cared that she'd been missing. Julie was too interested in Hugh's every move to even acknowledge Francine.

After slipping her feet back into her sandals, Francine gathered her billfold and novel and prepared to stand.

"Before I left for Paris I thought Dad was talking about getting you a cell phone," Ethan piped up and extended his hand to assist Francine to her feet. "If you'd had one, we could have called you and—"

"We decided it was too expensive," Francine said.

"Who's we?" Ethan prompted.

"Well, uh, Aunt Nora and me. But—but Uncle Tom's paying for so much for me already. My college tuition—"

"You're in-state at a local college. It can't be that bad. You need a cell phone," Ethan groused.

The group followed the hostess into the restaurant, which was decorated in a rich burgundy and teal that underscored the lowered lights, soft music, and elegant atmosphere.

Ethan grasped Francine's upper arm, leaned closer, and spoke in her ear. "Even if I have to pay for the phone myself, you're going to get one. What if you have some kind of an emergency and need help?" He paused. "You know what? I noticed an Alltel vendor by the front desk. That's who I use. I could add you to my plan in a snap. We might even take care of it before we leave the hotel."

"Well, if you insist," she replied. "But I can pay for it out of my allowance."

"You pay for all your own transportation and your own meals at school. And," he added, "I'll bet you also pay for your own clothes, too. Am I right?"

"Well…" Francine hedged as she maneuvered through the maze of tables and chairs and patrons.

"A good cell phone plan will cost a hundred bucks a month. Can you really afford that?"

"I…"

"Let's don't keep arguing about this."

"Who's arguing?" Francine brushed her thumb along the side of her thick novel and repressed a frown.

"We'll take care of it before we leave the hotel," Ethan repeated. "If that doesn't happen, you and I will go to the mall tomorrow and sign you up there. I don't want you to get lost again."

"I wasn't lost," Francine whispered and furtively glanced at Ricky.

The group stopped while the hostess scooted together a couple of tables near a fireplace. Ricky said something and laughed. Nobody joined him.

"I told Ricky I'd be at Addy's. I think he forgot. I didn't want to say anything because…" She shrugged. "Well, you know. I just hated to make him look bad."

Ethan stopped his griping. His mouth settled into a silent "Oh." He gazed toward Ricky and Marie. "I see," he said. "So you'd rather the whole group think you ditched us before you made Ricky look bad—or worse, I guess I should say."

Francine lowered her head, examined the cover of her novel, and didn't respond. "I like Ricky, actually," she explained. "I think he has a lot of good qualities."

After a sigh, Ethan said, "That's a big part of the reason you need a cell."

"What?" Francine peered at Ricky and tried to piece together how he affected her need for a phone.

"What I'm saying is, you always see the good in everybody—even if there's no good to see."

Puzzled, she looked up at Ethan. "You don't think there's any good in Ricky?"

"No, forget Ricky!" Ethan pulled on the center of his goatee. "This has nothing to do with Ricky—well, not really. What I mean is, what if some moron decided to hit on you while you were waiting for us? What would you have done?"

Francine opened her mouth, but Ethan held up his hand. "I'll tell you what you would have done. You'd have 'seen the good in him.'" His silky-brown eyes rounded, Ethan drew invisible quotes in the air. "By the time you realized what was going on, it might be too late. At least if you had a cell you could call me if you got in a bad situation!"

She looked toward their tables and remained silent. Ethan suddenly seemed obsessed with worries that some guy was going to take advantage of her. *Why?* Francine wondered. She was nearly twenty-one and had never had a problem with men approaching her. All the Casanovas proved themselves interested in women with more flamboyant beauty. Furthermore, she had long ago learned to use her natural reticence to spurn any guys interested in conversation-with-a-motive.

When the hostess pronounced her task complete and laid menus on the table, Francine took advantage of the shuffle to study Ethan. His mouth was set in a brooding line she didn't understand. Confused, she claimed a chair on the other end of the table from Ethan, but on the same side as he and Carrie were sitting. That way she wouldn't be forced to sit across from them and watch while they continued to fall in love.

Funny, she thought and pulled out her chair, *he's worried about my getting duped, and* he's *the one head-over-heals with the wrong kind of woman!*

Ethan's voice pierced her logic. "Why don't you sit here, Francine, on the other side of me?" he said. Although his statement was posed as a question, it left no room for argument. "I don't want you sneaking off without my noticing again," he grumbled.

Francine quietly did what he asked. While she had never been accused of having a short temper, Ethan's attitude was starting to rankle. A love song floating from stereo speakers challenged her growing ire. According to the artist, love was wonderful and beautiful…la, la, la.

Blah, blah, blah, Francine countered.

Ethan had been gone for six months, and now he acted as if she were six and he were her self-appointed manager. Of course, that was while he traipsed off into the great unknown with his new girlfriend! And then, *he* had accused *her* of sneaking off?

She picked up her menu and posed it high enough to assure herself some privacy. While everyone else discussed what they would be ordering, she read and re-read the menu, but she still had no idea what dishes were offered. All she could ponder was Ethan's insistence on getting her a cell phone. Then Ethan could connect with Francine immediately, any time, any where. Of course, that would assure that Francine was on his short chain while he was out with Carrie! She clutched the menu tighter.

An electronic voice from the right floated into the menu mix, "You have an incoming call." A chime resounded, and the voice repeated itself.

Francine peeped around her menu toward the feminine voice. Ethan retrieved his phone from his belt-loop holder and answered it. Francine glowered at the silver thing and decided now was a good time to take a turn in the ladies room. Lowering her menu-shield, she scouted out the restaurant. A sign near the fireplace read "Restrooms." The arrow beneath the word pointed the way.

Francine glanced around the table. The group was engrossed in conversation. She was especially relieved to see Marie talking to Ricky without a trace of irritation or impatience. Julie monop-olized Hugh. And Marie and Hugh appeared to barely know each other. Who could guess what happened between the two during their stairway escapade. *Hopefully nothing*, Francine thought. Looking back, she was now thankful that Julie had been spunky enough to chase them down.

While Ethan continued his cell conversation, Carrie concen-trated on what Julie and Hugh were discussing. Deciding no one would miss her, Francine slid from her chair and strode across the restaurant.

Ethan snapped his cell phone shut and said, "That was Dad, Francine! Believe it or not, he's around the corner. He wants to join us for dinner."

When Francine didn't answer, he looked up from slipping the phone into his holster. He encountered an empty chair. Ethan's face went cold, and he held his breath. He relived the panic he'd endured during that twenty-minute search for Francine.

Frantically, he scanned the room and caught sight of her pushing open the ladies room door. Her peach sundress sashayed behind her bare knees as if she were on a spring stroll and didn't have a care in the world. Releasing his breath, Ethan slumped against his chair and shook his head. Francine Ponce was like an ethereal being who floated from room to room with no thoughts to the affects her presence or absence might have.

Earlier, after Ethan and Carrie left the gift shop and independently toured the hotel, he decided the rest of the group might be missing them. Therefore, he'd called Marie's cell. Marie told him they were ready to eat, so they decided to meet in the foyer by the waterfall. From there, they'd go to Addy's.

He and Carrie arrived first. When the other group converged in the foyer, Ethan's first thought was for Francine, whom he didn't spot. He asked the group of four where she was. Ricky said he'd left her sitting by the staff elevator on the second floor. He didn't mention that Francine told him she'd meet them at Addy's.

Ethan scrutinized Marie's fiancé. He reminded Ethan of a cross between Herman Munster and a skinny Chevy Chase—on a non-funny day. Ricky's square head was on another planet, and nobody knew which one. Ethan rubbed his eyes and recalled he and Ricky traipsing all the way to the bench where Ricky said he'd left Francine, only to find it empty.

"Did Francine mention going anywhere when she got back?" he'd asked Ricky. Ricky shook his head.

Panic set in after Ethan asked three different staff members if they had seen Francine. After their negative responses, Ethan's mind conjured horrible scenarios. The worst one included some scoundrel pretending he needed help only to lure the gullible Francine into a hotel room for sinister purposes. Thoughts of someone taking advantage of his naïve and lovely Francine nearly took Ethan under.

For twenty minutes, Ethan tried to temper his alarm in the face of Marie's exasperation and Julie's indifference. While one of Francine's cousins tapped her toe, the other one flirted with Hugh. Carrie, on the other hand, had been a calm and cheerful pillar of support. "I'm sure we'll find her," she peacefully insisted as Ricky consulted with the assistant manager. He, like the other employees, claimed to have never seen Francine.

Carrie saved the day when she spotted Francine sitting in Addy's. Ethan had finally masked his worry and exasperation in mocking indulgence and decided Francine Ponce was going to have a cell phone—whether she wanted one or not. The knowledge that she'd told Ricky where she was going didn't alter Ethan's determination.

I'll put her on my plan, he thought as he picked up his menu, *and get us set up on the instant message option. That way I won't lose her again.*

Francine, forever sheltered on Central Park West, didn't seem to have one thought concerning the dangers New York City might pose for an artless woman as attractive as she. Ethan watched his sisters interact with the men at their sides. Never had he sensed the urge to protect them like he did Francine. Those two could take care of themselves. He'd seen them both tell hulking no-goods to get lost. And they knew how to put a cell phone to many good uses. He wouldn't put it past Marie to shove her antennae up a guy's nose if he didn't back off. But when it came to Francine, all a yahoo would have to do is pretend he desperately needed help. She, forever big-hearted, would gracefully sail into the middle of a trap before she ever knew what hit her.

At least if she has a cell she'll be able to call 911 if she needs it, Ethan thought and wished Nora would learn to keep her mouth shut for once. Nora shouldn't give a flip what few pennies Francine cost Tom Barrimore. Marie and Julie wasted thousands a year!

Ethan picked up the menu and purposefully calmed himself. *I've been gone six months*, he told himself. *Francine has done just fine without me or a cell phone.*

He studied the restroom doorway and decided to drop the whole thing for now. Francine was fine. She hadn't been lost—not really. And she'd survived in New York over half her life without incident.

No sense ruining this time with Carrie over friction with Francine, he decided.

"So, what are you going to order?" Carrie asked.

Ethan absorbed her engaging smile and decided to trust his culinary fate to the new lady in his life. "I don't have the foggiest idea. Why don't we both get your favorite?"

"Oh, that's easy, then," she crooned and fondled the emerald-and-diamond earrings now claiming her ear lobes. "We'll have the blackened salmon. It's to *die* for!" She lowered her hand and strategically tucked her hair behind her ears.

He touched the butterfly-shaped earrings and said, "You really like these, don't you?"

"I *adore* them," Carrie said and leaned closer. "I just wish someone would notice them so I can gloat!" She wrinkled her upturned nose in an endearing manner.

Francine's chair bumped Ethan's elbow, and he turned to discover her settling back at the table. "Hey, Franny," he said, "Carrie wants to gloat. Would you like to be her victim?"

"Oh you." Carrie hit at his forearm.

Ethan grabbed her hand and twined his fingers with hers. The fit was comfortable and good and felt so right.

He looked back at Francine, whose expression was impossible to read. "I bought Carrie some earrings," Ethan explained, "and she's wanting to show them off."

Carrie leaned across him and shamelessly pushed her hair away from her ear again. "See, see, see!" she exclaimed. "Aren't they as cute as they can be?"

"Yes, very nice," Francine said with about as much enthusiasm as she ever showed.

"In Franny talk, that means she likes them a lot," Ethan explained.

"I do," Francine agreed, her voice as calm as ever. "I think they're *very pretty*. They go well with your outfit and match your eyes."

"That's exactly what Ethan said," Carrie admitted. The light peck she bestowed on his cheek left Ethan wishing he hadn't negated the more passionate kiss in the chapel. "I think I'll wear green every day from now on!" Carrie finished.

"It's definitely your color," Francine agreed.

"And, I think peach is *your* color," Carrie said.

"I agree," Ethan said and meant it. "I don't think your eyes have ever looked bluer."

Francine looked down. "Thanks."

"Ethan and I are going to have the blackened salmon," Carrie said. "It's my favorite. You ought to try it."

"Okay," Francine meekly agreed.

Bless you, Carrie Casper, for being so nice to her, Ethan thought. Most women as sophisticated as Carrie wouldn't take the time to befriend someone as unassuming as Francine. But Carrie continued to prove her good character by offering warmth and encouragement to Ethan's childhood confidante. She steadily exhibited qualities required by a good pastor's wife. Ethan tightened his grip on her hand and came closer to confirming that she was most likely *the one*.

The pleasant Asian hostess who seated them approached the table and stopped near Hugh's chair. She touched his back and smiled into his eyes when he turned to face her. "Are you Ethan Summers?" she asked.

"I wish," Hugh said with all his usual charm.

The hostess response was almost as warm as Julie's focus upon Hugh.

Ethan chuckled and leaned toward Carrie. "I wish I was half as smooth as your brother," he said. "I've never been any good with one-liners."

"You're smooth enough as it is," Carrie purred. Her wink intensified her meaning. Ethan, distracted by Carrie's innuendo, barely registered Hugh's explaining his true identity.

"Actually, I meant to tell you when you seated us. I'm Hugh Casper. You might know my father, Darwin Casper?"

Ethan, now fully in-tune with Hugh's conversation, studied the black-suited hostess. Her eyes widened. Her gaze skipped to the oversized print of Darwin Casper hanging above the fireplace. Every Addy's Ethan had dined in featured a print of the founder's portrait. From the looks of it, Darwin Casper had only been about fifteen years older than Hugh was now when the image was captured. Their resemblance was astounding.

Carrie cupped her hand over her mouth and whispered toward Ethan, "Hugh just loves to do this. He gets a kick out of seeing the employees breaking their necks."

The hostess' mouth dropped open. "Oh my word," she breathed. "Does the manager know you're here?" She straightened her black skirt. "Oh dear, I've got to tell him!" she said and hurried away to fulfill Carrie's prophecy.

"Oh, I almost forgot." The hostess rushed back to their table. "I have a message for Ethan Summers."

Ethan raised his hand to catch the hostess' attention. "I'm Ethan," he said.

"Oh, okay then." She hastened toward Ethan and stumbled over a chair.

Hugh snickered.

"There's a gentleman at the front who's been asked to be seated with your party. A Mister," she examined a note tucked in her hand, "Mr. Tom Barrimore. We always check with the seated party before we allow someone to join them."

"Dad's here?" Marie quipped.

"Yes, he just called," Ethan explained and gave his nod to the hostess. "I guess you didn't hear me earlier. He's joining us for dinner."

"Okay! Okay!" The hostess bobbed her head. "I'll see him to your table then." She gawked at Hugh again and then scurried off.

Swiveling in his chair to face Francine, Ethan said, "Dad says he's got some exciting news. He also wanted to make sure you were here. Do you have any idea what's going on?"

Francine remained silently focused upon Hugh. A disapproving veil pulled her features into a negative pinch Ethan rarely saw. He frowned. Francine barely knew Hugh. Was she already drawing a bad opinion of him without getting to know him? Ethan, struggling to comprehend Francine's closed-minded behavior, restated his question.

The negative pinch disappeared. Francine looked at Ethan. "No—no, Uncle Tom hasn't said anything to me," she said.

Her soft blue eyes bespoke the untainted friendship Ethan had depended upon for years. Right now she appeared to be the same ol' Francine. Nothing different. Nothing going to be different. But Ethan's gut reminded him that if the last few days were anything to go by, looks could be deceiving.

Twelve

From the minute Tom Barrimore settled at the end of the table next to Francine, she held her shoulders erect. She noticed Marie treated Ricky with undefiled respect and Julie stopped blatantly flirting with Hugh. Carrie and Hugh were decidedly less extroverted. Hugh even stopped talking up the Asian hostess who continued to revisit their table and who insisted upon treating Hugh and Carrie like royalty. Francine noticed both Ethan's hands were free, so he and Carrie were no longer touching. She smiled to herself. Uncle Tom had a way of whipping everything into line.

The group had barely placed their order when Francine's mind centered upon the reason for his visit. Ethan said her uncle mentioned a surprise and he suspected that it involved her. Caught in the theme of the hour, Francine wondered if Uncle Tom had decided to go ahead and arrange for her to have a cell phone despite Nora's protest. Francine sipped her tart lemon water and anticipated the great relief such an announcement would bring. Ethan had morphed into an over-protective, Carrie-bedazzled stranger.

Francine could only imagine what life on his cell phone plan might be like. His bill would list every call she made and received. A year ago, that wouldn't have been a problem. But the way Ethan was acting now, Francine expected an interrogation if he didn't recognize a number. She had visions of his paging her every other hour, making certain another man wasn't looking at her—or she at him, for that matter. Francine gulped the lemon water.

If I didn't know any better, I'd think he was jealous or something!

She sputtered, and a small piece of lemon seed lodged at the back of her throat. When she tried to cough it up, the thing went down her windpipe. Francine's gasp sounded like the croak of a hoarse hen. She fell into mortifying rounds of gagging and choking that did exactly what Francine never wanted to do—draw attention to herself.

She plopped her water down, grabbed her linen napkin, covered her mouth, leaned forward, and heaved. A raucous bark erupted from her, followed by another…and another…and another. Her eyes watered. Her face heated. Her throat stung.

A chorus of concerned "Are you all right?" mingled with her hacking. When Ethan started whacking her back, Francine held up her hand.

"Stop it, Ethan," Uncle Tom demanded. "If the choking doesn't get her, the beating will!"

Ethan stopped, but left his hand on her back.

By the time Francine got control of the coughing, her hair had covered her face, and her sundress had ridden up past her knees. She began tugging on the dress at the same time Ethan swept her hair back.

"Hello in there," he teased. "Are you still alive?"

"Yes," Francine rasped, her face still warm. "I'm so sorry," she squeaked out. "I think I choked on a lemon seed."

"Here, drink some more water," Ethan offered. "Maybe it will clear everything out."

Francine took a few sips and began to breathe at a normal pace. She scanned the table's other occupants and was surprised to find her cousins were as concerned as Ethan.

"Are you going to live, girlfriend?" Julie asked.

Francine nodded and bestowed a weak smile upon Marie, who smiled back. At times Marie seemed to forget whatever game she was supposed to be playing.

Hugh extended the thumbs-up sign to Francine and Ricky waved. "Can't have you dying on us," he said.

"She's going to live," Ethan claimed.

Carrie leaned across Ethan and tapped Francine's arm. "Are you sure you're going to be okay?" she asked, her eyes full of genuine concern. "I'll go to the restroom with you if you'd like to do some more coughing in private."

Francine shook her head. "No thanks," she said and wished Carrie would make it simpler to dislike her. Most of the time, Carrie seemed like a truly kind-hearted woman who just happened to be stricken with a bad case of the beautifuls—along with a charming, although spontaneous tongue. Maybe Carrie really didn't mean that statement about her disregard for ministers. Perhaps she really was as perfect for Ethan as he seemed to believe. Possibly the person who was jealous was Francine.

Thankful her eyes had already teared from the choking, Francine mopped them with her napkin and hoped Ethan wasn't watching too closely.

"Well, I guess I need to make my announcement before Francine dies on the spot and takes all the fun out of it," Uncle Tom boomed.

Nobody laughed. Everyone silenced. The clink of silverware and low murmuring of guests filled their table's gap in conversation. Francine, keeping her focus on her uncle, knotted her fingers in her lap and prayed no one was still watching her.

Tom Barrimore, his blue eyes as shiny as his balding head, examined the group and said, "That was supposed to be a joke."

"Oh!" everyone said in unison and heartily laughed with the patriarch.

With a rare round of smiles, Tom placed his elbows on the table, made a tent of his fingers, and rested his chin on his fingertips. "I have just closed the deal on the purchase of the brownstone that adjoins ours," he said.

"No way!" Ethan exclaimed. "I didn't even know the Jacksons were selling it!"

"Yes." Tom nodded. "I've known for a couple of months and asked them to hold off putting it on the market until I made my final decision. They agreed."

Francine lowered her head and shot a glance at Uncle Tom from the corner of her eyes. She wondered if any of this actually had anything to do with her.

"After a little painting, I'm going to be leasing the ground floor and the second floor as one unit," he explained. "I'm giving the fourth and fifth floors to Nora for her own apartment." He unbuttoned the top of his shirt, loosened his red tie, and enjoyed a deep breath. "Of course, we'll create a connecting door from our house into that one, so she doesn't traipse through the bottom floors next door to get to her rooms. Also, I'm thinking about expanding the terrace across the tops of both houses."

"Cool!" Julie exclaimed.

"That just leaves the third floor," Tom continued. He reached toward Francine and touched her arm. "And most of that floor, I'm going to turn into a suite for you, my dear. You deserve one every bit as nice as what Julie and Marie now have."

Francine's gasp sounded as hoarse as the lemon-seed coughing spree. Her cheeks warmed. Her eyes widened. She silently stared at her uncle and barely registered that everyone else was staring at her.

"Your aunt and I have already discussed this," Uncle Tom affirmed. "She's scared to death you're going to move out on your own once you wrap up your degree and get a job. Mariette's gotten so used to you reading to her and sitting with her, she's ready to have a nervous breakdown. This way, you'll have your own apartment with us. And," Tom added, "if you wanted to go on to graduate school instead of getting a job you could do that, too." He nodded, and Francine suspected he'd already made the decision for her.

"Well, I—uh—I—" Francine, never certain what to say to her uncle, sputtered to a halt. She inspected her watch and snapped and unsnapped its clip. Francine hated being indebted to people. She already felt as if she owed her aunt and uncle her very life. Because of all the years they'd supported her, she was far more comfortable in the sewing room, her bedroom from her first night's stay. And Francine *had* entertained some fleeting notions of getting her own modest apartment once she finished school and got on her feet. She'd even wondered if she should settle near her mom and dad in Rockaway.

More than ever, she wished for her brother Wade, who was always so good at offering a dose of balanced common sense. If Francine accepted the gift, that was as good as saying she would stay at Central Park indefinitely. Thoughts of daily dealing with Aunt Nora nearly obliterated what was left of her appetite.

Ethan leaned toward her and cupped his hand to her ear. "Why don't you just say, 'thanks,'" he said.

"Thanks!" Francine whispered. Somehow, she managed to smile.

Uncle Tom's approving beam revealed his joy.

The waitress' arrival with their dinner ended Francine's need to say more. Even though she had some misgivings, she *was* stricken with her uncle's thoughtfulness. Maybe Ethan was right about his estimation of Uncle Tom's regard for her.

Francine glanced toward Marie and Julie and was hit with the unexpected. Marie's jealous glare made her want to crawl under the table. Francine couldn't imagine why Uncle Tom's eldest daughter felt such animosity toward her. When Francine first arrived at Central Park, both Marie and Julie befriended her. Somehow, as the years rocked on, their relationship had fractured—especially

Francine's relationship with Marie. She grappled with what Marie could find so offensive in her.

Marie and Julie had everything they could ever want. They had enjoyed their own suites since they were twelve. That was part of the reason there was no room for Francine to have another chamber. Her cousins commanded the third and fourth floors. They each even used a whole bedroom for their closets. Aunt Mariette and Uncle Tom claimed the fifth floor—except for the tiny room Francine had dubbed her own. The second floor housed Nora and Francine along with a small linen and housekeeping room. Ethan also enjoyed a sizable suite and study on that level.

Francine viewed the blackened salmon the waitress plopped in front of her and wondered why she'd let Carrie talk her into it. She really didn't care for fish that much. The smell of it did little to tempt her appetite. She'd far rather be eating soup and a salad.

She'd also far rather get a teaching job, rent her own apartment, and save graduate school for the future. But Francine suspected she wouldn't be enjoying those options.

"You know, Mr. Barrimore," Hugh chirped up. "I wouldn't mind leasing the bottom floors of your new brownstone." After pressing his fork into a piece of steak, he observed his sister. "Carrie, what would you say to our staying in Manhattan awhile? That would put us closer to the center of action. I've got a friend or two who'd like that. I was just talking to Yancey Bates this morning. Remember? He was trying to get me to take an apartment in New York. Besides, I imagine we're going to cramp Uncle Al's style before long anyway."

"Well, I…" Carrie hesitated and looked toward Ethan.

Francine, certain of Ethan's response, could have easily answered for him.

"I think that's a *wonderful* idea!" he crowed. He bobbed his head, and Marie and Julie joined his approval.

Uncle Tom lifted his graying brows. "That sounds fine to me," he agreed, "as long as you're willing to pay my price. These houses aren't cheap. I've got several million tied up between the two of them. The rent is a long way from free. Don't think I'll be giving you any cut." He shook his stubby finger at Hugh, his eyes full of a clever-yet-hard glint that underscored the reason for his Wall Street success.

"I want no cuts!" Hugh claimed, lifting his chin.

"Of course!" Carrie agreed. "We'd insist on paying the going rate. I wouldn't have it any other way."

"Great! I'll tell you what, let's eat and then talk about it some more. I'm starved." Tom picked up his steak knife and fork.

"Works for me," Hugh responded and tossed Julie a discreet wink.

Ricky exchanged a defeated glance with Francine. She suspected the two of them might be forming the "Casper Rejects Club" by Christmas.

Thirteen

~ ~

True to his word, Tom Barrimore made arrangements to freshen up the next door brownstone before he leased it. The work was in full swing when he left on his business trip to England, and everything was finished while he was still away. With Tom's approval, Carrie Casper arranged for the decorator to arrive the day after the painters moved upstairs to tackle Francine's quarters. By the end of August, Carrie had the last piece of furniture delivered, and the Caspers moved in.

The first item on their to-do list was to invite their neighbors over for a Saturday luncheon. While the invitation extended to everyone, only the young people accepted. Mariette declined due to a headache, as usual. And Nora had a previous engagement at church. That suited Carrie. While Mrs. Barrimore wasn't offensive, she never knew what to say or when the matriarch was in the conversation or out. As far as Nora Jamison was concerned, Carrie wasn't certain the queen of England could satisfy that rat-faced matron. The few times Carrie had been around Nora and Francine, she came away miffed. Nora treated Francine with zero respect, and Carrie believed Francine was one of the kindest young women she had ever met.

All during the decoration of their new quarters, Carrie had pulled Francine from whatever task she was involved in to ask her opinion of this color or that lamp or what print would best suit a particular room's mood. Patience personified, Francine had quietly given her opinion—but only after Carrie urged her to speak her mind. Once Francine made a few suggestions, Carrie decided her taste and judgment were impeccable.

Presently, Hugh remained in the garden room, visiting with his friend Yancey Bates. But Carrie, anxious to entertain her guests, stood near the front window of her new abode. She was ready to fling open the door as soon as she saw her friends descending their front steps and ascending hers.

Impatiently she checked her diamond-studded watch. When she looked up, Carrie noticed a movement from the steps next door. She hurried to the front door and pushed the latch down. The massive oak and leaded glass door swung open.

"Hello, everyone!" she called and waved gleefully. "Can you believe we're neighbors?"

With a ready smile, Ethan descended to the curb, turned right, and took Carrie's stairs two at a time. He stopped on the landing and extended a gift bag. When Carrie took it, Ethan offered the best present of all—a brief hug and the brush of his lips against her cheek. "I'm glad you're my neighbor." His warm breath tickled her ear, and Carrie shivered.

"So am I," she gurgled. When she first arrived in New York Carrie had hoped she would be wearing Ethan's ring by Christmas. That hope was gradually growing to certainty. The only problem was his dogged commitment to becoming a pastor.

But that can be remedied, Carrie thought. While she was falling in love with the man, she could not fall in love with being a pastor's wife. The only recourse was talking Ethan out of what he dubbed, "The Call." Carrie would far rather continue in her rich and idle lifestyle. Life could be one big party if Ethan would simply relax and forget his obsession with ministry.

Giggling, Carrie pulled aside the tissue paper and sneaked a peek into his bag. "Do you mind if I open it now?" she asked.

"No, go ahead! I wanted you to get mine first anyway." He looked over his shoulder toward the rest of the gang—Francine and Julie, Ricky and Marie—now striding up the steps. "They all brought something, too," he said.

Carrie, noting that each had a gift bag in their hands, decided it was only appropriate to open Ethan's first. She nudged aside the tissue and pulled out a monstrous Yankee Candle. "Oh yummy! Macintosh Apple! My favorite!" she exclaimed and didn't bother to tell him that she'd just decided the apple-scented candle *was* her favorite.

"Really?" Ethan's brown eyes, warm and inviting, made Carrie want to say whatever he wanted to hear.

"Absolutely!" Carrie said and decided this was a good excuse for another hug. She held Ethan tight and hoped he understood her interest in more. He had to be the slowest moving man on earth. Carrie could barely get him to peck her cheek, but she was beginning to think the best was worth waiting for. She fingered her emerald-and-diamond butterfly earrings. Ethan had put as much interest in the present as an engagement ring. Carrie reminded herself that he might move slowly, but his feelings ran deep.

"You guys will positively *adore* what Mr. Barrimore has done with the first and second floors!" she called to the others as they neared. "What a prince he was to let us pick the colors. Oh!" Carrie her puckered lips. "I guess all of you have seen it at one time or another." She inspected each of her smiling guests until her attention rested upon Marie's blank-eyed fiancé.

"Except Ricky!" she exclaimed. "That means he gets to come in first." She deposited her candle on the bench by the door and made a show of grabbing Ricky's arm and pulling him into the great room.

"Whoa!" Ricky's holler mingled with his laughter. "Marie, save me!" He looked for his fiancée, who never acknowledged his humor. Instead, she gazed past him into the home, her eyes hungry for the sight of another.

Carrie didn't have to guess who. She released her grip on Ricky and motioned for the others to follow. As Marie passed Carrie, she wondered if her brother took his interest in the opposite sex a little too far in the wrong direction. But Carrie couldn't quite blame Hugh this time. What man wouldn't take a second look at Marie Barrimore—especially when she purposefully placed her long-legged self in his space. Today, she wore a short skirt, spike-heeled sandals, and a tight cotton shirt. Carrie was certain Hugh would notice.

Julie's soft gray eyes as inquisitive as ever, strained over Francine's shoulder to see into the home. Even though Julie was an incurable flirt, she lacked Marie's sophistication and allure. Still, Carrie wished Hugh would spend less time watching Marie and more on Julie, who was legitimately available.

"Come on in," Carrie encouraged. "You're just going to love it!" She ushered the group in and was delighted when Julie gasped.

"This is way better than it was a week ago!" Julie exclaimed, inserting her hands into the hips of her low-riding jeans pockets. Today, her black-lace, snug shirt covered her bronze tummy for a change.

"Yes, it's lots better," Carrie replied and drank in the ambiance of the room all over again. The fresh paint and new furniture produced an odor somewhat like a new car smell. Carrie always reveled in anything new. "Two heads are better than one," she claimed. "Hugh told me he didn't care what I chose as long as he wasn't involved in it. So I relied on Francine. She made some wonderful suggestions." Hands on hips, Carrie turned toward Francine, who clicked the door shut.

Carrie found it hard to believe that someone so understated could approve such a bold color scheme. But Francine kept telling

Carrie that she thought the decorator was right—that the combination blended the best of her personality and Hugh's. The decorator had combined rich earth tones over a background of ivory or pale tan. She had also insisted that animal print was all the rage. Francine suggested the camel-colored couch and love seat—leather of course.

The wall over the marble fireplace featured a collection of tiger and leopard prints. The center one, a graceful tiger with exotic green eyes, commanded the center of attention. Francine had told Carrie that the tiger's eyes were much like hers. Carrie wondered if Ethan might think the same.

Out of the corner of her eye, she noted Ethan's spirited appraisal of the décor. Approval's glow heightened his Latin charm—as did the sheen of his black dress shirt. Carrie wanted to melt on the spot...until Ethan turned all the glow upon Francine.

"Hugh's in the garden room," Carrie told the rest of the gift-laden group. She pointed toward a wide entryway that opened into a sunny room full of plants. As part of Mr. Barrimore's closing deal, the former owners had agreed to leave the garden room as it was, except for the furniture. Carrie had delighted in having a ready-made haven of nature and gladly purchased wicker and wrought-iron furniture to fit the room's mood.

She was as anxious for Ethan to see that finished room as she was the rest of the house. With Marie, Ricky, and Julie meandering toward the garden room, Carrie started to approach Ethan but stopped.

Ethan, his attention all for Francine, touched her back and leaned closer to catch her every word. Carrie hovered near the marble fireplace, restored to its 1860s splendor, and kept smiling. Soon her mouth grew stiff. But it really didn't matter because no one noticed. Francine and Ethan were lost in each other. And Marie, Ricky, and Julie had found Hugh and his friend Yancey, in the garden room—if the boisterous laughter and Julie's shrill giggles were anything to go by.

Crossing her arms, Carrie examined Ethan and his childhood friend. A time or two, Carrie had felt some jealousy toward Francine—especially when Ethan seemed particularly focused upon the fragile-looking blonde, as he was now. The best she could tell, the guy hadn't even noticed the green-eyed tiger above the fireplace. Carrie was sure by now he would have mentioned that her eyes were as captivating as the cat's. But Ethan's focus remained on Francine.

Carrie had especially fought envy at the Worthingham Renaissance. The day was divine until Ethan nearly fell apart over Francine's absence. She began to wonder then if she had underestimated the relationship between the two. Even though she had put on a concerned face, Carrie nearly blurted out something about Francine being a grown woman who could take care of herself. By dinner, Carrie had been thankful she'd held her tongue. Ethan's doting affection ended her worries.

As with that evening, Carrie wound up reasoning herself out of the jealousy. After all, Francine's pale skin and heart-shaped face earned her a mildly attractive rating at best. Even her choice in clothing was usually nondescript. Today, she wore a simple denim skirt that fell nearly to her ankles, a pair of flats, and a cream-colored T-shirt. Thankfully, the thing wasn't peach.

Carrie examined her polished cotton capri set with rhinestones sprinkled across the front. She'd bought the suit yesterday and purposefully chosen green. After fingering her prized earrings, Carrie reminded herself that *she* was the one wearing Ethan's gems. All speculation vanished.

Ethan and Francine are just like any other brother and sister, she reasoned. Carrie wandered toward the lively garden room and refused to acknowledge that she and Hugh had *never* been as cozy as the two in the great room.

"Definitely not," Francine said with a firm shake of her head. "This color scheme is not for me. I prefer something softer." She shifted her golden gift bag from one hand to the other.

"Well, are you going to go to the furniture store like Dad said, or am I going to have to go for you?" Ethan pressed.

Francine set the bag on an end table, crossed her arms, and gazed around the stylish room. How could she explain to Ethan that she didn't want to continue to pile up what she viewed as debt to her aunt and uncle? Ever since that fated dinner at Addy's when Uncle Tom announced he was giving Francine a suite, she had debated dozens of ways to bow out of accepting the third-floor quarters. Unfortunately, none of the ways were graceful enough for Francine's taste.

"I see," Ethan said. His mischievous smile sparkled in his eyes. "It looks like I'm going to be in charge just like Dad said."

"Oh, so now the two of you are conspiring behind my back?" Francine softly challenged. She lifted her brows and didn't back down from Ethan. But then, she seldom backed down from Ethan. He was the only person besides her brother Wade with whom Francine could completely relax.

"Yes, as a matter of fact, we are," Ethan declared. "Dad says the decorator is due Monday. If you won't meet with her, I will. He's scared to death you'll go to the furniture store and pick out only the stuff that's on sale—whether it matches or you like it or not."

Francine laughed and looked down. She ran the end of her open-toed flat along the short-napped, ebony rug. "He knows me well, doesn't he?"

"Don't we all?" Ethan grumbled with a smile.

Francine, on the verge of an amiable retort, was interrupted by Hugh's merry voice. "Are you two going to join us? Lunch is almost on."

Uncrossing her arms, Francine swiveled to face the garden room.

Hugh, dressed in a red polo shirt, khaki shorts, and thick-soled sandals sauntered into the living room. He extended his hand to Ethan and the two enjoyed a warm handshake. Hugh then turned to Francine. As far as she knew, he was looking at

her the first time since that day on the terrace when he insinuated she was a beautiful woman.

"I'm glad you came, Francine," he said with a genuine respect
that surprised her.

Her first impulse was to look down. But the polished wood
did nothing to reveal whether Hugh meant what he said or if he
was just trotting out a new line. Francine decided there was only
one way to find out. She narrowed her eyes and didn't flinch from
studying the intent of his heart. Astoundingly, Francine noticed
none of the playboy innuendoes he'd lavished upon the Marie and
Julie. Hugh blinked hard and inched his head back. Francine, surprised he even noticed her scrutiny, looked down again.

"I want you to feel as much at home here as you do next door,"
Hugh added, his tone a bit uncertain.

Francine, more comfortable being a "Hugh Casper ignoree"
than a "Hugh Casper noticed guest," decided that etiquette
required she at least offer a handshake. She extended her hand
and tried to smile. A simple thanks was all she verbalized.

Apparently, that's all the encouragement Hugh Casper
needed. Before Francine realized his intent, Hugh took her arm
and guided her toward the garden room. A stranger sitting in a
fan-backed wicker chair proved to be their target. As they stepped
around Ricky's long legs and maneuvered past a maze of plants,
Francine shot a desperate glance over her shoulder in search of
Ethan. She spotted him freshly snared in Carrie's clutches.

A lot of help you are! Francine thought. In recent weeks Ethan
had nearly had a nervous breakdown over imaginary hotel
stalkers. He'd even foisted a pewter-colored cell phone off on
her. Now when Francine really needed him to run interference,
he was kissing up to Carrie. Or perhaps Carrie was kissing up to
him! Francine stumbled to a halt in front of the wicker chair and
tried to erase the image of Carrie's lips on the edge of Ethan's
goatee—dangerously close to his mouth.

"Francine," Hugh began, "this is my lifelong friend-turned-actor, Yancey Bates." He pretended to cuff Yancey's chin. "Be kind to the poor man. He's very sensitive."

The fellow had a boyish face and frizzy cropped hair. While he wasn't movie star handsome, his sparkling smile suggested a carefree spirit. Furthermore, this Yancey Bates had taste in clothes much like Ricky's—unmatched. Today, he wore a red-and-yellow floral print shirt and green plaid pants he had to have scratched up from the seventies.

Francine averted her gaze toward Hugh to keep from laughing. That was a mistake. Hugh was examining her with an expression of awe that made Francine forget she'd been amused at Yancey's wardrobe. Francine's face warmed. She considered crawling under the oversized glass-topped coffee table and covering her head with one of the magazines sprawled across the top.

Yancey stood, graciously took her hand, and bowed over it. Before she could jerk her hand away, he kissed her knuckles. "My lady," he murmured with a thick Shakespearean accent, "thou art as lovely as thy reputation hath made thee."

"Oh, cut it out," Hugh chided. "He's been in a Shakespeare play, and now he can't quit." He picked up a copy of *Good House-keeping* from the table Francine wished she was under and whacked Yancey over the head.

He straightened, blinked, gulped, and pretended to shift into a different mode. "Ah, the dame I've heard so much about!" This time he sounded like Humphry Bogart. His chilly fingers caressed her palm and gripped her hand longer than politeness dictated. "Hugh can't stop talking about your charms. Here's lookin' at you, kid."

The actor surveyed her for a moment. Feeling like a germ under a microscope, Francine purposefully looked past him toward a huge ficus. Maybe if she pretended he really wasn't there, he'd go away.

Despite her attempts, Yancey continued talking. This time, he dropped all pretense and a mellow, New York influx prevailed.

"The guy usually embellishes his descriptions of the women in his life, but in your case he hasn't said enough."

Hugh tossed the magazine back to the table and knocked over one of three unopened gift bags in the center. Francine remembered she'd left her gift in the great room and decided that slip of the mind would prove her blessing.

Why these two men of the world were picking on her when more attractive women were present was beyond Francine's comprehension. Whatever their reasons, Francine decided she had endured enough. So she used the same old trick she trotted out dozens of times before.

"It's nice to meet you," she said with no hint of warmth. She extracted her fingers from Yancey's and looked around. "If you'll excuse me," Francine continued. "I just remembered I left my housewarming gift in the great room."

"Okay," Hugh said. Francine assumed she was home free but soon discovered she was wrong. "I'll go with you to get it."

"Uh…" she hedged. "I also need to visit the ladies room. This house's layout is close to ours. I'm guessing there's a restroom near the stairs?"

"Yes, exactly," Hugh confirmed and thankfully didn't offer to accompany her on *that* trip.

The old "ladies room slip" usually did the trick. Francine had learned that most guys didn't argue with a woman with a full bladder. Once she found the restroom and dodged into it, Francine planned to slip out the front door and curl up with a book in her fifth-floor hideout. These guys would focus on Marie and Julie and never miss her.

Just as Francine was about to finalize her getaway, Ethan arrived at her side. He slid his arm around her back, eyed Yancey, and said, "Francine's every bit as beautiful on the inside as she is on the outside." While his words spoke one message, his tone communicated another: *Back off!*

Yancey retreated, clutched his chest, and feigned a shooting. "Ugh! He done got me! Right in the ticker!" he yelped with a southern accent and rolled his eyes back in his head. He staggered several paces to the side. "Ethel! Ethel! Go git Doc Hodges. And if'n you don' hurry, I'm a gonner, darlin'!"

Hugh laughed out loud, and Ethan's stern appraisal cracked into a mild smile. "You're an idiot, man!" Hugh said.

Francine wasn't even tempted to a lip twitch. She didn't know whether to kiss Ethan for being in tune with her plight or to smack him with a copy of *Good Housekeeping* for assuming she couldn't take care of herself.

Carrie's arrival ended Francine's deliberation. Miss Casper had the look of a woman possessing and possessed. She slipped her arm through Ethan's and purred, "It's almost one o'clock. Is everyone ready for lunch?"

"Lunch!" Yancey crowed. "I haven't eaten in weeks!"

Ethan dismissed his "defend Francine" mission and zoomed in on Carrie, whose captivating laugh resounded with the melodious charm of classical music.

Francine, stricken anew with Ethan's obsession with Carrie, forgot about her restroom escape and wondered how Ethan could be so convinced *she* was the naive one.

"Yes, let's eat, everybody!" Hugh declared. "Yancey and I have been scheming behind your backs. We have a fun project to run by you after lunch!"

Fourteen

"Our new housekeeper, Mrs. Krause, made both chicken salad and pastrami sandwiches," Carrie said and picked up a shiny brass bell from the end table. After giving it a merry jingle, she said, "I believe pastrami is the favorite of someone in the crowd."

"That will be me," Ethan admitted in a voice that communicated his gratitude. The smells of sandwiches mixed with some heavenly dessert in the oven, floated from the kitchen. Ethan's stomach growled. His mouth watered with thoughts of pastrami on rye with extra mustard.

He squeezed Carrie's hand. "You think of everything," he said.

"Well, when it concerns you," she responded.

Ethan couldn't stop the appreciative smile. "Did I tell you you look great in green?"

"Not today," she teased and wrinkled her nose.

"Well, I have now."

"I bought this outfit just for you," she admitted, "and for your earrings." She touched the diamond-and-emerald butterflies on her ears.

"I'm glad," Ethan said, convinced he had never met a woman more thoughtful—except Francine, of course. But then, few women could match her character. It wasn't even fair to use her as a measuring stick. Not to Carrie or anyone else, for that matter.

Carrie fussed with a cushion on the wrought-iron settee and then offered Francine a seat. She quietly took the seat, and Ethan bent toward her. "Are you comfortable?" he asked.

"Yes, thanks," Francine said, her expression wooden.

Ethan didn't know what to say next, or whether or not he should say anything. One minute Francine was congenial in the living room, and now she stared right through him. Confused, he opened his mouth to speak again but then chose to remain silent. The wiles of the feminine mind were beyond his comprehension. And the one woman he thought he could predict was proving herself unpredictable...*again.*

While Carrie flitted around the room, consulting with her guests, Ethan stood near Francine and observed his sisters. He didn't have to wonder why both of them—especially Marie—resented Francine. He never remembered Dad praising them as he did Francine. But of course, neither of them exhibited the maturity and common sense Francine showed, either. Both Marie and Julie had ditched college, and neither worried about how much of Tom Barrimore's money they spent.

Now Marie sat on the wicker love seat holding Ricky's hand and eyeing Hugh, who dragged a wrought-iron chair next to Julie's chair and laughed at something she said. Ethan wondered if Hugh realized what a crush Marie was developing on him. As outgoing as he was, he talked to everyone, just like Carrie did. Ethan figured he probably had no idea the impact he was having on the opposite sex.

But Yancey Bates was another case altogether. Ethan couldn't stand by and watch him come on to Francine without doing something to stop him. Yancey had just joined Hugh and Julie and was mimicking Humphrey Bogart again. Even though his antics were humorous, Ethan would prefer he *not* play up to

Francine. Feigning nonchalance, he purposefully positioned him-self between Yancey's line of vision and Francine.

Much to Ethan's aggravation, Yancey caught Ethan watching him. He smiled, stood, and ambled forward. Ethan didn't know whether to scowl or give in to a spontaneous chuckle over the guy's ridiculous clothes.

"Hey there, pard'ner," he drawled. "I guess we haven't been officially introduced. I'm John Wayne."

A humorous sputter beat out the scowl. Even though the dark-complected man looked nothing like John Wayne, he mim-icked an expression much like the movie star's. And his voice matched Wayne's every nuance.

"I'm Ethan Summers." Ethan extended his hand.

"This is a mighty fine group 'ere, don't ya think now, pad'ner?"

"Yes," Ethan agreed and looked over Yancey's green-plaid pants and red-and-yellow floral shirt. How he could have missed such a getup before now was a mystery. Ethan figured he'd been so focused on protecting Francine, he'd missed her suitor's ridicu-lous dress.

"Oh, don't waste your time on this crazy man!" Hugh aban-doned Julie and moved to Ethan's side.

Carrie rang her bell again, this time with less patience.

"Want me to go see what the holdup is?" Yancey asked and rubbed his hands together. "I'm starved."

"You're *always* starved," Carrie said and laid her hand on his shoulder.

"I'm a broke actor, what do you expect?" Yancey complained.

"Come on." Carrie motioned toward the kitchen. "We'll both go see what's wrong. If it's still going to be awhile, we'll fix you a snack."

The second the kitchen door swung shut, Hugh lowered his voice and spoke to Ethan. "Don't worry about Yancey," he com-forted. "He wasn't coming on to Francine. That's just his way. He's a clown."

Ethan frowned at the kitchen door, and his irritation began to ease. "I guess I'm a little protective of her," he admitted. "But she's just so innocent and naive, I feel like somebody's got to—"

"You don't have to worry about Francine Ponce," Hugh chided. "That woman can take care of herself."

Ethan raised his brows and posed a silent question.

"With just one look she can cut you to the floor, man. I'm telling you, she's tough."

"Francine?" Ethan questioned and darted a furtive glance toward the topic of their conversation. She serenely sat upon the settee, her legs crossed, her denim skirt touching her ankle.

"Yes, Francine," Hugh confirmed. "But even if she'd been snowed by Yancey, I wouldn't have let him…" Hugh trailed off and shrugged. "Well, you know," he assured, "there are women we chase and women we respect. I respect her."

"I'm glad to hear that," Ethan said.

"In some ways she reminds me of an angel," Hugh continued, his focus on Francine.

Ethan looked back at her. The city sunshine, weakened by haze, filtered through the row of windows lining the room. The golden glow illuminated Francine's white-blonde hair for a celestial effect that arrested Ethan. "I think you're right," he agreed.

"I wonder…" Hugh said, but didn't finish his thought.

Stricken anew with how pretty Francine had grown since he left for Paris, Ethan didn't press Hugh to complete his statement. Instead, he continued to appraise his childhood friend. Her beauty wasn't the drop-dead gorgeous variety as was Carrie's. Francine's attractiveness was simple and understated. Ethan stroked his goatee and wondered if she'd always been this pretty, and he just couldn't see it until after he'd been away. Either that or something was changing with Francine. Something he couldn't identify. Something that made him uneasy and half crazy at the thought of other men looking at her or taking advantage of her. Ethan could only hope that Francine would find a husband who deserved her due to his own high moral and ethical standards…a man who would appreciate not only her external beauty, but also the quality of woman that she was.

The kitchen door swung open, and Ethan was drawn to the fresh onslaught of delicious smells that reminded him he hadn't eaten in hours. Carrie and Yancey preceded Mrs. Krause, wide and round, who lumbered in pushing a painted serving cart.

"I've found the woman I'm going to marry!" Yancey crowed. "Any woman who can make a kitchen smell like that deserves my hand in marriage."

"If I were a woman, I wouldn't marry your hand—or the rest of you, either!" Hugh joked.

Ricky laughed the loudest. Carrie covered her eyes and shook her head. "That was really bad," she complained.

Mrs. Krause, old enough to be Yancey's mother, blushed, smiled, and made quick work of piling the garden room's large, glass-topped coffee table with sandwiches, two bowls of chips, and a tray laden with pickles, olives, cheeses, and fruit. A bottle of ginger ale surrounded by ice-filled glasses garnished with sprigs of mint remained on the cart's top shelf. A stack of clear glass saucers and linen napkins sat near the soda.

"Fill your plates, everybody," Carrie called over the oohs and ahs of a hungry group.

"Just wait!" Yancey said and popped a piece of cantaloupe in his mouth. "There's fresh cheesecake, too."

His stomach rumbled anew, and Ethan decided this was not the time to be shy. The second Mrs. Krause exited, he stepped to the cart, retrieved a plate, and realized no one had offered to bless the food. While Ethan had survived a time or two without the treasured tradition, eating without first praying always left him feeling a bit awkward and thankless.

"I guess one of us should say grace over the food," he said.

Yancey's jaw dropped. "What's the deal?" he joked. "Are you a reverend or something?"

"Actually, he is," Francine's soft claim ended Yancey's sarcastic grin.

"Oh," he said, while Julie and Marie giggled.

Carrie's demure smile smoothed the moment. "A wonderful way to begin," she stated generously…graciously. "Ethan, I think you're the perfect choice."

The group grew quiet. Only the sound of Mrs. Krause clanking dishes in the kitchen prevailed. Ethan bowed his head and was delighted when Carrie slipped her hand in his. *She's going to make a great wife!* he thought before offering the brief prayer of thanksgiving for the food and for new friends.

The group participated in a collective "amen," and began the lunch-time shuffle. Mrs. Krause reappeared and began setting up teak folding trays around the room. Carrie staked out two wrought-iron chairs placed slightly apart from the others for her and Ethan. She set her plate on the folding table between them. Ethan followed suit.

They were in an alcove of sorts, set apart by a line of hanging ferns. From the hanging bromeliads to the potted orchids, begonias, and exotic tropicals, this corner of the room was bedecked with nature's beauty.

Ethan gazed at Carrie and forgot his stomach's rumble. The abundance of plants heightened her allure. Carrie reminded him of Eve in the Garden of Eden. Ethan imagined himself taking their relationship to the next level and planting his lips upon hers. He didn't think she would mind in the least, not if her beckoning smile was anything to go by.

"Why are you staring?" she asked, the sunshine's caress highlighting her sandy curls.

"Because you're gorgeous," Ethan said and meant it.

"I thought you said you weren't good with one-liners." Carrie's eyes turned to molten fire.

"That wasn't a line. It was the truth."

She stood and stroked the side of his face with the tip of her cool finger. Her sophisticated perfume wove its spell. Ethan swallowed hard.

"Why don't I go get us some soda?" Carrie's husky tone increased his pulse. "You usually take care of the details. Now it's my turn. I guess we both forgot."

"Who can think of soda at a time like this?"

"Oh, you're *so good* with those lines," she responded.

Ethan, trying to remember where he was, watched Carrie sashay back to the food cart. He wasn't an expert on women's sizes, but Ethan figured she was a perfect size five...maybe a three. *Oh well,* he thought, *whatever size she is, it's perfect.*

Hugh stepped between him and Carrie, and Ethan strained to see past him. The effort was wasted, especially when he noticed what Hugh was doing. The guy was taking extra care to make sure Francine's plate was filled. Usually, Ethan did that sort of thing. If he didn't, Francine would wait until last when everyone else was through and the food was picked over.

After handing Francine's plate to her, Hugh dragged one of Mrs. Krause's tables to her seat and got her ginger ale. Her head bent, she sat down and deposited her plate on the table. When Hugh returned with the drink, she offered him an upward glance and spoke her thanks.

Ethan pondered Hugh's statement about Francine being an angel and wondered if Carrie's brother was developing a genuine interest in her. The thought struck Ethan with a perplexing set of emotions. His first reaction was the oddest. His gut tightened like it had when he thought that gold-watched businessman was going to approach Francine. Then Ethan convinced himself that if someone as respectable as Hugh were interested in Francine, she would be a fortunate young woman. Not only did Hugh have a good personality, he was filthy rich. Francine could hardly do better.

With this settled, Ethan noted that Julie also watched Hugh's attention to Francine. She sat by Yancey in one of the fan-backed wicker chairs and pouted over the scanty rations on her plate. Hugh's favoring Francine wasn't lost on Marie, either. She neared the wicker love seat where Ricky gobbled his chicken salad. Marie plopped her oversized saucer on the portable table with so much force a grape spilled onto the table and tumbled to the floor. Ethan decided that if Hugh were making a play for Francine, it would be the best thing that could happen to the sisters. Marie had no business allowing her eye to wander. And Julie was too big a flirt for her own good.

Ethan examined his meal. His hunger kicked in with renewed fervor. He tackled the mustard-laden pastrami, and his stomach growled its appreciation.

An icy glass of ginger ale appeared in his line of vision, and Ethan offered a smile to the woman attached to it. "I don't believe I've ever seen Hugh do that," Carrie mumbled and glanced over her shoulder.

"What?" Ethan asked.

"What he just did for Francine. Did you notice?"

"You mean that he helped her with her lunch and got her settled?"

"Yes, all that."

Ethan blinked and tried not to take Carrie's statement too literally. If Hugh were a true gentleman, this wouldn't be the first time he had helped a lady. Such manners were a way of life with Ethan. Today was the first day he'd even allowed Carrie to serve him, and he probably wouldn't have let her if his head had been clear. He suspected Carrie was simply exaggerating—like a lot of sisters did about their brother's vices.

"Well, I think he's probably just being a gentleman," Ethan explained.

"Hmmm," Carrie said. She sat down and thoughtfully munched a chip.

The next twenty minutes was consumed with eating, refilling plates, and praising Mrs. Krause. Yancey begged to know when the cheesecake would be ready.

"Mrs. Krause says ten more minutes," Carrie proclaimed. The kitchen door whisked shut behind her as Ethan picked up a tray from the food cart and proceeded to retrieve the used dishes scattered around the room.

"Good!" Hugh said and rubbed his hands together. "That's enough time for Yancey and me to tell you what we've cooked up."

Fifteen

The tray full, Ethan shifted his load to the cart's second level and turned toward the group. Everyone but Francine focused upon Hugh. He'd seen the look on her face too many times to count. Ethan suspected his "little sister" was on the verge of trying to make her escape. She would first excuse herself for a trip to the ladies room and then quietly vanish.

He settled on the settee beside her, touched her knee, and moved close. "Nice try!" he whispered.

"What?" Francine looked up, and Ethan couldn't remember a time when her eyes had been so blue—not even the day she wore the peach sundress. Whatever perfume she wore, it was soft and inviting. Nothing fancy or loud. Just like the woman who wore it. Maybe that was the reason Hugh was helping her.

"Uh…" Ethan stammered and tried to remember what he'd been saying.

"What's a nice try?" she repeated.

"Oh yeah, the escape," he said.

"Escape?"

"Yes. You were about to escape, weren't you?"

"What makes you say that?" Francine mumbled and looked past him.

"I know you!" Ethan claimed. "I know that look on your face. But it won't work. I've got you now." He looped her arm through his and clasped her hand "You're staying till we all leave." Her fingers trembled against his, and Ethan hoped he hadn't somehow upset her. He examined her features, and his reward was a shy smile. Ethan smiled back and experienced the same sensation he'd depended upon for years. When Franny smiled at him, the whole world was smiling for him.

"Do I have everyone's attention?" Hugh's sharp voice ended Ethan's dialogue with Francine.

Ethan turned his attention to Hugh and Yancey, standing side-by-side near the coffee table, and discovered every gaze upon him and Francine. "What?" Ethan said, wondering if someone had posed a question.

"We were just waiting on you two to join the class," Yancey said in a high-pitched voice that sounded like somebody's worst nightmare of a third-grade teacher.

Everyone laughed.

"Oh, don't bother with them," Marie said and waved toward Ethan and Francine. Her manicured fingernails glistened with frosty red. "They're always in another world. Let's just get on with it! I'm *dying* of curiosity!"

Julie scooted to the edge of her seat. Carrie, her arms crossed, stood in front of the row of ferns. Ricky reclined in the love seat and stared upward as if he really didn't want to be at the Caspers', let alone hear anything Hugh had to say.

"Okay," Hugh said and laid his hand on Yancey's shoulder. "You all already know that Yancey's an actor. As a matter of fact, he's heading out for a reading in about an hour."

"It's set in 1973," Yancey explained, and ran his hand up and down his clothing like a model on a game show. "I went ahead and dressed the part."

Francine's low chuckle instigated Ethan's darting her a glance. "So that explains it," he said under his breath. "I wonder what Ricky's excuse is?" He glanced toward the poor guy's brown slacks and pink shirt.

"Ricky has *never* looked that bad," Francine replied.

"Anyway," Hugh continued and rubbed the corners of his mouth with his index finger and thumb. "Along with being an actor and full-time clown, Yancey is also a playwright."

"Playwright," Yancey slowly added.

"And he's got a new script he wants to try to sell. But he also thinks seeing it performed will help him polish the final draft."

"Final draft." Yancey motioned like a queen waving to her constituency.

Without changing his expression, Hugh picked up the tried-and-true copy of *Good Housekeeping* and whacked Yancey on the head. "Would you cut it out?"

The actor blinked, gulped, and rolled his head back. When he snapped it back straight, his eyes were round, his lips were flattened together, and he began to talk like a chipmunk on fast forward. "Yancey Bates isn't sure of a few of his scenes and thought maybe it would help him to see it acted out. He was wondering if you would be his actors. The end."

Julie screamed with hilarity. Marie joined her. Ethan suspected the two were going to burst veins in their necks. They both fell sideways and shrieked. Carrie caught Ethan's eye, shook her head, and covered her face. While Ethan would have preferred to remain stoic, he couldn't deny his own laughter. Hugh doubled over, stumbled, and almost landed in Marie's lap. Ricky, who had been enjoying the moment as much as the rest, turned serious and glared at Hugh.

Francine punched Ethan and whispered, "That guy needs to be committed somewhere." But her eyes were full of giggles.

"Yep," Ethan agreed. "He'd have a ready-made audience."

"I think this all sounds like a blast!" Marie wiped her eyes and clapped her approval.

Ethan eyed Carrie. She was as intensely interested as Julie. "What a fun idea!" she stated. "I say we invite a few friends even, once Yancey gets it polished. It will give us all something to do the next few weeks."

The group's excitement increased. When the initial reaction subsided, Hugh searched the gang a moment before settling his gaze on Francine. "What do you think of the idea, Francine?"

She gripped Ethan's arm and straightened. "Well, it just all depends on what the play's about."

Yancey laughed out loud. "Oh! You're all going to *love* the title," he proclaimed. "It's called *Lovers*."

"*Lovers?*" Francine croaked as the others began an enthused discussion of the title.

"Isn't that the play you let Hugh and me read a couple of weeks ago?" Carrie asked.

"Yes," Yancey said.

"Oh my word, it's too funny for words!" Carrie covered her eyes and shook her head. "We'll have the time of our lives."

Ethan, caught up in the momentum, paid little attention to Francine.

Even Ricky's interest was piqued. "Where would we do it?" he asked.

"What about the room in the back that's supposed to be the library?" Carrie offered. "We haven't put anything in there, and—"

"*Perfect!*" Hugh exclaimed and pointed to his sister.

"What about a stage and scenery and props?" Julie asked.

"I'll take care of all that," Hugh said. "Not a problem."

"Okay, just a minute," Ethan cautioned and scooted forward. "Whatever we do, we need to make sure we don't, like, affix anything to the house. It needs to all stay portable." He imagined his father's disapproving stare if a collection of nail holes were inflicted upon his new paint job. "Dad's just spent a lot of money on this place, and—"

"Oh, Ethan…" Carrie strode across the room and squeezed her narrow hips in beside him. Ethan thought about scooting over but decided he preferred the tight fit. "Don't worry about a thing," Carrie admonished, "I'll personally make sure everything stays in order. Besides, your dad will be off in England, and we won't hurt a thing." She reached for his hand. "If we do, we'll fix it, okay?"

Ethan knew his smile was goofy, but he couldn't do a thing to stop it. "Sure, no problem," he agreed.

"What's the play about?" Francine's low voice punctured the revelry.

"Lovers!" Yancey said. "What else?"

She caught Ethan's gaze and issued a silent warning. He didn't have to hear one word from Francine to understand her meaning. With a title like *Lovers,* the possibilities were significant that some scenes could be R-rated. Francine's logic took hold, and Ethan heeded the still, small voice within that suggested he should proceed with caution. The last thing he needed was to be involved in something that would compromise his morals or his staff position at Manhattan Community Church.

In the middle of all his speculating, Ethan sensed Carrie's appraisal. He glanced toward her and debated the best way to pose his questions.

"Uh…it does have some, um, amorous scenes," she admitted, as if she'd been privy to the silent conversation between Ethan and Francine.

"So? I'm amorous!" Julie exclaimed and then flopped back and laughed at her own joke.

"Oh you are, are you?" Yancey shot back. "Want to tell me all about it?"

Marie rolled her eyes.

"If there's a problem," Hugh cleared his throat and his voice grew thoughtful for a change, "we can always tone down anything that makes anyone uncomfortable. You know," he shrugged and looked to Yancey for support, "I'm sure the Yance would be okay with just some kissing and that's it. I don't think the sexy scenes are the ones he's worried about anyway, are they?"

"Sure, that's right." Yancey nodded. "We can cut the racy stuff. Not a problem."

Ethan's shoulders relaxed. "That would be best," he admitted. "Even though this is a private deal, I don't need to be involved in anything that will, you know…" he shrugged, "make my boss uncomfortable if he found out."

"He's on staff at Manhattan Community Church," Francine explained, her even voice a beacon of certainty amid the volatile subject. "Right now, he's an associate pastor. He's supposed to be ordained next spring, and—"

"Oh, of course," Yancey said. He bowed his head and touched his forehead, his abdomen, and each shoulder. "Bless you, my son," he droned, his cooperative spirit swept aside in the face of evoking more mirth.

Marie and Julie didn't disappoint Yancey. They released bucketsful of shrill laughter.

Ethan's cheeks heated. He looked down. In the light of the mild mockery, an unexpected urge to participate in the play as it was overtook him. A coaxing voice suggested that a few amorous scenes with Carrie might be fun—*a lot of fun!* Never had Ethan been so tempted to forget the whole ministry thing and jump in…not only into the play, but also into Carrie's warm arms.

"Okay, Yancey," Carrie chided, her voice demanding no argument. "You've gone far enough. If we're going to do this play for you, there's no reason to make anyone uncomfortable. Let's just keep it as tame as possible." She raised her hand, paused, and looked at Ethan.

He nodded and hid all traces of the struggle within.

"A few kissing scenes can speak volumes. Let's just leave it at that. Okay?" Carrie said.

But what about the sexual overtones? Francine thought and stared at Ethan. *Will any adultery be implied? And what about the language factor? Does the play include any cursing…will anyone be required to take the Lord's name in vain?*

She scrutinized Ethan. He reminded her of a perch dangling on the end of Carrie's hook. All she had to do was look at him with those big green eyes and Ethan melted into a puddle. If there were passionate kissing scenes, Francine wagered those two would be in the middle of them. All these years Ethan had purposefully avoided such temptations.

Francine's stomach turned. She began to fear for Ethan's integrity. Simultaneously, Francine wondered if the play would be better titled *Samson and Delilah.*

While Francine toyed with her watch's clasp, a new thought swept aside her worries. Ethan was supposed to be enrolled in his final seminary class—an online seminar. From his last report, it was a doozy of a class that involved more than a hundred pages in researched material by semester's end. There was no way he would have time for a play.

With the excited group volleying ideas, Francine leaned toward Ethan. "Will you have time for this? What about your seminary class?" she whispered.

Ethan turned to face her, his eyes wide. He stared at Francine for several seconds before he finally spoke. "Oh no!" he gasped. "The last chance to complete registration was ten days ago. The class started last week. I completely forgot it!" He pressed his fingertips against the center of his forehead. "Oh man," he groaned. "I can't believe this."

Francine's soul grew numb. She said nothing. She didn't even blink. Ethan couldn't be ordained until he finished his academic requirements.

"There's a part for each of us," Yancey's voice floated through her horror. "You *will* take a part, Francine?"

Her hands dampened, and she sensed the pull of the vortex that had sucked Ethan up. Francine stood. Escaping was no longer an option. While she would have loved to flee with Ethan, she recognized that he was too far gone.

"N–no," Francine stammered. "I—I—this isn't—isn't—plays just aren't for me." She pressed her hands against the sides of her skirt and searched for something to reinforce her rejection. "I just started this semester. I'm—I'm in college," she said. "I don't have time. Besides, even a toned-down version sounds too risqué for me."

"But you haven't even read it." Yancey pointed his toes together and pretended to cry. He reminded Francine of a pouting clown.

"If you don't participate, we'll be short one person." Hugh stepped to her side, put his arm along her shoulders, and looked her squarely in the eyes, much too close for Francine's comfort. "*Then* what will we do?" His hazel eyes took on a pleading spirit she was certain had convinced numerous women to go along with his various schemes.

But Francine wasn't "numerous women," and she wasn't interested in any of Hugh Casper's schemes. Her back stiff, she stepped out of the circle of Hugh's arm.

Like a pack of hungry dogs after a helpless rabbit, the group verbally fell on Francine in an attempt to change her mind. Her heart pattering, she shifted her gaze from one determined face to another. Finally, her attention rested upon Ethan—the one person she had expected to support her simply because he always had.

But this time Carrie's fingers were twined with his. His expression attested that he'd already dismissed the forgotten seminary class for a more pressing matter. *Oh, come on Franny. Give it a try!* he silently urged.

And Francine understood that Carrie not only held Ethan's hand, she held his heart…and his mind.

The numbness in Francine's soul radiated to her limbs. "No!" she shouted, and the strength of her denial stunned her as much as it did the rest of the room's occupants.

Every protest was silenced. Every gaze rested solely upon her. She opened her mouth to say more but could only gasp for air.

"I—I can't." She dashed from the garden room. When she hit the great room, Francine sprinted for the front door.

"Francine!"

Ethan's voice did nothing to slow her.

"Francine!"

She didn't even look back.

"Franny!"

Wrenching the knob, Francine flung open the door, hurried onto the top step's landing, and slammed the door behind her. She raised her long skirt, grabbed the handrail, and raced down the stairs. The whir of traffic, the squeak of breaks, the disgruntled bark of a dog on a short leash only urged her on. Panting, Francine whipped to the left and tackled the twelve stairs going up to her uncle's brownstone. She couldn't reach her fifth-floor room fast enough.

The Caspers' door rattled open. "Francine!" The door's slam punctuated Ethan's call.

As much as she wanted to avoid a confrontation, Francine paused midway up and looked at her childhood friend. Even though she struggled to breathe, a greater struggle tore at her heart—the struggle to understand the hold the wrong woman could have upon such a man of God.

Her silent observation stopped Ethan, but only for a second. He descended the Caspers' steps and stopped opposite her. Only the handrail, warm against Francine's clammy palm, separated them. "I…I know you don't approve of this…" he started, his face a mask of confusion.

"Why would you think that?" Francine's subtle irony didn't stop his next words. An apathetic breeze, tinged with a hint of the approaching fall, ushered in the chilling words.

"But I really think it's going to be okay. I'll make sure nothing… We should at least read the play! I just wish you'd give it—"

"No." Francine clenched her jaw. "I don't feel right about it. It sounds like there's too much room for compromise."

Ethan yanked on his goatee. "If you don't approve, then I'll…" He looked down, worked his mouth.

"You'll what?" Francine inched toward him, desperately hoping he was going to say he'd bow out of the play.

A horn blasted from the street mere feet away. Francine jumped. A yellow cab zipped by. A cabby hung out the window, hurling curses at a wily tomcat who barely missed his tire.

"Francine, I—I've always trusted your judgment."

She jerked her attention back to Ethan.

He placed his hand atop his head. Ethan raised his face skyward and slid his hand down to cover his face. "I almost can't stand the idea of doing something you don't approve of."

"Then don't do it." Francine nodded with each word.

Ethan covered his face with both hands and rubbed. During the strained silence, her mind drifted across the street…to the sweet memories of her and Ethan and Central Park…to the days before Carrie Casper.

Finally, Ethan lowered his hands and looked Francine full in the face. The silken brown eyes that had encouraged her and supported her and bathed her in admiration were no longer limpid reflections of a guiltless soul. Francine flinched. She absorbed Ethan's dogged determination to do what he wanted, regardless of her misgivings. Ethan Summers had made his final decision.

Carrie won.

Sixteen

❦ ❧

"You never do anything to please me, Francine," Aunt Nora accused. "Any time I ever ask you for the slightest favor, you list every reason under the sun why it's impossible—and that's the way it's been since the first day you set foot in this house. You should remember who brought you here and be thankful enough to show me some respect!"

Francine bent her head over the paperwork on the rolltop desk. Furiously, she copied the quote from the *Turn of the Screw,* her favorite Henry James novel. She was only in her third week of this college semester, but Francine never wasted a day before tackling the term papers due in each of her classes. Because of her commitment to being early, she was usually one of the few students who wasn't stressing during the last month of school. This particular paper was for the final literature class she was taking to complete her English requirements. Aunt Nora's neurotic spiel was making concentrating hard, but not impossible. Francine had endured worse attacks and still aced a test or two.

"Just because they wouldn't do the play the way *you* wanted to do it, you won't cooperate with them? Marie says she asked you to take a part again last night, and you still refused." Nora softened her voice. "All I'm asking is for you to change your mind."

Her head lowered, Francine gripped her pen and reexamined her resistance to participating in the production that Ethan had flung himself into two weeks ago. The best she could gather, Yancey Bates had been true to his word and tamed the script. Marie had outlined the plot for her, and Francine still wasn't at peace about being part of it. As much as she wanted to be the timid Franny-mouse and adhere to the path of least resistance, this time she could not bend. This play—even though it was a just-for-fun endeavor—would compromise her standards. If she took the part they were trying to hoist off on her, she would wind up in a clutch with Yancey Bates—a man she had barely met. She refused to be involved in any kissing scenes with him. Not for the sake of art. Not to please Ethan and Carrie. Not even to halt Aunt Nora's badgering.

If only Uncle Tom were here! Francine bemoaned his absence anew. He was the one person in this family who would appreciate her logic.

Francine knew he would understand that she could not stomach allowing a man she'd barely met to kiss her fully on the mouth. She'd yet to kiss any man! Unless she counted the tender peck-on-the-cheek that Ethan bestowed after the senior ball…or the various high school basketball banquets…or the church Valentine's parties…or the single's retreat eighteen months ago.

Through the years, Ethan had always been there to act as her "big brother" escort. Always committed. Always reliable. Always eager to please her. Until now. Last week, Francine had even opted out of attending one of her professor's student parties because she didn't want to go alone.

She stroked her cheek and wondered how many times Ethan had kissed Carrie on the lips. By the play's end, there would be too many to count! The thought of seeing him and Carrie so close made her nauseous. Francine gritted her teeth. She gathered her paper, her book, her pen, and her folder. Standing, she hunched her shoulders and strode toward the library's doorway.

"If you don't cooperate," Nora despaired, "Marie will have to double up and play *your* part. That's too many lines for her to memorize!"

Francine had heard the argument a dozen times already. But she suspected that Marie's aversion for the part had little to do with memorizing lines and everything to do with the fact that she didn't want to kiss Yancey any more than Francine did.

"Aren't you even going to answer me?" Nora demanded.

Silence was Francine's only reply.

Still hunkered, she hustled the short distance to the staircase. Francine wagered there was no way Aunt Nora would chase her up two flights of steps. Her logic proved valid. While Aunt Nora might sacrifice Francine's morals for Marie's whims, she would never forfeit her own comfort—even to fight Marie's battles. While the elevator was always an option, Francine determined to out-run even its arrival.

At the top of the stairs, she nearly ducked into her old room but stopped herself. True to his promise, Uncle Tom had arranged for Francine's suite to be finished. The carpenters came first and created the doorway from one brownstone into the other. The decorator arrived after the painter. She'd been loaded with a plethora of ideas and accompanied by a man who hung wallpaper. The paint had barely dried when a truck full of furniture arrived. Three days ago, Francine moved all her belongings into her new suite.

Now she surged up the second flight of stairs and headed for the third-floor suite. Zooming past the elevator, Francine noted that the button was not lighted. That meant Aunt Nora had not yet boarded the elevator.

Sure she was home free, Francine trotted down the hallway. Past the restroom, she hung a left and whizzed through the open doorway into her suite. She shut the door, locked it, and slumped against the wall, her heart pounding in her temples.

A brass floor lamp near the sofa emitted a golden glow that blanketed the room full of finery, all coordinated in steel-blue and taupe and beige—some of her best colors. Even with Aunt Nora breathing down her neck, she couldn't get past her initial reaction of feeling like Cinderella at Prince Charming's palace. As Ethan had threatened, Uncle Tom commissioned him to consult with the decorator and purchase everything. Ethan knew her and knew her well. Francine loved everything, from the sofa's serene stripes to the brass bed's gray-blue comforter to the beige bath towels with her name monogrammed on the edges. Even the scattering of cucumber-melon candles, whose scent the room bore, represented one of her favorites. Francine was convinced she couldn't have done a better job herself.

The longer she listened for signs of Nora, the more convinced Francine became that her aunt hadn't even chased her via the elevator. After several minutes of being plastered against the door in rigid dread, Francine loosened her grip on her book and folder. But no sooner had she relaxed than another horror struck her.

What if Aunt Nora goes through Carrie and Hugh's apartment and tries to come in here through the other entrance? She imagined her feisty aunt, bent on out-smarting Francine, pounding on the downstairs apartment until one of the Caspers let her in. From there, she'd impose herself into the brownstone, hop the elevator, storm the hallway, and be in the middle of Francine's suite before she had the presence of mind to stop her.

But I always keep that door locked, Francine reasoned. Then, she recalled Carrie's discreet knock around five that evening. Profusely apologizing for the intrusion, she had asked to borrow a safety pin. Carrie and Ethan were going out for dinner and a movie, and Carrie's camisole strap had broken. Francine retrieved the safety pin and thought she relocked the door.

What if I forgot this time? Footsteps echoing from the home's stairwell heightened Francine's anxiety.

She slung her book and folder onto the couch, dashed past her private bath, and reached the door. After a quick check of the deadbolt, she confirmed that the door was indeed locked. Francine wilted against the wall and awaited Nora's attack through the closed door.

"Are you sure…no…up here?" bits of Marie's worried question floated from the hallway.

Francine frowned.

"Double sure," Hugh responded, his louder voice resonating confidence. "I just checked a few minutes ago. The coast is clear. Francine's not even in her suite." A solid knock on her door preceded silence.

Francine's eyes bugged.

"See?" Hugh claimed.

"I just don't want to get caught!" Marie's worried tones rose in volume.

"Caught? Who? You and me? Why are you always worrying about getting caught? We won't get caught. We haven't yet, have we?"

"Yet?" Francine mouthed.

"Julie doesn't even suspect," Hugh continued.

"Why should she?" Marie retorted. "She's all over you. As much as the two of you are kissing in that play—"

"Well, we've got to keep up appearances, don't we? After all, you're kissing Ricky in the play."

"Like I want to kiss him!" Marie snapped.

"Well, would you like to kiss me now?"

A long pause punctuated by a soft smack or two made Francine cover her warming face.

"Let's get into the room before this goes any further, okay?" Hugh's thick voice insisted.

"No wait," Marie panted.

"Wait?" Hugh asked.

"Yes, wait," Marie urged. "We need to talk first—before—before we go into the room."

Francine pressed her knuckles against her lips and couldn't imagine what room she referenced. According to the Caspers' lease agreement, all the third-, fourth-, and fifth-floor rooms were supposed to be off limits for personal use. Apparently Hugh and Marie had designated one of the rooms as their meeting place. Francine shook her head.

"Why would anybody need to talk at a time like this?" Hugh mocked.

"Because," Marie insisted, "I want to know how much longer we're going to keep this up. There's no reason for all this secrecy. My wedding's only six weeks away. I'm *dying* to break up with Ricky so you and I can elope. Just give me the nod."

"Elope?" Hugh gasped.

A fierce silence ensued. Francine covered her face again, held her breath, then clasped her hands under her chin. *This is worse than shameful,* she thought. *If Uncle Tom ever found out…*

A deep sense of duty insisted she inform her uncle. Francine's eyes bulged anew. *But what if he doesn't believe me?* A mixture of uncertainty over her brusque uncle and respect for who he was gnashed at Francine from all directions.

"W—well," Marie finally stammered, her voice wobbly, "isn't that what you said our—our first night together?"

"You can't be serious." Hugh laughed. "I never said—"

"Yes—yes, you did. You said—"

"No, I *didn't!*" Hugh's voice grew hard.

A sniffle was Marie's only reply. A broken sob followed.

Francine's eyes stung. Even though Marie spent more time condescending Francine than loving her, Francine still hurt for her cousin.

"Oh come on, Marie," Hugh soothed without a trace of his French accent. "It's not that bad, is it? So we don't get married. We're still having the time of our lives. And, when it's over, you'll marry Ricky and be so stinkin' rich you won't even remember me."

"But I wanted to be stinkin' rich with you—not that creep!" Marie's haunted cry echoed along the hallway.

"Ah, babe," Hugh charmed. "You know I'm not going to ever settle down. Let's just enjoy ourselves tonight and let the future take care of itself, okay?

"*No!* Don't touch me!" A thud rumbled against Francine's door.

"Marie!"

Francine jumped. Her palms moistened. If Hugh was trying to force himself onto Marie, Francine would have no choice but to intervene. Frantically, she searched her dimly lit suite until her gaze landed upon the ornamental poker propped against the marble fireplace.

"Get away from me!" Marie demanded.

"Marie!" Hugh barked again amid another round of door rumbling. "If you push me away again, I swear I'll go back to Paris on the first plane I can book!"

Francine had only taken a few steps toward the poker when a battery of hard footfalls descended the stairs. "So go to Paris!" Marie hollered and added a decree on the state of Hugh's character. She received his similar response, which attested that Hugh still stood outside the doorway. Francine stopped all progress toward the poker.

Hugh's frustrated pounding on the wall next to Francine's door sent another shock through her. She started again and simultaneously covered her mouth to stifle the squeak in her throat. Finally, Hugh's heavy footfalls faded down the stairwell. Francine collapsed onto her couch, covered her face, and rocked back and forth.

"Oh, dear Lord," she breathed, "what are my cousins coming to?" A silent sob wracked her body. "And what—what about Ethan?" she rasped. "Has he fallen, too?" She recalled his determination the day the play idea was introduced. His eyes had not been clear. They had been full of Carrie…of possible seduction. The magnitude of the Caspers' negative influence filled the room and stifled Francine. She rubbed the tears from her eyes and suppressed them from her heart.

With short, jerking movements, Francine snatched up the folder, book, and papers now scattered across the couch's cushion. She clutched them to her chest and clung to the only element of her life that was completely hers. She owned no part of the home where she stayed. The family wasn't even her original family. The one person in that family she thought she could always depend upon was abandoning her for a woman unsuited for him. The only thing Francine could call her own was the degree she was earning.

And Uncle Tom's paying for that, she thought. Even the hundred dollars in her billfold was part of her monthly allowance from her uncle.

Francine needed some space…some time of her own. She needed to get away from this house…from this family…and all the complications therewith. The public library beckoned. In the library, Francine could find a corner, open a novel, and lose herself in the lives of others. The desire wouldn't be denied.

She quickly and neatly rearranged her papers in the folder, laid them on the small desk in the room's corner, and retrieved her billfold from the mahogany dresser. Her fingers brushed the pewter-colored cell-phone Ethan had bought. Francine wrapped her fingers around the cell. She released it. The phone tottered against the dresser, bumped into her laptop gracing the dresser, and stopped.

I'm trying to get away from the people in this house, she thought. The cell phone was no longer an option.

Francine offered a token glance in the mirror and encountered a haunted-eyed blonde dressed in a crumpled sweatsuit. Deciding no one at the library cared about her clothes or her sloppy ponytail, Francine turned from the mirror.

She rushed out of her new room and into the narrow hallway. Head down, Francine had taken only a few steps when she nearly ran into someone bounding past her suite. Gasping, Francine looked up—into Marie's red-rimmed eyes.

"Marie!" she gasped.

"Have you seen Aunt Nora?" Marie cried. "I've looked for her everywhere. I need—" She hiccoughed over a sob. "I need to talk to her," Marie finished and scrubbed a tissue across her eyes.

"I was with her in the library a few minutes ago," Francine offered.

"I already tried there," Marie wailed.

"Have you tried her room?"

"Yes!" Marie's grief-stricken voice took on a sharp stab. "Oh, never mind!" She waved Francine off. "Just if you see her, tell her I need to talk with her. I'll be upstairs in my room." She continued her trek past Francine, but had only gone a couple of paces before she halted.

Her cheeks ashen, her eyes round, she spun back around to face Francine. Marie peered at the suite's closed door and then back at her cousin. "How long have you been in there?" she blurted.

Francine opened and closed her mouth and couldn't utter a word.

"How long?" Marie tripped forward and grabbed Francine's shoulders. Her manicured nails bit into her cousin's skin.

Clutching her billfold to her chest, Francine stared at Marie in wide-eyed silence.

"Did you hear anyone talking?" Marie demanded.

"I...I..." Francine's attempt to speak came out in a garbled rasp.

"You heard, didn't you?" No more tears seeped from Marie's eyes.

"I...I..." Francine slowly shook her head from side to side. The action was not so much a means of denial as it was a grappling for what to say.

"Don't lie to me." Marie's lips quivered. "I see it all over your face. You know, don't you?"

Francine tore herself from Marie's grasp and bumped into the wall. "I wasn't trying to lie," she affirmed and for once didn't flinch from her cousin's intimidating stare. "I just didn't know what to say."

"Well, I know what to say," Marie snapped. "I say you better not tell a soul." She furtively glanced up one end of the hall and then the other. "If Ricky finds out he'll call off the wedding."

"Y—you're still going to marry him?" Francine squeezed out the words.

"Of course," Marie replied, her eyes hard.

Francine, numb from the whole episode, hung onto her bill-fold as if it were the only link to sanity. At a new loss for words, she shook her head again and braced herself for Marie's usual antics: threats, manipulation, blackmail.

Instead, her cousin's hard eyes reddened, and she covered her face with her hands. Her hair fell forward in a satin-like curtain, and she shook with a new round of emotion. "Oh Francine," she piteously begged, "promise you won't tell anyone—especially not Dad. Oh my word, he'd probably never speak to me again!" She raised her face, a frantic plea sparking in her drenched eyes. She reached for Francine's hands and desperately gripped them and the wallet.

Considering her options, Francine imagined herself telling her uncle. She pictured Marie denying everything and Aunt Nora taking Marie's side. Finally, Francine pondered the likeliness of Uncle Tom eventually believing his daughter over Francine. That would leave Francine labeled a liar. Uncle Tom despised deception. She imagined the formidable patron forcing her to move out on her own. With no income and no support from her family of origin, she might very well be forced to quit college in order to support herself.

And Ethan would be no help at all, she fumed. *Carrie had him so tangled, he probably wouldn't even miss me!*

Through the years, Francine had adhered to a steady silence over an abundance of little secrets Marie covered from her father. As an adolescent, Marie had gotten Aunt Nora to sign substandard report cards. As a young adult, Marie had dropped out of college and not told her dad for months. The year before she received her trust fund, Marie moved out on her own, but she'd preferred shopping to working and overspent so much she was forced to move back home under the pretense of "missing the family."

Not revealing the present secret wouldn't be anything new. Francine would just do what she had done to survive in this household. She would remain silent and go with the flow. Francine wouldn't have to face her uncle. She wouldn't run the risk of being called a liar.

"I won't tell anyone," she agreed.

"Promise?" Marie urged.

"Yes—yes, I promise," Francine replied.

Marie's agitation eased. "I wish everyone were like you, Franny," she muttered. New tears puddled in her eyes and splashed onto her splotchy cheeks.

"What do you mean?" Francine squinted and tried to comprehend the shift in subject.

"You always keep your promises." Her cousin coughed over new tears, and then she ran up the hallway and turned the corner to the stairs.

Francine, still hovering against the wall, gazed up the hall until Marie's steps no longer pounded the stairs. Her bedroom door's muffled slam punctuated the awful silence—a silence that whispered Francine might one day regret her vow.

Seventeen

A quarter after ten, Francine returned home from the library—only because it closed at ten. She would have gladly camped in her corner until the next morning, but the straight-lipped librarians didn't look like they would take any argument. So Francine complied when the fifteen-minutes-until-closing announcement rang over the library's intercom.

Now she paid the taxi driver, hugged her Grace Livingston Hill novel, and scooted out the door into the damp night. The droplets of water clinging to her ponytail attested to the light shower that baptized her when she made the dash for the taxi. Fortunately, only a fine mist now christened the September night. The taxi puttered off, leaving a suffocating puff of smoke in its wake. Francine paused on the first step of the brownstone. She gazed up at the twin homes connected by an adjoining wall. The side-by-side structures towered into the night, mutely refusing to reveal the secrets hidden behind their windows.

For the first time in ages, Francine wished for the simpler life she'd left in Rockaway nine years ago. While her family hadn't been perfect, and the home had been far less fine, Francine couldn't recall the undercurrents and friction and veiled ventures that typified this household. All she could remember was a house full of noisy children who weren't sophisticated enough to hide a thing. During the summer, Wade and she spent more time at the pool than home. And when they came home at night, they'd fix themselves a sandwich and watch the younger ones for their mom, who was leaving for her evening waitress job. Everything went smoothly—except for the times Francine's father decided to come home.

But was even that as bad as I remember? Francine wondered.

The cool breeze stirred up the smell of wet Manhattan pavement. Francine hadn't bothered with a jacket when she left home, and her sweatsuit didn't block the chill. Shivering, she tilted her head toward the sky and allowed the frigid mist to caress her face. The street lights emitted a halo-like glow that seemed to radiate from a distant realm. She wished the water and light could cleanse her loneliness; they only increased the ache in her heart.

She trudged up the steps and considered her brother Wade again. Francine hadn't heard from him in a couple of weeks. They mostly stayed in touch via e-mail, with an occasional card or letter thrown in—usually from Francine to Wade. Once in awhile, Wade would call, often after Francine sent him a card. Aunt Nora usually discouraged Francine from calling him since the call was long distance and would cost extra money. The last e-mail Wade sent he commented on how much he enjoyed the assistant manager's position at a local diner in Rockaway. Even though Wade hadn't gone to college, he was a bright young man and a hard worker. Already he had his eye on the manager's position and didn't mind laboring to earn the title.

Francine paused at the doorway. The drizzle seeped into her soul and she shuddered. Longingly she gazed toward Central Park. The lighted walkways beckoned. Even though she never walked alone at night, the idea held promise despite the rain.

Francine needed a friend. The park, forever constant, was a friend she could depend upon.

Glancing at her wristwatch, she wondered if Wade was online. Sometimes at night she caught him on the internet, and they enjoyed an Instant Messenger conversation. Sighing, she decided a chat session with Wade posed fewer risks than walking alone at night.

She inserted her key into the door, opened it, and stepped into the opulence that had overwhelmed her as a child. Her survival instinct insisted she dart a furtive glance toward the piano room, then the library. The servants all left at eight o'clock these days. Aunt Mariette usually went to bed by nine. She hoped Aunt Nora was already in bed as well.

Francine didn't feel like being badgered over her thankless-ness in going to the library by herself rather than staying home with her aunts. Tonight, Francine had done something she'd never done by herself. She left a note in the den announcing her depar-ture and didn't ask a soul for permission. She was in the public library's corner, engrossed in the charming plot before she real-ized her error. Never had she left the brownstone alone without one or both of her aunts' approval. Francine could only imagine Aunt Nora's aghast reaction to what she would undoubtedly label "brazen independence."

Silently, Francine tiptoed across the giant raisin-colored rug and headed toward the stairs. While the stairs made less noise than the elevator, they also required that she pass the den. Since Aunt Nora usually didn't sit in the den at night, Francine decided the risk of being spotted was almost nonexistent. Feeling like the rankest of criminals, she tiptoed toward the stairway and had climbed the first step before a familiar voice stopped her.

"Francine?" Ethan called. "We're in here."

Still tense, Francine swiveled to face the person she once called best friend. Now he spent more time with Carrie than he ever spent with her. "Hi, Ethan," she said with as relaxed a smile as she could feign.

He hurried forward and joined her on the steps like he'd done many times through the years. "I tried to call your cell about six times, and all I got was your voice mail. Do you have it off or what?"

"Oh my cell…I guess I left it in my room," she admitted and avoided eye contact.

"Again?" Ethan exclaimed. "What good is it if you don't keep it with you?"

Francine shrugged. Not wanting to admit that she'd purposefully avoided all communication with the family, she searched for a solid and honest explanation that would preclude Ethan's pressuring her about the phone. This wasn't the first time Francine had failed to take the phone. Not yet in the habit of carrying it, half the time she honestly forgot the thing.

With the seconds stretching forth and Ethan silently awaiting an answer, Francine decided to resort to the trifling humor that had characterized their relationship for years. Their light banter had served as a dash of joy in the middle of life's darkest hours. Francine needed a dash of joy this cold and lonely night.

"I went to the library," Francine explained, and held up her book. "They put you in the library dungeon if they catch you talking on a cell phone."

Ethan's vague smile accompanied a mild reprimand. "Well, at least you could have put it on vibrate and stepped outside to call me back."

"Oh, but you don't understand." Francine widened her eyes in innocent horror. "There are all sorts of mean men outside the library door, just waiting for women with cell phones to come outside and return calls. Then they can pounce on them!" She inched closer to Ethan and hissed, "They're called the library mob! They also hang out at the Worthingham Renaissance." She nodded like a preschooler affirming the existence of the boogie man.

He narrowed his eyes. "You don't fool me with all this Franny-mouse act you put on, Francine Ponce," he teased. "You've got a mean streak a mile wide. Don't think I don't see it."

"Only when it comes to you, Ethan. You bring out the worst in me." Francine patted his cheek. Immediately, she lowered her hand lest she fall prey to the impulse to lovingly caress his face. But then she noticed the smudge of lipstick near Ethan's goatee. Hot pink. The shade Carrie most often wore.

"Wow, thanks for the compliment," Ethan said. "I always try to bring out the worst in people."

Swallowing, Francine studied her novel's worn fringes. She and Ethan had barely spoken in the last few weeks. He'd been too busy with Carrie and the play. She'd been absorbed by college. But that hadn't stopped Francine from wishing she had the right to shower sweet kisses upon his mouth and stroke his face, not just pat it in sisterly affection. But he'd granted those rights to Carrie.

"Don't you even want to know the reason I called you?" he asked with fond accusation.

"Sure," Francine said and didn't dare look up again.

"Dad's home."

Francine's head popped up. "He is? Already?" she gasped and detected a hint of dismay in Ethan's dark eyes. "I didn't think he was due back for several more weeks."

"He wasn't," Ethan said. "But he wound up cutting his trip short and didn't bother to tell any of us. He's waiting up for you, Franny."

"For me?" Francine squeaked. "Why would he do that?"

"Well, you're a part of this family, aren't you? He's seen everyone else. Now he wants to see you!"

Ethan lowered his mouth toward her ear. A trace of Carrie's sophisticated fragrance intensified the memory of the lipstick near Ethan's goatee. Francine recognized the scent—Estee Lauder's "Beautiful." The name befitted the woman and reminded Francine she would never measure up to Carrie's elegance.

"He's not in a good mood," Ethan whispered. "He found out about the play. Carrie was here earlier and let it slip. He went next door and wasn't happy with the stage being nailed to the floor."

"They nailed the stage to the floor?" Francine hissed back at his ear and couldn't stop the unexpected longing to be as beautiful as Carrie.

"Yes. Yancey did it. He says he didn't know he wasn't supposed to."

"But you specifically told them—I was there. I heard you." Francine's heart, hollow and cold, chastised her for rejecting her external appearance.

"I know. I know," Ethan said and backed away.

Francine covered her eyes with her hand and rubbed her temples with her thumb and forefinger. While weighing the implications of her uncle's presence, she reminded herself that her external appearance shouldn't be the factor that stimulated Ethan's love. A love based on looks alone was shallow and capricious. Francine, weary and worn, recognized that the Caspers' presence was starting to affect her own values. She detested herself for longing for a beauty she could never achieve in order to make Ethan love her. Before Carrie came, Francine had been certain Ethan would grow into loving her for who she was, not what she looked like.

"Thank you, Lord, that Uncle Tom is home," she mumbled and couldn't remember ever being so glad for her uncle's imposing personality. Strangely, his presence suggested that maybe things could go back to normal—back to the way they were before the Caspers' invasion. "Maybe he'll bring some stability back to this place," she added. Francine's hand went stiff. She lowered her head and gripped her neck. In her stress, she'd done something she almost never did—spoken before thinking. Her hasty words suggested Ethan needed a dose of stability. What he didn't know was that she believed the same of her own wayward heart.

"I'm sorry," she said. "I didn't mean to—"

"You didn't think the play was a good idea from the start," Ethan admitted. "I knew that. And well…"

She looked up at him and longed to see a tinge of repentance over that suggestive script.

"I guess, considering the way things have turned out, you were probably right."

"I'm glad you think so. That script was far too risqué for—"

"It's not so much that, you prude," Ethan said.

"So now I'm a prude?" Francine questioned. Not certain how to take this remark, she debated whether to be offended or to laugh. That is, if she *could* laugh.

"I'm just giving you and your library mob a dose of your own medicine," Ethan said with a broad grin.

Francine attempted a weak smile. "Oh…okay."

"But really, Franny, what red-blooded male *doesn't* enjoy a kissing scene or two?"

And what dedicated minister allows himself to be involved in a script that implies more is going on? Francine thought. This time, she risked holding his gaze past the token glances she'd limited herself to since he arrived home from Paris. While Francine still didn't want to take the chance of Ethan recognizing her love, she needed an answer to a question that had become her tormentor— especially after tonight's episode with Marie.

Sure enough, her silent inquisition uncovered the answer she'd dreaded most. Just beneath the surface of Ethan's veil of honor flickered the beginnings of the sensual flames blazing in Hugh's tarnished soul. Francine swallowed hard. Carrie's lipstick smudge seemed to glow in confirmation of Francine's assumption. Carrie's lingering perfume intensified. To make matters worse, Francine noticed another hot pink blur on the neck of Ethan's beige sweater. The man she had blindly trusted to never waver was slipping off a rocky cliff, and Francine was helpless to stop him.

"Uh…I didn't mean that to sound that way," Ethan amended. "Carrie and I aren't—aren't—" He stammered and backed away.

Francine narrowed her eyes and scrutinized him anew, in search of any scrap of dishonesty. Never had she doubted Ethan; the experience left her sickened.

"Good grief, Francine, what are you *thinking*?" he whispered. She looked down. *I don't know what to think anymore…*

"I'm not going to…to…" He sputtered to a halt. "I'm on staff at Manhattan Community Church. Remember? I've got a reputation. I…I…I've got a ministry. I…I…Carrie's not the kind of woman who would—"

While the admission swept away some of Francine's worries, she wasn't at peace. The lipstick was still an incriminating presence. Furthermore, the same question demanded an answer. *If that's really the way you feel, then why did you participate in the play in the first place?* The silent query hung between them until the air pulsated with tension.

"I guess you're right," Ethan finally admitted. "I probably shouldn't have—you know—it's just that I didn't really see the harm in—in—nothing immoral really happened in the play, even though it was implied. It was helping Yancey, and nobody but us knew. I certainly wouldn't ever be a part of a public performance like that."

Francine nodded. "Neither would I."

"Anyway," Ethan rushed, his voice tinged with shame, "none of that matters now. The whole thing has fallen around our ears. Dad's saying the stage has *got* to go. Marie says she was quitting anyway. I don't know *what* her deal is. She's not talking about it. My guess is she's throwing one of her silent fits because something didn't go the way she wanted. But who knows what?"

If only you knew, Francine thought. Marie's secret haunted her. Francine focused just above Ethan's eyes, guarded her expression, and didn't indicate even a scrap of knowledge.

"Besides that, just when Carrie and I were leaving the movie tonight, Hugh called Carrie's cell and told her he was bored and had booked an early flight back to Paris tomorrow morning. Just like that." Ethan snapped his fingers.

Francine held her breath and waited for Ethan to make a connection between Marie and Hugh simultaneously quitting the play. No connection came.

"Carrie says this is just like him." Ethan shook his head. "I really like Hugh. I think he's a good guy. As bad as I hate to admit it, I think he might be a little flighty sometimes."

"Flighty?" Francine repeated and marveled that Ethan could remain so blind to Hugh's true character.

"Yes. No pun intended." Ethan laughed. "You know, he's taking an early flight and he's flighty."

"You've been with Yancey too long," Francine said through a smile. "That was really corny."

"I think you're right," Ethan agreed. "But that guy's a *nut!*" He shook his head. "And his play is hilarious—just like Carrie said. I wish you had at least read it!" He chuckled under his breath.

Francine remained silent.

When Ethan's chortles died, he babbled on, "Anyway, back to Hugh, Carrie says she'll be glad when he gets married and settles down. Tonight she said she thought someone like you would be good for him."

"Like me?" Francine wheezed. She pointed her index finger against her chest and relived Hugh's attentions during their Saturday luncheon a few weeks ago. Francine had been mortified to take polite assistance from Hugh—especially because he didn't normally look upon a woman without ulterior motives.

Ethan nodded. "Carrie really respects you, Francine."

"She does?"

"Yes. I think she'd try to play matchmaker between you and Hugh if she could get away with it."

"No...no...oh no!" Francine vehemently shook her head, and her damp ponytail swayed from side to side.

Ethan chuckled. "Don't get all bent out of shape. He's outta here."

Good riddance! Francine thought and said, "Where does all this leave Yancey? Did Hugh even tell him he was leaving for Paris?"

"Who knows. Right now he and Julie are out on the town."

"Yancey and Julie?"

"Yep. They're a new item. You didn't know?"

"Uh, no. Does Uncle Tom know?"

"Yeah. He got here right before Yancey picked Julie up," Ethan said.

"Good grief," Francine mumbled and stroked the corner of the hardbound book. "I go to the library for a few hours and come back to all sorts of information. Do you think Uncle Tom approves of Yancey?"

"Do you think it matters?" Ethan's brows rose. "Julie is twenty-two. I have a hunch she's going to do what she wants."

"Yes, on the trust fund Uncle Tom set up for her," Francine mused. "Yancey is broke." She tapped her index finger against the maple banister.

"Hello out there!" Tom Barrimore's voice burst from the den.

Francine's shoulders stiffened. She peeked around Ethan to her uncle, who strode toward the stairs. His puffy cheeks had the red splotches that often accompanied his interactions with Nora.

"Are you going to keep Francine in a private powwow all night or let me talk with my niece?" He shifted his bulky frame, then eyed Francine up and down. His thinning hair, puffing around his ears, needed a trim. His disheveled white shirt and crumpled slacks spoke of a long plane ride. The bags under his eyes validated his gruff manner.

"Well, Franny, you're looking about the same these days," Uncle Tom said. "Somehow, I expected you to look more rested since you got the suite. Well, are you enjoying it or not?"

"Uncle Tom," Francine said and moved toward her uncle. "You know I am," she gently chided. "It's perfect! And it's *so good* to see you." Francine's words rang with unmatched conviction. She reached for his arm, and he clasped her in a short-lived hug.

"I stayed up because I wanted to talk to you specifically," Tom admitted.

"You did?" Francine asked.

"Why do you always have to look so confoundedly surprised?" he groused. "Yes, I did. Come in to the den and sit down." He motioned toward the room and began the march toward it. Then he stopped, swiveled, and examined his son.

"Ethan," he barked, "go get Francine a Coke. I'm sure she's probably thirsty. The library is the driest place on earth." Never doubting his son's obedience, Tom trudged toward the den once more.

"Oh sure," Ethan acquiesced.

"And take your time!" Tom shot over his shoulder.

Ethan's footsteps were the only response.

Head bent, Francine scurried after her uncle. She'd never crossed Uncle Tom and couldn't imagine living through the experience. The only time she'd ever gotten close to going against him was over the David Yurman watch last Christmas. Francine had dutifully worn the golden masterpiece every day since, and she dreaded the very thought of forgetting it. Now she was counting the days to her twenty-first birthday. Uncle Tom had given Ethan, Marie, and Julie their trust funds on that landmark birthday. Francine dreaded the thought of the same being bestowed upon her because it would only add to her sense of indebtedness.

"Have a seat!" he commanded and pointed toward the red velvet sofa.

Francine sat. A mug of hot cocoa, steaming on the lamp table, filled the room with a sweet, creamy fragrance. Francine would have preferred a cup of hot chocolate over a cola, but she didn't voice her opinion.

Tom lowered himself into the wing-backed chair nearest his mug and squeezed the arms like a king claiming his throne.

"Did you know anything about this play they were putting together?" he asked.

Gripping her book in one hand and her billfold in the other, Francine stared at the oriental rug she'd tripped over when she was eleven. She nodded.

"Did you know they nailed a stage to my floor?"

Francine pulled her tongue from the roof of her mouth. "N–no," she stammered. "Ethan just now told me. I don't think he knew about that either."

"Hmmm," Barrimore mused. "I hope not."

"I really don't think he did." Francine dared raise her gaze to meet her uncle's penetrating blue stare. Doubt vanished from his eyes. "Good," he said. "And what part did you play in their little production?"

"I d–didn't," she said and had never been so glad she'd followed her gut instincts.

"Doesn't surprise me." He never blinked. "Just what I figured. The only one of the bunch with a lick of common sense. I thought the same of Ethan—until now. He says he forgot to enroll in his last seminary class. Did you know that?"

"I didn't…until it was too late." Francine pressed her short fingernail into the corner of the novel's cover.

"What do you think is possessing him?" Tom raised his blunt fingers. "No, wait. I already think I know." Barrimore's sharp gaze met a target behind Francine. He leaned back in his chair, made a tent of his fingers, and rested his chin on the top. "If it weren't for the fact that these Caspers were so wealthy, I'd say they weren't worth the aggravation of all this upheaval. I've told Ethan for years not to rush into anything he'd regret later. He seems to be going a little faster than I'd advise on this one…but I think maybe he could do worse."

"Like Marie with Ricky?" Francine's barely audible question caught even *her* by surprise. Dreading her uncle's temper, she considered crawling under the camel-backed sofa.

However, his heavy-browed scrutiny spoke only confirmation. "Exactly," he said.

Eighteen

Eight weeks later, Carrie Casper settled into the corner of her leather sofa and watched the Victorian phone on her end table. The flames in the gas fireplace merrily flickered, dancing to a silent tune that celebrated fall's splendor. The cordless phone's brass trim reflected the gyrating flames and seemed to promise Hugh's call would come soon.

He had been in Paris almost two months now. While they had kept in close contact by e-mail, he had set an appointment to talk via phone today. Carrie couldn't imagine why. She checked her diamond-studded watch and tapped the couch's armrest with her freshly manicured nails. So far, Hugh was five minutes late. She'd give her brother ten more minutes, then get on with her day.

Carrie had promised Ethan she'd attend a church service with him tonight—a special Wednesday night event that ushered in the Thanksgiving season. Ethan was speaking. Carrie had only heard him speak two other times. This afternoon she planned to go shopping for a new outfit, enjoy a facial, and then get her hair styled. When Ethan looked into the audience, Carrie wanted him to remember who loved him.

While this church event was special to Carrie because it was special to Ethan, she cringed every time Ethan stepped behind a pulpit. She kept imagining a life of sitting in the audience while Ethan was forever taking the podium. The sensation usually magnified her determination to convince Ethan not to continue this pursuit of ministry. She figured the more gorgeous she kept herself looking, the greater her chances of swaying him to her opinions. Carrie couldn't deny that she was falling in love with Ethan. But the closer she grew to him, the more convinced she became that she would smother and die as a pastor's wife.

She eyed her leather skirt that had slid six inches above her knees. Carrie nearly choked as she imagined herself forever doomed to modest dresses that struck her knee and no higher. Last week, she'd purchased a new perfume, "Very Sexy." The erotic scent reminded her of a few of the passionate kissing scenes from Yancey's play. Carrie's midsection fluttered. Ethan's kisses stirred her as no others. In the midst of her revelry, Carrie imagined herself as a pastor's wife wearing the fragrance to church and someone asking her the name of her perfume. She lowered her arm and frowned.

Her string bikinis danced through her mind. She imagined being forced to submit to a one-piece number for the sake of "setting a good example" for the younger girls in the church. The thing would probably have a skirt on it!

"Oh gag!" Carrie stood and paced toward the stairway that led to her bedroom. Too disturbed to sit still, she abandoned her commitment to wait for Hugh's call and decided to get on with her day. If Hugh ever did get around to phoning her, he knew her cell number.

Carrie's heels had only tapped up the third stair when the telephone's shrill ring stopped her progress. She glanced back at her watch. *This is just like him,* she fumed. *Keeps you waiting until you decide to do something else, and then he calls.*

She trounced back toward the cordless phone. Carrie and Mrs. Krause had an understanding. If Carrie let the phone ring four times, then the housekeeper would answer it. Carrie retrieved the receiver on the third ring and flopped back into her corner in the couch.

"Hello, brother dear," she drawled.

"How did you know it was me?" he challenged.

"I know your ring." Carrie slipped her feet out of her suede heels and tucked them beneath her. She rubbed her hand against her cashmere sweater. Resting her head against the sofa, she eyed the green-eyed tiger over the marble mantel. "It's always about ten minutes later than you say it's supposed to be."

"Now, now, let's not get spiteful," Hugh said in a patronizing voice.

Carrie curled her toes, throbbing from the three-inch heels. "Well, some of us have a schedule," she fondly chided.

"Yes, it's a full-time job to catch a husband, isn't it?"

"Ha ha," Carrie returned. The sound of a faint whir from the kitchen testified that Mrs. Krause was preparing cappuccino for her afternoon break. Carrie hoped she remembered to make a cup for her as well. "Now, what did you want that you couldn't have shared over the internet? I'm waiting," she finished in a singsong voice.

"I just wanted to see what the…uh…weather is like in New York these days."

"The weather?" Carrie lifted her head and tapped her fingertips against her leg. She narrowed her eyes and focused upon a mahogany bookcase turned knickknack shelf. A porcelain replica of a pouncing leopard caught her eye.

After an oath, Hugh growled, "You have to explain everything to some people. Did Marie go through with her wedding or not?"

"Oh yes, now *that's* related to the weather, isn't it?" Carrie touched her forehead with the heel of her hand. "Why didn't I make that connection?"

"You haven't mentioned the wedding at all, and I started wondering…wasn't it supposed to have been two weeks ago?"

"Yes," Carrie answered and offered no other explanation. She didn't stop the sly smile from crawling onto her lips, slick with gloss. Occasionally, she couldn't resist the urge to purposefully exasperate her brother.

"And?" Hugh prompted. "Did they get married or didn't they?"

"Who wants to know?" Carrie stood and strolled toward the fireplace. She turned and backed up to the flames. The warmth penetrated her dark hose. A delightful shiver followed.

Hugh's sigh blended into a mixture of curses and loving threats.

After a satisfied chuckle, Carrie said, "Yes, she got married. The coast is clear. The weather is clear. No storms. All is peaceful."

"She did? Wonderful!" Hugh said.

"What happened? Did she take you a little more seriously than you wanted?" Carrie tapped the ebony rug with her stockinged toe and could only imagine what her brother had lured Marie into. The guy had a way with women that defied logic.

"That's nunya," he snapped.

"Nunya business?" Carrie taunted. "Now aren't we getting juvenile. Let me see, I imagine this one nearly backfired on you, considering the way you flew back to Paris like a pack of demons was after you." Hugh hadn't discussed his sudden trip off the continent, but when Marie simultaneously quit the play, Carrie deduced enough to piece together the story.

"Look, there's another reason I called," Hugh rushed, his tone intense.

"Okay," Carrie responded.

"Uh…" he hedged, "I'm not really sure how to say this. That's part of the reason I wanted to talk on the phone. I thought maybe I could say it easier than I could write it."

Carrie lazily eyed Mrs. Krause who entered the room with a mug of steaming liquid piled with cinnamon-specked whipped topping. The maid lifted the brew and raised her graying brows in query. The smell of cinnamon mocha cappuccino made Carrie's mouth water. A gust of wind rattled the windows on both sides of the doorway and reminded Carrie that this day held the kiss of winter. Today was a cappuccino day if there ever was one.

She nodded her approval and pointed to the end table near the phone. The housekeeper deposited the thick mug and saucer near the phone with the clank of stone pottery. She winked at Carrie, her chubby cheeks reminding Carrie of Mrs. Claus. Carrie told herself to give the double-knit-clad housekeeper a bonus. The woman was spoiling her, and that's what Carrie liked.

After a series of false starts and "ums" from Hugh, Carrie finally said, "Are you going to spill it," she stepped toward the cappuccino, "or am I going to have to guess?"

"I think you're going to laugh at me," Hugh said, his voice uncertain.

"Won't be the first time." Carrie picked up the cup and sipped the warm, sweet liquid. Her eyes rolled back in ecstasy. Mrs. Krause could do cappuccino to the max. Carrie greedily went for another swig, then licked the froth from her upper lip. At this rate, she was going to gain a few pounds.

"I can't stop thinking about Francine," Hugh admitted. "I think I'm...like...you know...falling in love with her."

Carrie sputtered over the cup. She inhaled a trickle of liquid and endured a series of compulsive coughs. The milky coffee sloshed against her hand and dribbled onto the rug.

"Have a heart attack, why don't you?" Hugh drawled.

Her response was more coughs. Carrie plunked the cup back into its saucer, shook her hand free of excess liquid, and covered her mouth. After a final bark and wheeze, Carrie gasped, "You're joking, right?"

"No, I'm serious," Hugh affirmed. "I came home thinking I was ditching Marie and wound up bumping into Francine. I can't quit thinking about her," he repeated. "I think she's the one I've been looking for. I mean, I can respect her, Carrie. *Really respect her.* She's not like any other woman I've ever been with."

"I told Ethan I wished you two would make a pair," Carrie rushed and bobbed her head. "I really did. I think she'd be so good for you."

"Yes, and maybe I'd be good for her. You know—get her out of her shell some."

"Exactly. It would be a perfect match." Carrie eyed the spot across the room where she had watched Ethan and Francine in their cozy talk mode the day she and Hugh invited everyone over for lunch. That day Carrie speculated if the two were more than mere siblings. Then two weeks ago at Marie's wedding, Ethan had actually been distracted by Francine, who walked down the aisle as a bridesmaid. Of course, the cream-and-white wedding colors had enhanced Francine's fair coloring. Her tea-length, off-white dress made her complexion glow and her blue eyes shine. Carrie couldn't deny that she'd been jealous when Ethan told Francine she looked stunning. She also couldn't ignore Francine's blush of pleasure.

Carrie moved back to the couch and perched on the edge. While she had honestly grown fond of the shy and innocent Francine, she would be far more comfortable if Francine were involved with a suitor. Even though logic insisted there was nothing but affection between Ethan and Francine, Carrie's intuition insisted that she shouldn't be so certain. If Hugh came back to New York and distracted Francine with his charm and money, she would be less of an influence upon Ethan—if for no other reason than that Francine might stop her perpetual encouragement about Ethan's ministry fixation. It seemed every time the three of them were together, Francine had to mention something pertaining to Ethan's ordination.

Caught in her own thoughts, Carrie didn't realize her brother had been talking until he demanded, "Well, aren't you going to answer me? Hello? Carrie? Are you still there? Did we disconnect?"

"I'm here! I'm here!" Carrie bleated. "Sorry, I spaced out on you there for a minute. What were you saying?"

Hugh's elongated sigh reminded Carrie of their childhood when the older brother barely tolerated his sister even though only two years separated them. "I was just asking," he repeated, "what you thought about me coming back to the Big Apple for awhile."

"I think it would be great!" Carrie exclaimed. She reached for her cappuccino and cautiously indulged in another swallow. Carrie imagined her brother snuggled next to Francine on the love seat opposite the couch while Ethan settled beside Carrie. This time Ethan didn't even look at Francine.

"Good! I've already booked a ticket for Friday."

"Oh, so you booked your ticket, and *then* called and asked what I thought?" Carrie turned down her mouth. "That sounds about right."

"Ha!" Hugh mocked. "You should know by now that when I see my woman I go after her. Not even you could stop me!"

Carrie hesitated in the middle of another swallow. She lowered the mug, studied the fireplace's merry blue flames, and compared her brother's romantic past with Francine's. Carrie didn't have to wonder if Francine was still a virgin. She'd be surprised if the young woman had even kissed a man.

An unexpected impulse to protect Francine couldn't be denied. If Hugh were truly in love with Francine and wanted to marry her, then Carrie would be thrilled to bless his endeavors. But if her brother was viewing Francine as yet another conquest… another notch in his belt…then he should stay in Paris. Even Carrie didn't have the heart to sacrifice the lamblike creature for the sake of her own progress with Ethan.

"All this sounds fine, Hugh," Carrie agreed. "But are you really playing for keeps? Or are you just after Francine because she's not easy?"

"Protective, are we?"

"Yes, we are," Carrie admitted. "I don't want you to hurt her, Hugh. She's a special lady. She doesn't deserve what—"

"What Marie got?" Hugh scoffed.

"Exactly. Whatever *that* was."

Hugh fell silent and Carrie gazed out the front window. A yellow taxi scooted to a halt at the base of the steps next door. A flash of white-blonde hair instigated Carrie's standing. She set her mug back in the saucer, hustled to the window, tugged aside the sheers, and peered outside. Francine opened the taxi door, slid inside, and pulled a rolling backpack in after her. Carrie caught a glimpse of an innocent face with a touch of cosmetics. The taxi door closed. The vehicle purred away.

An onslaught of sisterly protection surged anew. If Hugh was going to commit to Francine forever, then Carrie would support his decision. It would divert Francine's attention from Ethan and give Carrie a sister-in-law she could love. The match would also provide Francine an excellent husband. Even though her brother had played the field, he was a good catch.

"I just saw Francine," Carrie reported and released the sheers. "She had her backpack. She was taking a taxi. I guess she was heading for class. I think she has an afternoon class that meets on Wednesday."

"Really?" Hugh replied. "How did she look?"

"The same as usual," Carrie said. "Wearing sweats. Hair in a ponytail. Like she was about to take care of business. You know, about the same," she repeated with a shrug.

"Oh man, I wish I were already there!" Hugh sighed.

"Hugh," Carrie said, "you never answered me about what your intentions are."

"You sound like an uptight father from 1820!" Hugh teased.

Carrie placed her free hand on her hip. "Hugh Casper!" she rapped out. "You answer me now! Are you going to commit to her or not? And I mean forever! I mean, if you *do* get married, *no more women!*"

"Who wants to know?"

"Okay, that's it!" Carrie strode to the couch, then paced back in the direction she'd come. "You can't come here. I won't let you hurt her!"

"All right, already," Hugh acquiesced. "I'm just giving you a hard time. Of course I'm playing for keeps," he said. "Didn't I tell you? I'm a man who's falling in love!" He released a pining sigh. "I guess I might as well tell all. I haven't been sleeping much and my appetite is gone. Is this, like, what it's supposed to be like?" Mockery had left Hugh's voice, only uncertainty remained.

Carrie laughed.

"I knew you'd laugh!" he accused. "That's why I didn't…oh forget it!" he snapped. "Just forget it!"

"I always said when you fell, you'd fall hard," Carrie chimed. "And that's all I wanted to know."

"So you're happy now?"

"As a lark," Carrie agreed. "Listen, Francine's twenty-first birthday party is this Saturday night. Why don't you plan to go with me? I'm invited. They'll be fine with my bringing you. You'll be good for her even. Ethan says she's really uptight over all this focus on her—you know how she is. Anyway, I think Francine's brother Wade is even supposed to be there. And of course, Julie and Yancey…and Ethan and Francine's two aunts and uncle."

"What about Marie?" Hugh asked.

"She and Ricky are still in Athens. They won't be back until the middle of next week."

"Good. And Julie and the Yance—they're still a hot item?"

"Yes. I think Julie's going for a stay at Marie and Ricky's place next week—after they get back from Athens. Ricky's allowing Yancey to stay at the Worthingham Renaissance for free. Marie and Ricky wound up moving into the penthouse there. Did you know?"

"Ask me if I care," Hugh said and continued with his plans. "Anyway, I'll be there Friday. Don't worry about meeting me at the airport. I'll take a taxi."

"Works for me!" Carrie agreed before she and her brother closed the conversation with a lively round of banter

When she hung up, Carrie reached toward the table, dipped her finger into the cappuccino's cinnamon-flavored topping, and inserted it into her mouth. All the while, she hummed the wedding march.

Fate had such a wonderful way of ironing out life's difficulties. Once Francine fell for Hugh, there would be no question that Ethan would be all Carrie's. She slipped back into her suede heels and smoothed her fingers along the front of her short skirt. With a sassy giggle, Carrie inched the skirt higher up her thighs, released it, and tossed aside all worries about ever becoming a pastor's wife. Ethan's obsession was already wavering. After all, she'd managed to get him to forget to register for his last seminary class simply by being! And last week her pouting hints that she just wasn't ready to be in the ministry had resulted in Ethan's saying maybe he should consider postponing his ordination for a year or two.

Carrie examined her left hand and imagined Ethan's diamond on her third finger. Of course, the diamond *must* be surrounded by emeralds to match her earrings. She touched her ear lobes and reveled in the feel of the expensive butterflies. When Ethan slipped the ring on her finger, Carrie's Christmas goal would be met. After the engagement was secure and Francine was Hugh's conquest, Carrie would make Ethan forget he ever thought of becoming a pastor.

Nineteen

꿈

Ethan stood at the base of the stairs and waited for Francine to come down. The heavenly smells of roast beef and potatoes wafting from the kitchen underscored tonight's special occasion. The meal was Francine's favorite. Tonight was her night.

Classical piano music floated from the den's CD player. The clink of china and silverware punctuated the music as the staff readied the table. This evening crackled with an expectant atmosphere—much like Francine's senior ball. But tonight, her twenty-first birthday, seemed even more special. Even though Francine was legally an adult at eighteen, the Barrimores always treated the twenty-first birthday as a rite of passage into adulthood.

Ethan hadn't asked his dad about a trust fund, but he hoped his dad did as much for Francine as he did for him and his daughters. Francine had served this family far more than Marie and Julie—even more than Ethan. She deserved the respect of an equal share, although Ethan knew Francine well enough to suspect she would earnestly protest any monetary present.

Whatever the Barrimores chose to do, Ethan wanted to be the first to give her his gift before everyone else arrived. He didn't want to lose the impact of her pleasure due to the bustle of the evening. He tapped the long white box on the staircase handrail and smiled at the silver ribbon and bow. The jeweler had insisted this piece was the finest she had in stock. The price tag verified her claim. Ethan couldn't wait to see Francine in it.

He gazed up the staircase, checked his watch, and noted the guests were scheduled to arrive in ten minutes. "Maybe I'll go up to her suite," he mumbled and wondered what Francine's holdup was. She was almost always fifteen minutes early for anything. When another minute lapsed, Ethan could wait no longer. He took the steps two-at-a-time and was halfway up them when the elevator dinged. He paused, leaned over the banister, and eyed the elevator.

Head lowered, Francine stepped out and paused to fidget with her necklace. Ethan started to call to her but stopped the second she lifted her head. His eyes widened and Ethan held his breath. *Whoa!* he thought. Francine had never looked more beautiful. Tonight she wore a long blue sweater sprinkled with rhinestones over an ankle-length gauzy skirt. Besides that, she'd somehow piled her hair up in a droopy bun and allowed some tendrils to hang around her face. Even though her youthful face still bore the innocence Ethan had grown to love, Francine had somehow managed to pull off a look of sophisticated simplicity he'd never equated with her.

He looked down at his plain ebony sweater, gray slacks, and loafers. Ethan wished he'd at least had the foresight to put on a sports coat.

Francine had only walked a few more paces when she stopped to fuss with her necklace again—a short chain with a sparkling cross attached. Ethan decided his wanting to give her his gift early was a good idea.

"There you are," Ethan said, glad his voice sounded as carefree as ever. "I'd just about decided you were acting like Marie and Julie and were going to be late."

Debra White Smith

"Oh!" Francine said, her head popping up. "I didn't see you!"

"No, but I saw *you!*" Ethan said and stopped in front of her. With a jaunty grin, he continued, "I must say you are looking lovely this evening, Miss Ponce." He took her red-tipped fingers in his.

"Thanks," she whispered, her light-blue eyes pools of feminine mystery.

An unexpected ripple assaulted Ethan. The floor was no longer level. The smell of Francine's classy perfume intensified the effect. Like her appearance, the scent was something new and unexpected. Shocked beyond words, Ethan tried to jolt himself back to normal. He could do nothing but silently gaze at her.

The friend and confidante he'd counted on never changing had done just that. *But when?* Ethan thought. The last he remembered, Francine was rushing off to college wearing a ponytail and carrying a load of books. While she certainly hadn't looked like a guy, she hadn't resembled this knockout, either!

Except that day at the Worthingham Renaissance, Ethan reminded himself. *And at Marie's wedding. And then the afternoon Hugh said she reminded him of an angel.*

Hugh was a prophet. Never had Ethan viewed a mortal who looked more celestial. Francine earned the label angelic right now.

Francine's reddening face awakened Ethan to the fact that he must have done something to embarrass her. What, he couldn't know…unless speechlessly ogling her was license to blush.

I'm an engaged man, he reminded himself and released Francine's fingers. *Well, almost engaged,* Ethan corrected. And his soon-to-be fiancée would arrive any moment. For the life of him, Ethan couldn't remember what she looked like. Instead, his mind was intoxicated with the unexpected…white-blonde hair, a heart-shaped face, and pouty lips smothered in reddish gloss.

His Francine was all grown up! *Wow!*

"You're staring at me," she finally whispered. "Is it my makeup?" Francine touched her cheek. "I…I went and had it done this afternoon," she wobbled out. "It's too much, isn't it? I was afraid it—it was too much. I told the clerk it was too much, but she just kept on…and then my hair!" she worried. "I told the hairdresser I didn't want—"

"No! *Nothing's* too much or wrong. Everything's perfect!" Ethan exclaimed. "You look great! I've never seen you look so good! I didn't even know you *could* look this good."

A fresh, scarlet flush flowed to her hairline.

"Oh man!" Ethan rammed the heel of his hand against his forehead. "I didn't mean that to sound like…I was just trying to say—"

"No—oh, no! I didn't take it like that!" She vehemently shook her head.

Ethan, feeling like an awkward fifteen-year-old, shoved his present forward before he could say anything else boneheaded. "Here!" he said like a junior high kid giving his girl a corsage for the school dance. "This is for you."

"Already?" she squeaked.

"Y–yes," he responded. He eyed the sides of the short chain that had slipped under the neck of her sweater. "I think you might need it *now,* actually."

"Okay." Francine slipped a fingernail underneath the back fold. After wrestling the paper off the black velvet box, she pushed the lid up on its hinges and gasped.

Ethan peeked at the wide gold chain glistening against white satin, then drank in the pleasure on Francine's face.

"It's perfect!" she exclaimed. "Look!" She pulled on the chain she wore and showed Ethan the two-inch, gold cross attached to it. Two rows of glistening blue stones decorated the piece. "Wade gave it to me today at lunch. He wanted to buy me a chain, too, but I told him I already had *this* one."

She dropped the short rope around her neck. "Anyway, this chain just doesn't work. The cross is too big, and the chain isn't long enough for my sweater. But *your* chain…" She lifted the piece and held it up. Her fingers shook, and Ethan attributed the trembling to that of a gracious lady excited about a beautiful piece of jewelry. Seldom had he heard Francine babble as she was now. "It's perfect. Just the right length and…and…everything," she finished and looked back at Ethan with enough appreciation to knock a giant flat.

"That's what the jeweler said," Ethan admitted, "about the length, anyway. She said it was a perfect length for all sorts of occasions. It's twenty inches long, 18-karat gold. The jeweler said it was the best she had."

"I love it!" Francine whispered, her eyes brimming with moisture. "It's perfect…just perfect," she repeated.

"Hey…why do you want to go and cry?" Ethan chided, although he nearly burst with pride in knowing she loved the gift so much. "Nobody died here, you know."

"I know," she whispered. "I just—oh—thanks!"

Before Ethan could prepare himself, Francine wrapped her arms around his neck for a familial hug the two shared for many important moments—graduations, Christmas, homecomings. But this time when she pulled away, something inside Ethan whispered that he shouldn't let go. On an impulse, he brushed her cheek with the same gentle kiss he'd bestowed after each of the special occasions to which he'd escorted her. Usually the peck was short lived and chaste. This time the kiss lingered while the floor wobbled.

"You really look great," he whispered against her ear. And Ethan wasn't certain whether the shiver was hers or his.

When he backed away, Ethan found his answer. Francine's head was bashfully lowered as it always was when she became uncomfortable. She awkwardly toyed with the chain's clasp like a two-year-old unable to open a new toy.

Mortification swept across Ethan. The shiver had been all his. He allowed his masculine instinct to overrun common sense. If Francine even suspected what he was thinking, she would probably hide in her room and not come out for the whole evening. Francine was so innocent, so pure, she probably had never entertained one romantic thought—especially about him!

On top of that, Ethan had Carrie to think about. *She* was the woman he loved! *She* was his future wife! These thoughts of Francine were nothing short of traitorous.

He rebuked his wayward mind and finished off his self-incrimination: *You're acting like a rake! Get a grip on yourself!*

"I'm going to just step in here to the restroom and put my cross on this chain," Francine said. Her unsteady voice suggested that he'd upset her delicate nature. His self-disgust grew to mammoth proportions.

Before Ethan could offer to help with the chain, Francine plopped the piece back into its box and hurried away, her gauzy skirt swishing around her ankles.

Ethan told himself he should quit watching her. He watched her anyway. He absorbed the gentle sway of Francine's hips, the soft pile of pale hair, the graceful tilt of her shoulders. When the door next to the elevator snapped shut, he blinked hard, shook his head several times, and briskly rubbed his face.

This has got to stop! he told himself. *Francine is like my sister!*

The doorbell rang, and Ethan had never been so grateful. *Carrie!* he thought and hoped the caller was her, not Wade. While he was looking forward to visiting with Francine's brother, Ethan needed a heavy dose of Carrie Casper to remind him where his loyalties lay.

In a flash he recalled what he couldn't fathom minutes before. Carrie's image swam into his mind. Sandy-blonde curls, pouty pink lips, and a pair of exotic green eyes that made him forget his name. The woman was drop-dead gorgeous every day of the week. The bell rang again. Ike appeared from the dining room, hors d'oeuvre tray in hand.

"I'll get it," Ethan offered.

With a grateful nod, the silver-haired, tuxedo-clad Ike ducked back into the dining area.

Ethan reexamined his slacks and sweater and shook his head. *Oh well! Too late to change now,* he thought and strode toward the front door. The sooner he had Carrie by his side, the quicker he could eradicate his inappropriate reaction to Francine.

⁀ ⁀

Francine leaned against the free-standing sink while the room spun. The ringing doorbell blended with the buzz in her befuddled brain, and she couldn't even recall who the guests would be tonight. In one hand she clutched the black velvet box; in the other, the wrapping paper and ribbon. Her heart palpitated in her throat, and she could barely catch her breath.

She dared raise her gaze to the image in the mirror. A stranger stared back at her. This was the woman who had arrested Ethan's attention like the "same ol' Francine" never could.

The effect had been exactly what Francine hoped for. The appreciative glow in Ethan's dark eyes along with his silent "Wow!" had turned Francine's spine to jelly. The lingering kiss held promises she could only dare to wish for. When he whispered in her ear, she relished the shiver that tingled her skin and left her knees weak. At the time she suspected Ethan registered the reaction his nearness evoked. Now she didn't know.

That afternoon Francine had left the hairdresser's chair and settled in front of the cosmetic counter. She'd demurely hinted to the clerk that she needed to look smashing. The woman assured her that with the cosmetics she applied to her features and this hairdo she would turn heads for miles. Francine didn't explain that she only wanted to turn *one* head.

Now that Ethan had noticed, an unexpected reaction uncoiled within Francine. Her knees strengthened. Her heart rate slowed. Her breathing grew even. The glory of the moment paled in the light of brutal reality. Ethan hadn't been attracted to the *real* Francine—only to the work of art the cosmetologist and hairdresser created. Francine eyed herself with unexpected disdain.

If he isn't interested in the real *me, what kind of relationship can last on surface attraction alone?*

A quivering nausea suggested Francine had done the wrong thing. She should have made herself look presentable and nothing more.

She slammed the wrapping paper into the brass-plated receptacle, plunked the velvet box on the back of the toilet, and twisted the porcelain water knobs on the sink. Francine dampened her hands in the cold, hissing spray. She reached for the hand soap, furiously pumped, and rubbed her hands together. A thick lather coated her palms and released the essence of peaches that mingled with the smell of her new perfume.

The Oscar de la Renta saleswoman had guaranteed the new scent was perfect for Francine. Now she longed for the simple appeal of her dependable standby, Ombre Rose. That nonimposing fragrance fit the true Francine.

Seconds before she plunged her face into her opened hands, she reexamined her elegant image. *But, maybe this is what it will take to jolt Ethan into realizing I'm not his kid sister any more.*

Francine lowered her hands as this morning's logic surfaced with renewed force. She scrunched her toes, ensconced in blue and silver pumps. Her knees quivered anew. Desperate times called for desperate measures. If something didn't change and change soon, Ethan would very likely propose to Carrie. That was the *last* thing he needed to do—whether he realized it or not. She submerged her hands under the warming water until the lather slipped down the drain. Francine turned off the water and dried her hands on the thick towel hanging above the toilet.

No more thinking! she admonished herself. *You made your decisions, now live with them!*

After removing her short gold chain, she slipped off the cross and retrieved the new chain from the velvet box. With the old chain secure in the box, she slid the cross over the end of the new one. The stones glistened in the recessed lighting as if they were applauding Francine's determination.

With steady fingers, she fastened the clasp and then looked into the mirror. Wade's cross splendidly fit the fine chain. The high quality of Ethan's necklace made the cross look like a masterpiece. She barely twisted at the waist and watched with pleasure as the sequins scattered across her sweater winked in sequence with the blue stones on the cross.

The necklace and cross added the final touch to her look. This was a once-in-a-lifetime night. Her twenty-first birthday! Francine had never felt more special. And, she had to admit, she'd never *looked* so special.

She thought of Carrie's stunning looks and recognized that some of the magic lay in the makeup artist's hands. For the first time, she wondered what Carrie must look like without all the glamor tricks. Until now, Francine had assumed Carrie looked gorgeous from her first waking moment. In the face of Francine's transformation, her assumption was losing credence.

Without her makeup, she probably looks about like I do most of the time, Francine reasoned. A new confidence surged. She knew no matter how gorgeous Carrie looked tonight, she could hold her own with her.

While Francine didn't want a relationship with Ethan based on surface attraction alone, his noticing her new look just might instigate something deeper. She certainly wanted a different relationship than they had. A different relationship required a different approach.

A soft knock preceded Ethan's reticent voice. "Franny? Sorry to rush you, but Wade's here."

"Wade?" she repeated, her voice as elated as her heart. The name swept away her former confusion over the identity of tonight's guests. Francine mentally clicked through the short list. Wade Ponce stood out as the most anticipated.

"Okay, Ethan," she continued, "Tell him I'm—I'm coming!" Francine grabbed the velvet box and looked for a place to put it. After trying to make the box fit in the mirrored cabinet's narrow shelf, she opened the door to the petite linen closet on her right.

With a cursory glance, she tossed the box upon the stack of towels and snapped the door shut.

A final examination of her reflection elicited a smile. When Uncle Tom first insisted upon her party, she had protested. Francine, desperate to avoid any more indebtedness to her aunt and uncle, hoped to avoid the trust fund tradition by avoiding the party. But in the wake of Tom Barrimore's insistent scowl, her objections were short-lived. As usual, Francine complied. Besides, she decided if Uncle Tom was going to insist upon hoisting a trust fund upon her he could do it without the party.

Nonetheless, until this morning she had dreaded the evening with all its pomp. She would have far rather enjoyed a quiet dinner with Wade and Ethan at a small restaurant. Despite her original misgivings, Francine's spirits had risen to new heights as the day wore on. Now she was verging upon a serene case of the euphorics.

I'll remember this night forever, she thought, stroking Ethan's glittering chain.

Twenty

"If everyone is through with their cake, let's go to the den," Tom Barrimore said. "It's time for the presents."

Carrie stole one last bite of her German chocolate cake and a sip of her mellow coffee. In the bustle of the guests preparing to stand, she also sneaked another hard glance at Francine. Carrie had never been so taken aback by a woman's change in appearance. Francine Ponce gave the word "makeover" a phenomenal meaning. Someone had worked a miracle with her makeup and hair. The results screamed a less-is-more sophistication that insisted Francine could step into high-society circles with ease and grace.

Carrie observed her simple wool pantsuit topped with a Chanel jacket. She had been thankful Ethan had also chosen to dress down. Otherwise she would have suffered through the indecent torture of being the least elegant of the whole crew. Tom Barrimore and his wife both wore nice suits. Nora Jamison belied her sour disposition and donned a cheerful red dress with sequined buttons along the shoulder. Even Julie abandoned her hip huggers for a short-skirted number that shimmered beneath the chandelier and made Yancey Bates forget to be funny.

Despite the finery, Francine still shone brighter than them all. If she had looked this stunning the first time Carrie met her, she would have earnestly believed the younger woman was indeed a rival. Thankfully, Ethan's childhood friend had waited until now to pull her look together—*after* Ethan's heart was irrevocably committed. Tonight, he proved by every look, every touch, every action that he was all Carrie's.

He barely offered a glance toward Francine. Carrie's glee couldn't be greater. That meant the plan with Hugh would go even more smoothly. Besides, Carrie was growing to truly love and appreciate Francine. She would hate to view her as "the other woman." Instead, she preferred her recent tag as "future sister-in-law."

Ethan stood. Ever-the-gentleman, he assisted Carrie with her chair. Rising, she thanked Ethan and stifled a smile. Even though Ethan wasn't distracted by Francine, Hugh wasn't faring nearly as well. While Francine's brother Wade had sat on one side of her, Hugh claimed the seat on the other side. The poor guy had barely touched his meal for staring at Francine and forever striking up a new vein of conversation with her.

With Ethan close, Carrie followed the chatting group from the china and silver laden dining table. They left the scent of roast and spices, the company of the baroque dining table and matching sideboards, and passed through the doorway into the den. An urn of fresh coffee perched atop a silver tray extended a welcoming aroma. The pile of gifts in the center of the teak coffee table offered the assurance that the night was just beginning.

Hugh, dressed in a fine dinner suit that impressed even Carrie, walked a couple of paces behind Francine, who clung to her brother's arm. The cut of Wade's suit didn't even touch Hugh's, but he wore it like a slender prince.

Nothing about Wade and Francine attested that the two were blood relatives. While Francine was all composure and peace,

Wade's intense gaze revealed a soul that was driven and focused. Wade's hair was as red as Francine's was blonde. His eyes as green as Carrie's. His love for Francine as protective as Ethan's. All evening he'd eyed Hugh with suspicion and a hint of challenge. The woman definitely didn't lack for venerable knights to protect her honor.

Carrie stole a discreet glance toward Ethan. For the first time, she caught him gazing at Francine. The look wasn't that of a doting brother, but rather a male who appreciated the feminine image before him. Carrie's security wavered, and she decided to take action. After freshening up her bronze lipstick, Carrie had purposefully left her handbag near her dinner chair because she hated hauling the thing with her everywhere. Now she cheered her own foresight.

"I left my purse in the dining room," she mumbled and turned back toward the door they'd just walked through.

"Here, let me get it," Ethan offered.

"Sure," Carrie purred and followed in his wake.

Fortunately, they were the last ones to exit the dining room, so it was vacant—exactly what Carrie wanted. She examined the swinging oak door that led into the kitchen. The sounds of pots clanking, water running, and muffled voices testified that the staff was busy at work.

She hoped that nosy Ike Gentry didn't barge back into the room for something. Julie frequently complained about the family employee. His official position was doorman-on-call, sometimes driver, and always executive household manager. But Julie vowed the man was her father's secret watchdog as well. Carrie was slowly learning that nothing got past Ike's all-seeing eye.

Pausing near the den's entry, Carrie awaited Ethan. He pulled out her chair, gathered the leather bag, and approached Carrie with a smile that suggested they held a host of secrets. She couldn't wait to add another one to the list. The second he extended the petite handbag, she ignored the bag, gripped his arm, and tugged him toward the wall. They were safely out of sight from the den's occupants.

"Hey!" Ethan said over a chuckle. "What are you doing?" He didn't resist one step.

"Just making sure you don't forget me tonight after I'm gone," Carrie crooned and slipped her hands up the front of his sweater.

"Forget you?" Ethan responded. Still holding her purse, he settled his arms around her waist. "How could I ever do that?"

"Hmmm..." Carrie offered her lips, and Ethan accepted the gift. The kiss quickly deepened to the fiery exchange that always made Carrie yearn for more. The gentle plop of her purse at her feet accompanied Ethan's spreading his hands upon her back and pulling her closer.

Ethan wanted the kiss. He wanted it as he'd never wanted one of Carrie's kisses. *Or maybe,* he thought, *I need this! I need it to blot Francine from my mind.*

All during dinner, Ethan had purposefully honed his focus upon Carrie, and through staunch willpower he had resisted even the slightest glance at Francine...until they were passing into the den. Then, his willpower failed. His traitorous gaze had riveted upon Francine. He couldn't stop himself. The more he drank in her stunning appearance, the more he thirsted. The unexpected longing that attacked Ethan when he first saw Francine near the elevator had accosted him again.

Now he lambasted himself anew and desperately tightened his hold upon Carrie. When that didn't erase Francine's red-tinted lips and fascinating blue eyes, he increased the kiss' fervor. Carrie responded like a woman who longed for more passion. A warning voice urged Ethan to end the clutch. He'd never allowed an embrace to extend to this point, not even in the play. But he'd never been so frantic before, either.

Finally, Carrie's sigh awakened Ethan to the effects of his actions. Even if he remained Francine-focused and unstirred, Carrie was warming up—and fast. Just as he backed off the kiss,

Francine's familiar voice entered the dining room. At first Ethan was sure he was so eaten up with Francine he'd fabricated her voice. Nonetheless, he lifted his face from Carrie's and looked toward the entryway. When Francine appeared there in all her splendor, he started and tried to disentangle himself from Carrie.

"Ethan?" Francine repeated. "We're waiting on…" She turned and spotted him. "Oh," Francine whispered, her gaze settling on his lips.

The slick feel of lipstick across Ethan's pulsating mouth made him want to scrub at his lips. Instead, he tried to distance himself from Carrie, who seemed determined to remain in the clinging mode.

Carrie glanced over her shoulder toward Francine. "Oops!" she said and emitted a satisfied giggle that hinted at who knew what. Ethan resisted the impulse to cover Carrie's mouth with his hand.

A scarlet glow assaulted Francine's face, bled into her hairline, and reminded Ethan she was still innocent, even if she looked like a femme fatale. Nevertheless, the suspicion in her pale-blue eyes bespoke a full-grown woman who fully understood the implications of Ethan and Carrie's embrace.

He finally manipulated Carrie to a respectable distance and said, "Sorry."

Carrie giggled again. Ethan's forehead heated.

He recalled the night on the stairway a couple of months ago when Francine had candidly searched his motives in his relationship with Carrie. Until now, Ethan had purposefully repressed the memory of that conversation. He'd never felt so aghast that Francine would even *think* about sensuality, let alone suspect him of being involved on that level with Carrie.

The memory reawakened feelings of betrayal Ethan had experienced. If ever he'd thought someone fully believed in his honor, it was Francine. Now her knowing appraisal, silent and incriminating, reminded Ethan that his "little sister" was much more savvy than he wanted to believe and that she was once again doubting him.

If that wasn't enough, his masculine instinct insisted that Francine wasn't his little sister any more—nor had she ever been. Not really. She was a member of the opposite sex—and a very pretty member. Ethan was a guy—a very normal guy. And some perverse voice was insisting he should end the relationship with Carrie so he could pursue Francine.

But that's disgusting! he thought and nearly drowned in a fresh flood of self-reproach.

With feigned indifference, Ethan bent to retrieve Carrie's small bag from the floor and handed it to her. "Sorry," he repeated in Francine's direction. But this time, he kept his gaze lowered. "I didn't know you guys were waiting on us." She didn't respond. Ethan looked up. Francine was gone.

Carrie shrugged and smiled like a green-eyed feline satisfied with her latest meal. Ethan wondered if he was the main course *and* dessert.

"I guess we better go see her unwrap her presents," Carrie said. "Although…" she stroked her index finger along his mustache and goatee, "I'd much rather stay in here."

Ethan responded with a smile he hoped looked sincere and kissed her bronze-tipped finger.

"Look at you," Carrie said, simpering triumphantly. "You've got lipstick all over you." She unzipped her purse, pulled out a tissue, and stroked the color away. "There," she said, "all better."

"Thanks," Ethan replied and rubbed his fingertips across his mouth for a final test. Nothing slick remained.

As they walked back into the den, he prayed that God would deliver him from his own wandering thoughts. Ethan was a man of his word. He'd already told Carrie he played for keeps and that this was the deepest he'd allowed any relationship to go. In the past Ethan had scorned men who broke women's hearts after promising or even hinting at a commitment.

They neared the coffee table piled with presents and claimed the pair of folding chairs Ike had strategically arranged for them. Ethan purposefully ignored Francine, who remained the center of attention. He darted a furtive glance toward his future bride. Except for her blurred lipstick, Carrie was the image of the feminine ideal. On top of that, Ethan couldn't ask for a sweeter-natured woman. She was everything he'd ever dreamed of. The thought of breaking her heart left him nauseous...even though their kiss had left him cold.

Ethan squared his shoulders, stiffened his jaw, and decided to stand by his word no matter what new disloyalties his mind introduced. He'd heard married men talk about fleeting attractions to other women...about the temptations that presented themselves as viable possibilities...about their decisions to stand by their vows no matter how attractive the other opportunities appeared. Even though he had yet to state the wedding vows, the time to start proving his faithfulness was *now*. He was Carrie's man. He would *act like* Carrie's man. His honor dictated he had no other choice.

"Now that everyone's here," Uncle Tom began and slanted a pointed look toward Ethan, "Francine can open her presents."

Twenty-One

"I'll pass you the gifts, okay, Francine?" Hugh said.

"Sure," she replied and avoided eye contact with the man who had hovered over her all evening.

Wade nudged her, and she pretended she didn't register the silent innuendo. Even though she and Wade had previously agreed that he would pass her the presents, Francine didn't have the fortitude to argue with Hugh. He made her nervous enough without having to disagree with him.

Finally Wade spoke up. "Thanks for the offer, Hugh," he replied, his voice leaving no room for debate, "but Francine and I agreed for *me* to pass her the presents."

Forever desperate not to cause waves, Francine looked at her brother in silent appeal, begging him not to turn something so small into a territorial issue.

Wade's arrival had brought a startling surprise—a bag full of presents from her parents and siblings. With Ethan's direction, Wade placed each of the gifts on the coffee table. When Francine said she didn't know how she'd ever choose what present to unwrap first, Wade had offered to hand her the presents when it came time to open them.

Now she peered at the pile of multicolored gifts, whose number rivaled the last Christmas spread. She didn't know how to manage the situation. While the absence of a checkbook-sized gift brought mammoth relief, her brother's rising tension ushered in a new problem. She darted him another beseeching plea. Wade peered back at her, his green eyes as stubborn as ever. Either his color was high or he'd gained about eighty new freckles since he arrived.

As the evening wore on, Wade had gradually grown more and more defensive with Hugh's monopolizing Francine. Her brother wasn't the best at holding his tongue. All she could do was hope that Wade didn't cause a scene. Aunt Nora would never let Francine forget it.

She fixed her attention upon her red-clad aunt. Thankfully she was in the corner with Julie and Yancey, lingering by the stereo system. Upon entering the room, they had mentioned that they would put on some different CDs.

"Here, Wade," Hugh eventually said and took two presents from the top of the pile. "You hand Francine a gift and then I'll hand her one. Okay?" His voice was kind. His face lacked any hint of animosity. His friendly eyes begged Wade to relax.

Wade looked at Hugh, then the package, and back at Hugh.

Francine pinched her sweater and held her breath. She widened her eyes at Wade and barely nodded.

"Sure," Wade said and even threw in a sheepish smile. "Not a problem."

Francine never imagined feeling gratitude toward Hugh Casper. The relieved droop of her shoulders couldn't be denied. "Thanks," she breathed.

Hugh grinned like a pro star who'd just slam-dunked the final score for the NBA championship.

Two points! Francine thought and then wondered how many times he'd smiled at Marie that way. That overheard conversation between him and her cousin trickled through her mind.

Taking advantage of Wade's shift in attitude, Hugh began to chat with him. Francine assumed Hugh was working to win another conquest.

She directed her gaze downward, but that only exposed another situation Francine wanted to avoid. Sitting on the other side of the coffee table, Carrie crossed her legs and rubbed the tip of her pointed pump along the side of Ethan's leg.

Francine looked out the window to the glow of street lights on the damp, Manhattan pavement. Earlier today when her hopes were high, the rain had pattered a merry rhythm into her heart. Now the shifting droplets seemed the tears of a soul wretchedly in love. Francine tried to tell herself not to feel, but the self-imposed demand was empty. Her eyes stung. The evening was going flat—and fast.

Uncle Tom, who'd been helping Aunt Mariette pour herself a cup of coffee, invaded Francine's space. First, he laid his hand on Hugh's shoulder. "Great idea on those gifts, Hugh," he said and threw in a discreet wink for Francine only. "Francine needs all the help she can get. Knowing her, she'll take all night just to decide whose present she should unwrap first." He laughed at his own joke. For some reason, Tom had been in an unusually jovial mood from the evening's onset.

"Don't tease Francine, darling," Mariette coaxed as Tom took his seat in one of the wing-backed chairs. "She's nearly all I've got these days."

Francine lowered her head and offered her aunt an upward glance. Through the years she had grown increasingly fond of Mariette Barrimore. With her gray eyes and dark hair, Aunt Mariette also could have passed for Francine's mother's twin.

"I didn't even know you were listening to us, Uncle Tom," Wade admitted as he toyed with the bow on the present he held.

It was a long thin box snuggled in white shiny paper that resembled the packaging on Ethan's necklace.

"I don't miss a thing," Uncle Tom said with a good-natured smile. "Not a thing," he continued and scrutinized Hugh with a speculative gleam in his intense eyes.

Francine could only imagine what her uncle was thinking. Hugh Casper was worth a canyon full of money, and he was heaping plenty of attention upon Francine. She wondered if some of these facts had contributed to her uncle's buoyant mood. Francine, on the other hand, didn't want Hugh Casper—whether he was broke or lined in gold. She figured if she were lucky, his fixation was a fickle fancy that would wear off when the evening died.

"Did I hear you say you're in the restaurant business, Wade?" Hugh inquired across Francine. She'd noticed early in the evening that tonight he wore his mild French accent as suavely as he wore the Italian suit.

"Yes, as a matter of fact I'm the assistant manager at a restaurant on Long Beach."

Francine stroked her wide gold chain.

"Interesting…did you know my family's in the restaurant business as well?"

"No, really?"

She admired the way the lamplight reflected upon the gold's lucid surface.

"Yes, my dad owns Addy's. Ever heard of them?

"No way!" Wade exclaimed. "All of them?"

While Hugh and Wade continued their conversation, the memory of Ethan's presenting the chain stirred her soul. Still, Francine refused to look at him. What was the use? He'd ignored her all evening and then delayed her gift unwrapping with a kissing session that made Francine want to gag. Never had she been so bewildered. She was beginning to believe she had read more into his peck on the cheek than he ever intended. Maybe

Francine's aching heart was making her imagine Ethan's warmth where nothing but the usual friendship remained.

"Are you going to give her the gift, Wade?" Aunt Nora's prompting held the rap of a command. With the first bars of Mozart floating from the room's corner, the aging woman perched on the edge of the sofa near her sister, who languidly sipped her coffee.

"Oh sure!" Wade exclaimed. "I guess Hugh and I started talking and forgot all about the presents." Before passing the thin box to Francine, he looked at the tag. "This one's from Carrie and Hugh," he explained. This time his voice lacked the bristle it had assumed the minute Hugh settled beside Francine at dinner.

She accepted the present and noticed Julie and Yancey ducking out of the room. Yancey slid his arm around Julie's tiny waist and twirled her into a jaunty prance. Those two were in a world of their own.

Francine focused upon the task of removing the bow. All the while, she felt Hugh's gaze upon her. She didn't know what he was up to, but it was almost like he was picking up where he left off at that luncheon in late August. That day he'd assisted her with her sandwiches and chips. Tonight they'd filled their plates from the sideboard, and he'd made certain her plate was serviced with any morsel she desired.

When the oversized birthday cake arrived, flaming with twenty-one candles, Hugh was the first one who insisted she make a wish. The look in his eyes said he would like to fulfill her every dream. A tremor of revulsion spanned Francine's midsection then and now.

The gift paper slipped to the floor. Yet another velvet box wobbled in her unsteady hands.

She could barely look at Hugh Casper without reliving that dreadful conversation between him and Marie. *Is he after me now?* The question scared her almost as much as Ethan's marrying Carrie.

Francine gazed at the box that obviously held jewelry. That choice of gift seemed to be all the rage today. Francine felt Hugh's scrutiny intensify. The hair on the back of her neck prickled.

She didn't trust him—not even a little bit. And while Wade was here now to act as buffer, Francine didn't know what she would do when he went home Monday. Hugh was right next door! She had always counted on Ethan to intervene. But he was so wrapped up in Carrie Casper—literally—that Francine didn't think he would notice if Hugh drove a team of horses to the front door and abducted her in a barred carriage. The way Uncle Tom was acting, Francine figured he might applaud the abduction.

Hugh's fingers covered Francine's. His expensive masculine scent brought to mind a sun-kissed ocean bordered by inviting white sand. "Here," he tenderly murmured, "let me open it." The undertow in his words insisted that while the ocean might look placid, it held deadly currents.

Before Francine could protest, he removed the box from her grasp and flipped open the lid. A gold rope chain shimmered against cream-colored satin. While the necklace was a different design than Ethan's, it was every bit as expensive looking. Francine's dismay incited her gasp.

She didn't realize Hugh had leaned in so closely until she looked up. His face was inches from hers. His arm rested on the back of her chair. His hazel eyes beckoned Francine to read as much into the present as she dared. While the gift tag might have also featured Carrie's name, Hugh's silent appraisal insisted the sentiment was all his.

"It's 18-karat gold," he said. "The best they had."

"Wow, Franny!" Ethan exclaimed in the aftermath of the groups oohs and ahs. "That chain will match Wade's cross even better than mine."

Caught in a stupor, Francine broke her vow not to look at Ethan. She wanted to protest his claim, but the words lodged in her throat. Ethan's white-toothed grin contrasted with his dark skin in an alluring manner that Francine was certain he'd never used with her. His expression had never been so inviting. His eyes had never glittered with such an appreciative light. She couldn't recall a time when she'd wanted to kiss Ethan more than tonight...right now. She would have given ten years of her life to have been the one in his arms in the den. Fleetingly, she wondered what he'd think if he ever discovered just how deeply and ardently her love burned.

"You know, Ethan, I believe you're right," Aunt Mariette's delayed and listless agreement sealed the switch.

Before Francine could stop them, Wade and Hugh managed to remove the flat chain, slide the cross off, place it on the rope chain, and clasp it around her neck. During the whole process, Francine felt like a toddler grabbing for shiny baubles. At first, she tried to mutely stop the men. When that didn't work, she insisted upon refastening Ethan's chain back around her neck.

Once both pieces hung from her neck, she dared look back at Ethan, recklessly longing for him to notice her attachment to his gift. But Ethan was focused upon Carrie. He laughed at something she said and stroked her arm.

"I love it when you say that," Ethan gurgled.

Francine couldn't imagine what Carrie had said. *Probably some sickening endearment,* she thought. At last Francine admitted that Ethan and Carrie were as much in their own world as Julie and Yancey. Francine convinced herself that his recent appraisal was far more appreciative and inviting than it actually was.

I must be projecting my own feelings on him, she thought. *He loves Carrie, and there's nothing I can do to change that.*

Hugh pressed another gift into her hands. Francine absently grasped the present and looked toward the window again. Drops of rain pelted the pane like unrelenting darts.

Carrie meandered into the kitchen in search of her pre-bedtime glass of ice water. She held half a dozen vitamins and wondered for the hundredth time how she could convince Hugh to join her mineral-and-supplement regimen. "Stubborn, stubborn, stubborn," she mumbled, her fuzzy slippers tapping against her heels in rhythm to her decree.

She rounded the corner to pass through the garden room and encountered the topic of her thoughts.

"Still up?" she asked over a yawn.

"Yes." Hugh glanced from a line of playing cards placed along the glass-topped coffee table's edge. He wasted no time resuming his efforts at solitaire.

She checked the crystal clock residing on the lampstand. Eleven o'clock. Carrie had never seen someone drag out unwrapping presents like Francine Ponce. They'd finished dinner by eight, and didn't get through with the presents until nearly nine. Once the group visited for an hour, Carrie and Hugh came home.

Ethan had teasingly offered to walk her home. After the swift trip down one flight of steps and up the other, he'd ended the evening with a good-night kiss that left Carrie empty. Never had he kissed her like he did in the dining room, and she'd hoped for a repeat. His restrained brush of the lips and polite "good night" had been the epitome of anticlimactic.

So Carrie had retired to her room and read a spicy romance novel, all the while imagining the hero and heroine were Ethan and her. Now the time had come to down her vitamins and turn out the lights.

Her brother didn't appear to share her intent. The tense set of Hugh's jaw, the intensity of his focus suggested he wouldn't be retiring any time soon.

"What's got you so uptight?" Carrie asked. Lazily, she stroked the sash on her slinky housecoat and sat beside her brother.

Hugh's silent shrug prompted Carrie's chortle.

"What?" Hugh halted in the process of laying a card on the table. He fingered the deck in his hand and defensively eyed his sister.

"You're as uptight as a lion ready to pounce, aren't you?"

Hugh went back to his game. "Go swallow your horse pills," he mumbled.

The downcast droop of his mouth stirred Carrie's sympathy. She didn't have to wonder what had him all in knots. While Francine hadn't been rude to Hugh tonight, she hadn't given him any reason to believe he was making progress with her. The chain Hugh had been certain would leave her swooning had already been bettered by Ethan's earlier gift. Francine thanked Hugh for the necklace as serenely as if it had been a gold-plated trifle from Wal-Mart…and the thing had cost nearly a thousand bucks.

Hugh himself had admitted that Francine was different from any woman he had ever met. Tonight proved that his usual methods just might not work.

"Ever think about slowing down with Francine?" she suggested.

"Slowing down!" Hugh exclaimed and tossed the deck of cards upon the table. They fanned across the slick surface and bumped into the stack of magazines. "I'm going at a snail's pace, woman."

"Maybe for the ladies you've pursued in the past. But Francine's not them." Carrie snuggled into the love seat's corner and draped her red robe across her knees.

Hugh rubbed his face. "You can say that again," he mumbled and pinched his bottom lip. He slumped against the love seat, crossed his legs, jiggled his socked foot, and gazed toward the row of hanging ferns.

Carrie squinted and scrutinized his lean profile. The hungry point of his mouth sent a warning ripple across Carrie's mind. She knew her brother well enough to understand his ego didn't take a rebuff well, no matter how passive it was. For the first time since he admitted being truly in love with Francine, Carrie questioned his motives. This thing with Francine could easily be

Debra White Smith

nothing more than a challenge. Like a big-game hunter, Hugh could be pursuing the elusive prize. But Carrie could not and would not allow him to treat Francine as trophy game.

"And you're sure you love her?" Carrie blandly inquired. In an attempt to feign an indifferent air, she casually ran her tongue along the front of her freshly brushed teeth. Welcoming the mint sensation, she waited for Hugh to validate his love.

"You're like a mother hen when it comes to her, aren't you?" He cocked one eyebrow and studied his sister. "But that seems to be the reaction Francine has on everyone. The way Wade acted, I thought he was going to grab me and throw me on the floor just for looking at her."

"Maybe it was less the look and more the kind of look," Carrie offered and yawned again. Still, she waited for her answer.

"Was I *that* obvious?

"Only for anyone with at least one eye and half a brain."

Hugh rested his head against the back of the couch and stared at the ceiling. "I've never been at such a loss."

"You're going to have to go slow and easy," Carrie insisted. "Back off and let it build gradually. Otherwise you're going to scare her off."

He swiveled his head toward Carrie. "You'd be more comfortable if I *did* scare her off, wouldn't you?"

Carrie rested her hand in her lap and examined the six capsules nestled against her palm. "Like I already said, I'd love to have Francine as a sister-in-law, and I think she'd be good for you. I just sometimes worry that she might just become another conquest for you—and nothing else." She shrugged. "I mean, if you're *sure* you really love her—"

"*I do!*" Hugh grasped his sister's arm. "I really do. I *promise,* Carrie. This is the *real thing!*" The frenzied gleam in his eyes reminded Carrie of his claiming he couldn't eat. In Carrie's estimation the guy had lost about five to ten pounds. *Something* was spoiling his appetite. His emphatic expression insisted it was all about Francine.

"Okay," Carrie said and patted her brother's hand. "I believe you. I won't ask again."

Hugh shifted back into his corner. "Didn't Uncle Al say they were about to fire an assistant manager at one of the Boston restaurants?" Hugh rested his elbow on the love seat's arm and propped his temple against his fist.

Carrie wrinkled her brow and tried to recall any such reference. She also attempted to understand the shift in conversation. "I can't remember," she said. Another yawn assailed her, and she covered her mouth. The last thing Carrie ever thought about was her father's business. Like her mother, she was interested in the continuous cash flow and nothing more. "Why?" she asked.

"Francine's brother is an assistant manager at a joint in Long Beach." He leaned forward and retrieved his cards.

"So?" Carrie challenged.

"If you can't figure it out, then it won't do any good for me to explain it!" Hugh quipped. He gathered the cards into a stack and began to shuffle them.

Carrie recalled Wade and Francine's obvious devotion to one another. The two were undoubtedly close. She pieced together Hugh's logic and nodded. "So, you're figuring the shortest path to Francine might be through her brother. Is that it?"

One corner of Hugh's mouth twitched. "I like the way your mind works," he said and shuffled the cards again.

Twenty-Two

"You didn't have to do this, Ethan, *really!*" Francine insisted. She glanced over her shoulder at her gift-laden servant. While balancing her armload of presents, she opened the suite's door and stepped into the softly lighted chamber.

"I know…I know," Ethan patiently agreed and followed Francine into the room. "You don't ever want to put anyone out. You'd rather make eight trips to the den yourself than—"

A thump and plop interrupted Ethan's claim.

"Oh shoot," Ethan mumbled.

Francine instinctively dropped her load on the striped sofa and pivoted to help Ethan. "I told you I could have made a second trip," she admonished and bent to retrieve the trio of presents that stretched across the floor. Her mother's gift, a flannel robe, sprawled atop the slippers and gown from Sandra. Francine didn't have to look very closely to see that the gifts were gently worn. She figured they had been purchased at Goodwill or maybe a garage sale. But the tokens of love couldn't have been more valuable to Francine if they'd come from Neiman Marcus.

She scrambled to gather the nightwear as if she were once-again trying to protect it from Aunt Nora's acid remarks. "I don't think these are new," her taut-lipped aunt had stated. She extended her disapproval of the gown, the robe, the slippers, to include three Liz Claiborne sweaters as well. "You'd think my sister would have the decency to at least buy something new—even if she had to get it from the dollar store."

Francine rocked back on her knees and lovingly stroked the robe while Ethan deposited the sweaters and the rest of the gifts on the sofa. The presents brought back poignant memories of the family she'd left in Rockaway. The day Aunt Nora brought her to Central Park played through her mind. Francine had been so confused and distraught. All she wanted was to go back home to her mother and her brothers and Sandra. Even though she had never been her mom's favorite, Florence Ponce was still her mother. Francine dreadfully missed her that first year. Despite the anguish, she had somehow built a good life for herself here in Manhattan.

But after all these years, Francine still couldn't shake the regret at the contact she'd lost with her family of origin. At least she still had Wade, and Sandra tried to keep in touch. And maybe the others hadn't completely forgotten her. Wade said they were wanting her to come home for Christmas this year. The invitation was as precious as the gifts she now held. Francine snuggled her nose against the robe and was thankful for the freshly laundered aroma. She'd use the gown and robe tonight.

"That's your favorite present, isn't it?" Ethan's tender observation brought a sting to Francine's eyes.

She lowered the rose-colored robe in one hand and examined the matching slippers and gown she crushed against Ethan's chain and Wade's cross. "I can't say which is my favorite," she admitted and offered Ethan an assuring smile. "The gifts from you and Wade and the rest of my family all mean so much to me."

"Just as long as my gift is on the favorites list." Ethan offered his hand to help her stand.

Francine draped the robe across her forearm and accepted the kind gesture. "Oh, by all means," she rushed, rising to her feet.

"And Hugh's chain…" Ethan lifted the side of the chain and rolled it between his forefinger and thumb. "I guess it's on the favorites list as well?" He dropped the necklace. His black eyes, normally clear and readable, observed Francine in guarded speculation.

She mutely observed him and tried to decipher the meaning behind the odd question.

He'd been so wrapped up in Carrie all evening, Ethan barely acknowledged her existence since he gave her the chain. After the Caspers went home, she and Wade and her uncle and aunts had sat in the den visiting for nearly an hour with no sign of Ethan. Once Francine showed Wade to his room for the night, she went back into the den to retrieve her packages—only to discover Ethan awaiting her. She thought he'd gone to bed after walking Carrie home. Francine hadn't known how to react to his insisting he carry the gifts to her room.

Now he was standing in her suite posing questions that felt oddly loaded and looking at Francine with the wary eyes of a stranger.

"I guess I shouldn't have asked," Ethan finally said in a disappointed voice.

"Oh no!" Francine dropped her bundle on the couch and reached for the golden rope's clasp. "No, it's okay," she hurried. "You just reminded me to put the cross back on your chain. I liked it so much better, but I didn't quite know how to—"

"Here, I'll help you," Ethan rapidly offered and stepped behind her.

And this was the guy who said he thought Hugh's chain was better for the cross? Francine wondered. She had always prided herself in her ability to know Ethan's mind. But tonight the effort was wasted. She couldn't even begin to interpret his actions. One minute she thought he didn't know she was alive, and the next he was gladly helping her remove the cross from the chain he had suggested was a better match than his.

Once the switch was complete, Francine retired Hugh's gift to her silver-plated jewelry box. Then she looked in the dresser mirror to admire Ethan's chain and Wade's cross. Once again they were a simple duo upon her sweater.

"There!" she said brightly. "That's the best fit...two gifts from my two brothers," Francine added and couldn't imagine what had possessed her to say that.

Ethan wasn't her brother. She didn't even think of him in those terms. He was so much more...he was the man to whom she'd given her heart...the man she longed to marry. Francine clamped her hands together and cringed at the thought of his response. He'd probably affirm that she was the best sister he'd ever had. That left Francine as empty as the prospect of marrying Hugh Casper.

But Ethan remained so silent she thought he might have left the room without telling her. Francine turned to search the room and found him near the gas fireplace's mantel. His back to her, he held a butane lighter in one hand and a cucumber melon candle in the other. He clicked the lighter, touched the tip to the wick, and placed the flickering candle, back onto the marble mantel.

"Wade told me he's trying to get you to go home for Christmas this year." Ethan laid the butane lighter near the candle.

Francine blinked. "Y–yes, he mentioned that tonight—once. It was just in passing, so I wondered if he really meant that they really wanted me—"

"I'm sure they'll want you." Ethan laid his arm along the mantel and lowered his head. "Who wouldn't?" he asked, his hollow voice reminding Francine that his wayward father would never send him a Christmas invitation.

She didn't know what to say. While her heart was all for encouraging him, her mind offered no words. On top of everything else, she wondered how Uncle Tom and Aunt Mariette would react to the trip to Rockaway for Christmas. She dreaded the thought of telling them that she might have plans of her own. Once Aunt Nora heard of the trip, she would probably snap at Francine for the audacity of leaving Aunt Mariette's side. Uncle Tom's silent disapproval would probably be so heavy Francine would ultimately shrink from the very notion.

Finally Francine blurted, "I guess Carrie will spend Christmas here with you?" and was just as aghast over that remark as she had been over saying Ethan was merely her brother.

He raised his head, removed his arm from the mantel, and turned to face her. "Actually, she's hinting about a trip to Colorado."

"That sounds fun," Francine said, her voice flat.

"Of course, we'd stay in separate rooms." Ethan lowered his head and studied the oak coffee table, topped with an antiqued flower arrangement. His compulsive explanation of their sleeping arrangements was both embarrassing and awkward. A year ago, he wouldn't have even gone on such a trip without the safety of a group.

Despite her embarrassment, Francine couldn't stop looking at him. The lamp light's soft glow heightened Ethan's classic Latin appeal. As an eleven-year-old, she had often wondered why so many girls watched Ethan every time they went into public. Now she didn't have to wonder. And what was so refreshing was that Ethan seemed forever oblivious to his allure. She wondered if he even registered his dark brows, almond-shaped eyes, and square jaw when he looked in the mirror.

While keeping her features stoic, Francine shamelessly absorbed the impact. Even though she did appreciate his physical appeal, her love for him was based on so much more. She had never met a man of such solid character and strong morals…a man with such a heart for God and a commitment to doing His bidding.

At least, that's the way Ethan was before he met Carrie. The nagging worries wouldn't be denied. Nothing could be more romantic than the Colorado Rockies at Christmas. All Francine could do was pray that Ethan would stand firm in his morals until he saw just how shallow Carrie really was. She couldn't help but wonder if Miss Casper would have flown from Paris if Ethan had been only half as attractive. Mere physical attraction was no basis for a solid relationship.

The candle spread a cheerful and inviting fragrance across the room. The pleasing scent insisted all was well with the world. If only that were true. Her spirits low, Francine felt anything but uplifted. Instead, her back was stiff, and her throat was tight. But then, so was her heart.

Out of nowhere, a wave of raw jealousy crashed against Francine. The power of this unexpected emotion was so strong she nearly stumbled backward. *Oh, God, help me*, she inwardly groaned. *I will die if Ethan marries Carrie.*

Ethan broke the silence with a shocking question. "You really like Carrie, don't you?" he asked, then thankfully continued before she could answer. "She really likes you. I know that for certain."

"And you like her." Francine estimated that her whisper sounded more like a death sentence.

He didn't seem to glean that impression. Although his eyes were still wary, his smile was a bit more relaxed. "What makes you think that?" he teased.

Francine looked down at the cold fireplace and relived that awful moment when she caught Ethan and Carrie kissing. Hot remorse flashed across her. The fireplace blurred.

Shortly after she moved into the suite, Aunt Nora had insisted Francine not turn on the fireplace. She said the extra heat would undoubtedly be a luxury Tom wouldn't expect her to indulge in. Francine had dutifully obeyed. Although a few nights here lately she would have welcomed the flames, she was far from needing extra warmth now.

"I'm sorry you caught us earlier," Ethan admitted, his voice strained. "I shouldn't have let that happen."

"What—the kiss or getting caught?" Francine pressed her fingers against her lips in an attempt to stop any more inappropriate remarks. She didn't need a mirror to know her cheeks were fuchsia by now.

Ethan laughed. "Well, when two people are about to become engaged, I think a kiss or two is appropriate. Don't you?"

"So you really think she's the one?" Francine didn't pull her gaze from the porcelain fireplace.

"Of course!" he said, his voice a tad too enthused. "She's my dream woman."

Francine cut her glance toward Ethan. He no longer stood by the fireplace but now claimed the sofa. She couldn't decide if the edge to his voice was anxiety or an attempt to convince Francine that he was really in love.

"And she's okay with your being a minister?" Francine asked, voicing the worry that had nagged her since that day at the Worthingham Renaissance when Carrie made those horrible comments about clergymen.

"Uh…" Ethan fidgeted with the sofa's seam and looked away. "I'm really thinking about postponing my ordination until she's okay with all of it—even though I know she'll make a great pastor's wife. She's got such a good heart. But I don't want to rush her. I'm not sure she's ready to—"

"But you've worked toward this for years!" Francine, overtaken with sorrow, strode forward. Settling beside him on the couch, she gripped his arm. Now, it was *her* turn to sound anxious. "Ethan, you can't! You mustn't! What about God's call?"

"Maybe the Lord is calling me to marry Carrie first and then, when she's ready, I'll—"

"But what if she's never ready?" Francine leaned forward and peered into his very soul. What she had feared worst was happening. Ethan was so overcome by Carrie's feminine magnetism he was losing his ability to even hear the voice of God. Francine couldn't imagine that the same Lord who had called Ethan as a boy and directed him through all his studies and even given him a ministerial position would suddenly tell him to postpone his ordination. Francine had never been so possessed by such a fiery conviction. So strong was the feeling, she was even tempted to fall at Ethan's feet and beg him to reconsider.

I am the woman for you! The thought exploded across her agitation, and Francine held her breath to stop herself from speaking it. *I'm the one who can help you fulfill your call. Can't you see? I'm not just the same old Francine!* Her agitated cries metamorphosized into the heavenly wail of a breaking heart. *Oh, dear God, help him see!*

Panic flared in Ethan's eyes. He jerked his head back and began scrambling away from Francine. He sprang to his feet and fled toward the doorway.

"I can't talk anymore," he snapped. "I'll see you tomorrow—later." By the time he was passing into the hallway, he'd broken into a frantic sprint.

Francine covered her face with her hands and collapsed against the sofa's back. *What have I done?* she lamented. *Oh, Lord, please tell me he couldn't see what I was thinking!* A hot flood of mortification took her breath.

"What's the matter with Ethan?" Uncle Tom's voice erupted upon the room.

She jerked her hands from her face and straightened. Francine peered at her uncle and aunt who filled the room's entryway.

"He was just running up the hallway like the house was on fire or something," Uncle Tom continued. "He didn't even acknowledge us. Is everything okay?" He neared Francine. "Are you okay?" His heavy brows drew together. "Have you two had an argument or something?"

"Don't be silly, dear," Aunt Mariette murmured. "Ethan and Francine *never* argue."

"No, we didn't argue," Francine affirmed and stood to attention, "not really. I don't understand why Ethan was running." Her feet complained about the new pumps as she searched for anything to say. "I just—"

"Well, good. I guess we can chalk that one up to a man in love. They can do some really strange things, can't they, dear?" He smiled toward his wife, moved to her side, and bestowed a kiss on her forehead. Aunt Mariette slipped her hand along his back and returned the smile. Francine rarely saw her uncle and aunt in such an affectionate stance and attributed it to Tom's unusually good humor this evening.

Like a man with a purpose, he stepped back toward the door and snapped it shut. Francine, her mind still swirling in the wake of Ethan's departure, couldn't imagine why her aunt and uncle had come to the suite so late. Never had they visited her room at such an hour.

Twenty-Three

Uncle Tom, forever determined to get straight to the point, approached Francine. Without a word, he extracted a flat, wrapped gift from his shirt pocket and extended it to her. "This is your last gift from us," he declared.

A cold dread assaulted Francine. Wide-eyed, she looked at the thin gift wrapped in red. Her relief over the absence of such a package was too soon in coming. Not knowing how to react, Francine stammered, "But—but—you've already given me so much." She pointed to the pile of gifts on the sofa. Two tailored suits and a fur-lined coat crested the pile, each from her aunt and uncle.

"I know," Uncle Tom declared. "But this is the *important* present."

Aunt Mariette stepped to the back of the couch and rested her hands upon the top. "You've meant so much to me all these years, Francine," she quietly murmured. "This is the least we could do."

Francine shifted her gaze from her round-cheeked uncle to her thin-framed aunt. She once again observed the package, the size of a checkbook. Uncle Tom pressed the gift into her hands. Francine's fingers encircled the present, and her heart quaked.

"Tom wanted to give it to you when you got the rest of your gifts," Aunt Mariette explained, "but I told him we should wait until later. I was afraid it would be too overwhelming for you in front of everyone."

"After I thought about it, I decided Mariette was right. Besides all that, I was afraid you'd refuse to take it," Uncle Tom groused, "and then we'd have an argument in front of everyone."

She shifted her attention from the package to her patrons. Neither of them pretended that she wouldn't know what was inside. Aunt Mariette's softly lined face encouraged her to accept the honor. Uncle Tom's set jaw and stern eyes dared her to reject it.

"I...I don't know what to say," Francine stammered. Her heart hammered. The years of indebtedness swam before her. There was no way she'd ever be able to repay what her aunt and uncle had done for her...and now they had added a trust fund. At this point, she could only pray that it was a fraction of what the others got.

"Well, go ahead and open it," Tom said. "You might as well know up front, it's 500,000 dollars—the same as the other three."

"F–f–five hundred th–thousand?" Francine stammered. "*No!* Oh no!" She shook her head. "I—I can't! I simply can't," she wailed, feeling as if a crate full of gold bricks were being attached to her legs. She shoved the package back at Uncle Tom and released it. "I could never repay—"

"Who's asking you to repay a dime?" Tom bit out and barely caught the gift before it crashed to the floor.

"Don't be so gruff." Mariette slapped at his arm and moved to Francine's side. "I told you this would be traumatic for her."

"Traumatic?" Tom scoffed. "I know her well." He fidgeted with the change in his pocket. "She wouldn't take a piece of bologna from a king if she were starving. I almost never got her to take the watch last Christmas." He halted and peered into space for a second.

Then he appraised Francine again, his gaze as cutting as ever. Francine wished she could jump into bed and cover her head.

"I threatened to never speak to you once," he continued with renewed determination, "and I can do it again. I am your guardian, and I have been since you were eleven. I know what's best for you. If you want my good will, you'll take this offering, young lady."

"Well of course I—I want—your—your—" Francine struggled for every breath and blinked against a mortifying onset of tears. "I want your goodwill more than—more than anything," she squeaked out and sniffled. "I just don't—"

"There now, look what you've done, Tom," Aunt Mariette had never sounded so much like Aunt Nora. "You've made her cry." She snatched the red package from her husband's hand and placed her arm around Francine's shoulders. "Let's sit down," she insisted.

Dashing the hot tears from her cheeks, Francine obeyed. Aunt Mariette's floral perfume was as constant as Ike Gentry's presence at the brownstone.

"Now listen," Aunt Mariette continued in her soft and unassuming way, "one day you'll be glad you have this. Right now, it might seem overwhelming, but you'll be thankful you have a nest egg to fall back on." She lovingly slipped the thin gift into Francine's unsteady hands. "You don't even have to open it now. Just know that it's there, okay?"

Unaware of what else to do, Francine mutely nodded. She didn't really have a choice.

Uncle Tom released a grunt of expectation.

"Thank you," Francine wheezed and felt as if she'd just been bought for life. She imagined herself still here in fifteen years, still reading her aunt to sleep every night, still without a life of her own. Bleakly she wondered if she'd ever have the fortitude to stand up to her uncle on any front.

⌒ ⌒

Like Joseph fleeing Potipher's wife, Ethan rushed down two flights of stairs, into the entryway, and out the front door. But instead of fleeing a woman, Ethan was fleeing himself...his reaction to Francine. He couldn't fathom what he would have done if he'd stayed in her suite one second longer. When she'd leaned close to him, the urge to kiss her had nearly blotted out everything she said.

He slammed the brownstone's door and stepped onto the landing. Snatching at every breath, he welcomed the cold drizzle brushing his heated cheeks like a thousand icy feathers. The slap of tires on damp pavement accompanied the passing of several vehicles. The smell of the city reminded Ethan this was home. And home was across the street from Central Park. The park's lighted walkways beckoned him to lose himself in their twists and turns.

He ran to the corner and darted across the street. He barely registered the angry horn mere feet behind. Only when he was entering Central Park's patches of light and shadows did he allow himself to think about Francine. The very thought of her ethereal blonde hair, the slant of her delicate eyes, the fragile line of her heart-shaped face hurled him into a another headlong run. Blindly Ethan raced along the paved pathway, refusing to analyze the evening.

Finally, when his lungs burned and his feet protested that the loafers were not running shoes, Ethan crashed onto a park bench, propped his elbows on his knees, and rammed his forehead against his open palms. The clump of oaks behind the bench blocked the mist but offered heavier drops that had collected

⇜226⇝

upon weak, yellowing leaves. Sporadically, a wet dollop plastered his head and blended with the sweat trickling down his neck.

The smells of shrubbery and grass and fresh rain should have comforted and encouraged. Instead, they heightened his agony. Groaning, Ethan covered his face with his palms and scrubbed until his smarting cheeks couldn't take any more. He flopped back against the park bench, tilted his face toward the sky, and moaned, "Oh, Jesus, help me…"

Mental pictures of Francine played through his thoughts—a gallery of photos collected from years together. None of them resembled the woman who'd stunned him this evening. Eyes closed, he concentrated on the memory of the same sweet Francine the way she'd always been, especially before he left for Paris. His erratic pulse began to calm. His ragged breathing slowed to a manageable rate. His growing panic subsided.

If Francine hadn't revolutionized her appearance, Ethan would have gone through the evening without a problem. He fabricated the night as it should have gone, with Francine posed as her usual self. He'd have given her the necklace. She'd have hugged him. The kiss would have been—

"No," he corrected like a man talking in his sleep. "I wouldn't have even kissed her."

Then Carrie would have arrived. Ethan wouldn't have had a bit of trouble keeping his mind on her. Their kiss would have rocked the dining room. Now that his head was clearing, Ethan's gut stirred with the memory. The trip to Francine's suite would have been swift and helpful—nothing more.

"The end," he whispered and opened his eyelids. A cold drop flopped smack into the corner of his eye. "Oh man," Ethan bit out, his eye stinging. He stroked his eyelid until the discomfort subsided. A chill wracked his limbs, and his exercise-induced body heat began to fail him. Nevertheless, Ethan was determined to work through this problem and resolve the reason for his unusual reaction to Francine. He gazed across Central Park's shadowed acres toward the Manhattan skyline. The skyscrapers' late-night lights did little to inspire the needed solution.

On top of all that, there seemed to be no divine inspiration that would supply answers. But then Ethan hadn't spent as much time in prayer in the last few months as usual. Developing the relationship with Carrie had taken time from every aspect of his life. He attributed the answerless heavens to his own lack of communion with the Lord and mumbled, "I need to do better," but didn't take the time to assess how.

Instead, Ethan came to the only logical conclusion he could assume. *This thing with Francine is nothing but cold feet,* he told himself.

He'd heard several friends at school talk about how they felt just before they got engaged or married. A couple of them even shamefully admitted to having a secretive date "just to make sure" they were doing the right thing. One told Ethan he'd broken up with his fiancée out of sheer terror. When she married someone else a year later, he'd regretted his cowardice. Now his friend wished he'd gone through with the ceremony, but it was too late.

Ethan tried to imagine Carrie Casper married to another man. The very idea flamed his heart in hot disgust. Carrie was *his!* He wanted her as he'd never wanted another woman. She had led him to believe with every breath, every gesture, every expression that she felt the same and would gladly accept his proposal. Her only concern was that she wasn't quite ready to be a minister's wife. Ethan, buoyant in his budding love, had agreed to postpone his ordination until she was ready. That was only fair.

And that seemed to be the thing that had so upset Francine. Vaguely Ethan recalled her insisting he mustn't postpone his call, but he had been so enamored with the angelic woman only inches away he hadn't been able to fully comprehend her meaning or respond to her. Ethan decided Francine had simply been overreacting—despite the fact that overreacting wasn't her usual style. Once she got to know Carrie better, Francine would see just how suited her charming disposition was to ministry. Carrie just needed time to adjust, that's all. Ethan had waited years for his ordination. An extra year or two wouldn't kill anyone.

Another chill shook Ethan. He rubbed his hands together and stood. The sweat now coldly clung to his torso.

For the first time, he registered the faint lyrics of a Dean Martin swing classic echoing from the direction of the ice rink. He'd read in the paper that the park board decided to leave the ice rink open until midnight during the November–December holiday season. Ethan figured there were probably some couples in love still enjoying the romantic activity.

He imagined himself and Carrie floating along the ice together and smiled. Her curls hugged her face. Her eyes sparkled in adoration. Her sweet lips begged for more of his kisses.

I'm on the verge of asking Carrie to marry me, he thought. *Francine is out of the question.*

To finalize his decision, Ethan planned to shop for a ring Monday. Only a spectacular emerald surrounded by diamonds would suit Carrie. It would match her eyes…and the earrings she so loved. If Ethan couldn't find what he wanted, he'd have one custom made.

"Only the best for Carrie," he whispered and decided New Year's Day was the perfect time to present her the ring. He'd say something witty like "a New Year for a new engagement."

Two months would give him ample time to find the right ring. And if they extended their Colorado trip over New Year's, he could propose in the midst of the Rockie's fabulous atmosphere.

Ethan slipped his chilled hands into his pockets and started the lonely trek home. Before he had taken three steps, he finally allowed himself to admit that this reaction to Francine tonight hadn't been an isolated incident. Things hadn't been quite the same between them since he got home from Paris. He recalled how good it was to see her…how much he'd missed her while away. Next Ethan weighed his obsession with her disappearance at the Worthingham Renaissance, along with his aggravation over that businessman he thought was going to approach her.

Then there was the admiration he'd felt at Marie's wedding. Ethan could hardly keep his gaze off Francine that night. Even though she hadn't been nearly as glamorous as tonight, she looked every bit as pretty as she had at the Worthingham.

And tonight he'd also been eaten up with jealousy over Hugh's attentions to her. Before he left for Paris, Hugh said Francine reminded him of an angel. Tonight, Hugh's actions proved his claim. So Ethan had done his best to show the world Hugh's fixation for Francine didn't bother him in the least. He'd even suggested that golden rope Hugh gave her was a better fit for Wade's cross.

What a sham, he thought. His pace steady, Ethan acknowledged that he had some sort of a twisted problem. *Francine's supposed to be my sister,* he reminded himself and shuddered with self-revulsion. *The best thing that could happen would be if she married somebody like Hugh Casper,* he assured himself and tabulated some of the reasons a match with Hugh would work. Ethan convinced himself that the outgoing Hugh would help Francine overcome her shyness and give her financial security for life. Also, if Francine were happily married, it would ensure that Ethan could conquer this unexplained attraction for her.

Immediately, he began devising a scheme to protect Francine *and* his commitment to Carrie. Uncle Tom had repeatedly told him that the best means to avoiding temptation was to evade any activity or company that would place him in temptation's way. That motto had kept Ethan free of so many of the traps he'd seen his friends fall into—pornography, the partying crowd, and women who weren't suited for them. Therefore, the simplest solution would be to avoid Francine altogether. He would focus solely upon Carrie and no other woman. And if Hugh continued to pursue Francine and happened to propose, Ethan would encourage Francine to accept the golden opportunity.

Once he and Carrie were married, Ethan was sure he would be so ensnared with his new wife he'd be safe from temptation's lure. But for now and always, Francine Ponce would remain his little sister—and nothing more.

Twenty-Four

Francine, snuggling under an afghan in the den, finished the final lines of Dickens' *Great Expectations*. She stroked the last page and hated to see the end of yet another Dickens story. *Would that every author could be so great*, she thought and closed the book.

"What author do you want next, Aunt Mariette?" Francine glanced toward the sofa to find her aunt in a doze. Her brown hair curled around her face with the bounce of her new perm. Her head lolled against the back of the couch, her mouth drooped open. Aunt Mariette cuddled Daisy in the crook of her arm. The dog's light snores blended with her owner's.

As usual, Francine thought and checked her watch. Eight o'clock was but a few minutes away. They completed dinner over an hour ago. The staff would soon be leaving. Aunt Mariette would retire within the hour. Uncle Tom was still at the office. Aunt Nora had already gone to bed with a headache. Julie was spending more time at Marie's these days than at home. And

Ethan would probably sneak in after he was sure everyone was in bed.

Francine had seen him only on Sundays since her birthday party a month ago—and that was because he was part of the worship service. He left Sunday morning before she arose, spent the afternoon with Carrie, and returned to church for the evening service. His absence had been pure torment, which only increased by seeing him on the church platform and not being able to speak to him. The torture had increased until Francine had chosen to sit home with Aunt Mariette the last three Sunday nights.

Frowning, she pressed her fingers between her brows and tried not to think about the situation with Ethan. Despite her effort, one nagging thought prevailed: *Your best friend is no more.* Ethan hadn't even bothered to call the cell phone he'd hoisted upon her.

After their traumatic conversation a month ago, Francine prayed Ethan hadn't detected her love. As a result she gained an unexplainable peace that insisted nothing she had done clued him to her love. But lately she was inclined to believe that Ethan was purposefully avoiding her because he *did* know how she felt and was so disgusted he couldn't stand the sight of her.

The humiliation churned through her spirit. She wished she could hide from the whole human race, never to be seen again. Francine placed the book on the coffee table and covered her head with the afghan. She scrunched lower into the chair and hoped she might disappear. The smell of fabric softener did nothing to abate her stomach's rolling nausea. She longed for a 7-Up to ease the discomfort. The last few weeks, Francine had subsisted on 7-Up and soup. That was all her nervous stomach allowed her to hold down. She'd lost about ten pounds, and her pants were starting to bag on her. But so far, no one seemed to notice. And that was a good thing because Francine couldn't find her appetite.

On top of the strain of Ethan's absence, Hugh Casper had practically set up camp in their den. The guy appeared to be courting Francine like a beau in the eighteenth century. Several nights a week he arrived at their door. After Ike let him in, he'd sit in the den and chat with whoever happened to be there—usually Francine, Aunt Mariette, and Aunt Nora. While he blatantly showed favoritism to Francine, Aunt Nora was always so elated to see him anyone would think she was falling in love with him. The last thing the dowager tonight said before going to bed with her headache was, "I hate that I'll miss Hugh's visit. He's such a delightful boy."

Francine had remained silent, despite Aunt Nora's pointedly adding, "Some young ladies just don't know how lucky they are."

Since when is being chased by a womanizer luck? Francine thought. She threw the afghan off her head, pushed it aside, and stood. After folding the throw, she draped it over the back of the wing-backed chair. Francine gathered her book and headed toward the library.

I have done everything in my power to let the man know I'm not interested, Francine stewed. Silent hints and negative body language seemed lost on him. Francine was beginning to think she was going to have to bluntly tell Hugh to get lost. Until now, she hadn't possessed the valor for such a task. She'd never had to resort to blatant rudeness with any other man. But Hugh was by far the most thick-skulled of them all.

Entering the library, Francine wondered what she had already wondered dozens of times, *What does Hugh Casper want with me anyway?* Francine was miles removed from any of the glamor girls, like Marie, he must have chased in the past. And she *absolutely was not* going to have an affair with him!

In order to deter him, Francine had even begun washing off her makeup before dinner in hopes that he would see just how plain she really was. In her estimation, there was nothing more unattractive than a pale-skinned blonde with blonde lashes and eyebrows. Francine had often thought her eyes looked bald without the taupe eyebrow pencil and brown mascara she usually wore. But nothing seemed to deter Hugh—not even bald eyes. The guy told her two nights ago he liked her better without makeup because her eyes looked even bluer! So tonight she'd put on an extra layer of makeup.

"At least it doesn't look like he's coming tonight!" Francine huffed while laying the library book on the lamp table, on top of two other Dickens titles. She hiked up her sagging sweatpants and stepped toward the roll-top desk in the corner where her college text books sat. Finals were next week, and this was a good time to begin studying.

She'd never wanted to accept Wade's invitation to go home for Christmas more than now. Francine and her brother continued their steady e-mailing. Yesterday, Wade's e-mail had cryptically referenced a new, secretive job opportunity. He also implied that Francine needed to make up her mind about Christmas because if he did take the out-of-town job it might require him to work through the Christmas season next year. Therefore, this could be the last Christmas they could all be together for awhile. To add extra weight to his appeal, he threw in that Sandra was beside herself hoping that Francine would come.

If only I could just do what I wanted to do, she thought. Uncle Tom and Aunt Mariette were already making plans for their big Christmas party. As usual, they included Francine. Except this year, the pressure was higher because Marie was married and gone. And Julie and Ethan were home less and less.

Frequently Aunt Mariette mumbled, "You're just about all we have left, Francine."

The indebtedness to her aunt and uncle was about to make Francine's decision for her. The thin red present lying in her dresser drawer remained wrapped, but not undetected. The awareness of it traveled with her every step she made, forever insisting that she was not her own woman and never would be. Presently, she viewed herself staying in Manhattan for Christmas merely by default.

With a sigh, Francine pushed up her sweatshirt's sleeves and settled into the chair. Her children's literature studies would provide a welcome repose from her mental weight.

The doorbell's chime halted her opening the book. Francine's eyes widened. She stared at her watch. Eight o'clock was only five minutes away. Hugh had never arrived so late before. He usually showed up around five and sat until nine or ten. Even though he was off schedule, Francine sensed that the caller was Hugh. Her skin prickled along her spine. Her shoulders stiffened. She was nearly to the point of being able to detect Hugh Casper from five miles off.

She held her breath and listened. By the doorbell's second chime, Ike's predictable footfalls were crossing the entryway and nearing the door. Francine winced with every click of the doorknob. She dug her nails into the cover of the textbook and prayed for a reprieve.

"Hello, Hugh," Ike warily greeted. "We weren't expecting you this evening."

"Yes, I'm sorry I'm so late," Hugh offered. This time, he didn't bother to use the French accent. Francine wondered if he thought he was fooling her...or Ike.

Even though she and Ike had not discussed Hugh Casper, Francine recognized that the gray-haired employee doubted the young man. The look of reproach in Ike's intelligent eyes had been her sole source of support in rebuffing Hugh's advances—that and the memory of Hugh's appalling conversation with Marie. Everyone else in the family, including her uncle, remained delighted with Hugh's constant company.

"I'm assuming Francine is here?" Hugh asked.

"Yes. I believe you'll find her in the library."

Francine dropped the textbook on the desk and stood. How did Ike know where she was? She hadn't seen him when she left the den. But then Ike was as close to being omnipresent as any mortal Francine had ever encountered.

The men's footsteps neared the library, and Francine grabbed the back of the rolling office chair. Without contemplating her motives, she scooted the chair between herself and the door and tightened her hold. The men's shadows loomed in the entry seconds before they appeared.

When the two stepped into the library, Francine couldn't even look at Ike for the terror of observing Hugh Casper. He was dressed as he usually was in low-riding faded jeans and a turtleneck. With his retro, mop-style haircut, he looked like he should have been a member of the famous Beatles band. Neither their look nor their music had ever appealed to Francine. Her nausea returned with renewed fervor.

"Miss Franny," Ike stated. "Mr. Casper is here to see you." The statement was more a question. "Also, just so you know, your Aunt Mariette asked me to tell you she's going to bed now."

"Thank you, Ike," Francine acknowledged and focused upon the men's feet. Hugh's high-dollar sneakers claimed the fringe of the new Persian rug. Ike's shiny black lace-ups occupied the polished wooden floor.

"Would you like me to return with some refreshments?" Ike questioned.

Francine shifted her attention to the lean gentleman who had been her friend from the day he carried her rock-laden suitcase into the entryway. Ike's brown eyes suggested that if he returned with refreshments, it would be a good excuse to also check on her.

"Yes," she agreed and had never loved Ike more than now. "What would you like, Hugh?"

"Oh, nothing for me," he said and waved Ike away.

"I'd like a 7-Up, please," Francine said.

Ike raised his brows, and the deep lines around his eyes flexed in sequence. He took in Francine's figure and then said, "You're living on those these days, aren't you?" Even if no one else in the house saw Francine's weight loss, Ike wasn't fooled.

Francine lowered her head and shot him a look from the corner of her eyes. "Uh…if there are any of Katy's chocolate chip cookies—"

"I'll bring plenty," he agreed and whisked out of the room.

Hugh glared after him. "I didn't think he'd ever leave," he complained, then beamed toward Francine. "I've got some absolutely *wonderful* news," Hugh said in his French voice while waving a piece of folded typing paper.

Digging her fingers into the chair's back, Francine watched the paper flop with his movement. She couldn't imagine what Hugh Casper could know that was so wonderful and was equally challenged to even care.

"Come sit down. You'll be glad you're sitting when I tell you." Hugh motioned toward the striped sofa.

She hesitated, and Hugh hurried forward. He grabbed Francine's arm and drew her to the sofa. The whole time, Hugh babbled on about his own brilliance. "I think you're going to agree this was the most spectacular idea of the year," he claimed.

Silence was her only reply. Francine's jaw tightened. She stopped in front of the sofa's corner and came within a breath of refusing to sit. Hugh plopped onto the middle of the couch and looked up at her with the eagerness of a child at his first fair. A tinge of curiosity cavorted through her mind, and Francine lowered herself to the firm cushion. She tugged at one of the garnet-colored throw pillows and hugged it.

"Guess what this is!" Hugh chirped and unfolded the paper.

"What?" Francine asked, her voice wooden.

"It's an e-mail from Wade—your brother."

She leaned closer. "From Wade?" Francine queried, her defensive wall softening.

"Yes. Here!" Hugh shoved the message into her line of vision.

Francine, forgetting her indifference, released the pillow and gripped the paper. As she read the electronic note, the lamp's golden glow bathed the words in the aura of promise.

Hugh,

Consider this my acceptance. I'll be glad to report for work on January 2. No problem! Thanks again from the bottom of my heart! Please let me know when I can go public with this. I can't wait to tell Francine.

Yours,
Wade

The message's implications trickled into Francine's mind like a mountain stream, cool and refreshing. Hugh Casper had arranged for some sort of a job for Wade. Francine pulled in a lungful of the book-scented air, held her breath, and reread the note to verify her first impression. This answered the reason for Wade's ambiguous remarks in his last e-mail. Slowly exhaling, she riveted her attention upon Hugh—the man she had assumed was void of any humanitarian thought.

"This is about a job for Wade?" she asked.

"Yes." Hugh pumped his head up and down. "One of our Addy's in Boston was in bad need of a good assistant manager. The current manager—Lila's her name—didn't get along with the current guy at all. So I pulled some strings and got her to consider your brother. After they met and talked two days ago, Lila said he was perfect, and she gave the other guy his notice. That was part of the reason for all the secrecy. It's a small world, and—" Hugh shrugged.

"Of course, I understand," Francine agreed.

"Anyway, Lila really likes Wade's attitude and thinks he's going to be hard worker."

"Oh, he is," Francine assured. "One of the hardest workers I've ever seen." An unexpected rush of warmth spread through Francine's soul.

Hugh nodded and relaxed against the sofa like a conquering knight. "I talked them into starting him at 10,000 more a year than the usual salary, and..."

Francine rested the paper across the pillow and smiled at Hugh.

"...they're looking at putting him on track for a manager's position—if he's willing to take some classes along the way."

"He will be!" Francine claimed. "I *know* he will. Wade is a remarkable person." The increasing grin, all for Hugh, covered her face. "He just needs someone who'll believe in him, and—"

"Well, Addy's does, and so do *I*." His hazel eyes alight with triumph, Hugh caressed her features with his adoring gaze.

Her hands shaking, Francine covered her lips with her fingertips and scanned the letter again. All the while, she wondered if she had misjudged Hugh Casper. Furthermore, she began to suspect that his proclaimed interest in her was genuine and not just a frivolous flirtation. At least he was interested enough in her to help her brother.

She shoved the pillow back to its spot, folded the message, and pressed it next to her heart. "Do you mind if I keep this?" she asked, her eyes stinging.

"Not in the least," Hugh agreed.

"You don't know how much this means to me, Hugh." Francine inched closer. "I've worried off and on about Wade and even my other brothers and Sandra, my sister. There's no money for college, and—" the unopened trust fund upstairs drifted through her mind, "and something like this was exactly what Wade needed."

In her enthusiasm, Francine rested her hand on Hugh's arm while continuing to clutch the paper to her chest. "How can I ever repay you?"

Hugh laid his hand on top of Francine's and slid it to rest against his other hand. He wrapped her hand in both his and squeezed. His gaze embraced her in the way Ethan's did Carrie. Hugh's longing focus, heating with ardor, settled upon her lips and then roamed back to her eyes. Francine attempted to gently pull her hand from his, but he tightened his hold.

"Please," he begged, "don't shy away this time."

Francine's pulse quivered in her throat, and her startled mind tried to sort the implications of his actions.

"I might as well tell you, Francine," he said. "I've never felt for a woman what I feel for you. I—I've been about as patient as

I can. But now—now I can't hold back any more." He licked his lips, and his eye twitched.

Paralyzed with dread, Francine didn't speak.

"I don't think you're as unconscious of my love as you seem." Hugh paused, stared across the room, and swallowed hard.

Francine held her breath. Her previous dismay at the sight of Hugh returned tenfold. She could conjure no words to stop him and no strength to utter the words if her mind should form them.

"I guess what I'm trying to say…" Hugh hesitated and stroked her chilled cheek with the backs of his fingers, "is that you can repay me by becoming my wife."

"Your wife?" Francine's stomach rolled.

"Yes." He chuckled. "You should congratulate yourself, Francine Ponce. You've done what no other woman could do. You've irrevocably hooked me."

"No! Oh no!" Shaking her head, Francine yanked her hand from his and scrambled to her feet. She crumpled the message from Hugh against her damp palms. "I can—cannot believe you really mean—"

"But *of course* I mean it!" Hugh stood and rested his hands on her shoulders. "I mean every word of it, Francine. I love you!"

She released a garbled cry and stumbled backward until she bumped into the bookshelf. "No!" Francine repeated.

"Francine," Hugh persisted, his face bewildered, "do you understand what I'm offering?"

"I don't believe *you* understand, or…or…even *mean* what you're offering!" Francine moved away from the bookshelves and relived Marie's haunted claims of his offer of matrimony along with Hugh's emphatic denial. Perhaps Hugh's offer was his way of coercing yet another woman into his lustful clutches. This time, Hugh had chosen the wrong woman. Francine eyed the exit and prayed for a safe escape. Only minutes ago, she had begun to suspect that his interest was genuine. Now she wondered if Marie had been lulled into believing the same.

"I don't believe for one second you're serious about this!" she squeezed out.

"I've never been more serious in my life!" Hugh declared and raised his chin.

"Then get *un*serious," Francine countered and decided the time had come for blunt honestly. "I'm *not interested*, Hugh!" She observed the piece of paper in her hands. "And there's nothing you can do to make me interested! You can't even buy me with a job for my brother." She tossed the e-mail toward him and darted for the doorway.

"Francine!" Hugh exclaimed, his footsteps close behind. *"Francine!"*

Twenty-Five

Ethan opened the front door to the sound of Hugh Casper's frantic voice. "Francine, wait!"

Hugh's urgency propelled Ethan through the opening. With the crisp December air flooding past the open door, Ethan drank in the scene before him. Hugh stood at the library's threshold holding a piece of rumpled paper. Unaware of Ethan's presence, he gazed toward the stairway, where Francine pounded her way upward as if she were escaping an inferno.

"Please, Francine!" Hugh insisted and hurried toward the stairs.

Without a backward glance, Franny disappeared onto the second floor. The muffled sound of feet striking more stairs attested to her ascending to the third floor.

Ike, holding a tray laden with two cans of 7-Up, two glasses filled with ice, and some cookies, strode in front of the elevator. When he noticed Hugh, he slowed and scanned the entryway. His gaze rested upon Ethan, who realized he was standing by the ajar door. He swiveled to close the door when he caught sight of Tom Barrimore trotting up the brownstone's steps. His sleek white limo was inching away from the curb and into the Manhattan night.

"Hi, Dad," Ethan said and pulled the door wider for his father.

"Hello, Ethan." Tom's tired yet triumphant smile testified to another successful day on Wall Street.

Ethan turned and resumed his appraisal of the intriguing scene he'd interrupted. By this point, Hugh had pivoted to face Ethan. His disillusioned expression coupled with Francine's hasty retreat added up to one conclusion: Something disastrous had occurred.

The suit-clad Ike neared Hugh. "Do you still want the refreshments, Mr. Casper?" he asked. Even though his voice sounded as respectful as ever, his eyes reflected a less-than-enthused attitude.

The sudden realization of Ike's disdain shocked Ethan. He couldn't imagine what anyone could find annoying about Carrie's brother.

"Ike, there you are," Tom said from behind Ethan. "I know it's late, but I was going to ask you to see if Katy would get me something to eat before she goes home. I've not had dinner yet and I'm starved." Tom deposited his briefcase near his feet and was halfway out of his overcoat before he registered the room's tension. His alert gaze landed upon Hugh.

"What's with you?" he quipped. "You look like you just lost your best friend."

"I, uh…" Hugh hesitated and glanced over his shoulder toward the stairway. "Maybe we need to talk, sir," he finished and pulled on the neck of his sweater.

"Of course!" Tom replied.

Ethan closed the door and shrugged out of his leather jacket while Ike deposited the tray on an antique table near the piano room.

"Here, sir." Ike approached his employer. "I'll take your coat and case." He relieved Tom of his overcoat, picked up his case, then offered a one-handed assistance to Ethan in the final removal of his jacket.

"Better yet, Ike," Tom slipped off his charcoal-colored suit coat and loosened his red tie, "just get me a sandwich or two and bring them to the den. I'll take one of those 7-Ups if they aren't spoken for." He extended his coat toward Ike.

Accepting the burden, Ike silently inquired Hugh's desire.

"Like I said, I don't want anything, and Francine's gone to her room, I guess," Hugh replied. His shoulders slumping, he eyed the stairway again, looked at the piece of paper, and rubbed his forehead.

"Would you care for anything?" Ike asked, his attention on Ethan.

"I'll take a Pepsi." Ethan eyed the tray and noticed a plate of cookies near the 7-Ups. The subtle smell of freshly melted chocolate chips and warm walnuts tempted his appetite. "And maybe a couple of the cookies as well," he added. "Carrie and I just got home from dinner. She wasn't feeling well, so I'm home a little early tonight."

"I'll arrange everything, just as soon as I hang these up." Ike lifted the coats and hurried toward the closet tucked behind the staircase.

Ethan's plan to slip up to his room to avoid Francine wasn't necessary now. All month he had slithered into the shadows like some criminal. But the effort paid off. As he'd hoped, a steady diet of Carrie had distanced him from temptation. The only time he couldn't expunge Francine from his mind was during Sunday morning services, when his traitorous gaze sought her out in the crowd. Then there were the minutes before he fell to sleep when he was powerless to stop himself from wondering how her day went. And no matter how hard he tried, he failed to halt those dreadful dreams that promised heaven in Francine's arms.

Stiffening his shoulders, Ethan honed his attention to what Tom was saying.

"…in the den, we can talk." Tom graciously extended his arm toward the den, and Hugh strode forward.

Ethan marched after his father and entered the den as Tom settled into his favorite wing-backed chair and motioned for Hugh to take the other one. Ethan claimed the corner of the camel-backed couch and propped his ankle on his knee. The vague scent of rose potpourri tinged the air. For as long as Ethan remembered, his mother had harped at the maids to freshen the potpourri every week.

"Now, what gives, Hugh?" Tom questioned, the crease between his brows deepening.

"There's no sense beating around the bush." Hugh rested his head against the chair and stared at the chandelier. "I proposed to Francine."

Tom straightened and smiled. "Really?"

Ethan ground his teeth together and refused to allow himself to feel anything but satisfaction. This was exactly what he had hoped for. Francine would marry Hugh. He would marry Carrie. And this insane longing in his gut would cease to exist. Casually he rubbed his hand across the front of his ribbed sweater. The plan was almost complete.

He examined Hugh, who was in the middle of more details. "…so after I told her about the job…" Hugh held up the piece of paper and tossed it toward the coffee table in front of the sofa. The paper sashayed toward the floor and landed on the rug with an awkward swoosh. "…she asked me how she could ever repay me. I told her she could repay me by becoming my wife."

When Hugh showed no signs of retrieving the paper, Ethan did. He laid it atop the coffee table and skimmed it in the process. Wade's brief e-mail referenced the job Hugh mentioned.

"That's when she went ballistic on me and ran out of the room!" Hugh raised his hand. He leaned forward, propped his elbow on his knee, and rested his forehead against his fist.

Uncle Tom placed his elbows on his chair's arm. After making a tent of his fingers, he rested his chin on his fingertips. "You rushed her," he said and looked to Ethan for confirmation.

"I would agree with that," Ethan said and offered Hugh an encouraging nod. "Francine always needs time to process anything."

"Time?" Hugh groaned and raised his head. "I've been—been—" He flopped against the back of the chair, rapidly blinked, and pressed his lips together, "—courting her for two months! Surely she should have realized—"

"Francine has a very delicate disposition," Tom added with a solemn nod. "Things that don't shock most women send her into..." He shook his head. "Sometimes I think I still don't have her figured out."

But I do, Ethan thought and absently watched the flames flickering in the gas fireplace. *I know her well.*

"She gets embarrassed so easily," Ethan explained. "She was probably so overwhelmed by the compliment she just ran." He shifted his attention toward Hugh. "All she needs is someone to calm her down and talk to her."

"You really think so?" A veil of relief relaxing his features, Hugh leaned forward.

"That's a good idea." Tom scooted to the edge of his chair just as Ike entered the room with a tray of sodas and cookies.

"Katy is preparing your sandwiches, sir," he explained. "Meanwhile, here are the other things."

Tom nodded and paid no more attention to Ike. Claiming the can of Pepsi and a glass of ice before Ike set the tray on the coffee table, Ethan poured the fizzing liquid and tried to shove aside the notion that he should break his vow to avoid Francine. Perhaps he should try to talk some sense into her. Proposals like this didn't come every day, and she might not ever have a better opportunity for a better man. Ethan had always been able to sway Francine, especially when he appealed to her logic. As he sipped the effervescent soda, he wondered if his desire for Francine to marry Hugh was really for her benefit or for his own convenience.

"I think I'll go talk with her now," Tom said.

He hoisted his hefty frame upward and ended Ethan's debate about talking with her tonight. If his dad was going up now, Ethan determined to save his conversation for another day. With some luck, Tom would convince Francine she should marry Hugh, and Ethan wouldn't be forced to be alone with her. If their last encounter was anything to go by, the affects of connecting with Francine were too unsettling.

"But before I do go," Tom peered down at Hugh, "I want to make doubly sure you *are* serious in your proposal."

"I've never been more serious about anything in my life!" Hugh claimed, his French accent adding finesse to his vow.

"Good," Tom stepped toward Hugh, laid his hand on his shoulder, and looked him squarely in the eyes, "because I *will* get her to agree—I always do, you know. And once I do, there's no going back. Understand?" His question held the undertone of a threatening father who cherished his charge.

His eyes earnest, Hugh sat up straight. "Of course, sir!" he said over a compulsive swallow. "I'm committed for life!"

Francine gave the chair a final shove and backed away from the door that connected her suite with the home that Hugh and Carrie were renting. She double-checked the deadbolt lock and examined the back of the chair, securely wedged beneath the knob. Francine prayed the lock and chair would ensure Hugh couldn't break into her room. While she had always made sure her door was locked, the events of this evening sent her into a dizzy desire for safety.

Whether Hugh Casper was trying to lure her into an affair or he really was serious was anybody's guess. Whether Francine trusted him or not was no longer in question. She did not—especially not tonight.

Content with her efforts at the door, Francine hurried to her dresser and retrieved her cell phone. After checking to make sure it was charged, she put the phone on her nightstand beside her brass bed. For the first time since Ethan coerced her into taking the phone, Francine was thankful she had it.

She hastened to her dresser and retrieved the pink flannel nightgown Sandra had sent for her birthday. First, she would change into her gown, remove her makeup, and then snuggle into bed with a mystery novel that would raise her hair. Hugh's upsetting visit required drastic measures. Mary Higgins Clark usually so engrossed Francine she couldn't think of anything else until the novel was complete. She approached the bookshelf near the suite's main entrance and removed the new novel from the shelf. The glossy cover pulled her in and promised a story riveting enough to blot out Hugh and the whole wretched ordeal.

Francine strode back to her bed and tossed the hardbound book against the row of blue and cream pillows. She swiveled toward the bathroom, but a rap on her door stopped her cold. Francine's eyes widened, and she stared at herself in her dresser mirror. The pallid woman who gazed back appeared to have just undergone the gravest trauma.

Hugh Casper! she thought. *He chased me up here!* What little color Francine *did* have began to drain from her cheeks. Twin splotches of peachy blusher was all that remained. She clutched her gown and hovered in quavering silence. The chill in the room increased her shivering, and she wished for the fire Aunt Nora denied her.

Another knock made Francine jump.

"Francine?" Uncle Tom's encouraging voice floated through the doorway. "Are you up?"

She slumped and released her breath. "Y–yes," Francine squeaked out. Stumbling toward the door, she dropped her gown on the couch. Without hesitation, Francine turned the lock and opened the door for her uncle.

He eyed her with dubious intensity. "May I come in?" Tom queried.

"Sure." Francine swung open the door and allowed him to pass. She followed him as far as the couch and stopped near the armrest. Francine clutched the couch's arm and stood straight.

Head bent, Uncle Tom paced toward the fireplace, turned, and stopped. He studied Francine for several seconds, frowned, and looked back at the fireplace. "Are you cold, my dear?" he asked.

"Well..." Francine said, "I g–guess a little, maybe."

"Then why haven't you lit your fireplace? It's here for you to use, you know."

"Yes, but Aunt—Aunt Nora said I shouldn't—"

With a growl, Uncle Tom grabbed the butane lighter lying atop the mantel and lit the gas fireplace. The flames jumped in merry celebration, and he laid the lighter back on the mantel. "There!" he said. "Tell Nora I said you can burn the thing as much as you like. Understand?"

Francine nodded and lowered her head. She had no idea why Uncle Tom was here. She could count on one hand the number of times he had come to her room. The last time he came was to deliver the trust fund checkbook. Francine hoped he wasn't going to take her to task for not accessing the money. She also hoped he wouldn't chastise her if she used some of it for her brothers and Sandra.

The dark circles under Uncle Tom's eyes and his tired-looking tie and rumpled shirt indicated a long day at the office. The irritable tilt of his lips told her he didn't expect to be crossed. Francine cringed and eyed the pink gown sprawled across the couch's cushions and wished for her home in Rockaway more than ever.

"I've been downstairs talking with Hugh Casper," Uncle Tom said at last.

Francine moved in front of the couch and collapsed onto the striped cushions. She pulled the gown onto her lap and wadded the soft folds. Not knowing where this conversation was leading, Francine studied the antiqued roses and brass vase in the center of the coffee table.

"He told me he proposed to you tonight. Is that true?" His tone held the same nuance of disapproval he'd used when she tried to reject the watch last Christmas.

She mutely nodded while a hard tremor started at the center of her soul. Surely Uncle Tom wouldn't expect her to marry Hugh Casper. *But what if he does? How can I ever tell him no?*

"Hugh also says you declined his offer."

Francine nodded again.

"And he seems to think you won't even consider his offer. Am I right?"

"Yes," she whispered.

"Hugh's a little confused, and I can't say that I blame him… considering the way you turned him down. In his words, he says you went ballistic and ran out of the room."

Francine lifted her gaze to her uncle. She shook her head. "I— I couldn't get him to understand that I wasn't interested," she defended.

"Would you care to share why you aren't interested in even considering his proposal?" Uncle Tom's forehead wrinkled.

"I…" Francine grappled with what to say. In a flash she relived that conversation between Hugh and Marie and the promise she'd made to Marie that she wouldn't tell anyone about the affair. She considered telling Uncle Tom she thought Hugh Casper was a lecher, but she possessed no proof of the criticism. Finally she landed upon the one truth that she could voice.

"I don't love him," she admitted and squeezed the button on her gown until it bit into her fingertip. A comforting warmth, accompanied by the smell of burning natural gas, began to spread across the room, but it did little to ease Francine's cavorting nerves.

"Ah, love." Uncle Tom settled beside her on the couch. He extracted her hand from the gown and enveloped it between his in a gesture much like Hugh's.

"Listen, Franny," he began, "such proposals don't come every day. Even if you don't think you're madly in love with Hugh now, you can grow to love him over time. He's a good catch. I'm sure many, many women have tried. He's worth billions, Francine." Uncle Tom leaned closer and bore his icy blue gaze into hers. "That trust fund we gave you is mere pennies compared to what Hugh can offer. You'll be secure for life!"

Shaking her head, Francine rasped, "But I…I don't love him."

"Love will come!" Tom declared. "Besides, he says he loves you. By the looks of the poor guy, I'd say he's got enough love for the both of you," he coaxed.

"No—no, he—he doesn't." Francine tugged her hand from her uncle's and adamantly shook her head. *He doesn't love me at all,* Francine thought. *He just wants me in that sick way he wanted Marie. If I were stupid enough to marry him, he'd probably find another woman he wanted on our honeymoon.*

"Are you disputing my word?" Uncle Tom demanded, his tone taking on a hard edge.

Francine jumped. She hunched her shoulders. Never had she stood her ground when her uncle's voice went hard. But this time a surge of courage rose from within and urged her not to crumble. This was her life on the line. Marrying Hugh Casper would mean emotional death. Her stomach threatened to unload her light supper, and she wished for the 7-Up.

Even though she stared straight ahead at the ivory-colored wall, Francine sensed her uncle's ire rising. She also detected his wordless attempt to bend her will to his.

Oh dear God, help me! she cried and somehow conjured the strength to resist.

"The least you could do is give Hugh a chance to prove himself," Tom said, his steady words rumbling with disapproval.

"No," Francine quietly asserted.

"No?" Uncle Tom spewed. "No? Just like that?" He snapped his fingers in front of Francine's face, and she tucked her chin against her chest. "You refuse to even give it a chance? Have you lost your mind?"

She crossed her arms and huddled toward the couch's corner. Francine wondered if Uncle Tom was already counting his commissions should the Caspers choose him as an investment consultant. Her marrying Hugh would probably result in exactly that. Aunt Nora mentioned last week that Ricky Worthingham's parents had shifted some of their capital to Tom's management since Marie and Ricky's marriage.

Uncle Tom stood and began pacing in front of her like a panther ready to pounce on his prey. "Of all the hard-headed, stubborn, insubordinates I've ever met," he growled, "you top them all! I took you in as my own. I've treated you like a daughter. I've given you every advantage in life imaginable. Most young women your age would *die* for half of what you have! And you return all that kindness with a cold and constant refusal to even consider marrying the man I think you should marry?"

Francine bit her lips. Silent tears slipped from her rapidly blinking eyes and dropped onto the gown she still gripped. The temptation to tell her uncle everything almost couldn't be denied, but she simply could not break her word to Marie.

Besides, she thought, *even if I do tell him the truth, Marie and Hugh both would probably deny it.* From there, Francine mentally detailed the natural sequence of events. Carrie would be furious that Francine slurred her brother's name. Ethan would most likely take Carrie's side. And Francine could only imagine Aunt Nora's part in the whole mess. She would probably lecture Francine for a year about the ills of lying.

Uncle Tom stopped pacing. Francine, her head still lowered, observed his leather shoes and braced herself for another assault.

"You have pushed me to the limits of my patience," he growled. Once again he silently compelled her to do his bidding. "You are showing me a side of you I never imagined existed.

When it comes down to it, you're more stubborn than Marie and Julie both put together. I have never—"

A sob erupted from Francine. She covered her face and began to rock back and forth. "Oh please—please just go!" she begged.

Uncle Tom responded with deathly silence.

Francine released a series of broken wails and then managed to control herself long enough to speak. "I'll pack my things and go back—go back home to Rockaway as soon as this semester is over," she rushed. "I'll get out of your life and out—out of your way and ask for nothing. They want me home for Christmas, and I'm going. I'll be gone by the end of next week and you won't have to—have to look at me anymore. Just please, please st–stop!" Francine released a cough and continued her rocking.

"You're going home for Christmas?" Tom asked, his voice incredulous. "Without asking me?"

"Y–yes," Francine replied. "I'm going home." She lowered her hands and used her gown to mop her face. The very words brought comfort to her throbbing soul and promised a new start without the pressures and complications of Central Park. Unless the atmosphere changed, Francine might not even return. The thought brought a surge of relief as well as bucketsful of fresh worries.

"Humph," Uncle Tom said and trudged toward the fireplace. When he stopped, he turned around, and she felt his glare.

Francine considered how she was going to survive away from Central Park. She glanced toward her dresser's top drawer where lay the trust fund. She had been considering using the money to help her family. But now she loathed touching a penny of it. Aside from that money, Francine had quietly saved a few thousand dollars out of her weekly allowance. That money would aid her in renting her own apartment near the college.

Furthermore, she considered a teaching position that had been offered her starting in January. The elementary school was willing to let her begin with an emergency teaching certificate until she finished her degree. Francine had turned down the offer because the combined weight of finishing school and teaching had seemed far too great. Now she determined that she had no choice. She could not continue at Central Park under Uncle Tom's disapproval. The very thought made her feel as if she were suffocating.

"You know," Uncle Tom said, "I think going to Rockaway is probably the smartest thing for you to do right now."

Francine quirked her brows and dared observe his face. His calculating stare suggested more was coming.

"You haven't been home since we got you. I'm sure you've forgotten how bad it is. A few weeks there, and you'll remember what poverty is really like, and maybe you'll appreciate what we've done for you and what Hugh Casper is offering."

Somehow Francine managed to hold his hard gaze. The fierce eyes that usually guaranteed her compliance did nothing to change her mind. Instead she gained new determination with every second that passed.

"I am not for sale," she simply stated, her cheeks cooling with the drying tears. "I'd rather live in poverty my whole life and be—be my own woman than be filthy rich with a man I don't love and have no capacity or intention to love." Her soft voice held the strength of her resolve.

Tom blinked. His mouth twitched. A ripple of surprise scurried across his features. He looked down, straightened his shoulders, and marched toward the doorway. "I'm going downstairs to tell Hugh to be patient," he said. "I still believe you'll come around given time, especially after the visit to Rockaway has taken its toll."

"But…" Francine stood and watched her uncle's retreat. She slumped back onto the couch, shook her head, and sighed. Her Christmas trip couldn't come soon enough.

Twenty-Six

Ten days later Francine sat in the den with her aunts and awaited the arrival of Uncle Tom's white limousine. This morning at breakfast her uncle informed her that he was arranging for Ike to drive her to Rockaway. Since Francine had planned to hire a taxi, her first intention was to protest the luxury. Uncle Tom's silent dare stopped her from offering one peep of resistance.

She lowered her Agatha Christie novel and glanced toward her aunts, both tucked into the wing-backed chairs, both engrossed in reading of their own. The smell of applejack potpourri mingled with the aroma of Mariette's raspberry tea, steaming on the lamp table. An orchestra's rendition of "I'll Be Home for Christmas" floated from the corner stereo. Francine allowed her gaze to roam the luxurious room bedecked in holly and wreaths and holiday finery. She attempted to remember the details of the less-than-ritzy home in Rockaway. Francine recalled her last Christmas at home. She and Wade and Sandra had decorated a tired pine tree with faded tinsel and strings of popcorn.

Now all she could do was imagine the embarrassment of arriving at her parents' humble house in her uncle's glossy car.

Francine could already sense the potential friction of the "long lost daughter" returning like a queen while the rest of the family struggled to survive.

But little do they know I might be struggling on my own once I leave them, she thought. Her fingers flexed against the book, and she avoided looking at her aunts again. No one knew her intention to move near her college—not even Aunt Mariette. It was for her sake that Francine had wavered in her initial determination to leave Central Park.

Furthermore, when Francine inquired about the teaching job, she'd been informed that the position was already filled. That blow had further weakened her resolution. Francine's only option now involved applying for a part-time job on campus and trying to stretch her savings as far as she could. The temptation to dip into the trust fund was great. But she left the checkbook in her drawer and prayed every night for God's divine provision for her future. She hoped the trip home would empower her to continue with her plans to move. She certainly needed to get away from Hugh Casper, even if that meant disappointing Aunt Mariette.

Hugh had continued to visit Francine as if she never rejected his proposal, and Uncle Tom had persisted in his silent coercion. She could hardly wait for Ike's arrival with the limo. Hopefully Hugh or Uncle Tom wouldn't arrive in an attempt to block her leaving.

Intending to sweep all these worries from her mind, Francine sharpened her concentration on the mystery novel she hoped would dash aside her anxieties. So far the words only blurred into the musings of her distracted mind.

"We're going to miss you, Francine," Aunt Mariette pined as she had the last several days. "Daisy and I won't know what to do these next couple of weeks. I'm already wishing for you to come back home."

Francine closed her book and attempted a smile. Daisy hopped out of her owner's lap and padded toward her second-favorite person in the household. Francine tapped the sofa cushion, and Daisy hopped to her side. She stroked the dog's velvety ears and observed her aunt. While Mariette's softly lined face brought back memories of cozy afternoons reading by a warm fire, it also reminded Francine of the mother who awaited her arrival. She glanced toward her leather luggage, purse, and laptop case sitting just inside the den. A mixture of anticipation and doubt overwhelmed her. For the first time, Francine wondered if she might regret leaving Central Park.

"I'll miss you, Aunt Mariette," she affirmed.

"If you have half an ounce of common sense, you'll miss Hugh Casper as well," Nora mumbled, never once taking her gaze from the *Reader's Digest* she clutched in bony hands. Nora's fiery-red house dress perfectly matched the shade of her thin lips now pulled into a disapproving line. "I really thought you had more sense, Francine."

"Oh Nora," Mariette softly chided. She fiddled with the neckline of her velour pantsuit and eyed her sister. She continued as if Francine weren't present, "You and Tom need to let Francine make her own choices. She'll come to the right conclusion on her own if you'll just leave her alone. Anyone can see Hugh is a good catch. Francine has eyes." Mariette smiled toward her niece.

Francine shrank into the couch's corner. This was the closest Aunt Mariette had come to saying she sided with her husband. Francine imagined herself returning to Central Park and the whole household ganging up on her. Without knowing it, Aunt Mariette had just given Francine one more reason to rent her own apartment.

The front door's opening instigated a dutiful "woof" from Daisy. Nora lowered her magazine and gazed into the entryway. Francine, certain the person must be Ike, scooted to the couch's edge. Before rising, she turned and peered past the nine-foot Christmas tree covered in tiny red lights. The tree left only a two-foot strip of window uncovered, but that was enough for Francine to determine that no white limo was parked at the curb.

"It's just Ethan," Nora stated without expression. "Looks like you don't get to escape as soon as you'd hoped."

Pretending she didn't hear Nora, Francine focused upon Daisy and stiffened. She and Ethan hadn't exchanged a word since her birthday party. This morning, when she got up, she wondered if he would allow her to leave without even a goodbye. Initially, the notion both relieved and pained her. When she endured breakfast with no sign of Ethan, the pain overrode the relief. However, she'd wondered what she would say to him if he did arrive for her departure. Francine couldn't come up with one appropriate word. She was beginning to think the two of them had nothing left to say to each other...but at the same time she prayed the assumption wasn't so.

Ethan's footsteps halted inside the den. His presence filled the room...and Francine's heart. She didn't dare take her focus from Daisy. This was the closest they'd been since the night he helped her take her birthday packages to her suite. Francine hadn't even hinted to Ethan that she was seriously thinking about moving out on her own. He was so wrapped up in Carrie, she wondered if he'd even care—or notice.

"Hey, I was hoping I'd catch you still here, Franny."

"Of course she's here," Aunt Mariette said. "Ike isn't due for another half hour."

Her head lowered, Francine darted an upward glance toward him. The short-lived glimpse revealed that Ethan looked as great as ever. His fashionably faded jeans were topped with a black sweater that made his dark eyes appear full of promises and mysteries. Achingly, Francine knew the promises and mysteries were all for Carrie. She pinched the hem of her knee-length skirt and told herself not to feel.

"Uh...Mom, do you mind if Francine and I have a private chat in the library?" Ethan asked.

Francine's attention riveted upon him. The last thing she needed was a "private chat" with Ethan.

"Of course, dear," Mariette agreed and picked up her book. "We've all said our goodbyes until we're weary. I'm already missing Francine, and she's not even gone yet. Aren't you, Nora?" Mariette directed a heavy-eyed gaze toward her sister.

Nora vaguely nodded and continued her reading.

With a jolly smile, Ethan approached Francine and offered his hand to assist her standing. Francine wondered what he would do if she refused to go with him. Ethan hadn't bothered to ask her if she wanted to talk with him in the library. Instead, he'd asked Aunt Mariette's permission and assumed Francine would comply with his wishes.

But isn't that the way it always has been? Francine questioned. *I just go along with everything everyone wants and do my best to keep the peace, even if that means my own discomfort.* The disturbing thoughts were short-lived and potent. She stored them in the back of her mind and decided to revisit them later. For now, Francine chose to continue keeping the peace. She placed her hand in Ethan's and stood while Daisy abandoned the couch for Mariette's chair.

Ethan didn't want to release her hand. Something inside him insisted he hang onto his childhood friend and not let her go. He released her hand anyway. This meeting wasn't about Ethan and Francine. It was about *Hugh* and Francine.

He stopped at the den's doorway and allowed Francine to pass before him. She wore an oversized sweater and a corduroy skirt that stopped at the center of her knees. A pair of dark tights and sensible flats finished the outfit.

He compared Carrie's short skirts, high heels, and bare legs to Francine's demure attire. While Carrie's long legs were always appealing, he had to admit that Francine usually looked more appropriate—especially for ministry events. Absently, Ethan wondered how to approach the subject with Carrie. A few hints might be in order before the church Christmas banquet next week. He wondered if Carrie would consider a nice pantsuit. The idea struck him to make the purchase himself and infer that she might enjoy wearing the new suit for the banquet.

Maybe I'll ask Francine what she thinks, Ethan mused.

But the second Francine stepped inside the library, lowered her head, and shot a brief glimpse toward him, he forgot all about Carrie and her inappropriate wardrobe. Franny crossed her arms and took on the uneasy stance he'd seen her use any time she was uncomfortable. And Ethan realized he wasn't dealing with his "Francine tease." He was dealing with Franny-mouse. He couldn't remember the last time she'd acted so shy with him.

Perhaps the first day I met her, he thought and strode toward the recliner.

That day flowed through Ethan's mind. She had been so small and helpless and scared. Ethan's brotherly instincts kicked in from the beginning of their acquaintance. Soon, their relationship blossomed into the easy friendship he'd counted on ever since. Francine hadn't felt the need to be shy with him since those early days…until now.

Ethan started to sit in the recliner. When he noted Francine hovering near the bookshelves, he chose to walk behind the recliner instead. He laid his hands on the back of the overstuffed chair. Once he realized he was using the chair as a barrier between himself and Francine, he fidgeted with his belt loop, thought about moving closer to her, and then rested his hand back on the recliner.

He possessed no idea how to begin the conversation. An awkward silence descended upon the room. Only the faint strings of the Christmas classic "Sleigh Ride" offered a reprieve from the hush. The whole month of December, his mother always insisted upon the continual playing of holiday music. The tradition had become a family hallmark, as dependable as Francine Ponce always spending Christmas at Central Park.

But this year, his Francine was going away. For some reason, Ethan couldn't quite get over the feeling that she might not be back. A hollow emptiness filled his soul, and he told himself his worries were in vain. Francine would never move out until Dad gave his permission, and he seemed as attached to her as ever.

Ethan silently drummed his fingers along the back of the recliner, stared at the stack of novels on the lamp table, and attempted to rein his mind into the task at hand. He had promised not only Hugh, but also Carrie and his dad that he would talk with Franny regarding Hugh's proposal. They all seemed to think Ethan could influence her more than any other. Ethan still clung to the belief that once Francine married Hugh and he married Carrie, his out-of-character attraction to her would die.

Presently, her appeal was far from dead. And he couldn't even blame it on the power of a professional makeover this time. Francine's hair was in a simple ponytail; her makeup, far from dramatic. She wasn't even wearing that sophisticated perfume she'd worn the night of her birthday party. All Ethan had detected when she passed him was a hint of her usual soft scent.

Despite it all, Ethan's mind still suggested he should wrap his arms around Francine in an embrace that offered more than brotherly affection. He tugged on the neck of his sweater and wondered why Ike didn't set the thermometer at least ten degrees cooler. This encounter was swiftly becoming as distracting and stressful as the last one, and Ethan hadn't even spoken yet.

Twenty-Seven

"When are you and Carrie leaving for Colorado?" Francine's question barged into Ethan's thoughts.

His gaze snapped straight to her blue eyes, which were as cool as the New York sky.

"We aren't," he simply stated and hoped his attempt to cover his attraction to Francine was successful.

"Oh." Francine looked away and ran her fingertips along the edge of the bookshelf. Her silent curiosity couldn't be denied.

"I...I...I heard you weren't going to be here for Christmas, so I decided I should stay," he explained. "Marie's gone now and is throwing her own Christmas parties. Julie might as well be gone, as much as she stays at Marie's. I just couldn't see leaving Mom and Dad alone these next couple of weeks. They'd be going from a full house to an empty nest in one year. Of course, we'll all be here Christmas night for the big family bash." He shrugged. "Everyone but you."

"And Carrie's fine with all that?" Francine's voice sounded as disinterested as her expression looked.

Ethan shrugged again. "Sure," he said. "I guess she'll have to be."

She examined the books and didn't offer a response.

Ethan didn't reference Carrie's pouting fit over his decision against the Colorado trip. It had been their first quarrel. However, he'd stood firm. Not only was the Christmas issue a problem, Ethan had also begun to worry about the appearance of his traveling alone with a gorgeous woman to a Colorado resort. He had never allowed himself to be placed in a situation where gossip could abound. After a few of Pastor Steve's well-placed hints, Ethan realized his pending mistake. The last thing he needed to do was compromise his reputation, especially after deciding to postpone his ordination.

Looking back, Ethan wondered why he even agreed to the excursion in the first place. The memory of Carrie's kisses, of her passionate green eyes hinted at a reason Ethan chose to ignore. Ironically, when he also told Carrie he was worried about the appearance of their traveling alone, she hadn't shared his concerns. At the time, he chalked it up to naiveté and didn't care to revisit that assessment.

"I'm glad you aren't going off by yourself like that," Francine finally said. "I was afraid it wouldn't look good. I mean—even though you were getting separate rooms and all…" Her gaze still averted, she pressed her fingertips to her lips.

"Yes, I know," Ethan admitted with a comforting tone. "After I thought about it awhile, I came to the same conclusion."

Francine looked him full in the face. "I'm so glad," she said. Her posture shifted. Her expression grew less guarded. Some of the reticence faded, and Ethan caught glimpses of the Francine he'd grown to depend upon. The way his gut tightened, Ethan didn't know whether he should be glad she was relaxing or more wary than ever.

"I guess I can propose in New York as easily as I can in Colorado," he said with an attempt at a carefree smile. "This is probably one of the most romantic cities in the world, and it has an unmatched park." He gestured toward Central Park. "What more could a woman want?"

Francine crossed her arms again and hunched her shoulders. Ethan had never seen her so without expression. Maybe this was the reason Hugh was on the verge of howling at the moon. Ethan couldn't imagine trying to woo a woman who was as emotionless as Francine was now.

"Have you already gotten the ring?" Her barely discernible question held little interest.

"Yep." Ethan stroked the recliner. "I had it custom made. It's an emerald surrounded by diamonds—a *big* emerald," he added and nearly winced at the price he'd paid.

"I guess it's one-of-a-kind." Francine peered past him.

"Of course," Ethan acknowledged and decided now was as good a time as any to introduce the reason for this visit. "I understand Hugh wants to buy an engagement ring, too."

Francine ducked her head and didn't answer.

Ethan could almost hear Carrie, Hugh, and his dad urging him to push a little more. "Aren't you even going to give the guy a chance?" Ethan asked.

"You think I should marry him, too, Ethan?" Francine lifted her gaze to his, and this time her eyes held the ache of a soul betrayed. "Of all people, I thought—" She shook her head and turned her back to him.

Confused, Ethan shifted his feet and was propelled to move closer. The last thing he wanted was Franny upset with him. He stepped around the chair, neared her, and placed his hand on her shoulder. "Franny?" he said.

Her back still to him, Francine lifted her head. "Tell me the truth, Ethan. Did Uncle Tom ask you to talk me into marrying Hugh?"

"Uh...actually, if you want the *truth*—"

"That's all I ever want."

"Well, Dad's not the only culprit. Carrie and Hugh also asked me to talk with you. Carrie likes you so much she wants you to marry Hugh almost as much as *he* does."

Francine heaved a deep breath. "I'm not going to marry him," she said, her voice as solid as a brick.

Ethan imagined himself having to face Tom Barrimore and repeat this conversation word for word. While instinct insisted he shouldn't pressure Francine, his father silently persisted.

"Why not?" Ethan asked.

"I already told Uncle Tom. *I don't love Hugh.*"

"And you don't think you could grow to love him?"

"No, Ethan. He's…he's…he's…" She swiveled to face him and didn't flinch from looking him full in the face. "He's a flirt," she said. "I don't think I'd trust him on our honeymoon even. You saw how he acted with Julie and Marie. As soon as he'd met them—boom," she waved her hand. "He had Julie kissing him and had Marie…well, I don't know if you noticed, but Marie *wanted* to!"

"Oh that," Ethan said and shook his head. "Hugh's just got a personality that attracts women. He can't help it. But that doesn't mean he's not serious about *you!* Think about it, Francine. The guy's worth billions. You'd be set for life. Besides," he gently punched her arm, "we could be in-laws."

"Just what I always wanted," she mumbled and stepped away from Ethan. Before he realized her intent, she was halfway to the door.

"Francine, wait!" Ethan called. "I—I'm not through."

His claim only increased her pace.

"Franny!" Ethan repeated. He whipped in front of her, and stopped in the doorway.

She halted mere feet away. Her heightened color and hard stare presented a side of Francine that Ethan had never been the target for. Baffled beyond words, he wrinkled his brow, silently observed her, and grappled with something to say.

Finally, she looked down. "Please let me go." Her soft voice held a determined edge.

"I'm sorry," Ethan hurried. "I guess—it's just that—"

"I'll tell you like I told Uncle Tom. I'm not for sale. I really expected more from you, Ethan."

Ugh! he thought. *What a low blow.*

"I'm sorry," he repeated. "I was just trying to help."

"Who? Uncle Tom or me?" She gripped the back of her neck.

Ethan stroked his goatee and chose not to answer.

"Are we through now?" she asked and looked past him.

Through? he thought. *No, we're not through. There's all sorts of stuff I want to tell you, but I'm not sure I even understand it all.*

"Hey, don't be mad at me, okay?" Ethan urged. "Especially not right before you leave."

Her mouth relaxed.

"Is this any way to begin your Christmas holiday? Look, it's me—Ethan." He laid his hands across his chest and infused his words with a smile. "You aren't supposed to be mad at me, are you?"

Her stare turned into a graceful glance. "Sorry," she mumbled. "I'm just tired of everyone pushing me about Hugh. It's getting old."

"So I won't push anymore, okay?" He lifted his hands, palms outward. "Even if Dad threatens to decapitate me—that's okay. I won't mention Hugh ever again. Deal?"

Francine chuckled and nodded. "Deal."

The urge for Ethan to bid farewell at a closer range grew to mammoth proportions. He dared step within inches of Francine and placed his hand on her left shoulder. "I didn't leave the church this morning just to talk about Hugh anyway," he admitted. "I wanted to tell you goodbye and let you know I'll miss you."

Francine toyed with the hem of her sweater and didn't respond, but neither did she push him away by expression or body language.

"Christmas won't be quite the same without you, Franny," Ethan continued and doubted that his words could sound more affectionate. A sixth sense insisted Carrie would not approve. He could almost hear her saying, *Back away, Ethan.*

Instead of backing away, he rested his other hand on her right shoulder. And before he heeded caution, Ethan pulled Francine close for an embrace he promised himself would duplicate all the chaste hugs they'd shared through the years. When Francine latched onto him, the promise failed. The hug lengthened. Ethan rested his cheek on her temple and reveled in her sweet perfume. The fragrance reminded him of yesterday's roses and tomorrow's dreams. And he tried not to remember that tomorrow's dreams belonged to Carrie Casper.

The mellifluous Christmas music still wafted from the den, and Ethan was tempted to swirl Francine around the room. He didn't. Instead, he tuned into the primeval rhythm pounding through his soul that insisted he should tighten the hug. An alarmed voice whispered a dire warning about the consequences. He refrained. Francine Ponce, forever pure and sweet, probably believed this was just another hug from her "big brother." But it was swiftly turning into more—much more—for Ethan. He closed his eyes and hung on.

Thoughts of an emerald surrounded by diamonds plagued his conscience, as did images of his wife-to-be. This encounter was a betrayal of the worst variety. His honorable side urged him to run. Ethan couldn't budge. He shamelessly absorbed Francine's essence. He wanted to tell her how much he'd missed her these past few weeks…how much he appreciated her faithful friendship through the years…how much he wished her all the happiness in the world because she, of all women, deserved nothing less. But Ethan didn't say any of that. He couldn't—not without admitting a few more things that defied his mental abilities.

Finally, he lifted his face and brushed her temple in a light kiss. Ethan stifled a groan as he relished the achingly poignant sensations flooding him. "No matter what the future holds," he rasped, "I'll always remember our times together, Franny. You're the best." He inched away and was sorely tempted to repeat the kiss, but this time on her lips.

Peering into her calm eyes empowered him to resist. Francine was as innocent as ever...as unstirred as ever...and that made Ethan despise himself anew. His marriage to Carrie couldn't come soon enough.

Francine averted her gaze and finally spoke, "You're the best too, Ethan." And he was sure he imagined the wobble in her breathy words.

"Miss Franny," Ike's voice floated from nearby, "Mrs. Barrimore said you were waiting for me in—"

Ethan jerked from Francine and swiveled to face the doorway. Ike Gentry stood a few feet away, his keen gaze shifting from Francine to Ethan, and back to Francine. "I'm sorry." He respectfully nodded. "I didn't mean to interrupt."

"Oh no, that's quite all right," Francine said with a nonchalant smile. "We were just saying goodbye, that's all."

"Right," Ethan affirmed. "Like always," he added and forced his tone to sound as carefree as Francine's.

Ike nodded. "Of course," he said, his lined face registering nothing but acceptance of the usual routine. "Are you ready, then, Miss?" He checked his watch. "I'm a few minutes early."

"Sure," Francine affirmed and shoved up the sleeves of her sweater. "I've been ready awhile. My luggage is sitting in the den, and then there are two boxes by the front door. Aunt Nora and I went through some of Marie and Julie's last year's stuff and came up with some hand-me-downs for Sandra," she explained.

"Good," Ike said.

Ethan slipped his hands into his jeans pockets and silently observed Francine's heightened color, the excited sparkle in her eyes, the elevated resonance of her rushed words. Undoubtedly she was thrilled to be going to Rockaway for Christmas.

" 'Bye again, Ethan," Francine said and graced him with a light, sideways hug.

"Goodbye," he said and fought hard to keep his voice steady. "Be good, okay?"

She broke away from the hug. "I will," she said and followed Ike toward the entryway. At the door she paused and dashed him a bashful glance. "Merry Christmas," she whispered.

"Merry Christmas to you, too," Ethan returned.

Then she was gone. Ethan moved to the sofa and collapsed onto it. He propped his elbows on his knees, closed his eyes, and cradled his face in his hands. He detected a trace of Francine's perfume and relived those agonizing moments in her arms.

The den CD player now proclaimed the merry notes of "Jingle Bells," which accompanied the muffled sounds of Francine bidding her aunts farewell. Even Nora rose to the occasion and wished her well for once. The front door swished open. The sounds of traffic and his mother's bemoaning Francine's departure filtered into the library. The door snapped shut.

Ethan opened his eyes and lowered his hands. Even though he was going to miss Franny this Christmas, he couldn't deny that she probably needed this trip back home. *I'm thrilled for her...I guess.* Ethan couldn't help but wonder where his father was this Christmas. Ethan lost track of him somewhere in L.A. several years ago. He shook his head and pressed his forefinger and thumb against his eyes. He'd long ago sought and received peace over his father's abandonment. *No sense in opening old wounds,* he thought and studied the Persian rug's floral design. But he couldn't ignore the new wound pulsating in his spirit. Strangely, he felt as if he were being abandoned all over again. This time by Francine.

◠ ◡

Once the luggage and boxes were loaded into the limo's trunk and final farewells were exchanged, Francine collapsed onto the vehicle's backseat. The warm interior and soft leather enveloped her shaking frame and helped to calm her scattered senses. When Ike closed the door for her, she released her purse and laptop case to the floor, then flopped open the Agatha Christie novel she'd been trying to read in the den before Ethan arrived. Desperately she grabbed onto every word in the hope of expunging Ethan's hug from her psyche. The embrace refused to be removed.

Francine thought her heart would break when Ethan tugged her close. His simple kiss sent her senses reeling. His whispered reference to their past, his telling her she was the best nearly brought her to the point of uttering just how much she loved him. Francine had stopped herself within a breath of the dread mistake and had somehow managed to put forth what she hoped was a cool demeanor. Her ability to appear undisturbed was her only salvation.

Oh God, help me, she prayed, *I've got to get him out of my system. He's going to marry Carrie, and I'm going to have to attend the wedding. You've got to help me!*

Ike slid into the driver's seat and glanced into the rearview mirror. Francine sat right behind him and straight in his line of vision. Without ever taking his gaze from her, he cranked the engine and snapped his door closed.

Francine, confused by Ike's odd staring, looked out the tinted window and pretended interest in the patches of snow that lined the pavement.

"Do you ever plan to tell him?" Ike asked.

Blinking, Francine cut her gaze back to the rearview mirror. Ike's discerning brown eyes spoke more than she ever dreamed he knew. Her initial astonishment swiftly faded. In the years she'd lived at Central Park, not much got past Ike Gentry. Francine wondered why she thought this detail would miss his detection. She closed her book, fanned the pages, and considered pretending ignorance. But that would be less than honest, and Ike wouldn't buy the act anyway. Francine toyed with the zipper on her suede coat and remained silent.

"If he marries that Carrie Casper, it'll be the worst mistake he's ever made and you know it," Ike grumbled. "I can't help but think it would make a difference if he *knew*."

Francine's eyes stung. "I can't tell him," she said before touching the corner of her eye. A series of rapid blinks did little to abate the stinging. *If only everything were that simple,* she thought. *But if I tell Ethan I love him, that doesn't change his love for Carrie. It would only make him pity me—and pity is the last thing I want from him.*

Ike sighed. "I apologize," he said. "It's just—oh, never mind." He shifted the limo into gear, and sped forward, his attention now on the task at hand.

Francine allowed herself the luxury of one whimper and then retrieved a tissue from her purse. After a series of blots and a stern round of self-talk, Francine snuggled into her seat and peered out the window. The crowded New York streets provided the distraction her sore heart needed. From there, she created her plan.

Once she arrived in Rockaway, Francine purposed to forget Ethan Summers. She would reembrace her family and savor the childhood memories that would awaken from years of slumber. She and Wade would spend hours talking. She would take Sandra under her wing all over again. And Francine would do whatever she could to assist her mother. By the time she moved into her new apartment, her life and thoughts would be all for her original family. There would be no room left for Ethan. And Central Park would be nothing more than a hazy remembrance on the canvass of her mind.

Twenty-Eight

An hour later, Francine sat forward, her attention riveted upon the passing scenery. Once they entered Rockaway, she had pulled Wade's directions from her purse and detailed the travel instructions to Ike.

Francine stared at the slender houses built wall to wall. Somehow her memory had failed her. She didn't recall the layers of grime that covered her childhood neighborhood. Ike, as dependable as ever, struggled to dodge old vans, abandoned cars, and motorcycles parked almost bumper to bumper along the narrow street. Her heart ached for the children running in the streets. School was out for the Christmas holidays, and many of the kids had no place to turn but poverty-scarred neighborhoods.

"Are we close yet?" Ike asked.

"The next block, I'm sure," she answered while looking in every direction for a familiar landmark. "I can't believe how much things have changed."

Snow covered the ground and rooftops. Splotches of gray soot marred the white blanket. Noon approached, and with it, the rush of people scurrying along the sidewalk.

Two old men standing by a barrel in which a healthy fire blazed gave the unusual vehicle a quizzical look. Francine wished she could inch toward the floorboard. A taxi would have been so much less ostentatious.

"There, Ike, just past the bar on the corner." Francine put her hand to her mouth. "Oh no, that was Mrs. Conway's home. She hated liquor and now her place is a *saloon?*"

"Are you sure you'll be safe here?" Ike asked with a frown.

"Of course," Francine said and doubted her own assumption. "I mean," she countered, "I don't remember any problems when I was a kid."

Ike pulled along the curb and claimed two parking places with the long limousine. "I'll have to get your luggage in quick and be on my way." He checked his watch. "Mr. Barrimore wants me back by one-thirty. He has an important luncheon with the mayor." He shifted and peered over the backseat. "But I don't like the idea of just dumping you off like this in this neighborhood." He squinted and gazed out the window.

"I was fine here for eleven years," Francine said and bolstered her failing courage. "I'll be fine now. This is my family, remember? They'll watch out for me."

Ike clicked off his seatbelt and opened his door. Refuse littered the street and the haze blowing from New York City tainted the air with a smell like burned rubber. He looked back at Francine like a father not wanting to abandon his child. "If I had my way," he commented, "you'd still be back at Central Park. Christmas won't be the same without you."

Ike's words held all the regret of Ethan's.

"Thanks." Francine bent the edge of Wade's instructions. She started to tell Ike she'd be back after Christmas, but stopped herself. Chances were high she wouldn't.

Before Francine could conjure up something else to say, two boys came bounding from the house. Francine recognized them from the photos Wade had e-mailed her. These two rascals were none other than the twins who'd been almost a year old when she moved to Central Park. The smaller one, Max, jumped up on the limousine's hood and peered in at Ike. The chubby one, Jeff, jerked the door open and yelled, "Is that you, Francine?"

Francine laughed. "Say hello to my brothers, Ike," she explained. "Yes, it's me!" she called. "Want to help me get my things?"

"Nah," said Max, "we don't do nothin' for girls." He backed out of the door, scrambled to the front, and began pulling his barefooted brother off the car.

Ike stepped from the vehicle and opened Francine's door. She secured her purse and laptop, scooted out of the car, and lowered her feet into the slush covering the pavement. When she emerged into the cold air, Ike clicked her door shut, paced to the trunk, and pressed a button on his key ring. The trunk sighed open. Her shoes grinding against the dirty street, Francine stepped toward the trunk and grabbed the handle of a piece of her luggage.

After a disapproving mumble, Ike tried to brush aside her hand. But Francine refused to relinquish her hold. "I've got to get used to taking care of everything myself," she admonished and lifted the weighty case out of the limo. "My family doesn't have a staff, you know."

"Okay, okay," Ike acquiesced. He warily eyed the mischievous waifs now into a game of king-of-the-mountain with the car's roof as their goal. "Do you think they're always like this?" he asked.

Francine shrugged and plopped her leather luggage on the curb. She examined a trio of boys across the street who looked every bit as mischievous and relentless as her younger brothers. "Let's hope not," she breathed, but she couldn't have sounded more doubtful.

"I'm looking forward to you being back home," Ike said as he heaved out her other piece of luggage. "The whole staff is going to miss you—especially me."

She tried to stop the unexpected tears, but to no avail. "Thanks," Francine squeaked out. "I'll miss all of you as well."

After patting Francine's back, Ike deposited the suitcase on the curb near the other one. He shot a playful glance toward her. "What do you have in this thing, rocks?"

His kind teasing chased away her sentimental tears. "Believe it or not, I do. It's the same collection I brought to Central Park. I was planning on giving it to those two characters." She pointed toward the car's hood.

Ike grabbed the two boxes full of hand-me-downs and Francine assisted him in closing the trunk's lid. "Looks like they've got grit all over the top of the car. I'm going to have to run it through a car wash before I pick up Mr. Barrimore."

"I'll get them off," Francine said with more bravado than she felt. Prying the boys off the car offered a good initiation into her new way of life. By the time she herded them to the front door, Francine was out of breath and challenged nearly beyond the realms of every childhood development book she'd ingested.

When Max and Jeff exploded into the house, they both hollered, "She's here! She's here!"

A sixteen-year-old blonde bolted from the doorway and plastered Francine with a tight hug.

"Sandra!" she exclaimed and braced herself. "I'm so glad to see you!"

"Oh my word!" Sandra exclaimed and pulled away from Francine. "I was so excited, I ran out here barefooted. Yikes! The snow is cold." She shifted from one foot to the other and shoved her hands into her faded jeans pockets.

"Max and Jeff are barefooted, too," Francine said and eyed the gray sky, pregnant with more snow. "It's a wonder you don't all catch pneumonia!"

The boys exploded back outside and headed toward the limo again.

"No! Stop them!" Ike hollered.

Francine pivoted to face Ike, now loaded with one of her cases and both boxes.

Sandra, hugging her midsection with one arm, inserted her fingers between her teeth and released a whistle loud enough to shatter glass. Max and Jeff ignored the ear-piercing command and continued straight for the limo's hood. Sandra picked up a limb recently fallen from the street's only tree, an old elm slowly dying from the town's polluted air. With a holler, she charged the boys.

Max and Jeff yelped like a pair of frightened puppies and ran for the house. Sandra dropped the stick and brushed her hands. "That oughtta keep 'em out of trouble for awhile," she determined.

"Whoa!" Ike exclaimed and Francine turned in time to see the top box tottering toward the edge.

Sandra came to the rescue. She extended her arms and caught the box as it toppled from Ike's control. Sandra's grunt, the rounding of her blue eyes accompanied her exclamation, "This thing weighs a ton!"

"Both boxes are full of clothes for *you!*" Francine proclaimed.

"For me!" Sandra gasped. "Oh my word, I can't wait!"

Francine quickly assessed Sandra, clad in a tight sweater and jeans. Even though Sandra strongly favored Francine, she was slimmer than Francine had been at sixteen. Chances were high Julie and Marie's size six and size eight hand-me-downs would fit.

They moved inside the dilapidated home, void of Christmas decor, with Ike close behind. Francine followed Sandra's lead and set her purse, laptop, and suitcase near the parlor door. The small parlor, filled with odd pieces of furniture, opened off the entrance. A chill completed the cluttered room's uninviting atmosphere. A musty smell, coupled with the aroma of something burning, completed the welcome.

Francine tried not to compare this house with the one on Central Park West. She also attempted to talk herself into feeling as if she'd come home. Frantically, she scanned the stained walls, the streaked windows, the dust-laden light fixtures, but found nothing that stirred poignant memories. Her only response was the hollow ache of an empty heart.

"Is that you, Francine?" a harassed voice called from the end of the short hallway. The clank of pots and pans punctuated the question.

"Yeah! She's here, Mom!" Sandra's rowdy crow rattled the rafters.

Francine shied toward the hall wall, winced, and covered her protesting ear. Ike, rising from depositing his load, directed a grim stare at her. She looked down at the tired carpet and refused to answer his silent petition that she not stay.

"About time," the matron bellowed. "I didn't think you'd *ever* get here! We've been waitin' on you so we can call Wade to come home for lunch! Get out of the stew, Jeff!" she yelled, then fell into a series of dry coughs.

A dull thud preceded Jeff's yowl. A smack accompanied Max's yelling, "I ain't in the stew. Why you slappin' me?"

"Because you need to get outta here, now! Can't you see, I'm busy!"

Sandra bounded down the hallway and hollered, "Come on, Francine!"

Francine edged toward the kitchen. Ike's firm grip on her shoulder halted her progress, and she turned toward him.

"Are you sure you want to stay two weeks?" he whispered. "I could come back and pick you up tonight at…" he checked his watch, "…at eight."

"I'm staying," Francine insisted and wished her wavering resolution were as strong as her voice. So far, all the emotions she expected to feel for her childhood home were not surfacing. She could only hope the renewed relationships would make up for her lack of connectedness with the house.

Ike's expectant expression stiffened. "Well, all right," he said and dubiously gazed toward the kitchen. "I guess I don't have a choice. I've got to go or I'll be late." He glanced at his watch once more.

"I'll be fine," Francine assured. "I promise. Please don't worry."

"That's something I *can't* promise," Ike admitted and gazed into the parlor. His flinch reminded Francine of someone who'd smelled soured milk. He walked out the doorway without another word.

Francine stepped toward the kitchen, hovered near the entry, and gazed at the woman who had birthed her. Florence Ponce, dressed in a faded duster, stood in front of a sink full of dishes. She handed a platter to Sandra, who'd crawled onto a kitchen stepladder and stood in front of an opened cupboard.

While her mom's profile and features reminded Francine of Aunt Mariette's, she was as scrawny as Aunt Nora and nearly as wrinkled as Ike. This broken woman, ten years Mariette's junior, was a mere shadow of the person Francine had hugged goodbye when she left for Central Park.

Oh Mother...Francine thought. Her heart swelling with sorrow and bottled-up love, she moved forward with the full intent of offering her mom an embrace and some assistance.

As soon a Sandra placed the platter on its shelf, Florence's rough voice slapped Francine in the face, "Tell Francine to get her stuff upstairs!" The harsh tone was worse than Aunt Nora's on a bad day.

Francine slunk into the shadowed hallway and experienced an unexpected flashback to another day, another year, another Christmas. Her mother had been slaving over the kitchen sink, yelling at Francine to take Sandra and Wade upstairs to get them out of her way. As usual, Francine had complied without a word of protest. She learned at an early age not to express her opinion. The results usually involved a blow. She touched her face and relived the sting of her mother's hand upon her cheeks. Francine blinked against the burn in her eyes.

"I don't know why she was so set to come here for Christmas," Florence harped. "She's done just fine without us all these years. Seems like she could have waited until later. This is the worst time of year for me!"

"Sshh! She's going to hear you. She's just in the hallway." Sandra's aghast whisper intensified Francine's discomfort.

Her limbs shook. *But Wade invited me!* she countered and crossed her arms. Her dismay mounting, Francine shook her head and recalled overhearing a conversation between her mom and Aunt Nora. Her aunt had arrived with news that Florence's estranged sister, Mariette and her husband, Tom, were offering to take in one of Florence's children to lighten her load. Francine's mother had insisted they couldn't have Wade and Sandra because they were her favorites. The twins were still too little. That only left Francine.

I was the castoff, Francine thought and wondered how she could have ever forgotten what her first home was really like. Her worries over the white limo mocked her. Florence Ponce hadn't even been watching for her. And Sandra and the twins weren't sophisticated enough to be offended by the flashy vehicle.

Even though she hadn't talked to her mother in years, Francine decided not to approach her. More dark memories flooded her mind and marred any faith for the return of the fantasies she had mistaken for life in Rockaway. She recalled Uncle Tom's grave prediction that a season in Rockaway might help her appreciate what she had at Central Park. Francine decided her visit was still too young for her to fully admit that Tom might have been right about that—or his insisting she marry Hugh Casper.

If I had Hugh's money, at least I could help my family, she thought and imagined a new house, a new car, perhaps a couple of staff members to ease her mother's load. She could pay for college for Sandra—and Wade, too, if he still wanted to go. Even with her trust fund, Francine couldn't touch what she could do with Hugh's wealth.

She collected her scattered senses and refused to continue thinking in this vein. Even helping her family wasn't worth sacrificing her happiness and losing her self-respect. *I don't love him,* she reminded herself. Nonetheless, Uncle Tom's claim that she could grow to love Hugh nibbled at her protest.

Francine stuffed these musings, along with the pain her mom's attitude was inflicting, and searched for the stairs. The doorway to her left proved to be the opening for a narrow stairway she had forgotten. She turned toward the parlor door and picked up one of the boxes, her purse, and laptop seconds before Sandra stormed the hallway.

"Mom's in a bad mood," she whispered, her deep-blue eyes as convincing as her words. "Don't listen to anything she says. She's been like this for three days. Dad left for work Friday and hasn't been back since. The house payment's due, and he was supposed to bring his check home."

Francine spotted a toppled whiskey bottle near the kitchen's entry. Beside it lay a crunched beer can. The harshness of grim reality annihilated the final traces of Francine's "fond memories." At least at Central Park Uncle Tom came home every night, Aunt Mariette never yelled, and Aunt Nora wasn't half as caustic as her younger sister—even on her worst day.

"We'll just stay out of her way for awhile, okay?" Sandra said with a weary smile that suggested dodging mom was business as usual.

"Sure," Francine agreed and wondered how her younger sister kept such an upbeat demeanor with so much negativity surrounding her. *Maybe Mom doesn't slap her,* Francine thought. *After all, she and Wade have always been the favorites.*

Sandra scooped up Francine's smallest case. The sisters wrestled their burdens up the steep, narrow stairs, down a cramped hallway, and into Sandra's tiny room. A pair of twin beds claimed the room's center. A doorless closet spilled forth a web of old clothes and rundown shoes. One sagging chest-of-drawers offered the room's only other storage space. A hanger on the door's back served as a second closet for Sandra's worn wardrobe. The room had a peculiar smell, like lemons mixed with moldy bread.

"You can have that bed." Sandra pointed to the left. "This one's mine." She dropped Francine's suitcase on the bed and eyed the box Francine held.

Francine deposited her laptop case and purse on the bed and set the box on the room's only chair—an ancient straight-back with peeling green paint and back dowels that had come unglued.

"I'll unpack later," Francine said and opened the box's snuggly folded flaps. "Right now, let's see if any of these clothes fit, okay?"

Sandra clambered off her bed, hung over the box, and gasped at the contents. "Oh my word!" she breathed and held up the first outfit, a Calvin Klein denim jacket with matching jeans.

"I thought you'd like those," Francine quietly commented.

"Like them!" Sandra laid down the first set and grabbed the next one—a two piece, knit suit with short skirt and long-sleeved blouse. The set still bore the Neiman Marcus tag, and Sandra latched onto it. "Aaahhhhh!" she hollered. "It's brand-new! And it cost nearly 300 dollars! My friends are going to turn neon green and die with envy! And I am so not kidding!"

"And just think, we left another box just like this one downstairs," Francine said.

Sandra yelped and tossed the knit suit on top of the box still full of undiscovered treasures. "Let's go get it now!" she squealed. "I think I'll dump them all on the bed and roll around in them."

A spontaneous laugh, so strong it took her breath, gurgled from Francine. She hurried after Sandra, and a warm glow filled the hollow ache in her heart. Even if no one else but Wade welcomed her, even if all her remembrances were only wishful thinking, Francine was glad she'd come home for Sandra's sake.

Twenty-Nine

Francine delved into her savings to pay half the house payment her still-absentee father had skipped. Wade coughed up the other half. She had also bought groceries, and the smell of freshly baked sugar cookies evidenced her mother's putting the food to good use. Francine eyed the gingerbread men dangling from the artificial Christmas tree that claimed the parlor's corner. After purchasing the tree and new decorations, she had further provided money for a modest supply of Christmas presents. All the while, she told herself she needed to quit spending. She would have few funds to support herself next semester at this rate.

Florence's attitude had softened with every blessing Francine bestowed. This morning, she'd even called her "dear" at breakfast. That was *after* Florence slapped Max and Jeff. Sadly, the abuse had become such a way of life that the twins barely acknowledged it.

Hovered in the parlor, her laptop balanced on her knees, Francine logged on. She remembered the barrage of questions from her suspicious mother about long distance charges that might accrue from connecting to the internet. Finally, Francine had promised her mother she'd pay the whole December phone bill for the privilege and freedom of using the internet. Then and only then did Florence Ponce go back to her laundry room duties and leave Francine in peace.

While she awaited the internet's connection, Francine cherished the silence that enveloped the shabby room—something she'd taken for granted at Central Park. In Rockaway, silence was a rare commodity and as precious as pure gold. Presently, Wade was still at work, so he wasn't available with his incessant chatting about how wonderful Hugh Casper was to land him the job in Boston. The twins were down the street playing, and Sandra had gone to a friend's to show off her new clothes.

Once her e-mail box opened, Francine scanned the long list of received messages for the one name she longed to see: Ethan Summers. But his name was absent. She counted the days until Christmas and came up with three. Even though Ethan never said he was giving Carrie the engagement ring on Christmas Day, Francine figured that was the logical choice.

A collection of dead hopes and unanswered prayers littered her spirit and compelled her to accept the inevitable. Ethan would marry Carrie. From there, it wouldn't matter *who* Francine married. Her heart would always belong to Ethan, and he would be forever unattainable.

I might as well marry Hugh and make everyone happy, she thought and reminded herself just how much his fortune could help her family.

Her mother had informed her yesterday there was no money for an exterminator. The kitchen roaches were beyond nauseating, and Francine rewashed every glass or plate before use. Finding a roach in her coffee this morning had prompted Francine to call the exterminator herself. Enough was enough! The bug annihilator was due two days after Christmas.

When she refocused upon her laptop, she realized six of her e-mails were all from the same person: Hugh Casper. Francine's face flexed in amazement. Why she thought she would be free of his presence in Rockaway was now a mystery to her. He had left two messages on her cell phone, mailed her a romantic Christmas card, and now she was facing half-a-dozen e-mails.

With a resigned sigh, Francine admitted that the guy was finally wearing her down. Maybe he really *was* in love with her, and perhaps such a love could tame even the most wayward of men. She ignored the memory of Hugh's interactions with Marie, opened the e-mails one by one, and scanned them. The first five consisted of a combination of chatty news and forwarded funnies. The last one made her back go rigid.

Francine,

Since I haven't heard back from you, I'm assuming you must not be checking your e-mail. I also left a couple of voice mails on your cell phone. Ethan gave me your number. I hope that's all right. Did you get my voice mails, or do you have your cell turned off? Anyway, I just wanted to let you know that Carrie and I arrived in Long Beach today and will be spending the next few days with Uncle Al. So I'm only about twenty minutes from you now and was hoping maybe we could get together. How does tomorrow sound? That's Thursday.

"Thursday?" Francine whispered. "Today is Thursday!" She shoved up the sleeve of her oversized sweater and read the next line.

If that's okay with you, I'll be at your parents' house around four o'clock.

Francine checked her watch. "Three-thirty!" she yelped, her face growing cold.

I typed in Wade's home address on MapQuest and got directions to your home. I thought maybe we could drive back to Long Beach for dinner. There's a great restaurant here—not an Addy's, believe it or not. I know

that's probably almost sacrilegious but I thought we'd
live dangerously. Smiles. Anyway, it's called Etienne's
and has pasta and seafood to die for. It's an upscale
restaurant, so you might want to dress up. If I don't hear
back from you, I'll take my chances and be there at four.
Looking forward to it.

Forever yours,
Hugh

Francine stared at the e-mail. Her mind roared. She checked
her watch again to affirm that her first estimation hadn't been
erroneous. Hugh Casper would arrive in thirty short minutes. He
may have even left his uncle's by now.

She looked around the dilapidated room to the marred walls,
the has-been furniture, the torn drapes, the light fixture covered in
dust. The rickety chair in which she sat squeaked with the shift of
her weight. A roach trotted up the wall near the Christmas tree.
Francine shivered.

What if I'm just not here when he comes? she thought and then
rolled her eyes. *As determined as Hugh is, he'd probably sit here until
I came back!*

But is that so bad? She gnawed on her lower lip. *Maybe if he
sees where I really come from, he'd be turned off for good. Then I
wouldn't have to worry about him chasing me anymore.*

She stared at the computer screen. "But is that what my family
needs?" she whispered. Groaning, Francine pressed her fingertips
against her temple, and her mind gyrated in a jumble of con-
flicting thoughts. She relived her uncle's astonishment that she
wouldn't even consider Hugh. Uncle Tom's admonition marched
through her mind like a banner of truth:

> *Listen, Franny, such proposals don't come every day. Even if
> you don't think you're madly in love with Hugh now, you can
> grow to love him over time. He's a good catch. I'm sure many,
> many women have tried. He's worth billions, Francine....
> That trust fund we gave you is mere pennies compared to
> what Hugh can offer. You'll be secure for life!"*

Francine studied the worn room. Even the sugar cookies couldn't annihilate the home's musty odor. Hugh's money could change all that and more.

If he would really settle down, she reasoned, *maybe I could stand him until the love came.*

She imagined her uncle's beam of approval and her decision was made. *The least I can do is give the guy a chance.* Her thoughts jumped to the clothing she'd brought with her to Rockaway. Francine packed only two suits for church. One of them would have to do for the restaurant.

She checked her watch again and prepared to get off-line when a small box in the lower, right corner popped up. It read, "You have a new e-mail from esummers@emancc.com."

Francine's heart lept. Forgetting Hugh's pending visit, she breathlessly waited for the message to download. Her palms moistening, Francine opened the e-mail and devoured Ethan's words.

> Hi, Franny! How are things with you? Everything is going well here at Central Park. Everything is business as usual for Christmas. Mom and Dad just hosted their last Christmas party two nights ago. That one was for Dad's major clients. Hugh and Carrie came. They've been talking to him about some investments, by the way. Ricky's parents were there as well, along with Marie and Ricky. His folks have already placed a chunk of money with Dad for his investing. Dad's really doing well these days. I'm glad.
>
> Now, we only have the Christmas-night family party left. I'm already missing you.

She stopped and reread the line, absorbing the nuance of every word. Ethan missed her! Since arriving in Rockaway, Francine had been working from dawn to dusk to help her mother, so stopping herself from thinking of Ethan hadn't been an insurmountable task—as long as she was so exhausted at night she immediately dropped off to sleep. But now her heart swelled with a consuming love, more intense than ever.

Her pulse thudding in her throat, she continued to read his message:

> Mom said you left your presents for us under the tree. I didn't even think to give you my present before you left. Okay, I'll be honest. I didn't buy it until yesterday. J

Her imagination spread its wings. Francine imagined a dozen different novelties that Ethan might have purchased her—each in 18-karat gold, each as dear as the last. She stroked the wide gold chain lying against her sweater.

> Dad and Mom said they let the gift thing slip, too, so I guess you'll have Christmas here when you get back home.

Francine's lips trembled. Ethan fully expected her to return as planned. So did Ike and the staff, along with Aunt Nora, Aunt Mariette, and Uncle Tom. Suddenly the whole idea of getting an apartment no longer seemed so easy. Francine would have to go back home to get all her clothing. She imagined the family's reaction when they realized she was moving out…their coaxing and perhaps some tears. For the first time, Franny began to doubt her ability to make the break from Central Park. She had never been able to go against what the family wanted for very long. Why had she lulled herself into believing getting an apartment would be any different?

> We've invited Hugh and Carrie here for the family Christmas party. They've gone to their uncle's in Long Beach for a few days. I didn't mention it the other day, but Carrie got a little miffed over our not going to Colorado for Christmas. I don't think she's over it. Oh, before they left, Hugh mentioned that their Uncle Al is actually living with a woman. Carrie didn't act like it was any big deal. That bothers me. I'm hoping that this

uncle isn't somehow influencing her. She's such a sweet-
heart and seems a little naive at times, I guess. At least
she seemed that way over the Colorado trip. She didn't
understand why I thought it would look bad or why
Pastor Steve hinted that it wouldn't look good.

Francine shook her head. *Ethan, if you still can't see her morals
aren't what yours are, then you're the naive one,* she thought and
resigned herself to Ethan's fate. The man was irrevocably blind
when it came to Carrie Casper.

Well, I'm looking over this e-mail now and seeing
that I rambled terribly. I just wanted to touch base with
you and wish you Merry Christmas!

Blessings!
Ethan

"Merry Christmas, Ethan," Francine whispered and stroked
the screen. Her index finger lingered upon his name, and she
imagined being in his arms once more. A delightful quiver radiated from her soul, only to be followed by a cold dash of harsh
reality. Ethan belonged to Carrie, and he always would.

Her gaze trailed to Hugh's name listed just above Ethan's.
Maybe it was time to fully admit that Uncle Tom really was considering her best interest.

Francine checked her watch again. Five more minutes had
lapsed. Hugh would be here in twenty-five minutes.

Deciding to respond to Ethan's e-mail later, she closed her
internet connection. After a series of key clicks, she shut down
the computer and headed upstairs to change into her suit.

"Mother," Francine called and hustled across the kitchen
toward the laundry room. She glanced at her watch for the fourth
time in four minutes. Hugh was due to arrive in exactly one

minute. "Mother?" Francine repeated and inched open the laundry room's door. The smell of bleach and detergent merged with the fresh application of Francine's Oscar de la Renta perfume. The roar, wheeze, and tumble of an ancient washer and drier blotted out all other sounds.

Her back to Francine, Florence Ponce stood in the midst of piles of laundry. A pair of cabinets over the washer and drier sagged open, revealing a mesh of mismatched socks and torn towels too frayed to use. Iron in hand, Florence manned a tired ironing board, pressing the wrinkles from a blouse. After a day of heavy house work, Florence would go to the same cafe waitress job she'd gotten when Francine was eight. The grim reality only confirmed that Francine's going out with Hugh was the right choice.

Francine moved closer and touched her mother's slumped shoulder. She jumped and faced Francine. "Good grief! You scared me to death!" Florence glared at her eldest daughter with the same green-eyed stare Nora used when most vexed. "Why didn't you *say* something before you touched me like that?" she demanded with no trace of the endearing tone she'd used over breakfast.

"I did," Francine said and looked past her mother's disapproving gaze. "You didn't hear me."

"Well, okay then. What did you want?" Florence examined Francine from head to toe. The bags under her eyes suggested she needed a nap, not an eight-hour shift at a twenty-four-hour diner.

Francine fiddled with the pocket of her jacket. Her suit was a snazzy NR1 design that Aunt Mariette had given her last Christmas. She estimated the suit cost more than her mother made in a week.

"I was hoping you were going to offer to help, but it doesn't look like you're dressed for it," Florence said and smoothed the front of her worn duster.

"I…got an e-mail," Francine explained, "from a…a…a friend. He's going to be here any second now. He wanted to take me to dinner. I was just going to tell you I'd be leaving."

"Well, does he have a name?" Florence barked.

The doorbell's broken chime mingled with the dryer's groan.

"That's him now," Francine said and whirled from the room, only to come face-to-face with Sandra, dressed in Julie's denim jacket and jeans.

"Oh my word," Sandra oozed. "When I was coming in, there was a man driving up in a red Ferrari. I think that's him at the door!" She took in Francine's striped suit and fresh makeup. "Do you *know* him?" she gasped.

"Yes," Francine responded and sidestepped her sister.

"Are you, like, going out with him or something?" Sandra squeaked from behind.

"Yes," Francine said and cast a quick glance over her shoulder. Both her mom and Sandra followed her through the cluttered kitchen like two hounds hot on the trail.

"What's his name, Francine?" Florence insisted during the doorbell's second ring.

"Hugh Casper," she said. As she hit the hallway, Francine wanted to groan. Her busy mind projected the coming sequence of events, which involved her mother asking Hugh in for a chat and some roach-coffee while Sandra ogled him. Francine had planned to swiftly slip from the house without Hugh's getting even a peek into the disheveled interior.

"You should see his car, Mom!" Sandra exclaimed. "It must have cost 80,000 dollars!"

Try 150,000 dollars, Francine thought. That fact alone might send Sandra into a shrieking fit. Francine halted at the door and placed her hand on the knob. She rested her finger against her puckered lips and said, "Sshh. He might hear you."

Her dark-blue eyes rounding, Sandra nodded.

"If he has time, I'll invite him in," Florence whispered and smoothed her callused hands along her frizzy gray hair. "He has money, right?"

Francine offered a resigned nod.

"Why don't I call the preacher while he's here, and you can marry him before he gets away," she pressed.

Francine's cheeks flashed hot. "Please, Mother," she begged, "don't...don't..." She looked toward the sad parlor, then back to her mom.

The doorbell's ring preceded a round of loud knocks.

Florence's brows rose. "You don't want him in here, do you?" she asked. "You're ashamed."

"Look at this place," Francine whispered. "It's a mess."

Florence Ponce's disgust took on epic proportions. "A woman in your position can't be so picky," she snorted. "Maybe it will do him good to see how much we need his money. Let the poor man in, Sandra!"

Sandra barged past Francine and shoved her hand off the knob. All grins and giggles, she whipped open the door.

As predicted, Hugh Casper stood outside. His face glowed with a broad smile and a rosy-nosed testimony of the frosty temperature. "Good afternoon, ladies," he said and met Francine's gaze.

Francine swallowed hard. "Hello, Hugh," she answered. Not certain how to act, she toyed with the strap on her handbag and groped for words to fill the tense silence.

"Aren't you going to introduce us?" Florence asked.

"Oh sure," Francine said. "This is my mom, Florence Ponce, and my sister, Sandra."

"Nice to meet you," Hugh said, a gust of wind playing with his hair. "I believe I saw Sandra coming into the house. She looks so much like you, Franny, I thought she was you for a few seconds there."

Sandra giggled again.

"Please come in," Florence said and poked at Sandra to move out of the doorway. "I can put on some coffee."

Francine gritted her teeth and endured the inevitable. She could only pray that the parlor was currently free of wildlife.

Hugh stepped inside, and Sandra closed the door behind him. "Actually," he said, "I can't stay. I made reservations." His longing gaze alighted upon Francine. "I'm assuming you got my e-mail?"

Francine nodded. "About thirty minutes ago," she admitted.

He took in her appearance. "You got ready quick—or were you already going out?"

"No." Francine looked down and cut him a glance out of the corner of her eyes. "I got ready."

"So that means we're on?" he asked.

"Yes," Francine replied and didn't have to look at Sandra to know the ogling had begun.

Hugh offered his hand to Mrs. Ponce. "I can see where Franny got her beauty." His warm voice and appreciative appraisal sounded as genuine as his French accent.

Florence touched her haggard cheek and beamed. "I always thought Francine and Sandra took mostly after their father," she said.

Hugh inserted his hands into the pockets of his wool overcoat. His bronze-colored turtleneck complemented his looks, and he appeared nearly handsome. The way her mom and Sandra were gawking at him, he might as well have been Elvis Presley.

"If we have reservations," Francine began, "I'll get my coat now."

"Sure," Hugh agreed.

Within half a minute, Francine hovered near the front door, waiting on Hugh to take his leave. "Well, it was good to meet you two," he said. "I know you're enjoying Franny being home, but it's tragic for us. We miss her so much in the city." Hugh lifted his hand in a broad gesture. "She's the center of attention at Central Park."

"Oh, but—" Francine shook her head.

"At least it looks like she's the center of *your* attention," Florence said, her voice softer even than when she'd called Francine "dear" this morning.

Francine's shock melded with amazement. It would appear no one was immune to the vapors of money.

"I will say she has a wisdom and generosity none of the rest of us have. But I've got to stop rattling." He paused to smile at Francine, who was ready to crawl into a corner and cover her head. "We've got reservations, and I've got a few surprises."

"But do you have any *brothers?* That's what I want to know!" Sandra blurted, her flirtatious simper underscoring her meaning.

"Sandra, *please!*" Francine pleaded.

"Don't scold her," Hugh admonished and beamed at Sandra as if she were the queen of England. "If I had a brother, I'd mail him to you," he said and turned to Florence with a confidential air. "That's from Shakespeare."

Forgetting her embarrassment, Francine wrinkled her brow and scanned her mental file labeled "Shakespeare." "I don't believe he said anything like that, did he?" she quietly asserted.

"Well, he should have!" Hugh retorted and winked, his sparkling hazel eyes testifying to his mischief.

Florence and Sandra laughed out loud. Francine couldn't deny a chuckle herself. Maybe this date with Hugh wouldn't be so bad after all.

Thirty

Hugh pulled the Ferrari into a parking lot and gassed the powerful vehicle toward the new brick restaurant's portico. "I'll let you off and then park, okay?" he asked.

"Sure," Francine agreed and ran her hand over the dashboard's leather finish. *Wade would drool a week over this car,* she thought and couldn't deny that even the car's new smell seemed more refined than the less expensive makes.

"Do you like?" Hugh questioned, his eyebrow cocked at a suggestive angle that insinuated he was talking about himself...and not the vehicle. Francine had chatted more with Hugh on their half-hour trek than she had in all the times he'd visited her. Now she wondered if he was getting a little too enthused about their date.

"I was just thinking Wade would drool over this car," she said, keeping her attention firmly upon the vehicle. "He loves Ferraris."

"Actually, this one's my uncle's. He just got it last week. He's going to sell his other one. It's nearly a twin to this one, only a couple years older. Maybe I should arrange for Wade to have the old one as a bonus with his new job."

"No!" Francine said. Her toes curling, she stared at Hugh.

"But I'd do anything for you," he said with an adoring gaze.

"I mean, I—I don't want to seem ungrateful, but…but…I could never repay…" She twisted the tie of her suede coat and gazed downward.

"Maybe one day it won't matter," Hugh asserted, "especially if we're all family."

Francine gazed out her side of the car and didn't respond. Hugh's every expression, his every word, his every gesture insisted his offer of matrimony still stood. All Francine had to do was whisper a simple yes, and he'd understand exactly what she meant.

Her stomach churned. Her appetite vanished. And she began to do what she should have done the second she read Hugh's e-mail: Francine started praying for divine guidance.

All the way here, Hugh had talked about his new involvement in an inner-city charity that fed the homeless, provided them with Bibles and a place to worship, and empowered them with job opportunities. Francine's opinion of Hugh was improving with every minute.

He might not be all bad. She stole a glimpse of him and reminded herself that God was in the business of changing hearts. Maybe Hugh was in the process of such an alteration.

When the Ferrari halted under the portico, Hugh leaned across Francine and pulled on the door latch. She averted her face. The door clicked open, and the frigid coastal air along with the sounds of Long Beach Christmas traffic filtered inside. Francine thought Hugh had shifted back into his seat when she turned her head and reached for her purse. She thought wrong. He was still very much in her space, his face about six inches from hers.

"You smell like you did the night of your birthday party," he said. "What is it?"

"Oscar de la Renta," Francine replied, her voice unsteady.

"Remind me to buy that company tomorrow, okay?" His devilish smile wouldn't quit.

Francine looked away and couldn't help but wonder if Hugh had used that line on other women. She also began to wonder if she was duping herself into buying Uncle Tom's claim of growing to love him. Even if Hugh was in the middle of a change, Francine wondered if the "ghosts" of all the other women would plague their marriage and prohibit her from offering him her untainted respect. How could she love a man she couldn't fully respect? And how could she respect a man who had been such a flagrant womanizer?

Maybe if he really changed, she told herself, *God's grace would be there for us.*

"I guess I'll just wait here for you then?" she said and inched open the door.

"Sure," Hugh responded, his confident tone turning to uncertainty.

She didn't look at him again. Francine climbed from the vehicle, closed the door, and walked toward the expansive glass entryway. A prominent sign to the left of the doors read "CLOSED" in bold red. Francine squinted, pivoted toward the purr of the Ferrari, and realized the parking lot was empty. She wondered when Hugh would recognize the same.

But he said we have reservations, she thought.

Hugh turned off the vehicle's engine, got out, slammed the door, and walked toward her. His stride, the tilt of his chin suggested he had been born with plenty of money and confidence. She marveled that he could have sounded so unsure of himself when she slipped out of the car. His wool coat billowed in the gusty breeze, and he sprinted the rest of the distance toward Francine. With his hair frightfully mussed from the wind, his cocky smile back intact, Francine didn't have to question any more why so many women found Hugh alluring. His carefree personality and silver tongue made him more attractive than perfect features would have any day.

Despite it all, she tried to imagine a lifetime with Hugh Casper and couldn't come up with any matrimonial motivation save his wealth.

"Are you ready?" he asked and rubbed his hands together.

"It's closed." Francine pointed to the sign and hugged her coat closer.

"To the public, but not to us," Hugh explained with a wink. He stepped to a brass button and pressed it twice. The mildest distinction of a buzzer penetrated the wind's bluster. A section of blonde hair whacked Francine in the eyes, and she wished she'd had enough time to twist her hair into a knot.

"I arranged to rent the whole restaurant...and a few other specialties," he explained.

"You—you what?" Francine stammered.

"I rented the whole restaurant for us." Hugh turned up his coat collar. "Now tell me you're impressed," he teased.

Francine's mouth fell open.

"I guess that's a Francine Ponce version of ecstatic," he mused. "Is this as excited as you ever get?"

A man dressed in a tuxedo appeared on the door's other side and ended the opportunity for Francine's response. But she couldn't conjure a thing to say anyway. The host twisted the lock and swung the door open.

"Welcome to Etienne's," he said with a deep bow. His dark skin was the color of the richest chocolate. His square jaw, handsome features, and athletic frame suggested he should be doing fitness advertisements on TV. The gold name tag near his lapel read "Etienne McKnight, Owner."

Francine stopped herself from gaping again. Hugh had not only rented a whole restaurant, he had arranged for the owner to serve them. She couldn't imagine what he had paid for these privileges. Probably more than several of her mother's house payments.

She entered the restaurant, which was filled with the smells of gourmet food, to the sound of a band playing a classic love song. Francine assumed the music was piped in until Etienne ushered them from the foyer into the elegant restaurant's sitting area. Near the corner, a live band performed "Endless Love." On the restaurant's furthest wall, a huge window offered a breathtaking view of the coast. The wind stirred up the sea and tossed vivacious waves against the rocky coast. The westward sun, unseen but not undetected, threw yellow beams upon the dancing white waves and offered a golden kiss upon the whole scene.

Hugh took Francine's hand and urged her forward. His fingers upon hers made Francine wish for another...Ethan Summers. Feeling like a traitor, Francine tried to pull her hand away, but Hugh tightened his grip and smiled into her eyes. Francine reminded herself that Ethan was within a breath of marrying Carrie. Hugh's touch, gentle and warm, represented a logical alternative to spending the rest of her life alone.

Silently, she strolled by Hugh to the expansive bay window that offered a close-up view of the ocean's splendor. Light faded in the eastern sky as the sun rested its chin on the western horizon. Like a travel brochure's picture, the silhouettes of three gulls flew along the indigo canvass.

Francine, captured by the view, barely registered someone freeing her of her coat and purse. When Hugh's arm slipped along her shoulders, Francine was jolted from the enrapturing view. He held two flutes of something bubbly and pale.

The rejection was on her lips when he said, "Sparkling grape juice. Want some?"

"Sure," she said, surprised by his thoughtfulness. She accepted the gift.

"So, you like my view?" a rich baritone voice inquired.

Francine glanced to the left and encountered Etienne's encouraging expression.

"It's incredible."

His smile deepening, he observed Hugh. "Your table is ready when you want to order."

Francine looked where he pointed and noticed a table for two, replete with china, candles, and a fresh bouquet of roses.

"Are you hungry yet?" Hugh asked.

"Actually, no," Francine answered and sipped her effervescent juice, the tart chill teasing her tongue.

"I thought maybe you'd like to open my Christmas present first and then…maybe we could dance awhile?" He lifted his brows in query.

She examined the bubbles popping on the top of the juice and wondered if dancing with Hugh would be even half as special as dancing with Ethan at her senior ball. That night had been a magical awakening of the love pulsating through her soul. Maybe something magical would also happen between her and Hugh.

"Okay," she said with a tiny nod.

Hugh's heightening expectation grew nearly tangible.

Francine's hand quivered, and the crystal flute wavered. A cautious whisper insisted she was wading in over her head. She eyed the huge waves pounding the rocky coast. Their distant rush and crash could still be detected despite the glass barrier and the band's melody. Francine imagined getting caught in the grip of those icy waves. A shiver sent goose bumps along her arms.

"So…let's do the Christmas present first, okay?" Hugh's encouraging question diminished her apprehension.

"You got me a Christmas present?" Francine queried, as if the information were still new. Her mind raced with what it might be. An engagement ring topped her list.

"Of course," Hugh replied. "Wait right here and I'll go get it, okay?"

Francine hugged her middle and watched Hugh hurry to their table. He set his crystal glass atop the white tablecloth and retrieved a black package from one of the chairs. On his way back to Francine, she decided Hugh's narrow hips and broad shoulders didn't hurt his appeal.

Maybe that's what Marie liked, too. The thought barged in and refused to leave. Francine studied the plush burgundy carpet and resisted a grimace. A distant whisper suggested she was allowing herself to be charmed by a pro who didn't mean a word of anything he said.

Francine compelled herself to remember her family's dire living conditions and how happy Uncle Tom would be if she announced her engagement to Hugh. When Hugh extended the gift, topped with silver ribbon and bells, thoughts of Marie vanished.

She shifted her crystal flute to her left hand and wrapped her right hand around the moderate-sized gift. Hugh smiled into her eyes. The moment froze like a paused video. She observed Hugh's alluring expression, his twinkling eyes that eagerly anticipated her response.

What will it imply to him if I accept this? she questioned. *Am I crazy to think he loves me enough to never cheat on me?*

The internal warning grew stronger. And this time it involved Francine escaping while she still had the chance. Then she remembered her family again. She shut out the whisper and took the gift.

Hugh relieved her of her sparkling grape juice and placed it on the nearest table. "Go ahead. Open it."

"You make me feel terrible," Francine explained. "I have nothing for you."

"It doesn't matter. You've already given me more than I ever dared hope."

Francine's lifted brows posed the wordless question.

"You actually came out with me!" he exclaimed like a man who'd won the lottery. "I arranged every bit of this based on one unanswered e-mail. As far as I knew, you could have not even checked it!" He laughed. "Talk about taking a chance!"

Francine joined in his chuckles and toyed with the package's tiny bells. The band struck up the first melodious chords of "Silver Bells," and she didn't think it was a coincidence.

"And on top of going out with me, you've actually started treating me like maybe…" His voice husky, Hugh didn't finish.

She touched the ribbon and searched for something to say. As usual, silence was her only option.

"You're even wearing my chain." He politely lifted the side of the golden rope and rolled it between his index finger and thumb. When he released it, he said, "I don't know if you really understand just how much I love you. I love everything about you. I even liked it when you caught my fib about Shakespeare," he teased.

She grinned and was nearly convinced the guy had really made a turn for the better. Francine had heard of his type finally falling in love. And once they really were smitten, they were loyal husbands and committed family men. Francine admired the sheen of the low lighting upon the glossy paper and wondered if Hugh Casper's love was strong enough to carry them both until her love kicked in.

"Anyway," Hugh said and tapped the top of the gift, "this will remind you of our first real date together."

Francine, curious about the package, began peeling the tape from the end. The present was too large for a ring or any other jewelry. That relieved her. While she was considering life with Hugh, she didn't want to be pressed into making the final decision now or even accepting another expensive gift.

After the present's ends were free, she removed the tape on the back. The paper slipped off an ancient leather-bound book. She opened the cover and peered at the title page for several seconds. Before she attempted to speak, Francine realized she was holding her breath.

"Oh my word!" she gasped and was stricken with how much she sounded like Sandra. "Is this what I think it is?"

"If you think it's an autographed copy of *A Christmas Carol*, you're right."

Francine's whole body began a slow quiver. "I can't believe this!" she whispered.

"It's a first edition," he offered with a glow of pride.

She held the book to her nose and inhaled the smell of antique pages. Francine closed her eyes and savored the moment. "How did you know I like Dickens?" she asked. Her attention all for Hugh, she lowered the book.

"I saw his books on the table in the library and just knew," he explained. "You're always reading. So I assumed..." He stroked her cheek, and his fingers held the chill of the ocean. "I'm so glad you like it, Francine," he whispered. "The book was given to my great-great-grandfather when Dickens was in America after the Civil War. It's been passed down through the years. Before my grandfather died, he gave it to me."

"I shouldn't take it," she protested and tried to place the book back into his hands.

"No." Hugh held up his hands. "It's yours no matter what. I want you to love the book as much as I love you."

Francine cradled the heirloom to her chest and was mesmerized by the reverent adoration in Hugh's eyes. *What I would have given for Ethan to look at me like this?* she thought. *But this is the way he looks at Carrie.* The force of her own regret created twin puddles in her eyes.

"Hey, don't cry," Hugh crooned. He placed his hand on her shoulder and propelled her closer to the window. When they stopped, they were in a snug niche, not visible by the band that was now playing "Evergreen."

Francine didn't realize until it was too late that Hugh had backed her into a corner and was moving in closer all the time. A flash of heat rushed from her feet to brow. And with the heat came snatches of the conversation Francine overheard between Hugh and Marie.

> *"Let's get into the room before this goes any further, okay?" Hugh insisted.*
> *"No wait," Marie panted.*
> *"Wait?"*
> *"Yes, wait. We need to talk first—before—before we go into the room."*

"Why would anybody need to talk at a time like this?"

"Because I want to know how much longer we're going to keep this up. There's no reason for all this secrecy. I'm dying to break up with Ricky so we can elope. Just give me the nod."

"Elope?"

"W-well, isn't that what you said our—our first night together?"

"You can't be serious." Hugh laughed. "I never said—"

"Yes—yes, you did. You said—"

"No, I didn't!"

The memory, suppressed but not forgotten, worked like a dash of cold water upon her confused mind. The internal whisper, once distant and faint, now burst upon Francine's thoughts. *Run!*

The spell was broken.

Francine, using the book as a shield, held it up between Hugh and herself. "W–w–wait!" she gasped. "You're moving too fast!"

"Oh come on, Francine," he begged, his breathing ragged. "Just one kiss." His voice thickened. "I've waited so, so long." Hugh's gaze roamed her features like a ravenous bear ready to devour its latest victim.

"No!" Francine asserted.

Hugh ignored her and pressed closer.

Francine shoved the book against his chest with a thud. *"Stop!"* she commanded in a low, urgent tone. "I'm not ready for this!"

"Okay." Hugh held up both hands. Blinking, he backed away.

And with each step, Marie's disenchanted cries echoed through Francine's mind. There was no doubt he had lied to Marie. There was no doubt Hugh had been with numerous women the way he had been with Marie. There was also no doubt he wanted Francine in that way, too.

Hugh stopped backing up and examined her, his gaze as hot as ever. "I thought maybe you were warming up to me," he coaxed. "Don't you love me at least a little?"

Francine hugged the book. "I know about Marie," she said and couldn't believe the admission slipped from her tongue.

A rush of chills covered her torso, much like when she was in the presence of God. Perhaps her own words were an answer to her heavenly petition in the parking lot. If Hugh came clean and expressed repentance, then maybe he really was changing. If he didn't…

"What about Marie?" Hugh finally asked. "And what does she have to do with—"

"You know what I'm talking about," Francine continued, her gaze as steady as her words.

"No, I don't." Hugh shook his head, his blank expression amazing Francine. For the unsuspecting, it would have been as convincing as his French accent.

"I'm talking about *you* and *her*," Francine continued, her quiet voice inflexible.

"Marie and me?" He rubbed at his brow. "Look, I don't know what she's told you, but—"

"It's not what she told me," Francine ground out. She marched from the corner and passed Hugh. Francine scanned the restaurant for any sign of Etienne and spotted him exiting the kitchen with a tray of hors d'oeuvres.

"Francine?" Hugh's wary question barely penetrated her resolve.

Without another glace at him, Francine strode toward Etienne. Hugh Casper was everything Francine knew he was from the day she met him: a lying, selfish playboy and nothing more. Presently she even doubted his involvement in the charity. His "love" for Francine hadn't changed a thing about him. If he would lie to her now about a woman, he would lie to her after the wedding.

He doesn't love me, she told herself. *He's just after me. I don't know what possessed me to even consider—*

Images of her family's wretched existence stormed her mind. Her aching love and devotion for them had pushed her beyond the realm of common sense and almost beyond the reach of God's urgent voice.

She stopped near the smiling Etienne and decided from the respect oozing from his countenance that he was more honorable on a bad day than Hugh Casper could be at his best. "My purse and coat," she said, still gripping the Dickens classic, "where are they?"

"On your chair, ma'am," Etienne explained, a disappointed wilt to his mouth.

Francine looked at the table topped with a pair of flaming candles. As predicted, her coat was draped across the back of her chair. Her purse was leaning against the chair's leg. She pressed the heel of her hand to her forehead and said, "Of course. Why didn't I notice them?"

She looked back at Etienne. "Would you please call me a taxi?"

She didn't tarry for his answer. When Francine reached the table, Hugh was awaiting her. He looked her squarely in the eyes and said, "You are the only woman I have ever seriously proposed to, Francine Ponce."

"I don't believe you!" she snapped and wrestled into her coat. "You're lying about that just like you're lying about Marie." *You told Marie you'd marry her!* she added to herself.

"No, I'm not!" he snapped, his face reddening. "I've never proposed with the intent of following through."

"Oh, but you have proposed with the intent to get what you want?"

He worked his mouth and remained silent.

She bent to retrieve her purse. "Goodbye, Hugh," she said and didn't bother to look at him.

"Francine, if you leave now, your chances with me are over. Are you sure that's what you really want? I seriously doubt there'll be another man with my...my assets who will—"

Francine pivoted toward Hugh. "I'm not looking for assets, Hugh," she stated without a blink. "I'm looking for character."

Carrie sat in her uncle's ultramodern coastal home. She snuggled into the corner of the posh sofa and lazily leafed through a copy of *Cosmopolitan,* her favorite magazine. The garland-laden gas fireplace provided heat as well as delightful flickers that played across the magazine.

She paused on a page with Christian Dior written in bold letters across the top. The silver-lipped blonde model wore a black evening gown studded in sequins. The plunging neckline went to there while the skirt's slit rose to here. Carrie smiled. The gown was nearly an exact replica of the one she'd bought for Ethan's family Christmas party. If that baby didn't tempt him to take their relationship to a more physical level, then the guy was hopeless.

She retrieved her mocha latte from the twisted-iron end table and sipped the brew. Uncle Al's housekeeper knew how to whip up a heavenly brew. Already, the liquid was soothing her taut nerves. She needed some space from Ethan as well as something to help calm her irritation.

Ethan's calling off their Colorado trip had angered and disappointed her to the point of a screaming fit, but all Ethan got was the mild pouting. Carrie reserved the screaming for her bedroom. Considering what her plans for the trip had been, she couldn't fathom why Ethan was so worried about the looks of things. If it weren't for the passion in his kisses, she might think the guy was a prude.

"Well, he's a preacher," she said under her breath. "What should I have expected?" Carrie sighed, set her coffee down, and rested her head on the back of the couch. The crystal light fixture's angular planes blurred. She shut her eyes. *Who'd have ever thought I would get tangled up with a preacher! Of all the people!* She lifted her head and grabbed her latte. She gulped the liquid and reveled in the warmth that oozed down her throat and filled her stomach. She gazed past the deck's glass doorway. In the distance, the angry ocean slammed into the sandy beach. The winter white caps, fierce and intimidating, eroded the sand.

"Hmmm," Carrie purred. Her lips resting on the mug's rim, she savored the creamy aroma and estimated Ethan was wearing down nicely. Once they became engaged, they were as good as married—in Carrie's estimation anyway. And she entertained no plans to wait until after the wedding to consummate their love. Once that was achieved, permanently prying Ethan from the pulpit would be an afterthought.

She replaced the mug on the end table and examined the silver-lipped model once more. Somehow, the pale blonde took on Francine Ponce's understated appeal...all blue-eyed and innocent. Carrie seldom talked to Ethan without his mentioning Franny—even after Hugh's distracting her. A time or two she had even wondered if Francine had somehow influenced him to call off the Colorado trip to stay home with her for Christmas. But her going away didn't fit the logic of that theory. The model's smile took on a triumphant edge. Carrie flipped the page with a snap.

A high-pitched jazz tune pierced the tranquil room and announced a call coming in. Carrie looked toward her leather bag sitting on the corner desk, then stood and padded toward it. She retrieved the phone and flipped open the lid. Hugh's name flashed across the screen.

"So, are you eloping now or what?" Carrie asked into the phone. Hugh had left their uncle's in the hopes of wooing Francine closer to marrying him.

"Fat chance!" he said and released a round of oaths.

Carrie grimaced and inched the phone away from her ear. "Watch it! You're burning my virgin ears!" she exclaimed and pulled out the straight iron chair.

"Yeah, right," Hugh chided.

Tucking one leg beneath her, Carrie lowered herself into the chair. "So what happened?" she asked and toyed with the zipper at the neck of her velour jogging suit.

"It's over! That's what happened!" Hugh snorted. "I'm going into New York City for the night. Don't wait up for me. Tell Vicky when she gets home I'll pick up Uncle Al from the airport in the morning as planned."

Ethan had driven their uncle to JFK this morning to catch a plane for an overnight business trip to Tennessee. When Al got back home, they were all going to have a family celebration with him and his girlfriend, Vicky, who was only ten years older than Carrie.

After a thoughtful pause, Carrie dubiously said, "Okay, but what's on the agenda between now and then?"

"It's none of your business!" Hugh blurted.

Carrie blinked with the force of his edict. "Hugh," she rested one elbow on the glass-topped desk and leaned forward, "just because you and Francine might have argued, that doesn't mean you need to go out and do something rash. Now listen," she lectured, "Francine is a slow mover. You knew that when—"

"It's off, Carrie!" Hugh exclaimed.

She huffed and covered her eyes. If Hugh and Francine really were on the outs, then that left the fragile blonde unattached, which meant she was more likely to influence Ethan. Carrie's stomach knotted, and she envisioned ripping that blonde model out of her magazine. Ethan had been beyond distracted the day Francine left for Rockaway. Carrie wondered where his mind was until he called her Franny. She lowered her hand and scraped the desk's glass top with her sculptured nails.

"Whatever you do, keep it low key," she admonished. "Whatever happened today, your chances of Francine changing her mind will be over if you do something stupid and she finds out—"

"When have I ever done anything stupid?" he said, a wicked smile in his voice.

"Just make sure you cover your tracks, okay?"

"I've got to go. I'm hitting traffic," Hugh said and ended the call without giving her a chance to reply.

Carrie looked at the phone, shook her head, and wondered if her capricious brother even knew how to cover his tracks.

Thirty-One

Christmas Eve morning Francine bent over her suitcase, which was sitting on the floor in Sandra's room. She pulled a lipstick from her cosmetic bag that had been tucked inside the suitcase. Beneath the bag lay the autographed Dickens novel. Somehow, she had arrived home from Hugh's date with the novel in hand.

By the time the taxi dropped her off, her mother was at work. Sandra was on the phone. And Max and Jeff were still out running the streets.

Francine had been able to hide the book without explaining its presence to anyone. She'd shoved the heirloom inside her suitcase and planned to return it to Hugh through Carrie. Simultaneously, Francine had prayed Hugh Casper meant what he said about withdrawing his proposal. She didn't ever want to speak to him again.

She looked over her shoulder toward Sandra's closed door. Her sister had gone to the bathroom for a shower five minutes ago. Francine estimated she still had a good ten minutes on her own.

She slipped the lipstick into her pants pocket, removed the novel from her suitcase, sat on the foot of her bed, and opened the book to the title page. There, Charles Dickens name was scrawled in black ink.

She fingered the signature and lifted the book to her nose. Francine inhaled and cherished the scent. Hugh had said she could keep the book no matter what. She was tempted to take him at his word.

Then a new thought struck her. *What if the book is as much of a fake as Hugh? Maybe he even forged the signature!*

Without another thought, Francine went back to her suitcase, knelt beside it, and snatched Hugh's Christmas card from the bottom. She flopped open the envelope's flap and whipped out the card. A picture of a man and woman sitting in front of a flaming fireplace graced the front of the card. Hugh's signature claimed the inside.

Francine held his signature up to the one in the book. They proved so evidently different that she dismissed her previous doubts. After close scrutiny of the autograph, Francine deduced that time had indeed faded it. The "s" even bore a watermark.

"Okay," she said and stuffed the card back into the envelope. "I guess this is the real deal." The growing temptation to keep the book nearly overwhelmed her. With a groan, she ran her index finger over the yellowed page and knew she couldn't. Her conscience wouldn't let her. This was a family heirloom. Even if Hugh didn't want it, his parents would.

"Easy come, easy go," she breathed and placed the book back under her cosmetic case. When she shut the top of her suitcase, the door creaked, and Sandra exploded into the room.

Francine stood from her suitcase, retrieved the lipstick from her pocket, and leaned toward a cracked mirror hanging on the wall.

"Boy, that water is cold. Makes my teeth hurt when I brush them." Sandra flopped onto her bed and dumped her faded pink nightshirt and shampoo next to her. "I made the mistake of brushing my teeth after I took a shower and used up all the hot water." Her hair wrapped in a towel, she pulled her terrycloth robe closer and shivered. "I promise, I think the wind is blowing right through that bathroom. It's a wonder we don't all die of exposure.

"When you get through," Sandra said, "I'll do my makeup there."

"I'm through," Francine replied and moved away. She glanced toward the window and noted the thick cord tied to the handle. She smiled and imagined Sandra's ecstatic reaction when she learned about the secret. Francine stepped toward the window, but Sandra's energized voice altered her plans.

"While I'm painting my face, tell me more about Central Park," Sandra said. "Oh!" She clapped her hands once. "Does that yummy Hugh Casper live close?"

"Sometimes," Francine said and settled back onto the bed. Images of Hugh dashed aside her pleasant musings about Christmas surprises.

Makeup bag in hand, Sandra stepped to the full-length mirror and dropped to the floor. "I don't think Mother is ever going to forgive you for breaking up with him," Sandra claimed.

Francine ignored her sister's comment. She had been forced by her mom's interrogation to explain that she and Hugh were no longer an item, nor had they ever been.

To keep from having to talk about Hugh anymore, she began drawing word pictures for Sandra on everything from Daisy's favorite dog food to the famous people whom Uncle Tom had helped invest money. She even detailed her cousins' parties and vacations to exotic places.

"You know, Sandra," Francine finished, "I might be able to get Uncle Tom to let you visit sometime. Would you like that?"

"Would I!" Sandra exclaimed and applied the final coat to her lip gloss. "I'd give a year of my life for that!"

Francine nodded. "Let's don't push it, okay?" she said. "Let me handle it. The smoother you are with Uncle Tom, the more likely you are to get what you ask for. We'll just see how it unfolds."

Considering her dwindling savings account, Francine had resigned herself to going back to Central Park. She also planned to access her trust fund on behalf of her family. Sometime during last night's tossing and debating her options, Francine had decided that if she couldn't have Ethan, she could be just as miserable under Uncle Tom's thumb as she could be on her own. At least with this plan, she would keep her trust fund and use it to assist her family.

Francine picked at the sleeping bag atop the bed. A profound gloominess overtook her. Visions of Carrie Casper tantalizing Ethan…leading him from his mission…haunted her. Uncle Tom's disapproval wrenched her heart. But the deepest pain was Ethan's lack of attention, the loss of his daily kindness, and the lack of his continual assurance of her worth to him.

Oh Ethan! she inwardly wailed. *We could have been so happy together!*

Her present misery was topped only by having to respond to Ethan's chatty e-mail with one of her own. Francine had felt like the biggest fake of the century. Every word she typed had been full of information but lacking in the professions of love her heart so longed to express. She had yet to receive a response back, and she pined for his e-mail while dreading the absence of love.

"Hello in there!" Sandra's hand appeared before her face.

Francine blinked and looked up at her.

"What in the world are you thinking about?" Sandra asked. "You look like you just lost your best friend."

Stunned, Francine didn't answer. Instead she stood and searched beside the bed for her penny loafers. The silence stretching, she inserted her feet into the shoes.

"Hey, you okay?" Sandra asked and gripped Francine's arm.

"Sure," Francine said and hoped her smile didn't look as forlorn as it felt. On a whim, Francine went back to her suitcase and pulled out the bottle of Oscar de la Renta Eau de Toilette she'd bought for her birthday party. That night she'd hoped Ethan would fall in love with her looks…her fragrance…her. Now she doubted he even remembered.

"Would you like to have this, Sandra?" she asked.

Sandra's eyes bugged. "You bet!" she said and accepted the gift. She lifted the gold-toned lid from the spray bottle and inhaled. Sandra rolled her eyes. "This is the stuff you had on when you went out with Hugh, isn't it?"

"Yes," Francine acknowledged and stifled a moan. Every conversation with Sandra went back to Hugh Casper.

"Maybe if I spray this all over my body I'll catch someone like him!" she said and hustled toward her closed door. On the back of the door hung one of Marie's hand-me-downs—a pantsuit replete with a wide silver belt and a short-waisted jacket. "As soon as I dry my hair, this is what I'm wearing today." Sandra misted the outfit up and down, huffed in a deep breath, then released a rafter-shaking sneeze.

Francine giggled. "You're crazy," she teased.

"Well, somebody's got to laugh around this place," Sandra said, her animation dying with every word. She replaced the top on the fragrance bottle.

Her features settled into an expression every bit as forlorn as Francine's smile felt. She ducked her head and turned her back to Francine. "Dad's going to be back home between now and tomorrow," she said with conviction. "He never misses Christmas." She placed the fragrance on the top of the aging chest of drawers. Then she trudged past Francine and began gathering her makeup from the floor.

"I heard Mom crying before I went to sleep last night," Francine said. She crossed her arms and leaned against the marred wall. "Nothing ever gets better here, does it? It's the same as it was when I moved to Manhattan ten years ago."

"I just pretend he's someone who stops by…not even a friend." Sandra waved her mascara container and attempted a chipper smile. "Maybe like a meter reader." Her hollow declaration intensified the room's despondent aura.

"But Sandra, he's supposed to be our *father!*"

" 'Supposed to be's' don't count in Rockaway," Sandra said. With her makeup in her stained bag, she stepped back to the chest of drawers and laid it next to the fragrance.

Once again Francine eyed the piece of thick cord tied to the window handle and decided her surprise would chase away Sandra's gloom. She pushed up the sleeves of her cotton sweater and rubbed her hands together.

"I have a secret," Francine confessed.

Sandra pulled her hair dryer out of the top drawer and looked at Francine. "You're full of surprises," she said, "like billionaires who drive up in Ferraris."

"See that string tied to the window handle?" Francine asked. Ignoring the reference to Hugh, she pointed toward the frost-covered window.

Sandra mutely eyed the window.

"Our Christmas dinner is out there."

"What?" Sandra exclaimed. She dropped the blow dryer, climbed over her bed, and examined the knot.

"Remember Mother saying yesterday she wanted a ham to go with the chicken tomorrow…and some pumpkin pies, but she didn't have the money?"

"Yeah," Sandra said.

"Well, Wade and I sneaked out last night at midnight and took a taxi to the all-night grocery store."

"You guys went out at midnight in *this* neighborhood?" Sandra exclaimed. Francine chuckled under her breath. "It's not like we walked the streets or anything. Besides, Wade is good protection. The taxi pulled right up to the front door and waited outside the store while we shopped." She squeezed past Sandra's bed and joined her at the window. With a grunt, Francine inched the window upward. "This is heavy with the box tied to it."

She looked at Sandra who was so mesmerized with the whole idea she hadn't a clue about assisting her sister. "How did you get it out there?"

"Wade helped," Francine explained. "You slept like a log through the whole thing."

Sandra laughed, and her merry eyes showed no signs of the memories of her father. "Wade always says I could sleep through a hurricane."

"That's what he said last night, too," Francine said. "Would you like to help now?"

"Oh sure!" Sandra exclaimed. "Here!"

With a series of heaves and grunts, the sisters lifted the window all the way. They propped the window open and leaned out to view the box, dangling three feet beneath the second-story window.

"When I told Wade I wanted to put it out the window, he nearly made me put it in the fridge because he leaves so early every morning and couldn't help me now. But I didn't want to put the stuff in the refrigerator because I knew Mother would find it this morning before I got up," Francine explained. "I wanted to be the one to give it to her. I enjoy seeing her face when she's surprised. So I talked Wade into using some of the twins' cord they tied around the dining table last night, and the great outdoors made the perfect refrigerator."

They wrestled the box, bound in cord, through the opened window. Laughing, the two sisters fell back on Sandra's bed. "Franny, you're the best," Sandra said when she caught her breath. She looked at her sister for several seconds while tears reddened her eyes. "I wish we had all those years back when you were in Manhattan." She blinked at the tears. "Not that I would have wanted you to miss the opportunity." Her voice grew solemn. "But it would have been so much fun to be together."

Francine sat up, drew her sister close, and said, "I wish that too." She tightened her arms around Sandra's back and rested her cheek on the towel, still wrapped around hair as blonde as Francine's. The icy air filtering in from the city smelled of exhaust and ushered in the honks and lurch of traffic. The sounds weren't much different than at Central Park.

A new sense of peace began in the center of Francine's heart and spread outward like a warming coal newly alive. All these years she had wished for her family, forever believing they had abandoned her. But from their viewpoint, in a sense she had abandoned them. Wade had succeeded in keeping in touch, and Sandra tried. And while Francine didn't think she would ever lose contact with one of her children the way her mother had, she recognized the back-bending load her mom was carrying. She understood how a woman of her temperament might fall into a pattern of not contacting a daughter who had far more privileges than the children still at home. While none of Florence's circumstances were an excuse for the neglect, they were a *reason* that assisted Francine in coming to terms with the hurt.

Suddenly, Uncle Tom's overbearing ways seemed a small price to pay for the privilege of helping her family. A small price indeed. Besides, nothing at Central Park seemed half as bad as the chaos and raw dysfunction of her Rockaway family. Francine would be glad to get back home. Uncle Tom had been right. It had done her good to see just how bad her family's circumstances were, but not for the reasons he'd hoped.

"If I have my way, Sandra," Francine said and stroked her sister's back, "you'll be a regular visitor at Central Park from now on."

Sandra sniffed and dried her eyes on the edge of her sheet. "I'm almost afraid to hope," she whimpered.

As soon as Sandra finished dressing, the sisters shared the load on the heavy box of food and did their best to descend the stairs without toppling head over heels. Amid giggles and anticipation, they managed to arrive at the bottom with the box and their heads still intact.

Francine slammed into her sister as they tried to reclaim their grip on the box.

"I'm so glad we're going to be together for Christmas," Sandra said. "Otherwise, who'd knock me silly?"

"This Christmas is going to be *perfect!*" Francine encouraged, and a fresh, festive spirit began to chase away some of her disenchantment over Ethan.

Sandra's face grew solemn. "Especially if Dad decides to stay gone." Her whisper was barely audible.

Francine didn't answer. She had really hoped to see her father. Given his behavior during her childhood and now, she didn't really understand why. But the desire was there nonetheless.

They strolled into the kitchen and set the box on the counter, near where Florence Ponce was hunched over a pan of fragrant bacon—more of Francine's blessings.

"Merry Christmas, Mother," Francine said and slid an arm around her shoulders.

Sandra grabbed a kitchen knife and started sawing on the twine. "Francine and Wade sneaked out last night and got us a ham!" she crowed.

Florence's head snapped up. Her eyes were swollen and red. Because of the cooking, the room felt slightly warmer than the others. But Florence Ponce was shivering.

"Mother!" Francine exclaimed. "Is the house warm enough? You look so cold."

"Don't worry about her none," a familiar voice growled from the corner.

Francine spun around and recognized the man who went with the voice. Her father, his face rough with gray-blond whiskers, lowered his *New York Times* and looked over the top. His pale hair was thinning and now mixed with silver. His red face was fuller than Francine recalled and flushed with the presence of alcohol. Blue eyes, as pale as her own, demanded she look away.

She did. *He doesn't even act like he recognizes me,* she thought.

"The danged power costs too much to keep the heat more than sixty-two or three," Howie slurred. He picked up a brown bottle sitting on the table and took a long swig.

Jeff and Max blasted into the room and circled the table like two wild hyenas. Howie Ponce buried himself back into his paper.

Sandra gripped Francine's hand. Florence went back to her bacon and her weeping. Francine's gift was forgotten.

"I can't stand all this noise," Howie snapped. "The garbage that woman cooks ain't worth all this upheaval. I come back 'ome thinkin' I'm gonna get some peace and I wind up with…" He yanked up his bottle and hurled it at the twins.

The bottle splashed beer all over the dining table, then crashed against the refrigerator. Amazingly, it missed the twins and didn't break. Max and Jeff looked like two puppies who spied the neighborhood bulldog. They screeched and dashed toward the hallway.

Howie glared at Francine. "Well, don't just stand there, clean up the mess!" he snarled.

She jumped, and Florence shoved a towel into her hands. Francine began her task. She started at the refrigerator. After throwing away the bottle, she recalled the reason the very smell of alcohol made her nauseous.

"Ha!" Howie's coarse laugh sent a jolt through Francine.

She turned to face him again and prepared to dodge another missile.

"Here's an article that's somethin' to see! Ha!" He repeated like a pirate relishing a sick joke. Howie lowered the paper and sneered at Francine. "The society pages," he said with falsetto mockery.

Francine moved toward the cabinet and gripped it for support. This person wasn't her father and had *never* been. In her childhood he had never done anything but tell her she was worthless. And he had expected her to wait on him hand and foot. Even with all his faults, Uncle Tom was a hundred times more caring than this yelling brute. Sandra's saying Howie Ponce was like the meter reader was a generous estimation.

"Christmas surprises abound from the Wor–Worthinghams," Howie read. "Marie Barrimore Worthingham, the recent bride of billionaire Ricky Worthing–Worthingham, was caught in flight with 'er lover, Hugh C–C–Casper."

Sandra gasped. Florence turned to face her husband. Francine's horror switched from her father to what he read. She clutched her towel and prayed what she was hearing was something he was making up in his diseased mind.

"Marie knows 'ow to attract the money!" Howie paused for a belch and shot a cunning glance toward his captive audience. "Hugh is said to be one of the heirs to the Addy's restaurant billions. A cl—close friend of the new Mrs. Worthingham reports that Marie is leaving her…her 'usband for Casper. The two are seen 'ere before they boarded a flight for Paris. What a roman—romantic city to spend Christmas in—espe-specially for a new bride!"

Howie flopped the paper on the recently dried table. "Ha!" he repeated. "Looks like that side of the family is more trashy than—than this one! What did I tell you, Florence?" he jeered. "And 'ere you sent our daughter off to live with them!"

He stood and jabbed the center of the paper with his index finger. "Read fur yourself!" he demanded. "I'm going to the back porch for my c–cigar. I've had 'bout all the high society I can–can stomach." He shot a bleary glower at Francine and stomped from the room.

The second the kitchen door slammed, all three women darted to the paper. Francine only needed one glance at the color photo to confirm every word of what her father read. The photographer had caught Hugh and Marie from the side as they strode into the airport. Hugh's arm was around Marie's back, and she leaned into his embrace like a lover.

Numb disbelief struck her speechless. Francine scanned the short article plastered on the front of the society page. All she could think was, *Thank You, God, I didn't agree to marry him!* Francine's next thoughts were for Uncle Tom and Aunt Mariette and how this must be ripping out their hearts.

The telephone's ringing jarred the trio from their mute fixation upon the paper. Francine knew before Sandra even picked up the kitchen phone's receiver that the call would be for her.

Thirty-Two

Ethan paced Carrie's living room. Her housekeeper had admitted him and told him she would notify Carrie of his presence. That was fifteen minutes ago. He checked his watch and noted that ten o'clock was only a few minutes away. He wondered if Carrie might just now be getting up.

She had arrived back at Central Park yesterday evening after a few days with her uncle. Hugh was supposed to follow today. She and Ethan had shared dinner last night, and she promised him a Christmas he wouldn't forget. Ironically, Carrie didn't know that he couldn't forget Francine. Last night Christmas with Carrie had been at the bottom of his list of concerns.

He sat on the leather sofa, propped his elbows on his knees, and looked at the black lacquer coffee table. At last Ethan admitted what he'd known since he arrived home from Paris. His friendship with Francine was no more. Her e-mail yesterday had sounded as stilted as her goodbye when she left for Rockaway. Ethan didn't even have the heart to answer it. He settled into the corner of the sofa and stared into space. A tide of confusion jumbled his thoughts and skewed his logic.

Carrie's cheerful greeting yanked him back to the reason he was here and reminded him of another crisis far more scandalous than his confusion over Francine. His gaze landed on the *New York Times* he'd dropped on the center of the table when he arrived.

Ethan stood and turned to face the woman who would be his fiancée in just over a week. As usual, she looked like she'd just stepped off the pages of a fashion magazine. But today her outfit was more daring than anything Ethan had ever seen her in. Her tight leather pants left nothing to the imagination. Neither did the cowl neck sweater that suggestively drooped to reveal more cleavage than was appropriate for any pastor's wife.

"Do you like my new outfit?" Carrie crooned and pivoted before him. "Uncle Al's girlfriend gave it to me for Christmas. What do you think?"

"You look—you look great," Ethan squeezed out the words, then coughed.

She moved in close and slid both her hands up his face in a gesture that once sent him into a spin. But today the move annoyed. He gently covered her hands with his and inched them away from his face.

Carrie puckered her lower lip, tilted her head, and simpered, "No kiss this morning?"

"Not right now, okay?" Ethan replied.

"So what brings you over so early?" she asked and daintily covered a yawn. "You look like you've already been for your run." Carrie rubbed the sleeve of his sweatshirt. "Is it cold out this morning?"

"I guess you could say that." Ethan stepped to the coffee table and picked up the newspaper. He turned to the front of the society section and held it under Carrie's view. His gut tight, he said, "You didn't know anything about this, did you?"

"*Oh no!*" Carrie shrieked and grabbed the paper. Her widened eyes and opened mouth answered Ethan's question.

"My brother is an idiot!" she spewed and ripped the paper from Ethan's hands. "How could he do this? Why would he do this? Now there's no way Francine will even *look* at him again!"

"And well she shouldn't." Ethan crossed his arms.

"Well, if he was going to go off and have another fling with Marie, he could have at least had the decency to keep it quiet." She slammed the paper onto the couch. "I told him two days ago not to do anything stupid!"

"*Another* fling?" Ethan asked and placed his hands on his hips.

"Oops!" Carrie covered her lips with her fingertips. "I guess I spilled that little secret, didn't I?"

"How long have you known?" Ethan demanded, his stomach burning.

"Well, I just assumed, and Hugh never denied it. I really think they broke up and that's the reason he went back to Paris a few months ago."

Ethan's face went cold. "And you knew about all this even before he proposed to Franny?"

"Well, yes." Carrie shrugged.

"And you didn't say anything?"

She lifted her hands. "What? So I tell the world and ruin his chances with Francine? You know she wouldn't have even considered him if she knew he'd had an affair with Marie."

"Yes, I know," Ethan mumbled. He staggered sideways and landed on the couch's arm. His legs extended for support, he braced himself against any new revelations. Slowly he allowed his attention to travel up the length of Carrie's legs, toward her sweater, then to her immaculately made-up face.

Carrie huffed. "Now, he's gone off and ruined all chances forever! Oh shoot! I thought Francine would have been so good for him. If he was dead-set on doing this—why did he have to let it hit the paper?"

She marched across the room and kicked at a table. "Oh well." Carrie raised her hands. "I hope he'll at least have the decency to marry Marie—especially after he's taken her away from her husband. But who knows!"

Ethan felt as if he were in a slow-motion movie and every detail of Carrie's words and expressions were being engraved upon his psyche. "What I *do* know is that all this is terribly immoral," Ethan said.

"Well, I guess so," Carrie admitted. "But even at that, people will forget—especially if Hugh and Marie get married. People have such a way of forgetting these types of things a few years down the road. Then it won't matter anymore."

"What about Ricky?" Ethan questioned. He pitied the man he had scorned and who Francine had insisted possessed good qualities. But then she always saw the best in everyone.

"Humph, that idiot?" Carrie laughed. "You think he'll even realize she's gone?"

Ethan didn't smile.

"Oh sorry." She bit her bottom lip until the smile was no more. "I'm sure he's gone back home to mama and won't be any worse for wear. Somebody will marry him again. He's too rich to stay single too long."

"And my aunt and uncle?" Ethan stood and couldn't stop his rising ire from distorting his features.

"I imagine they are disappointed, aren't they?" Carrie's voice softened and she stepped back to Ethan's side. "But if Marie divorces Ricky and marries Hugh, they'll get over it."

"No, I don't think so."

When Carrie tried to slip her hand into the crook of his arm, Ethan moved out of her reach.

"There's more news besides this today," he explained and wondered if there was any way the jeweler would allow him to return a custom-made engagement ring. "Julie eloped with Yancey Bates," he finished.

"Well, that doesn't surprise me!" Carrie shook her head.

"It did my parents. They never expected her to do something like this and exclude them from it. They think maybe Marie influenced her."

"Probably," Carrie mused.

Ethan considered Carrie's appearance once more and wondered why he ever convinced himself she would make a good wife. The answer surged from the bottom of his being and left him disgusted with his own weakness.

He relived that day at the Worthingham Renaissance chapel. Carrie had plainly said she didn't respect clergymen and then talked her way out of it. Next he faced another grim reality. He had allowed her to so distract him from enrolling in his final seminary class. And on top of that, he had even promised her he'd postpone his ordination. He had nearly also allowed her to entice him on that trip to Colorado. In the past he had never done more than group dating. Somehow he had permitted himself to be lured into compromising his reputation. Now he could only imagine what other plans Carrie might have had.

A holy fire cleansed his soul and burned away the last traces of the invisible blinders marring his vision.

"You're no different than Hugh!" Ethan accused. He stumbled backward and gaped at Carrie.

"Excuse me?" Carrie asked. Hands on hips, she narrowed her eyes and studied Ethan.

"Francine knows," he mumbled to himself.

"Francine?" Carrie's thin brows arched.

"She knows everything. I know she knows…about you… maybe even about Marie and Hugh. That's why—"

"Francine knows *what* about me?" Carrie snapped.

"That you…your…that…we—you and I aren't—"

Carrie's face grew crimson. "Are you breaking up with me, Ethan?"

"Yes." His mouth dry, Ethan nodded.

"What does Francine have to do with it?" Carrie demanded and stomped her spike-heeled shoe.

"N–nothing. I guess…I don't—I don't know." Ethan rammed his hands into the sides of his hair and tried to make sense of the information bombshells exploding one at a time.

"Are you breaking up with me because of her?" Carrie hollered. "Because of something she's said?"

Ethan lowered his hands and stared at the red-faced vixen prancing before him.

"That little two-faced—"

"Don't start blaming Francine for—"

"I'll blame her if she's the cause!" Carrie stormed within centimeters of Ethan. "You're in love with her, aren't you?" she screamed.

"No," Ethan said and thought he was telling the truth. But with his denial came the conviction that he didn't understand his own heart.

"You're lying!" Carrie bellowed. She kicked her pointed-toed shoes across the room. One crashed into the cold fireplace. The other one slammed into a knickknack shelf and toppled a porcelain leopard. The animal smashed onto the hardwood floor and shattered into hundreds of shards.

Carrie ran in place and screamed like a wild woman. "I have been an idiot!" she roared. "I see the way you look at her…the way you protect her…the way *she* looks at you. I suspected it from the start, but I talked myself out of it."

Ethan staggered backward. Each of Carrie's claims hit him in the gut like a physical punch. He stopped when he slammed into the wall. And Ethan finally understood that his attraction for Francine wasn't a sick fascination.

It was love. It was pure love. And it was perfectly natural and perfectly honorable.

Francine wasn't his sister. She had *never* been his sister. They'd been friends from the start. Most normal brothers and sisters weren't half as close as they were. Their relationship had been more—much, much more. At least to him.

"I've got to go," Ethan said and fled for the doorway.

"I hate you, Ethan Summers!" Carrie shrieked. "Do you hear me? I hate—"

He slammed the door on her final edict.

⌒ ⌒

Francine sat in the Barrimores' den and fanned Aunt Mariette, who had finally relaxed after an exhausting sobbing spell. The minute Francine walked into the home, Mariette had fallen into her arms and cried as if both her daughters were murdered. Francine joined in her crying and couldn't deny that a few of her tears involved the relief of being home.

Sandra hurried back into the den with another cool compress. Francine accepted the cloth and gingerly placed it upon her aunt's forehead.

Mariette shifted on the sofa, sighed, and whimpered, "I'm so glad you're back home, Franny. And I'm glad you brought Sandra." Her eyes drooped open and she gazed up at the sisters. "She's as big a help as you are. It's like I've got two daughters all over—over again. She's even wearing Marie's old outfit." She gulped and clutched the neck of her housedress. "This is the worst Christmas I've ever had!" she wailed.

Francine, perched on the sofa's edge, patted her aunt's hand. Sandra hovered near her head. "It's going to be okay," Francine crooned and observed the Christmas tree. Decked with red lights, the tree still claimed its merry place by the window but had lost its allure. Francine sighed and wished the holiday were already behind them.

"Both my daughters are gone...just gone!" Mariette wept. "We don't even know where Julie is right now! And I was hoping Marie would give us a grandchild by next Christmas. Now... now..." She shook her head and hiccoughed. "The whole church will know. It's the most disgraceful thing I've ever heard of!"

"And we all know whose fault it is!" Nora's rigid tones invaded the room.

The sisters turned, and Francine never thought she'd ever be glad to see her caustic aunt. But after a week in Rockaway, even Aunt Nora's grim face was a welcome reprieve. Anything was better than roach-coffee and flying beer bottles.

Nora, her lids rimmed in red, walked into the antique-laden den and sat in the wing-backed chair. She frowned at Francine, her green eyes hard. Her unspoken message was clear. Aunt Nora blamed Francine for this mess with Marie.

She started to protest when Nora shifted her focus to Sandra. "Lord help us, there's two of them now," Nora mumbled and shook her head.

"Yes, Sandra came for a visit too," Mariette said. "I don't know what I'd do without either one of them right now."

Mariette released Francine's hand and weakly grasped Sandra's. "She got my tea and keeps bringing me fresh compresses."

Taking the cue, Sandra reached for the china cup sitting on the teak end table. She plumped up the pillows behind her aunt and offered the lady the tea that was steaming with the fragrance of fresh raspberries.

"Thank you. Thank you so much, dear," Mariette said and accepted the gift. After a brief sip, she continued, "I told Ike to arrange for Sandra to have Francine's old room."

Sandra dimpled into an ecstatic smile.

"Oh, that's not necessary," Francine said. "She can sleep with me. We didn't intend for anyone to be put out."

"Nonsense," Mariette said and touched the cloth on her head. "She deserves her own space while she's here." She closed her eyes again and tilted her head toward the velvet sofa. "Maybe she'll be like you and never leave us," she said. "The Lord knows we need some joy around here."

Francine shot a silent "Calm down!" to Sandra, who was on the verge of jumping into a cheer. Although she bottled her enthusiasm, Sandra's face shone.

Daisy's worried bark echoed from the entryway and Francine stood.

"Daisy is as upset as we are," Mariette said. "It's like she knows."

"She's just worried because you're crying," Nora claimed with an unspoken "oh brother" dripping from her words. "Dogs don't know things like this."

Francine stood and strode toward the entryway. "Hello, Daisy," she said and clapped her hands toward the rat terrier hovering near the doorway.

The dog yelped and dashed to Francine. She scooped up the canine and scratched her ears. Daisy panted, licked Francine's hand, and yapped some more.

"She's missed you," Mariette said. "We all have. It's been dreadful around here without you—just like we thought it would be."

"Apparently Hugh thought it was dreadful too," Nora said. She leaned back in the chair and rested her elbows on the arms. "If you'd just done the decent thing and obeyed your uncle and gotten engaged to Hugh, none of this would have happened." Nora pointed her finger at Francine's nose. "Now look what you've done. This whole thing is your fault!"

Francine stopped petting Daisy and eyed Nora. For the first time in her life, she didn't lower her head in the face of Nora's disdain. Instead, Francine held her aunt's gaze and decided the time had come to speak.

"I don't believe my engagement to Hugh would have stopped him and Marie from doing what they wanted to," she quietly said.

Nora gasped and went rigid. Movement from Mariette snared Francine's attention. Her aunt had lifted herself up on one elbow and was watching Francine in wide-eyed astonishment. A puddle of tea rested in her tottering cup's saucer. Francine licked her lips and glanced at Sandra. While her sister possessed no background to understand the significance of the moment, she knotted her fingers and looked from Nora to Francine and back again.

"Are you refuting my word, young lady?" Scooting forward, Nora prepared to stand.

"I believe she is." Uncle Tom's voice boomed from the doorway.

Francine jumped and turned to face her uncle. Daisy barked and squirmed in her arms.

Tom Barrimore's eyes, suspiciously swollen, nailed Nora in an intense glower. "How dare you blame Francine for this!" he barked. "I think she's the most level-headed person in this whole household. She's the only one who's shown one lick of sense in the middle of this whole mess."

Nora cowered into the chair's corner and didn't look above her brother-in-law's chin.

"The blame rests with my daughters and these men they've gone off with! And with me!" Tom rammed his index finger against his chest. "I didn't have character enough to see past the money. I should have never encouraged Marie to marry Ricky in the first place. She didn't love him, and I knew it. But I thought..." His attention trailed toward Francine, and his eyes begged her forgiveness. "I thought the love would come."

While Uncle Tom's disdain had been unbearable, his humility was overwhelming. Francine shook; her shoulders hunched. She couldn't prevent the broken sob from bursting from her soul. Someone took Daisy, and Francine covered her face with both hands.

Uncle Tom patted her back and pulled her close. "Oh Franny," he said, his voice thick. "I can't tell you how sorry I am."

Francine leaned into him and rested her head on his shoulder, covered in a starched white shirt. She breathed in his familiar peppermint smell.

"Ethan says Carrie told him Marie and Hugh had an affair before she got married. You knew, didn't you?" Tom asked.

Francine nodded.

"Why didn't you tell me?"

"Because I pr–promised Marie I wouldn't—wouldn't tell," she choked out.

"And you always keep your word," Uncle Tom said. He stroked her hair and rested his chin on her head. "I should have trusted you," he admitted.

"It's okay," Francine squeaked and scrounged through her pocket for a tissue. She came up empty-handed. Someone shoved a box of tissue under her nose, and she grabbed a handful. When her tears were drying, she realized that "someone" was Sandra and that she also held Daisy.

"Hey," Francine said with a watery laugh, "that's not fair. Daisy never likes strangers."

"Sandra's not a stranger," Uncle Tom asserted. "She's family!"

Thirty-Three

One week later Francine sat in the sunroom on top of the Barrimores' brownstone. She studied page 83 of her Agatha Christie novel. The words "Chapter Eight" claimed the top. The problem was, Francine couldn't remember reading chapter seven.

She shifted in the settee and reached for the styrofoam cup of hot cocoa she'd prepared for herself minutes before. Francine sipped the liquid, closed her eyes, and welcomed the warmth that slipped into her stomach just as she'd welcomed the solitude of the sunroom. She eyed her novel and closed it. Francine had read chapter seven twice. She refused to read it again. Her thoughts had been so wrapped up in the events of the past week she hadn't been able to absorb one syllable of the plotline.

Julie and Yancey, all laughter and newlywed joy, had surfaced two days after Christmas. Even though Uncle Tom wasn't wild about Yancey, he had to admit that Julie had married for love, not money. The guy couldn't even support himself, let alone her.

Hugh and Marie, brazenly unrepentant, were still in Paris. Poor Ricky was seeing a counselor. And Uncle Tom had forbidden Nora from mentioning the subject in his presence.

Francine swallowed another sip of cocoa, stood, and stretched. She laid her novel on the snack bar and debated what to do with the free afternoon that stretched forth like an empty chasm. Sandra was sitting with Aunt Mariette. Francine wasn't so certain that her aunt didn't enjoy Sandra's company more than her own. Sandra was much more talkative and had Aunt Mariette laughing out loud this morning. Uncle Tom had agreed that since Francine would be away from Central Park more and more with her upcoming teaching schedule, Sandra should move in and enjoy the privileges Francine had known. Florence Ponce readily agreed.

Francine idly wondered if Wade had responded to her last e-mail. He started his new job in two days, and he was ecstatic about the opportunity. Francine had worried that her rejection of Hugh would cause him to end Wade's job opportunity. But apparently Hugh had left with Marie and not looked back. Wade's last e-mail stated that the restaurant manager called him yesterday to confirm his arrival January 2. That's when Francine quit fretting about Wade's future.

She stretched again and set her hot cocoa on the snack bar. After gathering her denim jacket from the back of one of the patio chairs, Francine slipped it on and retrieved her cocoa and book. The trek to the elevator was short, but the New York winter was setting in.

When Francine placed her hand on the doorknob, a flash of blue from the right snared her attention. Ethan had just exited the elevator and was striding toward the edge of the terrace. Francine's fingers tightened on the knob.

All week she and Ethan had kept a polite distance like two strangers who didn't know whether or not they would like the other. The Christmas gift exchange had been stiff at best. The Christmas-night family bash had been canceled. Christmas afternoon, Francine and Sandra went back to Rockaway to spend the day with their mother. This time Francine took her trust fund checkbook and explained her plans to help. Florence Ponce wept during the whole conversation. Both Francine and Sandra had been relieved that their father was conveniently absent…again.

When they returned to Central Park the day after Christmas, the details of Ethan's breakup with Carrie were trickling from Aunt Mariette. No one in the household seemed to have the whole story. Even Mariette reported that her husband's knowledge was limited. Because of Carrie's absence, Francine had mailed the Dickens novel to their Uncle Al with a cryptic note attached for Hugh.

The dark circles under Ethan's eyes implied he wasn't handling the breakup very well. Francine wanted to talk to him about the lost romance, but she didn't quite know where to start. So she remained polite but reserved. The last thing her raw heart needed was Ethan's bemoaning the loss of his "perfect woman." Whatever happened between them must have been traumatic. Carrie had relinquished her lease Christmas Eve and spent the rest of the holiday at her uncle's.

Francine gazed at Ethan in his blue sweater and faded jeans. Shoulders slanted, he inserted his hands into his pockets and looked toward Central Park. He seemed oblivious to the cold.

Ike's question the day Francine left for Rockaway barged into her mind: *Do you ever plan to tell him?*

"No—oh no!" Francine had whispered and vehemently shook her head. "I'm not telling him!"

Maybe this is the answer to your own prayer. The thought seared its way through the center of her mind and wouldn't be ignored. During the past week, Francine had prayed like never before. She petitioned heaven for a miracle…that maybe somehow, some way Ethan would return her love.

I wonder what he would say if I just told him? Francine stumbled away from the door and hastened to the far wall. *I can't tell him!* she argued with herself. *What if he laughs at me? What if he thinks I'm crazy? We've been like brother and sister. What if he's disgusted?*

She collapsed back onto the wicker settee at the same time the door swung open. Something wet and warm soaked through her jeans. But Francine was so focused upon the man entering the room she just shoved her cup of cocoa onto the counter and didn't bother to look at the mess.

"Hey," Ethan called and stepped inside. "I didn't know you were in here. I was just coming in to make myself some coffee. I came up for some quiet time and found out it's cold up here." A swoosh of chilled air accompanied his closing the door. He rubbed his hands together.

Francine, overtaken by the quivers, barely nodded and didn't even attempt to speak.

Ethan approached the snack bar, turned his back to her, and removed a styrofoam cup from the dispenser. "Looks like you've already got some hot water going here," he said, helping himself to a cup of water from the coffee maker. He reached for the instant coffee, and with his every move Francine's heart pounded in growing fierceness.

She told herself to stop watching Ethan, but she couldn't. He held her in his power, and all she could do was hunger to feel his thick, dark hair beneath her touch…to experience his lips upon hers. Simultaneously, Francine had never been so scared in her life. Not even the day she arrived at Central Park could compare to her current fright. She knew beyond all doubt that the answer to her prayers had come. And the answer involved her taking a risk.

Like a person on the verge of death, Francine's life flashed before her. For the most part, she had never taken action in her world. She had meekly gone along with the flow and made everyone happy…except when it came to the Hugh Casper business and participating in that play. Other than that, Francine had allowed life to happen to her…allowed other people to dictate how that might happen.

"I don't even like blackened salmon," she mumbled, shaking her head, *but I ate it anyway because that's what Carrie liked, and she wanted me to have it.*

"What?" Ethan turned to face her. His coffee steaming on the snack bar, he leaned against the counter and crossed his arms. "Did you say something about blackened salmon?" he asked, his brows raised.

Francine stood and approached the snack bar. She laid her book near the fruit basket and reached for a roll of paper towels. "I guess I did," she replied and tore off a fist full of paper towels. She blotted at her jeans, now cooling from their cocoa bath.

When she didn't offer to expound, Ethan chuckled. "Is there something on your mind?"

She tossed the damp paper towels in the trash can at the end of the counter and grappled with what to say. "I…uh…" she hedged and wondered how one went about telling a man she loved him. Francine watched him out of the corner of her eye. He still leaned against the counter, his arms crossed, his attention upon her. Francine allowed her gaze to drift to his eyes. Guarded yet expectant, they glistened at her.

Francine tried to breathe, but the effort resulted in a series of broken gasps and short huffs. *It's now or never!* she thought.

"I was j–just thinking about my life," she explained. "I've been thinking about it a lot lately, I guess." Her smile felt as wobbly as her knees.

"So have I." Ethan rubbed his goatee and looked away. "I've been wanting to talk to you," he said, "all week, actually. But I— I just didn't exactly know where to begin."

"Me, too," Francine admitted.

"How many ways would you like to tell me I've been a fool?" he said, his lips twisting.

Francine twined her fingers and wrestled with what to say.

"When I showed Carrie that newspaper article, she wasn't even worried about the morality of the situation or even about Ricky. She said everyone would get over it. Her main gripe was that her brother got caught. I should have seen her real attitudes from the start. The clues were out there in the open for all the world to see." Ethan closed his eyes and shook his head. "I have been a fool."

"Oh Ethan…" Francine said.

"You knew all along, didn't you?" he asked.

"Well…"

"When did you realize it?" Ethan shook his head.

"I…I guess I suspected when I first met Hugh but—okay—I believe I knew the day I met Hugh. It just seemed so obvious. Carrie…I knew about Carrie the day in the chapel."

"Yep," Ethan acknowledged. "And that's when I should have known, too. Right?"

"Well…"

"Do you know what I've been doing this week?" Ethan asked. Francine shook her head.

"I've been spending as much time as I can in prayer. Here I thought I was close to God." He waved his hand. "Even had a 'call' on my life!" Ethan drew invisible quotes in the air. "And I essentially got knocked over by a pretty face and went off the deep end."

Francine covered her lips with her fingers. *I can't stand this!* she thought. *What if he's about to confess—*

"Wait a minute!" Ethan held up his hands. "I didn't mean that the way it sounded. I promise, Francine, Carrie and I *never—*"

"I believe you," she rushed.

His face settled into a mask of disbelief.

"I really do," Francine said. "But I've got to be honest. The two of you got really…uh…close." She coughed over her embarrassment.

"You know what happened?" Ethan said, his mouth firm. "Carrie Casper came after me."

What single woman wouldn't? Francine thought.

"But this time I was so…carnal," he spat, "I didn't run! I don't think I've ever been so disgusted with myself in my *whole life!*"

"I'm a little disgusted with myself these days, too," Francine admitted.

"You?" Ethan looked at the ceiling and laughed. "You're perfect! What's there to be disgusted with?"

Francine's cheeks flashed hot. She looked down and repeated the statement that began this whole conversation. "I don't like blackened salmon."

"Oh, so we're back to the salmon." Ethan chuckled. "Now that's a serious flaw if I ever heard one. Ooh!" His eyes dancing with the tease, he wagged his head from side to side. "You should beg forgiveness!"

She rolled her eyes. "No, you idiot," she said, "you don't get what I'm saying."

"Should I?"

"Well, yes! What did I eat when we went to Addy's at the Worthingham Renaissance?"

"I have no idea, but let me guess." Ethan stroked his temple. "Blackened salmon!"

"Yes!" She spread her hands. "And I don't like it. Do you know why I ate it?"

"No, why?"

"Because Carrie insisted that I have it."

"Do you have to bring her into this?" Ethan grimaced.

"This isn't about Carrie. It's about me," Francine explained. "My whole life I've let everyone make choices for me. After going back home to Rockaway, I realized a lot of it involved my family. My father is a…" Francine rubbed her palms together and really didn't want to go into all that pain at the moment.

"He's nothing like Uncle Tom," she explained.

"Neither was my dad," Ethan admitted. The two shared a wordless but powerful glance. "I wouldn't be where I am now if it weren't for Tom Barrimore. I know he's not perfect," Ethan explained. "He has a tendency to be a little controlling."

"I hadn't noticed," Francine said.

Ethan chuckled. "Yep. But I'm on the verge of being ordained, here, and Dad has played a huge part in all of it."

"You're still going to pursue ordination?" Francine asked.

"You bet." His lips set, Ethan nodded. "As soon as I wrap up this last course in the spring, I'm scheduled for the church's summer district assembly."

"I'm so glad." Francine covered her heart. "I was *so worried!*"

"I know you were," Ethan said, his voice tender. "And I appreciate that more than you'll ever know." The tiniest flicker of awareness wavered in his gaze—just enough to give Francine a dash of courage.

She locked her unsteady knees. Ike's question propelled her forward. *Do you ever plan to tell him?* Francine opened her mouth and decided she would never again eat blackened salmon for anyone. Neither would she continue in silence when her heart bade her speak her love.

"I love you," she confessed.

"What?" Ethan leaned toward her, his eyes bulging, his mouth open. "What did you just say?" he asked.

"I said, I love you," Francine whispered. This time her admission came easier.

Before Francine could register his intent, Ethan grabbed her. Before she could breathe again, he pulled her close. Before she could react, Ethan pressed his lips against hers.

Francine's eyes popped open. A tide of pent-up longing exploded through her soul. She held Ethan tight, closed her eyes, and kissed him back. He didn't have to say a word to reveal his love was every bit as powerful as hers. The realization rocked the terrace.

When he lifted his face, Ethan showered Francine's cheeks in a trail of kisses. All the while he murmured, "I love you, too. I love you, too. Oh Francine, you don't know how much I love you. I think I started loving you the day you moved in."

She laughed, and his own joy mingled with hers. "I feel the same way," she explained. "I think I had a case of hero worship until my senior ball, and then..." She shook her head. "But I didn't realize it until you were in Paris, and then—" Unexpected tears blurred her eyes.

"Oh Francine," Ethan groaned, "what have I put you through?"

"Pure misery," she confessed.

"And on top of all my stuff with Carrie, everyone was trying to push Hugh off on you." He stroked the nape of her neck and then trailed his fingers toward her ponytail.

"Let's don't even talk about any of that," Francine said and decided now was not the time to confess that she'd actually considered Hugh's proposal, even if only for a brief season.

He tugged on her ponytail holder, and Francine's hair fell to her shoulders. The smell of her freshly shampooed hair mingled with Ethan's cologne. "Hmmm," Ethan said. "I like this." He laid both hands on either side of her head and trailed his fingers in her hair. "I've wanted to do something like this since the night of your birthday party. You bowled me over that night." He propped his forehead against hers and peered into her eyes.

"I tried to," Francine admitted, and clung to Ethan to keep from collapsing.

Ethan pulled away. "You mean that was all for me?"

"All for you," she admitted. Francine lowered her head and dared an upward glance.

"It worked," he said, his mouth quirking. "I couldn't think of anything else but you."

"But that's when I caught you and Carrie kissing in the dining room."

"In the first place, *she* kissed me. And I didn't stop her because I was trying to get you out of my system."

Francine shyly aimed a whisper at Ethan's ear, "I hope I'm in your system for good now."

"You're there to stay," Ethan asserted.

"What will the family think of us?" Francine asked, resting her head on his shoulder. "How will we ever tell Uncle Tom?"

"He already knows."

Francine jerked back and looked into Ethan's face.

"I told him how I felt yesterday and asked if he'd be opposed to my, well, you know, asking you to marry me."

"Yes!" Francine exploded.

Fresh laughter ignited Ethan's features. "Dad said the same thing. He said it was the smartest idea he'd heard in ages."

"I do, too," Francine replied. "I really do!"

About the Author

Debra White Smith continues to impact and entertain readers with her life-changing books, including *Romancing Your Husband, 101 Ways to Romance Your Marriage, Friends for Keeps, More than Rubies: Becoming a Woman of Godly Influence,* and the popular Seven Sisters fiction series. She has 40 book sales to her credit and close to a million books in print.

The founder of Real Life Ministries, Debra touches lives through the written and spoken word by presenting real truth for real life and ministering to people where they are. Debra speaks at events across the nation and sings with her husband and children. She has been featured on a variety of media spots, including *The 700 Club, At Home Live, Getting Together, Focus on the Family, John Maxwell's Thrive Ministry, Moody Broadcasting Network, Midday Connection,* and *Fox News.* She holds an M.A. in English.

Debra lives in small-town America with her husband of 22 years, two children, and a herd of cats.

To write Debra or contact her for speaking engagements, check out her website:

www.debrawhitesmith.com

or send mail to

Real Life Ministries
Debra White Smith
P.O. Box 1482
Jacksonville, TX 75766

The
Austen
Series

First Impressions

When Eddi Boswick is cast as Elizabeth, the female lead in a local production of *Pride and Prejudice*, she hesitates. Dave, the handsome young rancher cast as Darcy, seems arrogant and unpredictable. Accepting the challenge of playing opposite him, Eddi soon realizes that he is difficult to work with on and off the set.

But when a tornado springs out of nowhere, Dave protects Eddi...much to her chagrin. And he is shocked to discover an attraction for the feisty lawyer he can't deny. Sparks fly when Eddi misinterprets his interest and discovers the truth he's trying to hide.

Will Eddi's passionate faith, fierce independence, and quick wit keep Dave from discovering the secret to love...and the key to her heart?

The
Austen
Series

Reason and Romance

When Ted arrives, Elaina assumes he can't be interested in her. But Ted surprises her. Attracted by his charming personality, Elaina dreams about love. But then comes shocking news. Has she made a mistake?

The handsome Willis hints at engagement...and Elaina's sister, Anna, is delighted. But when he is called away, he doesn't leave a forwarding address. Broken-hearted, Anna falls into depression. Will she love again?

Readers will be enraptured by this story about the joys and follies of infatuation and how faith in God reveals true love.

Seven Sisters

Second Chances

When Marilyn meets her charming neighbor, her heart awakens. But when she learns Joshua is a pastor, she cuts off all contact. She will not lose her heart again.

Joshua is making a new life free from his sinful past. When he begins to receive mysterious letters, he realizes that his secret—and life—are in danger.

The Awakening

Supermodel Kim Lowry has it all: beauty, wealth, and a budding faith that seldom interferes with her plans. When a secret admirer sends love notes, Kim is flattered. But as the letters become more possessive, warning signals flash.

Joining a mission outreach, Kim's high-profile status conflicts with coordinator O'Donnel's vision for a quiet trip. Sparks fly as their lifestyles clash and they battle an undercurrent of passion. When the notes start appearing again, Kim turns to the only person she can trust...or can she?

A Shelter in the Storm

When Sonsee realized she was in love with longtime friend Taylor, discouragement gripped her. He'd made it clear romance was not in his plans. To find peace, Sonsee relinquishes her heart and future to the Lord. But then her father is killed, and Taylor is the suspect. As the search for the murderer intensifies, Sonsee enters a maze of betrayal and greed that leads to a long-held family secret. When the killer makes a desperate move, Sonsee faces the ultimate challenge.

To Rome with Love

Melissa gazed into velvet-brown eyes. Kinkaide hadn't changed. His expressive eyes and vibrant smile brought back memories of love. She stepped back. Nothing could break the barriers surrounding her heart. And now he was standing before her, believing she had accepted his invitation for a cruise. Despite his broken promises, hope stirred. What if...

For Your Heart Only
Come with me. We'll fly to the stars. Lawton's soft invitation lingers in Jac's mind as she grapples with his disappearance, his desperate phone call, and the dread filling her heart. Using her private detective skills, Jac locates her secret love. But when another attempt is made on his life, Jac and Lawton spring into action. Uncovering a 35-year-old mystery, they plunge into a dark tangle of greed and vengeance. Drawn together for survival, they wrestle with their feelings for each other—and the past that keeps them apart.

This Time Around
Journalist Sammie Jones has two problems: R.J. Butler just became her boss, and he wants to woo her back to their former relationship. But struggling with the aftermath of abuse, Sammie's only desire is to create a safe haven for herself and her son. When Sammie stumbles onto a drug-smuggling operation, her instinct for a story lures her into a world of murder, madness, and greed. Turning to R.J. for advice, Sammie's heart begins to open. But when the painful past erupts into the present, she faces the hardest decision of all...

Let's Begin Again
From her beautifully decorated house to the set of her television show, everything Victoria does exudes talent and confidence. She's been a Christian since childhood, and in her tidy world only one problem stands out: Why doesn't Tony make their marriage a top priority?

Tony is frustrated. If he can't measure up to Victoria's standards now, what happens when she discovers his past? Tony can't get past the shame in his heart. Until he is shot at. Until he is plunged into a deadly game. Until circumstances strip away the lies.

Torn apart by dark secrets and conditional love, can Victoria and Tony find the strength to meet the deadly challenge and face the past together?

Variety is the spice of life! *101 Ways to Romance Your Marriage* gives you a host of "I love you because" ideas and "how to wow your spouse" dates to help keep your love blazing. Turn your ordinary marriage into an extraordinary love affair! Three sections in this book will help you and your spouse create special moments to keep your hearts entwined:

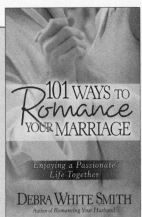

- *Making Your Hero Sizzle* delivers innovative and exciting ways to romance husbands.

- *Making Your Lady Swoon* provides unique and easy-to-do suggestions to charm wives.

- *The Hero and the Lady* offers creative, heartwarming activities couples can do together.

From simple gestures to fun weekend getaways, the ideas in this book are sure to add zest to your love life. Marriage can be the exciting, satisfying experience God intended!

Early days in a relationship are exhilarating, but they can't touch the thrilling love affair you can have now! Cutting through traditional misconceptions and exploring every facet of the Bible's message on marriage, *Romancing Your Husband* reveals how you can create a union others only dream about. From making Jesus an active part of your marriage to arranging fantastic romantic interludes, you'll discover how to—

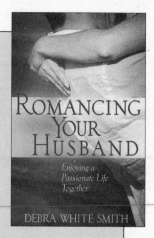

ROMANCING
YOUR
HUSBAND

*Enjoying a
Passionate Life
Together*

DEBRA WHITE SMITH

- make romance a reality
- "knock your husband's socks off"
- become a lover–wife, not a mother–wife
- find freedom in forgiving
- cultivate a sacred romance with God

*Experience fulfillment
through romancing your husband...
and don't be surprised
when he romances you back!*

CROSSINGS®
THE BOOK CLUB FOR TODAY'S CHRISTIAN FAMILY

A Letter to Our Readers

Dear Reader:

In order that we might better contribute to your reading enjoyment, we would appreciate your taking a few minutes to respond to the following questions. When completed, please return to the following:

Andrea Doering, Editor-in-Chief
Crossings Book Club
401 Franklin Avenue, Garden City, NY 11530
You can post your review online! Go to www.crossings.com and rate this book.

Title _____ Author _____

1   Did you enjoy reading this book?

❏ Very much. I would like to see more books by this author!

❏ I really liked_____

❏ Moderately. I would have enjoyed it more if_____

**2   What influenced your decision to purchase
this book? Check all that apply.**

❏ Cover
❏ Title
❏ Publicity
❏ Catalog description
❏ Friends
❏ Enjoyed other books by this author
❏ Other _____

3   Please check your age range:

❏ Under 18   ❏ 18-24
❏ 25-34   ❏ 35-45
❏ 46-55   ❏ Over 55

4   How many hours per week do you read? _____

5   How would you rate this book, on a scale from 1 (poor) to 5 (superior)?
_____

Name_____

Occupation_____

Address_____

City_____ State_____ Zip_____